AMAN J. BEDI

CITY OF JACKALS

This paperback first published in Great Britain in 2026 by Gollancz

First published in Great Britain in 2025 by Gollancz
an imprint of The Orion Publishing Group Ltd
Carmelite House, 50 Victoria Embankment
London EC4Y 0DZ

An Hachette UK Company

The authorised representative in the EEA is Hachette Ireland,
8 Castlecourt Centre, Castleknock Road, Castleknock, Dublin 15, D15 XTP3,
Republic of Ireland (email: info@hbgi.ie)

3 5 7 9 10 8 6 4

A CIP catalogue record for this book
is available from the British Library.

ISBN (Mass Market Paperback) 978 1 399 60992 0
ISBN (Ebook) 978 1 399 60993 7

Typeset by Deltatype Ltd, Birkenhead, Merseyside

Printed in Great Britain by Clays Ltd, Elcograf S.p.A

www.gollancz.co.uk

Praise for Aman J. Bedi

'Aman has created such a richly detailed, darkly gritty world, and Kavi is such a compelling, sharp, and original heroine'
Sunyi Dean, *Sunday Times* bestselling author of *The Book Eaters*

'An impressive debut in every sense – this grim and relentless exploration of colonialism, power, resistance, and courage will leave readers shaken'
Samit Basu, author of *The Jinn-Bot of Shantiport*

'With *Kavithri*, Aman J. Bedi presents a striking examination of class, caste, and colonialism by way of wondrously creative magic and an underdog you can't help but root for'
J.T. Greathouse, British Fantasy Award-nominated author

'*Kavithri* is majestic: a pacy, visceral tale . . . powered by a heroine with lashings of charm and grit in equal measure'
David Wragg, author of *The Black Hawks*

'The worldbuilding and character work is absolutely stunning, and it keeps a joyous tone even when it goes to some very dark places'
Peter McLean, author of *Priest of Bones*

'An exhilarating ride through a vivid and violent world, *Kavithri* is simultaneously brutal, triumphant, and astounding'
Sarah Beth Durst, award-winning author of The Queens of Renthia series

'A masterfully detailed epic adventure in a lush, vibrant setting'
K.S. Villoso, author of *The Wolf of Oren-Yaro*

By Aman J. Bedi

Ghosts of Ethuran Series

Kavithri
City of Jackals

For Nisha.
You've got the whole page to yourself this time.

Part One

Chapter 1
BOSS-1

Boss, they called her now.

Akka, the Raayan word for big sister, if they really wanted something from her, or if they weren't employees of the Imperial Rickshaw Company. But while Kavi sat behind Massa's old desk and smoked her beedis and stared at the map of the city and organised steam-rickshaw allocations and haggled with un-scrupulous mechanics over the cost of repairs and maintenance and dealt with a whole host of unforeseen, time-consuming setbacks and headaches, she was their boss.

'Captain?' Brigadier Thordali said. 'What do you think?'

To this man, however, ever since he'd recruited Kavi's people to hold the Kraelish at the chokepoint in the park, she was the captain of the Taemu battalion.

Kavi fought to keep her expression neutral, resisted the urge to whoop and holler, and nodded. 'And accommodation?'

Thordali, seated in the chair opposite, straightened and rapped his knuckles on the desk. 'Military barracks, until we find a more permanent solution.'

The hint of a grin slipped through a crack in Kavi's com-posure. Three months they'd spent negotiating for this. Three months since the Kraelish assault, when the city of Azraaya had come under attack – for the first time in centuries – by its old

Imperial masters; and in the aftermath of which the Taemu had helped with the rebuild: as labourers for construction, as look-outs on the wall, as part of the clean-up crew, and of course, as steam-rickshaw drivers. And now, it was finally happening.

'How'd you convince them?' she asked.

'The military is not the Council, and the generals are not fools,' Thordali said with a wry smile. 'There are people in the city besides you and me who want this to happen.'

He was talking about Dharvish, a young politico running for the Azraayan seat on the Council in the upcoming elections, who constantly reminded people that the Taemu had fought for the city. She'd attended one of his rallies when she'd first learned of him and was surprised by his honest, passionate rhetoric: *Raaya is not just one people, it is a collection! Call the Gashani down from the hills and mountains. Give Ethuran back to the Taemu, those lost children – those people robbed of their home, dragged across continents, used as meat grinders by the Empire.* She was stunned when people around her nodded and applauded.

He spoke about equality. He called out the corruption rampant in the Council. He was fearless. Naively so, and it was only a matter of time before someone in power shut him up. But for now, it worked in her favour.

'Thank you,' Kavi said to Thordali now, voice thick with emotion.

'We should be the ones thanking you.' Thordali adjusted the collar of his uniform and stood. 'It will take a couple of days to finalise the papers – we will require each auxiliary to sign, stamp, or thumbprint them.'

And with that, the Taemu would become official auxiliaries in the Azraayan army. They would have their own unit, with her as captain, and each of them would receive stipends and fully-funded accommodation. They would need to attend regular training sessions at the military campus, but could otherwise carry on with their steam-rickshaw work and remain on stand-by.

Kavi's chair scraped the floor as she stood out of respect. 'Of course.'

'I look forward to working with you, Captain,' Thordali said.

'Likewise, sir.' This changed everything. It finally made the Taemu a legitimate part of Raayan society. A small part, barely a cog, but enough to secure them a future in this country.

He nodded, donned his hat, and strode out the door.

Kavi collapsed back into her chair with a loud sigh and a large smile plastered on her face.

Sravan, her erstwhile bodyguard/secretary, poked his head into the office. 'He's still waiting.'

She groaned. 'Send him in.'

'Boss will see you now,' Sravan said.

'Boss? Hah? What boss? Who is boss?' Subbal Reddy, proprietor of Reddy's Dead Body Disposals, waddled in, purse tucked under one arm and jowls wobbling as he shook his head in pantomimed disappointment. 'You can't control! Every day these fellows are hanging around outside my business – eating, drinking, urinating.' He counted the offences on his fingers. 'Kavithri! What are you going to do about my business? My customers can't even walk to the – *aiyo*!' He slapped his head and searched the office for a solution.

Kavi smothered the stub of a half-smoked beedi into an ash tray, exhaled with exaggerated slowness, and reached for her cup of tea.

Almost a year had passed since she'd failed the tests in Bochan. Since she'd met Bithun and trained to fight for a place at the Vagola, the Raayan college for mages and Blades. And now, finally, *one more week*. She clenched her jaw. The start of the academic year had been delayed by a couple of months – a consequence of the Kraelish assault on the city – but a week from now her training at the Vagola would begin, and Chotu (with Salora's help) would take over the running of the rickshaw company. Until then … she sipped her lukewarm tea and glanced at Subbal Reddy over the rim of the cup: the man was now talking to the empty divan, glancing at her through the corner of an eye while he beseeched it for guidance: 'What should I do? Tell me. Who's going to … if only Massa was here.'

Kavi suppressed a wince. She was not Massa, had none of the man's charisma or confidence or magnetic energy; but she was doing her best. The problem here was the narrow street the two businesses shared. It wasn't enough to accommodate the number of steam-rickshaws and drivers she'd put into service. When they weren't out and about in the city ferrying its citizens, the rickshaws and their drivers loitered in the street outside the office, which, sadly for Subbal Reddy, was also the entrance to his place of business.

From what she'd learned from Massa, and via several uncalled-for and involuntary interactions during the last few weeks, she'd reached the conclusion that Reddy was a man of many faces. He was, at any given moment:

An irredeemable adulterer.

An incorrigible gambler.

And an indulgent and doting father.

'Reddy-sir, please,' Kavi said and gestured to the empty chair across the desk.

His gaze softened, and he ceased his discussion with the divan. He liked it when people called him 'sir'.

'I have no place to move my people to,' Kavi said.

He bristled. 'Now, look—'

'But I can offer you a kind of *recompense*.'

'Recomp?' He pursed his lips and considered. 'How much?'

This was what he was after. He didn't care that the drivers loitered outside his shop front; it was shuttered during the day and pissed on by drunks at night. In fact, she had a feeling that his shop front was exactly that: a fucking front. For what? She couldn't care less. 'You're aware that I will be joining the Vagola as a Blade soon?'

He threw a couple of pathetic-looking jabs at the space in front of him. 'Fighting-girl ah, you? Yes, yes, I know.'

'And you know, as a student, that I am allowed to invite two guests to attend the Blade-lock tournament?'

His mouth fell open into the shape of an 'O'. 'You mean ...'

Kavi nodded. The tournament was an annual tradition at the Vagola, held during the first term alongside its lectures and exams. It was not open to the public, only to the city's elite, the Vagola faculty, and to guests of the participants. According to Salora, students from the Department of Blades and Warlocks would pair up and fight in an elimination style tournament – any student, first year to third, could enter – where the winners were awarded an obscene amount of cash and would have their names carved into the walls of the Vagola. The Blade-lock tournament was usually accompanied by raucous banquets, miscellaneous revelry, and copious amounts of gambling. 'I'm sure your son would love to—'

'All the matches?' he said.

'All. Even the ones I don't fight in.'

He stroked his chin, shrugged, pretended nonchalance, but she had him.

'You, uh' – he jerked his head at her – 'you don't have friends or family you want to invite?'

'No.' She had no desire to allow the only family she had left watch her get beaten bloody; and as for friends, she got along with Salora, but they weren't really friends, and Bithun was in Bochan, so, no. She had no friends. They were all dead.

'Deal.' He flashed her a thumbs-up, adjusted the purse tucked under his arm, and stomped out the door.

She sighed and turned back to the ledger and map spread open on her desk. They needed to find a new steam-rickshaw mechanic for maintenance because the current one – she'd learned after the scoundrel had absconded – had been over-charging her. She needed to find a contact in the municipal office so they could stay up to date with road closures and repairs. And she needed to figure out a more efficient way of scheduling the drivers instead of the free-for-all *everyone just tell me when you want to work* system that was in place.

Kavi scratched her head, tsked, folded up the map, stuffed it in between the pages of the ledger, and slammed it shut. She reached for Massa's beedi case and slid the artificed match-stick out the side. She lit up a beedi. Winced as the first drag singed its way into her chest. And sighed as she exhaled and the tamakhu eased the pressure at the base of her skull.

Her brother Chotu, who insisted that she call him Chotu and not the name Appa had given him – Khagan – had banned her from smoking in his presence. *I know you can heal, but it's still a bad habit. Makes you stink, Akka. Makes the place reek. I cannot.*

Kavi grunted as she arranged her feet on the desk and the ashtray in her lap. She'd not told him that her contaminated maayin would kill her in another six years. She'd not told any of the Taemu. No point worrying about something now when they'd have to deal with it later anyway. 'Double-worry', as Massa would say.

She took another drag and flicked the ash off the tip.

The re-established Imperial Rickshaw Company – which she'd briefly considered renaming until Ratan reminded her that the misleading name (Raaya was, after all, no longer a part of the Empire) had stayed the same for close to three centuries – had breathed new life into the Taemu. Given them purpose. Meaning. They'd gone from living hand-to-mouth, abused and humiliated on a daily basis, eking out a living as rubbish-pickers, drain-cleaners, grave-diggers, servants, beggars, to wearing the khaki shirts of the city's rickshaw drivers with pride. If Ratan was to be believed, stories of what the Taemu had done during the Kraelish attack had spread, and the other Raayan rickshaw drivers had taken the Taemu under their wing and initiated them into their cultish group. Wearing the khaki shirt, it turned out, was something of a religion. The Taemu even behaved like true-blooded rickshaw drivers: accelerating like maniacs, swerving through traffic, and spitting, swearing, and haggling like they'd been doing this their entire lives. They loved every minute of it.

The only *real* issue she'd had was the incident with Sravan – the big man who'd fought at her side during the Kraelish attack; who, despite his considerable bulk, was among the gentlest and most thoughtful Taemu she knew (the man was an incorrigible kitten collector). It was why he no longer drove steam-rickshaws and now acted as a pseudo-bodyguard for her. A job he took much too seriously. Sravan had had a disagreement with a customer who'd refused to pay the settled-upon fare, and when Sravan had protested, a passing city guard had arrested the big Taemu for 'attempted extortion of a citizen'.

They'd dragged him in front of a judge, who'd forced him to kneel while he (the chootia judge) lectured Sravan on civilised behaviour and mocked the Taemu in front of the court:

'Do you know how to count?'

'Yes, sahib,' Sravan had said, eyes on the ground.

'Oh? So you went to school?'

'No, sahib.'

'Did your parents not have the money to send you?'

'No parents, sahib.'

'Of course, how foolish of me,' the judge said. 'So then, where did you learn?'

'Hessal – a Taemu elder, taught me.'

'A Taemu elder!' The judge turned to his staff. 'We should get this elder to teach at the university.'

They laughed.

He laughed.

The case had got a lot of attention, and the court, that day, was crowded. Not everyone was happy with the Taemu re-insertion in Azraayan life, despite the support of Dharvish and his followers, and a loud group – *most vocal, usually means most idiotic*, Massa had once said – had shown up to watch a Taemu get put in his place.

But when the judge had called upon the customer to press charges, the man, previously indignant, had mysteriously changed his mind. He stepped in front of the judge, soaked in sweat, licking his lips, cradling a heavily bandaged forearm, and he scraped and bowed and said it was all a misunderstanding, that he did not wish to proceed. And throughout, he cast furtive and fearful glances at the audience where Kavi stood with Chotu at her side, and she stared back, unblinking, reminding him of the simple threat she'd made at his home the previous night as she twisted and fractured each finger and thumb: *if my man is charged, is sent to prison, I will find you, and I will break* (crack) *your arms* (crack) *your legs* (crack) *and I will leave you* (crack) *alone and friendless* (crack) *deep within the slums, to fend for yourself.*

Was it excessive? Yes.

Had she gone too far? Fuck, no.

She'd made a promise to Hessal: she'd sworn to protect their people. But what she'd decided – alone, in the aftermath of the Kraelish assault on Azraaya, in the vacuum left behind by the friends she'd lost, the truths she'd learned, the family she'd found – was that when she was done, when her maayin had eaten her from the inside out and booted her soul back to Hel, that she would leave her people in a better place. With a better life.

This, then, was to be her purpose.

The sunlight that filtered into the office dimmed, then disappeared as a collection of dark rain clouds blotted out the sun. She took another drag and exhaled.

Chotu didn't agree with her methods. Said she was behaving like Appa.

Gods, that had stung.

They lived together now; shared the spare room on the second floor of the rickshaw company. She'd been teaching him how to read and write; some history, basic arithmetic – he loved numbers. He'd sit hunched over his little slate with a piece of chalk and scribble and erase and scribble and erase, and then he'd stop, look up at her, and his face would light up. *I solved it, Akka.* Then, hungry for more, *Can I learn something harder? Please?* Salora had volunteered to take over his tutoring, Meshira bless her.

He'd told her, not long after he moved in, about what had happened to Appa and their brother Kamith after Appa had sold Kavi to the beggar crew in Dyarabad.

They'd travelled. West first, to see if they could find work in the farms and villages on the Tholar delta. When they were rebuffed, often violently, Appa decided their best option was to stowaway on a ship to the Hamakan Isles. He believed the Hamakans were free of the prejudices that gripped the Raayans on the peninsula. 'All outsiders are treated the same in Hamaka,' he'd said.

They could start over. He would find work. The boys would find work. In the meantime, while they made their way to the coast, they still needed to eat, and since no one would give him work, and the local scavengers maintained a vicious monopoly on the rubbish heaps and dens, Appa was forced to steal.

Chotu had been keeping an eye on their belongings the day Appa and Kamith were caught.

Later, he was in the crowd watching when their hands were severed at the wrist. 'So they will never steal again!' the village elder had announced to cheers.

They bled to death in the village square. Tied down and powerless. No one would touch them. No one would help or tend to their horrific wounds. When he tried to stop the bleeding, when he squeezed rags into their wrists and pleaded with them to keep their eyes open, the villagers kicked him, offered him the same fate.

Chotu hung his head; said he should have done more, but he was too small, too weak.

'You are not weak,' Kavi had said, holding his face in her hands and peering into his eyes while she fought to keep tears from spilling out of her own. 'You. Are not. Weak.'

A muffled yelp startled her out of her reverie. She blinked. Outside: shouts, scuffed feet, thuds, and the unmistakable sound of glass shattering. Kavi frowned. A disagreement among the drivers? It'd never happened before. She stood. The beedi hissed as she stubbed it out.

A head peeked into the office – with a face Kavi didn't recognise – and withdrew. 'Boss, she's here.'

'Thank you, Deva,' another stranger's voice said. And ducking his head, a man stepped into Kavi's office.

Chapter 2
BOSS-II

His beige linen shirt, open at the collar, rode up his large shoulders, and he righted it with a sharp tug on the hem. He checked all four corners of the office before his eyes finally settled on Kavi.

He smiled.

She stared.

His large, bloated forearms were covered with row after row of thin, pale scars that ran from the insides of his elbows to his wrists. More scars, overlapping and blending and merging with each other, ran across the circumference of his thick neck.

'Can I help you?' she asked, and to be safe, 'Sahib?'

Still smiling, he walked up to the desk and placed a thick sheet of paper on it. 'Read it, please,' he said, in perfect, unaccented, educated Raayan.

Kavi glanced from the paper, which was some sort of stamped, official document, to the man, who nodded in encouragement, while outside the sounds of the scuffle continued to grow louder.

It was hard to tell the man's age. He could've been in his thirties, or fifties, or sixties, depending on the angle – it was his skin. She swallowed. The skin on his face had not aged evenly. Some patches appeared to have aged faster than the rest.

She picked up the document. Read. And snorted. 'What is this? Who are you people?'

'My peers, the few still alive, call me Grishan,' he said. 'My business' – he lingered on the *ness* – 'and my men are collectively referred to as the Tivasi.'

Her brows shot up. The Tivasi were the second largest gang in Azraaya. *Agoma, human trafficking, brothels, ring-fighting, extortion, and to top it all off they're in deep with the politicos*, Massa had said. *These chootia are not like the Dolmondas, they don't walk around with a sign that says 'I'm a Tivasi'. The only time you find out you're dealing with them is when they either want something from you, or you fucked with the wrong – Kavi, just stay away from the Lantern district, and you'll be fine.*

She licked her lips, and read the document again, this time with a creeping sense of dread.

Signed and stamped by a Councilman Nashik Faria, it declared that the Imperial Rickshaw Company owed the city 57,235.75 rayals in overdue fines due to incomplete steam-rickshaw licensing and invalid road permits. It went on to state that if the amount was not paid by (a date three weeks past) the company would be declared insolvent and therefore property of the city, available for purchase by any party willing to pay the aforementioned amount. This party, added at the bottom of the paper in blue ink, was *Grishan Ltd.*

'We were not notified—' The commotion outside flared up again: more shouts, thuds, moans, this time accompanied by laughter.

A gruff voice outside the door said, 'Fucking dogs think they can fight.'

What the Hel? Kavi skipped around the desk, was about to step around the man but he blocked her path with an arm.

'I own this place now,' Grishan said, and pointed to the

document in her hands. 'I would like you to acknowledge the transfer of ownership by signing the document, to prevent any disputes or complications down the line. Also, due to the illegal nature of the *business* you've been running, and your failure to pay the fines, the Council will nullify your agreement with the army. Criminals are not allowed in the Raayan military.'

Her eyes bulged. Everything she'd worked for, everything she'd promised her people … 'We were never told about these fines.'

He shrugged his shoulders. 'Irrelevant. Sign it, and get out.'

'What – why do you even want it?' Kavi said, inching away so the man didn't loom over her. She needed to think. Surely this was illegal – she grimaced, of course this was illegal. The man was a Raeth-damned gangster who, from the looks of it, had the favour of a councilman.

'I needed a new warehouse,' Grishan said.

'A what?'

'Warehouse.'

And you couldn't find anywhere else?

He read the question on her face. 'I find it distasteful.'

She blinked.

'Taemu scuttering around the city, acting like they're the same as the rest of us.' He tugged on the hem of his shirt then adjusted the collar. 'Your people have forgotten where you belong. I'm here to remind you.'

The audacity, the ease and confidence that made this man believe he could just show up and take. The veins on her neck stood as she forced her lips into a smile.

'Sahib, I think you've come to the wrong place.' She crushed the document into a ball and tossed it at his feet.

The change in the man's face was instantaneous. The light went out of his eyes. The skin around his neck and cheeks twitched and tightened. His mouth thinned to a straight line. He snapped his fingers. 'Deva.'

Two men – two Tivasi gangsters – stepped through the door, dragging a third, much larger man on his knees.

Kavi's stomach dropped.

The man on his knees, his face swollen and bloody, met Kavi's eyes. 'Sorry, Akka,' he said and averted his gaze.

A prickling engulfed her spine as she took a step in his direction. Sravan. Why was he apologising? *You've done nothing wrong.* She clenched her fists. 'Leave him alon—'

Grishan swung at her.

An open-handed blow with barely any back-lift that she began to lean away from, confident that she'd dodge, when his entire arm seemed to contract in mid-air and the speed with which it hurtled at her face doubled.

His open palm caught her flush across the face. Spun her head around with a loud *smack!* and knocked her off her feet. Sent her stumbling to the ground where she scrambled to stand but lost her balance and fell back down to her knees.

She tried to flex her jaw but found she couldn't move it. Her ears rang. Lights floated in front of her eyes and exploded. For a heartbeat, she lost track of what was up and what was down. Panic set in. Her rage slipped through her fingers. The air caught in her throat.

Breathe, a voice whispered in her head.

BREATHE.

She swallowed the blood in her mouth. And took her sword's advice. She gulped down air as she searched the office for where it sat, propped up in a corner behind the desk. She hadn't drawn the sword, hadn't used Drisana since the Kraelish assault on the city.

Come, Drisana urged. It wanted to fight. It wanted to taste the blood of the men who'd hurt their people. *Get up.*

She took a shuddering breath. What was she doing? It was just one hit. She'd dealt with worse. So much worse. Get up. Get the fuck up.

'Deva, keep her on her knees,' Grishan said.

A pair of rough hands squeezed down on her nape while a knee was shoved between her shoulder blades.

She grunted. Tried to force her way upright. And gasped as the knee dug into her spine and forced her to stop squirming.

They dragged Sravan deeper into the office. Positioned him so he was facing Kavi, with Grishan standing between them.

'Akka,' Sravan muttered.

A gangster slapped the back of his head. 'Shut up.'

Enough.

Heal me, she commanded, and her Jinn responded.

Blue tendrils of Nilasian maayin, invisible to everyone but her, tore their way out of the bruised skin on her face.

Him. Take it from him. It would shock them. Confuse him. And buy her enough time to get this bastard off her back. *Now.*

The maayin lunged at Grishan, and was rebuffed.

Kavi's eyes bulged.

A mage. The man was a fucking mage.

'I could remove you from the premises,' Grishan was saying. 'But you'd just keep coming back, wouldn't you? Like a leech, you'd live with this fantasy of revenge, even find a purpose in it.' He gestured to one of the gangsters holding Sravan.

The gangster offered Grishan a small knife, like the one the guava vendors used to slice their fruit.

'Please,' Grishan said, accepting the knife, 'save us both the trouble, and don't bother.'

The skin on his knife-arm contorted, like something crawled

beneath it, and when he lashed out at Sravan, his arm was a blur.

He handed the knife back to the gangster, clean, as if it hadn't even been used.

Kavi frowned at Grishan. What was wrong with his arm? She glanced at Sravan, and the moisture in her mouth, her throat, evaporated.

She tried to speak, but a thin film covered her tongue and smothered the words she tried to form. All she could manage was a low, pleading moan.

From where she was kneeling, it looked like Sravan had grown another mouth under his jaw. And from this new grinning mouth, oozed thick, dark blood.

His throat had been slit from under one earlobe to the other.

Sravan's wild eyes searched the office. He coughed. Blood dribbled down the sides of his mouth. His nostrils flared as dark, red bubbles expanded and popped with each wheezing breath.

Vomit burned its way up Kavi's throat, she swallowed it back down. Gagged. And let it spill down the front of her shirt. Her ears rang with a keening that rose in pitch. Someone was weeping, drawing ragged breaths, and sobbing. Time folded in on itself: the present merged with the past and forced her back into the ruins of Ethuran, where she walked through blackened streets filled with flies and rotting food and muck that came up to her knees and haunted corpses that hung by their necks and swung back-and-forth in the wind while more mutilated bodies naked bloated lined the alleyways where broken things plates toys pets crunched underfoot and the smell, oh, the smell of charred flesh of congealed blood and old vomit and stale piss and shit that clung to the bodies and clogged her nostrils and she sobbed and cried and wiped her face and wept and walked and swallowed the bile and pain and ignored the hollow inside her where her mother once lived – her mother. She moaned.

Amma.

Her chest shuddered. Amma. She cried out. Fell to her knees. Just like Sravan, they'd taken her mother from her, and all she could do while they brutalised her, slit her throat, and bludgeoned her to death, was hide. Hide. And watch.

It's OK, Kavi, her mother's voice whispered in her ear. *Don't look at what the bad men are doing – Shhh, it's okay. It's okay to hide.* Then in the same breath, her father growled, *That's all you're good for. Stand and watch while they slaughter everyone you love.*

You left us, Appa. You sold me. You don't get to talk.

A low-pitched gurgle filled her ears and Kavi stared at the floor between her knees. At the floor of the rickshaw company. She squeezed her eyes shut. Those were just memories. She was no longer in Ethuran. She was ... where *was* she?

Her head lolled. The air and the men who walked through it turned sluggish. The temptation to succumb to catatonia and let whatever happen, happen, called to her. She sighed. Reached for it. And froze as a pulse of alarm from her sword jolted her upright.

Sravan's head had begun to tilt back with its own weight, tightening the skin, widening the wound. The gurgling came from his throat.

Grishan stood over him, a lit beedi in one hand. 'Boys,' he said, and shoved the beedi into the mouthlike wound in Sravan's throat, 'smoking kills.'

His men chuckled.

Grishan made a satisfied grunt and plucked the beedi back out. Flipped it so the orange burning tip faced Sravan, and plunged it back into the wound where it went out with a wet hiss.

Sravan convulsed, and Grishan, gathering a bunch of Sravan's hair, pulled the big Taemu's head back, all the way, until it seemed like it would fall off.

There was a soft crack, and the wheezing and gurgling stopped.

Grishan stepped back – not a drop of blood on his fingers, his hands, or his clothes – and gestured to a gangster who set a chair down for him to sit in. 'Bring the brother,' he said.

'No.' Kavi's shoulders slumped. 'Leave him.'

Grishan lifted the crumpled-up document off the floor. Flattened it on the desk. And handed it to her.

'Pen in the top drawer,' she said in a hoarse whisper.

Her hands shook, and she struggled to grip the pen, but – with a chest that felt like it had caved in – she eventually signed the document, and robbed her people of their purpose.

Grishan studied her signature, and when he was satisfied, folded the piece of paper and tucked it into his pocket. He waved away the gangster who had his knee on Kavi's back.

Would they hate her? She'd dragged her people out of their stupor, yanked them out of the darkness and shown them what lay on the other side, and now she was responsible for sending them back to their old lives.

She kept her eyes averted from Sravan's stiff, kneeling body.

But they would still have lives to go back to.

'What—' She swallowed the bile at the back of her throat. 'What if I get you the money? The fifty-seven thousand you paid.' She already knew the answer, but she wanted it confirmed. Needed that last nail to be hammered in.

Grishan stroked his chin. 'When?'

She jerked her head back. Her mouth worked. 'I can—' She could ask Bithun. He would help. 'A few weeks. Maybe—'

'Where will you get it from?'

'I can borrow it from a friend.'

He winced. And shook his head. 'No. I don't want borrowed money. It needs to be *earned*.' He uncrossed his legs and tugged on the hem of his shirt. Licked his lips and leaned closer to Kavi. 'Why don't you come work for me? I've heard you don't mind twisting arms, or' – he smiled – 'fingers, if you need to. I could use that sort of ruthlessness. I will pay you a thousand rayals a month, and, in seven or eight years, if you save well, you will be able to buy this place back from me.'

She clenched her jaw. He was mocking her. What was she even thinking? And even if he was serious, she'd be dead before—

'I've decided.' Grishan slapped his thighs and stood. 'Starting today – no, starting tomorrow, you will work for me. As one of my enforcers. Yes?'

No, she wanted to say. But as he loomed over her, as fresh beads of sweat burst out across her forehead, she was overcome with this need to hide, to do whatever was necessary to keep the man's unfathomable capacity for violence in check, to keep his face from undergoing that terrifying change. All she could do was nod. And repeat. 'Yes.'

Chapter 3
ENFORCER

'What's his name?' Salora said, gnawing on the wrong end of a pencil.

Kavi sat hunched over in an interview chair in Salora's office, deep within the bowels of the Artificed Hydraulics Building where Azraaya's artificers kept their offices and stored their artifacts. She'd spent a sleepless night organising her people's return to the slums. Their old huts, by some perverse miracle, stood empty and unused, and once she'd ensured that everyone had a roof over their heads, she'd retraced her steps, collected Sravan's body – Grishan had smiled and assured her it would remain 'unmolested', frozen on its knees, partially decapitated – and arranged for a cremation. The Taemu had stood and watched, deep into the night, as the smoke from the pyre filled the sky above.

'Grishan,' Kavi said. The man was a mage, no question about it. The only time maayin failed to affect someone was if another Jinn had claimed them – if they were a mage themselves. As for his class ... *Biomancer*. There'd been an entry describing their abilities in the *Diary of an Unknown Mage*:

Dangerous, lethal, and batshit insane. Its mages could enhance, modify, and strengthen parts of their bodies.

Status: inactive
Countervail: lifespan
Jinn: Raktha

Suman, the artificer who'd administered the third test to Kavi in Bochan, had told her that Raktha only chose Taemu as its mages, and that in the aftermath of the Methun Revolt three centuries ago, the Taemu Biomancers had been rounded up and executed. The slaughter had shocked their Jinn, Raktha, into silence, and it had not chosen a mage since.

Until Kavi.

Had Suman lied to her? No. Even Drisana, in the visions she'd shared with Kavi, had called Raktha her people's Jinn. Maybe Grishan wasn't a Biomancer. But then what else could he be? The way his muscles had contracted, the inhuman speed with which he'd moved, it was the only explanation.

'His last name?' Salora asked.

Kavi squeezed her temples and sighed. 'He didn't give me his last name.'

The Taemu had insisted that Kavi, along with Chotu, use Hessal's old hut.

She'd hesitated. The others believed that the Taemu elder had been killed by the Kraelish, but it was Kavi who was responsible for her death, who'd used Hessal as a countervail when she'd escaped her imprisonment and torture.

Her brother had wept, wiped away his tears, and fallen into a deep sleep. She'd tried to sleep too, but as she dozed off a hypnopompic projection of Hessal had stepped out of the walls, walked into a corner, and stood, hunched over, as it judged, accused, and then whispered: *You were supposed to protect them. You were supposed to protect us. You were supposed to protect me.*

There was no sleep to be had after that. She'd sat and stared at the small idol of Drisana until sunup, when she splashed her face with water, tidied up her hair, and walked down to the army base where she begged for an audience with Brigadier Thordali.

The brigadier had averted his eyes, squeezed her shoulder, and said with a pained expression on his face, 'My hands are tied, I'm sorry.'

'And the councilman who signed the document?' Salora said, snapping her back to the present.

'Nashik Faria.'

Salora flung the pencil across the office. 'Hel! If it was one of the others—' She ground her teeth. 'I could've talked to them, sent a petition. But not him.'

'Why not?'

'You don't know who he is?'

Kavi thumbed an earlobe. 'Should I?'

'He's the councilman responsible for – who was accused of – instigating the Ethuran massacre.'

Kavi sagged. Her insides churned, but all she could manage was an exhausted nod. Everything always came back to Ethuran. Three centuries ago, the Kraelish had slaughtered her people in its fields as punishment for their defiance – for fighting along-side the Raayans in their doomed revolt. And thirteen years ago, the Raayans, out of fear and hatred, had massacred the Taemu in its streets and homes. Kavi, barely eight years old at the time, had watched, hidden inside the walls of their home, as they yanked her mother by the hair, knocked her to the ground, punched, kicked, dragged her by the ankles, slit her throat, and bashed her head in with a rock.

'He's barely seen in public anymore.' Salora said. 'Some sort of bone disease. But if he's put his name on that contract, it means either the Tivasi have something on him, or—'

'Or he's the one making the decisions.'

Salora nodded. 'I'll hire Chotu, say he's a manservant. It'll give him something to do and keep him away from the Tivasi. You … just do whatever this Grishan needs. I'll think of something to get you out of this.'

Kavi could hear it in her voice. The woman was lying; she was as lost as Kavi was.

But at least she was trying. Kavi had expected Salora to cut off all contact after she'd fulfilled her obligation to Bithun and helped Kavi use the Venator – the artifact that had reunited her with Chotu, which had once been used by the Kraelish to hunt the Taemu.

Salora was, after all, Massa's friend, not Kavi's. But the artificer had remained in contact and offered to help manage the rickshaw company once Kavi began her training at the Vagola.

'Thank you,' Kavi said.

'How're the others doing?' Salora asked.

They'd gathered around Sravan's pyre, angry, eager to fight. 'Chootia took us by surprise,' Jiboo had said. 'Most of us were away, working, it was four against twenty.' He'd turned and spat over his shoulder as the others nodded and muttered in agreement. 'We can fight them, Akka. We've faced far worse.'

'And then what?' she'd asked, softly.

'Then we take back the rickshaw company.'

'There was a councilman's signature on that document. Do you understand what that means?'

'Fuck the councilman. The company is ours.'

'Grishan and the Tivasi have the backing of a sitting member of the Council,' Kavi had said, louder. 'They can turn the entire city against us, and they will have the law behind them – the city guards, the military, the Vagola – there's nothing we can do while the Tivasi have his backing.'

Jiboo had stuck his chest out. 'We'll fight them too.' And the others had echoed him. 'We want to fight, Akka.'

'No.' *I cannot lose any more of you.* 'No,' she'd said again into the silence.

'Kavi?' Salora said.

Kavi blinked. 'Yes – no, they're fine. They just need to adapt.'

Outside Artificed Hydraulics, in the kind of stunningly bright sunlight that seemed to single out insomniacs for special attention, Kavi squinted at a scrap of paper that Grishan had handed her.

The Golden Caterpillar, 132 Lantern district, opp. Naadan's Bookshop, it said. The address he'd asked her to report at for her new job as a Tivasi enforcer. And underneath: *Ask for Deva.*

She tucked the paper back into her pocket and gazed up at the monstrous building. A strange feeling of familiarity emanated from the place. A nostalgia, almost.

Ever since her abduction and torture at the hands of a Kraelish mage – a sickly, tormented man called Jarard – the suppressed memories of her horrific childhood had returned in fragmented bursts. Some pieces, like this nostalgia, would eventually fit with another fragment and make sense. She swallowed and lowered her eyes.

The Kraelishman, Jarard, had drained her for blood, and once the cylinders storing her blood were full, he'd methodically tested the limits of her self-healing. He'd sliced off her eyelids, her earlobes, her fingers and toes; he'd sawn off her arms and legs, crushed her organs, and forced her to use other people as countervails, killing them in the process. People like Hessal.

But Kavi had escaped, and in the subsequent assault on the city had rallied the Taemu to fight the Kraelish through the streets and alleys of Azraaya. But as they fought, more men and women

– Raayans – had joined her under the blood-soaked banner that Chotu carried. Brigadier Thordali had recruited her battalion of irregulars to defend a chokepoint against the Kraelish and buy the military time to detonate an artificed weapon. They'd made their stand. They'd held. Until the warlock, Ze'aan, arrived and decimated her people. And after a lifetime of keeping it chained, Kavi had lost control of the berserker and butchered the Kraelish left standing in the chokepoint.

'Kavi,' a familiar voice said, 'what did Salora say?'

Kavi turned to face a bespectacled man in a flatcap who leaned against a steam-rickshaw. Ratan had found her in the slums the previous night and had insisted on ferrying her around while she sorted things out for the Taemu. He owned his own vehicle, so the Tivasi had no claim over him. Asking Salora for help had been his suggestion.

'Kavi?' Ratan repeated.

She shook her head.

He sighed. 'Where to now?'

'The Tivasi.'

He jerked his head at the rickshaw. 'Get in.'

'No. It – I want to walk.'

Ratan crossed his arms. 'Have you eaten?'

She looked away.

He sighed and slipped into the driver's seat of the rickshaw. 'You know how to find me?'

'Rickshaw stand outside the Picchadi stadium.'

Ratan nodded. Pumped the lever to start the rickshaw. The vehicle sputtered, spat, and came to life. He squeezed the brakes and twisted the accelerator. 'I still work for you,' he said. 'Remember that.'

'Thank you,' she said, tried to force a smile, failed, and instead waved as he sped away.

Chapter 4
ENFORCER

Agoma Dream

She stopped at a hawker centre and bought herself a bread-omelette – eggs beaten with chilli, coriander, and cumin powder, tossed with sautéed onions and tomato on a hot plate then laid over a slice of pan-toasted bread. The hawker dramatically finished it off with a sprinkle of salt and white pepper and passed it to her on a folded piece of news pamphlet.

Kavi bit into it, savoured the spice, the texture – the soft, velvety egg vs. the crunchy, buttery bread – and sighed as the warmth from the first morsel spread through her core. She walked and ate; her hunger a temporary distraction from the grief and despair that had kept her up all night.

Azraaya, on the surface, seemed to be recovering from the attempted Kraelish invasion. The rebuild was in full swing, shops and businesses were open, and the streets were once again alive. Kavi licked her fingers clean and dropped the makeshift plate into a large rubbish bin that sat outside a construction site.

But the city had changed. She could see it in the furtive glances people cast over their shoulders – eyes that slid almost subconsciously in the direction of the scaffolded walls the Kraelish makra had breached. Unlike the structures on the ground, the walls would still take months to fix.

In the meantime, Azraaya held its breath while the country

prepared for a full-scale Kraelish invasion. It signed new treaties with Hamaka and Fumesh, and extended the armistice over the disputed eastern border with Nathria. It severed all diplomatic ties with Kraelin. Fortified and reinforced its northern borders. And waited for the results of an 'ongoing' investigation into how the makra had gotten so close to the capital unnoticed.

Kavi stepped around a stray cow and crossed the street.

Her guess was that the components were transported into Raaya and then assembled in secrecy. Likewise the soldiers and their equipment. It made sense. But no one was asking for her opinion about things, and now she had more immediate concerns to attend to.

Do whatever they need, Salora had said.

Yes, she'd keep her head down, bite her tongue, and do what the Tivasi wanted her to. Salute, grovel, scrape, and bide her time. She'd take the money Grishan promised to pay her each month and share it with the other Taemu. If there was one thing she'd learned from being in the gutter ... she frowned. Grappled with the thought. Tried again, and yawned. Either way, what she was trying to logicise was that *eventually* an opportunity would arrive, and all she needed to do was—

A steam-rickshaw's screeching *honk!* startled her off the footpath and into an alleyway.

She clutched her chest. Swore. A person could get killed if they weren't paying attention on Azraayan streets.

After that, she forced herself to remain grounded; fought to keep her mind from wandering off and focused on getting herself in one piece to the Golden Caterpillar.

The Lantern district was still lurching awake as she wandered into its belly. Most of the businesses – agoma dens, fighting rings, and brothels like the Golden Caterpillar – would only open its doors after sundown, but the subordinate businesses, the ones that relied on foot traffic to the main attractions to thrive, had already raised their shutters. Restaurants and hawkers, beedi and paan kiosks, rum dens, money lenders, physicians specialising in 'sexual health', shops that sold various paraphernalia: ring-fighting equipment, brooms, coconuts, trousers, chicken, teapots, massive steel thalis, headgear, chappals, henna, and, for some bizarre reason, books.

She found Deva smoking and chatting with a chaiwallah in the shadow of the wide, four-storeyed Golden Caterpillar.

Kavi clenched her jaw, smothered images of Sravan's wound and the emotions they evoked, and strolled up behind the man. 'Sir-ji,' she said. 'Boss sent me.'

Deva glanced at her and flashed the 'two cups' sign at the chaiwallah. 'You're late,' he said, voice gruff and throaty from what she assumed was a lifetime of filter-less beedis.

'Boss didn't give me a time,' she said.

He shrugged. Offered her a cup of tea.

She hesitated.

'Take it,' he said, thick beard twitching as he spoke.

Kavi accepted. Gripped the rim of the cup with thumb and forefinger and brought it up to her chin. She inhaled the heady mix of spice and tea leaves, and blew over it, sending ripples across its surface.

'The boss is an accommodating man.' Deva waved the chaiwallah away. 'On days that you are training – when you're required to be present at the Vagola, you will be excused from collection. Instead, in the evenings, you will work here.' He jabbed a thumb at the brothel at his back.

Kavi tensed. 'He said I was to be an enforcer.'

Deva nodded. 'You will keep an eye on the clients, ensure peace is maintained, and deal with any disturbances.'

'A bouncer,' she said, relaxing.

'If that's what you want to call it.' He sipped his tea and gestured to the shops that surrounded the Caterpillar. 'On days that you're not training you will collect protection fees. I will prepare a list for you – names of businesses, dates, amount owed, et cetera.' He pointed at the shop that sold books. 'Come, it's their turn today.'

Kavi fell into step beside him. 'So, I just ask them to pay?'

'Ask, request, demand – whatever you have to do.' He cracked his neck. 'Get us our money.'

'And what if another gang tries to extor— collect from these shops?'

'Then do what these businesses are paying us for. Protect them.' Deva stopped at the entrance to the bookshop and indicated for her to hand over the teacup. 'This one owes us three hundred rayals,' he said, stepping back.

The book shop, it turned out, was a treasure trove of pornography: playing cards with semi-nude Kraelish women painted on the backs; rows of wood carvings on a shelf tagged 'self-pleasure'; charcoal impressions of couples engaged in intercourse, each selling for a mind-boggling fifty rayals; and the books themselves, mingled among a legitimate collection of novels were spines with titles like: *The Snake in the Sari*, *Pervert Pundit*, *Midnight Rowdies*, a large volume called *Fornicate like the Gods*, and another one called *Sexual Chutney*. She should've known.

Kavi narrowed her eyes at the shopkeeper. The man sat on a stool behind a counter, reading a news pamphlet while he bit and spat his fingernails onto the floor.

She cleared her throat. 'Tivasi collection.'

He glanced up, adjusted his spectacles, and peered into her eyes: at the blood-red irises unique to her people. 'Get lost, bleddy Taemu,' he said, and returned to his reading.

She sighed. Studied the man while he gnawed on his thumb.

She had no quarrel with him, he hadn't hurt her or her people. But, 'Bhai, I don't want to do this either, but if you don't pay me they will just send someone much worse. Someone who will not hesitate to hurt you.'

He folded the news pamphlet and slapped it down on the counter. 'And what else will you take along with my money? Hah? My books? My cards? My—'

'Just the money,' Kavi said, hands raised in placation. 'Three hundred rayals. That's all.'

'That's all?' He leaned back and made a face. 'There is no *that's all* with you chootia. The money goes to the Tivasi. But for you? What extra things will you take from me?'

Kavi clenched her jaw. She didn't have time for – wait, hold on, maybe this could work. 'You have a knife?'

'A knife?' He rummaged under the counter and pulled out a kitchen knife. 'Of course I have a knife!' He said, outraged.

She walked up to the counter and snatched it out of his hands.

'What—'

'I'll pretend to stab you in the hand,' Kavi said, 'but I'll miss on purpose.'

'Pretend?'

'Yes, and when I do, you cry out in pain, "*Aiiyo, my hand!*", like that, then you give me the money.'

His mouth worked, and he stared at her, flummoxed. 'But I don't want to.'

'Then you'll actually get stabbed.' She mimicked the potential stabbing. 'Choose.'

'But why?'

She lowered her voice. 'Deva's outside, wants to see if I can collect.'

Understanding lit up his eyes. 'You want him to think—'

'Yes.'

'That you are not afraid to—'

'Yes.'

'So you really only want their money?'

'Yes.'

He brought his hand up to his face. 'What if you *miss* your miss?'

'I won't,' Kavi said. But for his reaction to be authentic, it had to feel like she might.

'Can I just give you the money?'

'Too late for that.'

The shopkeeper swallowed and bobbled his head. 'As long as you're only taking the money, and leaving my—'

She grabbed his hand. Slapped it down flat. Flipped the knife and drilled it into the counter.

It struck the wood with a bone-rattling *thunk* and the shopkeeper stared, goggle-eyed, as the handle jutted out and wobbled between his fingers.

'Now,' Kavi whispered.

The man opened his mouth, and he let out a loud, warbling, 'Aiiiyo!' He held his hand up to the light and twisted and turned it. 'My hand!'

She gestured for him to keep going.

'How could you! You – you cold-hearted bitch!'

'Relax,' she whispered.

He cradled his uninjured hand, scowled at her, and howled, 'Fucking Taemu!'

She rolled her eyes. 'Just hand over the money.'

He passed her three crisp hundred-rayal notes.

'Thanks,' Kavi said. 'I'll see you next week.'

'Was it good?' he whispered. 'My performance?'

'Oh, yes, very realistic.' She paused. 'Let the other shop-owners know, tell them there's a new enforcer who will *only* collect what the Tivasi are due.'

Outside, Deva stood with a teacup in each hand and watched her as she strolled up to him.

She tucked the money into his shirt pocket. 'Three hundred.'

He passed her her tea, counted the money, glanced at the bookshop, then gave her a respectful nod. 'I think you'll do just fine.'

And she did, during the day, at least.

Some shopkeepers couldn't see past what she was; they spat in her wake and flung their money at her; some, like Naadan the bookseller, called her Collector-memsaab and made small talk whenever he saw her. To her surprise, some knew her: *Taemu swordmaster*, they called her; the girl who survived the Siphon; the woman who fought the Kraelish. A street-sweeper even saluted, called her *Akka* and showed her the red band tattooed around his arm. She had no idea who he was, but she told him not to salute her anymore.

She learned that Grishan, and the Tivasi by proxy, were universally feared in the Lantern district; that the act of collecting was a ritual where both parties had to play their parts: the shop-owners had to protest, she had to coax or threaten, they had to curse and swear, and only then hand over the money. When she wasn't collecting, Deva instructed she hang around, in case something came up, so she borrowed a book from the bookshop, a retelling of a Raayan epic from a fresh point of view (the maharaja's accountant's anthropomorphised pet donkey) by literary sensation Abhilash Varma, and read in the shade of the Caterpillar.

On the surface, just like Azraaya itself, Kavi pretended like she'd recovered from all that had happened. But then the sun would sink behind the minarets and domes, the temples and the walls, and she would slink back home to her hut and wait for Chotu to return. He was the only one who knew the truth. The bags under her eyes, the chronic exhaustion, the missing hours where she just wasn't there; the headaches, the nightmares, the seizures – on their second night in the hut, she'd opened her eyes to find herself curled into a foetal position, whimpering, with Chotu's bleeding hand in her mouth. 'To save your tongue, Akka,' he'd explained.

She'd dreamed that she was in the walls of their home in Ethuran: knees held tight to her chest and hand clamped over her mouth, watching Grishan slit Sravan's throat.

The next night she awoke screaming, drenched in sweat, and scampered on all fours into a corner. She was back in the darkness, with the man who'd cut her into pieces, with the scraping of saw against bone, her nostrils clogged with the metallic scent of blood.

The night after that, the men and women she'd slaughtered as the berserker appeared. Their shattered armour clanked and rattled as they ambled closer; their bones twisted into unnatural shapes and angles, their wounds and lacerations oozed pus and gore; the dismembered crawled, while the ones the berserker had decapitated walked with a pink mist where their heads should've been. Together, they boxed her in, made it hard to breathe, to think.

Chotu urged her back to her sleeping mat. Cushioned her head in his lap, brushed the hair off her face, wiped the sweat off her brow, and asked, voice thick with concern and worry, 'What happened, Akka?'

She found it hard to explain. Words refused to attach themselves to thoughts and feelings. All she could manage was a lie. 'I'll be okay. Tired. Mourning for Sravan.' For Massa. For Elisai. Haibo. Kamith. Appa. Amma.

Each morning, her memories of Ethuran, her time as Jarard's prisoner, and of the handful of minutes she'd given the berserker control of her body, so vivid and alive the night before, would wither, fall away, and leave her empty. She told herself that it was over, it was all in the past. That was then, this was now.

The lie got her through the day.

'Akka,' Chotu said, the night before her first day of training at the Vagola. 'Brought you something.' He pressed a small, flat disc into her palm, and shuffled away.

Kavi sat cross-legged on her sleeping mat, and stared at the black disc, no larger than an eyeball. 'Agoma?'

'It will help you sleep,' Chotu said, not meeting her eyes. 'Help you cope.'

She flinched. Agoma could only blunt or tranquilise, it could never fix. She licked her lips. But he was right, she needed to sleep, and tomorrow was important. 'Where did you get this?'

He shrugged.

'How much?'

'I had some money.'

'Ask me first,' Kavi said, 'next time.'

Chotu bobbed his head.

Her mouth was dry as she lifted the agoma disc, rearranged her hair, and positioned it over her nape. Jarard had used agoma on her. Had pressed it into her sternum while she begged him to leave her mind alone. His disc had looked different, and what it had done to her was not normal; was not how the artificed drug normally worked. She shuddered, took a shallow breath, and pushed it down, wincing as something sharp punctured her skin.

The agoma hit the back of her head first. Then her neck,

then it travelled all the way down to her legs: a cascading wave of relaxation that slackened the muscles around her bones and made her feel like she was floating.

Chotu guided her head onto the folded-up piece of cloth she used as a pillow while the thatched roof of the hut withered away into a clear night sky; an entire array of stars spread out just for her.

'You have to create your experience,' she heard Chotu's muffled voice say.

That's right. A user could control their agoma dream, or if they wanted to, relive a memory.

A beach. I want to be on a beach.

The stars flickered out, and the darkness transformed into the dome of a clear blue sky.

Beneath her: soft sand. At her back: the trunk of an ancient coconut tree. Before her: a pale blue ocean.

She leaned against the tree, clenched her toes in the sand, and shivered as the air – between breaths – turned icy-cold and a wave of goosebumps rippled across the skin on her forearms. She blinked, and the sky, so bright and peaceful just a heartbeat ago, vanished, and once again left her in the dark. Kavi forced herself upright. This wasn't what she wanted, this—

Her feet, of their own accord, forced her forward. The sand beneath them lost its texture, turned into something softer, colder … *ash.* She was walking on ash. Ash that clung to her naked, blistered feet as wind swept across a plain and whipped and coated her skin with it.

Cold.

So cold.

She hugged her chest and gazed up at an enormous full moon. The sky was cloudless, but the moonlight drowned out the stars, all except for the brightest, and these shimmered and danced as they watched her continue her journey across a flat, lifeless plain.

A memory. She was in another fragmented memory. She was nine again, scrawny, terrified, lost in the Deadlands after the massacre at Ethuran.

Kavi relaxed, allowed herself to sink into her own body – she wanted to know, she wanted to remember – and let
the
memory
take
over.

The oppressive, unrelenting heat of the day had caused the skin on her face and neck to peel away, and she fought the urge to scratch and pick; instead, she stuck and unstuck her tongue from the roof of her dry mouth and, 'Ahhh,' she said, just to hear her voice, like she'd been doing every few minutes to re-assure herself that she was still alive, that she was not in Hel.

Because Appa said there was no sound in Hel.

Her lips trembled, and she wiped her eyes on the inside of her elbow.

She'd taken the tunnels, just like he'd told her to. She'd not drunk the contaminated water in the stream, because he'd asked her not to. So where was he?

Where was she?

She stifled a whimper, scanned the horizon, and froze.

What is that?

In the distance, under the pale light of the moon, a boxlike structure squatted in the grey ash.

A house? A hut?

She sped up. Knocked her bruised knees against each other as she rushed, shivering, to the structure.

It *was* some kind of hut. A hut made entirely out of metal

with two eye-like windows and a massive gash in the lower half – as if a giant fist had punched its way out – that served as a door. She stared at the jagged edges of metal as she stepped inside, where a column of moonlight lanced through another hole in the roof and lit up the barren interior.

Her shoulders slumped. It didn't look like anyone lived here. No beds, no pots or pans, no jugs of water.

She blinked. Rubbed her hands together. It was warm inside.

There was no fire, but it was warm.

And the closer she got to the walls of the hut, the warmer it got. She dropped to her knees, crawled into a corner, and latched onto a piece of twisted, warm metal.

Strange hut.

Strange warm hut.

Her body soaked up the heat, the tension from her muscles oozed out; she sniffled, her chin quivered, and she burst into tears.

She hugged the piece of metal tighter, bit her knuckles, and sobbed in silence. Until a tune, wordless and nostalgic, wriggled its way out of a formless memory, and she found herself humming it. She clenched a fist and gently thumped her chest to add the percussion she knew was part of the song.

Where had she heard it before?

It comforted her, took away her fear, but also filled her with an unspeakable rage that she felt in her stomach, in her bones, in her chest – she would never hear this song again, she would forget it when she woke up because someone had done something really bad.

The tune lulled her to sleep, and then it, too, sank back into the sludge her memory was turning into. Her last thought, as she gave in to exhaustion, was that one day she would find that someone who'd taken the song from her, and she would make them hurt.

She dreamed of blood-splattered walls and floors, of the sounds of violence – screams and pleas and sobs and through it all a sinister wheezing that went on and on and on until she woke, blinked bleary eyes and squinted at the sunlight.

Her throat was raw and itchy. She was thirsty, she was hungry. And she was still lost.

She sat on her haunches in the shade of the metal hut and ran a hand across its dull red surface.

Still warm.

Why?

Only things that were alive were warm. Right?

The notion should've scared her, but she found it reassuring and oddly familiar.

She leaned her head against the hut and stared with empty eyes at the swirling grey ash that covered the plain. She should leave, she should stand up and start walking.

But which way?

West.

She cocked her head. The urge to head west was real, tangible. She licked her lips. 'It's you, isn't it?'

The soft whoosh of breeze cutting through ash was the only response she got.

'You'll be alone if I go,' she said.

Silence.

'What's your name?' She turned and faced the hut; placed both hands on the scratched and worn metal. 'Should I give you one?'

She frowned. Tried to think of a name and came up empty. 'I can't think of one now, sorry.'

A gust of wind dashed across the plain, and the hut creaked.

'I don't want to leave you.' It made her heart ache, the thought of it being alone in the waste, but she didn't have a choice, she had to go. 'We'll meet again, I promise, and I'll have a name for you then.'

Kavi stood. Flattened the beads of sweat on her forehead with her palm, but instead of walking out into the sun like she had thirteen years ago, she leaned against the hut, which she could now tell was the severed head of makra, and let the fragmented memories Jarard had unlocked merge

with

each

other.

Her time as a girl in Ethuran: the school she'd attended, the other children, the rust-coloured buildings and the narrow streets she'd played in; her father in the fields, her mother teaching the others to hum the old Taemu songs.

Everyone had forgotten the words to the old songs, but Amma, for a reason that was still unclear to Kavi, remembered the tunes. And she taught this to the other Taemu. Hummed it to them first, and then encouraged them to join her. Kavi would sit, clutching her mother's hem, and quietly hum along. She remembered her heart soaring at the angry, violent songs, where men hummed from deep within their throats and women thumped their chests to create a furious percussion; remembered feeling warm tears on her cheeks when they switched to the sad, haunted melodies that filled her with loss and sorrow and loneliness.

Then there was the aftermath of the massacre, the time spent lost in the Deadlands. In the vast stretch of land on Raaya's northern border, covered entirely in grey ash, where nothing lived or grew; whose only visitors were deranged scavenger crews who risked death to explore the area in search of relics from the Retreat or artifacts that predated human civilisation – like the makra head she now stood beside. A leftover from the ancient war from Drisana's visions? It had to be. Only something equally monstrous and horrific could've ripped its head off and torn its face open.

That morning, when she'd left the makra head and walked with the sun at her back, like she imagined the makra had told her to, she'd run into the scavenger crew that had saved her and brought her to the refugee camp set up for the survivors of Ethuran.

Kavi sighed. Sank back down to her haunches, gazed up at the ruined makra head, and ran her fingers along its twisted and dented surface.

'Are you still out here?' she whispered. 'Are you still alone?'

Chapter 5
BLADE

None of the other first-years in the Vagola canteen spoke to her. They watched, they muttered, they whispered and pointed, but kept their distance.

Kavi collected her plate of food – two idlis and a golden-brown vada with a pottle of sambhar on the side – and sat on the free bench next to the toilets. She let the hum of conversation and the clatter of steel plates and utensils wash over her as she ate.

On the surface, the Vagola was a university for mages, with separate departments dedicated to each class and where novices had to complete a three-year programme before they could be considered fully-fledged warlocks, healers, or artificers. In reality, it controlled all things maayin related, and had grown into one of the most powerful organisations on the subcontinent. Even Blades were managed by the Vagola. A warlock's countervail – complete immobility for the duration of their cast – left them extremely vulnerable, so having a trained bodyguard familiar with Harithian maayin was still considered useful.

Real Blades, however – an altogether much more violent and dangerous creature than the glorified bodyguards-in-artificed-armour they'd been reduced to – were a tradition that predated the Retreat. During the era of the First Mages, warlocks had learned to forge a maayin-based bond with a warrior who could

"

share their countervail. The result: increased manoeuvrability for the warlock; enhanced speed and strength for the warrior, their Blade. Some academics even speculated that the Blade gained a heightened awareness of maayin – there were stories of bonded Blades and warlocks breaking sieges and toppling entire cities all on their own. But at the end of the day, that's all it was, speculation and stories. The knowledge of forging the bond had been lost during the Retreat, during the four-odd centuries following the collapse of the First Empire from which no recorded history remained.

Kavi sighed. Her initial plan had seemed so simple: pass the tests, be confirmed as a mage, and join the Vagola as a novice so she could use the artifact called the Venator to find her father and brothers. But she'd failed the tests and had instead fought in the Siphon to gain admission to the Vagola as a Blade cadet.

Candidates for the Blade programme at the Vagola were usually recruited from military academies and active duty, but the Siphon gave those without military experience an opportunity to earn a place by surviving a three-month crash course that culminated in an event where entrants fought and died for the entertainment of paying spectators. Kavi had survived. She'd won a spot at the Vagola as a cadet. And with Salora's help, she'd used the Venator and found her brother, Chotu.

And now, she got to live the life she'd always dreamed of: a student, albeit not the kind she'd imagined, at the most prestigious institute of learning in Raaya; with access to all the learning and knowledge that had been out of her people's grasp for so long. With a well-paid career of protecting absent-minded warlocks (*Sir-ji, avoid the banana peel*, she'd have to say, or *Sir-ji, please, that fish curry is seven days old, don't eat it!*) awaiting her upon graduation.

She was, of course, a mage in her own right: an Azir, a hybrid mage chosen by two Jinn – Raktha, the supposedly dormant Biomancers' Jinn, and Nilasi, the Healers' Jinn – which had corrupted her maayin and caused it to behave in ways that defied the Vagola's rules and paradigms.

Which was why she could never reveal to them that she was a mage. Worst-case scenario, as Bithun had suggested, they'd kill her on the spot. Best case, she'd be kept alive in a laboratory somewhere and experimented on until her contaminated maayin eventually killed her. So as far as they were concerned, she was a dud. A dormant Azir who they couldn't use and who was no threat to them. And she intended to keep it that way.

Either way, it'd been a while since she'd been reminded of her Taemu otherness. The rickshaw company and the people she'd surrounded herself with since the Kraelish invasion had shielded her from it, and she'd almost got used to it. Almost.

She let her gaze wander around the packed canteen – it would've been nice to make a friend. There were people in her life she could trust, but none she could confide in. The Taemu looked to her for leadership. Chotu was her younger brother. Salora was friendly enough, but still very much an enigma. And Bithun – her patron, mentor, and friend – was too far away. She missed Elisai's honesty, Massa's wacky sense of humour.

The vada was fresh and crunchy with pieces of onion buried inside, and she took her time with it.

One thing she couldn't deny, much as she'd have liked to, was that the agoma Chotu had given her the night before had helped. She was alert. Her mind was clear. And for the first time since Grishan had upended her world and unravelled her plans, she could step out of the frame and look back at the picture.

And the picture did not look good.

Her people most likely resented her for capitulating to

Grishan, for Sravan's death, and for prohibiting them from fighting the Tivasi (who she now worked for). Sravan's death had also ripped the scabs off old wounds that had never fully healed, and now every night they oozed and bled into her nightmares. Then there was the thick, cloying guilt for being here at the Vagola, starting a new life while her people had been sent back to their old one. All that in sharp contrast to the tingling in her belly, the excitement – she'd made it into the Vagola. Unbelievable.

Despicable.

What kind of monster would be excited for something while the people she loved suffered?

A fucking selfish one, that's who.

Kavi mopped up the crumbs on her plate, licked her fingers, and was halfway out of her seat when a tall, broad-shouldered woman, a first-year like her, based on the uniform, slipped into the seat opposite.

'Enjoy your meal?' the woman said.

Kavi allowed herself a glimmer of hope – maybe the woman saw her eating by herself and decided, fuck these bigots, I will rise above them and befriend the Taemu – until she spotted the woman's cold, dead-eyed smile. 'Yes, did you?'

'It was average, the warlocks have a much nicer canteen.' The woman rested her elbows on the table. 'I'm Vaisha. I was selected from the military academy in Dyarabad.'

Okay? Kavi started to stand again, when the woman's hand snapped out and latched onto her wrist.

'Sit,' Vaisha said. 'I'm still talking.'

Kavi put the plate down. Sat. Studied the hand around her wrist. This was clearly someone used to Taemu who kept their eyes lowered and backs bent, who expected a *yes, memsaab*, and an *of course, memsaab* from her, and whose parents had probably celebrated after the massacre at Ethuran, whose grandparents may have even owned indentured Taemu.

'Tell me,' Kavi said, mirroring the woman's humourless smile. 'Are you particularly fond of that hand?'

It was only for a heartbeat, but Vaisha's eyes flashed with surprise, and she withdrew. She leaned away and clasped her hands together. 'When it is your turn to choose a mentor, I hope you will remember what you are.'

'And what's that?'

Vaisha ignored her. 'Because the rest of us do, and we'd be disappointed if you made the wrong choice.'

What the Hel was she talking about? 'Sure, I'll do my best.' *Now get the fuck away from me before I do something I'll regret later.*

Vaisha stood. 'I knew you would understand.'

No one else tried to stop Kavi when she left her plate in a large tub labelled 'Used dishes', then queued up with the other first-years to collect the weapons they'd left with an attendant at the entrance to the canteen.

When it was her turn, the attendant handed Kavi her sword, checked her name against a long sheet of paper, explained in a dry and tired voice that the students had been divided into three groups of sixty-one, and – he brought the sheet of paper closer to his face – told her she was allocated to group one.

After that, it was just a matter of following the signs that led them to the 'Department of Blades and Warlocks'.

The paved footpath they followed was lined on both sides with trees – banyan, mango, jujube, coralwood, gulmohar, jackfruit – and the occasional man-made pond where massive monitor-lizards lounged and watched Kavi pass with dispassionate eyes. Some of the trees had large woodblock prints nailed into their trunks: colourful images of a stoic Blade who stood with arms crossed while her cunning warlock stroked his long moustache and pointed at the words, *Participate in the annual Blade-lock tournament!* Underneath, smaller lettering warned students that to enter they must, *have a minimum 90% attendance record across all lectures and classes.*

Kavi thumbed the hilt of her sword as she walked. Drisana had gone silent after Sravan's death. No amount of prompting or cleaning or polishing could get the sword to speak to her. Now Drisana was just another person – if the consciousness inside the sword could be called a person – whom she'd disappointed.

Laughter filtered down from the large group ahead. Kavi cracked her neck and pretended not to stare at the woman with the broad shoulders who was clearly its leader.

The other students deferred to Vaisha. Agreed with everything she said. Nodded. Smiled. And when Vaisha looked their way or gave them attention, their backs visibly straightened, their eyes sparkled, and their faces flushed with admiration.

Kavi stopped a man chewing on a toothpick as he walked past her. 'What's the deal with all this?' She gestured to Vaisha and the students fawning over her.

The man pulled out his toothpick and glared at the piece of food on its tip. 'Old nobility.' He flicked the food off and shoved the toothpick back into his mouth.

The old nobles, like the sahibs, were a dying breed in Raaya. When the Kraelish abolished the monarchy (executed the royal family) the nobles used their resources to set themselves up as trading houses. Some thrived, some failed, some went into the tea plantation business, others disappeared into poverty.

'And?' Kavi said. There had to be more to Vaisha than just that.

He shrugged. 'She's good with a longsword.'

Really? That was it? Kavi shook her head. 'Thanks, carry on.'

It made no sense. How could you idolise someone like Vaisha? A hero came from nothing, was someone who faced failure and stood back up and scraped their way out despite the odds. Not some bhaenchod born into wealth and success. Or some woman who'd never had to spend a cold night staring at an empty plate.

Kavi scowled and spat.

Maybe she was being bitter, but Vaisha could trip and fall into a ditch and get mauled by these fucking lizards that were everywhere.

The part of the Vagola Kavi was familiar with – the domed building with the lecture theatres and the manicured lawns that surrounded it – turned out to be a small subsection of a much larger campus, where each discipline had its own dedicated area.

The group trudged past the School of Healing: a collection of multi-storeyed buildings where the smell of antiseptic and vomit stung Kavi's nostrils and where apron-clad students clutched books to their chests as they scurried between lectures. Conversation fell away when her group of cadets walked through the Artificers' College with its myriad laboratories, windowless towers, and eery silences in which students staggered around as if in a daze. Chatter picked up again as they passed the library, a long, flamevine-covered structure that made her heart flutter with anticipation. Then they passed the faculty residence, the gymnasium, a swimming pool, warehouses for defective artifacts, weapons storage, meeting rooms and, finally, the Department of Blades and Warlocks, which consisted of a single bloated building the size of the Picchadi stadium.

Outside, boisterous groups of cadets sat or stood in huddles. Some ate, some stretched, some clapped and shouted encouragement at a woman who was apparently on her two-hundred-and-eighty-ninth push-up.

A man strolled up to the first-years. Long, slicked-back hair, bags under his eyes, thick layer of stubble on his face. 'Group one, follow me. Two and three, wait here,' he said, not bothering with introductions, and led Kavi's group inside the building, through a series of corridors, and out onto a wide courtyard.

He arranged them into neat rows that faced a dais – pausing to chew out a cadet for the spilled food on their uniform – where Vagola staff were busy erecting a blackboard.

More men and women, all wearing dark training shirts and trousers, and all equally battle-scarred, strode into the courtyard and walked onto the dais.

Kavi, buried in the back row, wiped clammy hands on her crisp, new uniform and stared at the Gashani woman who towered over the other instructors; at her tattooed chin, the twin fangs that trailed down each corner of her mouth, and at the scars that knitted their way across her forearms. The last time they'd spoken to each other had been in Bochan, after Kavi had failed the tests to become a mage.

Taemu, where did you learn to move like that? She'd asked Kavi.
Can you use a weapon?
Any experience in hand-to-hand combat?
With some training, I think you can be a Blade.
Greema cracked her neck, glanced at Kavi, expressionless, and adjusted the pair of swords she wore on her hip.

Chapter 6
BLADE

The Boy

'All right, all right, that's enough,' the man who'd led them into the courtyard said, ushering the Vagola staff away from the blackboard. Once they were clear, he used a piece of chalk to scrawl seven names onto its surface.

He flung the chalk aside. 'Your first task' – he slapped the board – 'choose your mentor.'

Ah, so this was what Vaisha had been hinting at.

The man exchanged a glance with Greema, who raised an eyebrow.

'Okay, fine.' He scratched the stubble on his neck. 'My name is Rathore. First-year coordinator. I deal with any issues the instructors may have. You? If you have any issues? Take it up with your mentor. They will be your guide and your teacher for the rest of the year.

'Now, the tradition of choosing a mentor goes all the way back to—' Rathore frowned. 'Actually, I don't know, it's just how it's always been done. I did it' – he cocked a thumb at the six other instructors – 'they did it, and you will too. Why, you ask? Why do you have to pick a teacher you know nothing about?' He shrugged. 'Maybe it's to teach you to trust your gut. Maybe it's to teach you responsibility. Who knows? Either way—' He began matching the seven names on the board – one of which was his own – with the instructors on the dais, but Kavi had stopped listening. She'd already made her choice.

'Now, one at a time,' Rathore said. 'Write your name.' He pointed at a cadet in the front row. 'You do know how to write, yes?'

The man checked over his shoulder then slowly nodded.

'Excellent, come up here and write your name under your mentor.'

One by one, they went up on the dais – many hesitated, glanced from one instructor to the other, before Rathore suggested they 'stop wasting time' – and wrote their names on the blackboard.

By the time it was Kavi's turn, there were long columns of student names scribbled under each of the instructor's names, except for Greema's, which remained blank.

Kavi picked up the chalk. So, these fuckers were too good to work under a Gashani tribeswoman. And what Vaisha had said earlier, *remember what you are ... we'd be disappointed if you made the wrong choice*, made sense now. The other students didn't want to share a mentor with her.

She'd expected more from this place but was not surprised. The Vagola was a microcosm of the outside world, and just like everyone else here, she had her part to play. Best not to disappoint. She wrote her name on the board under Greema's.

'All right,' Rathore said when everyone was done. 'Your mentors will now take over.'

The group split up: cadets followed their mentors to different corners of the courtyard, but Kavi stayed put. Greema strode in her direction.

'Memsaab—'

'Ma'am,' Greema said, 'or sir.'

'Ma'am. Good to see you again.'

Greema inclined her head. 'It's—'

'Chootias,' Rathore said, shaking his head at the other cadets as he walked up behind Greema and peered at Kavi. 'The rest of your cohort are all bloody chootias. Did you know your mentor won the tournament thrice as a student? Back-to-back-to-back when everyone was rooting for her to lose? No? Did you know her warlock was an archmage? That she once fought—'

'Rathore,' Greema said in a low growl that shut the man up.

Kavi stared at Greema, who seemed taller, larger, more intimidating.

'I want her to understand how lucky she is,' Rathore said.

'I know, sir,' Kavi said.

He cocked his head. Narrowed his eyes at her. 'You fought in the Siphon.'

It wasn't a question. But she nodded.

'Which school do you use?'

'I—' Kavi tugged on an ear. *Use* a school? 'I'm not sure.'

Rathore's brows shot up. 'You got this far on just the basics?' He turned to Greema. 'Will you teach her the Gashani school?'

Greema shrugged. 'If she wants to learn.'

He grinned. 'Now wouldn't that be something to see.'

'Rathore …' Greema said.

'Yes?'

'Your cadets are waiting for you.'

Once the man had left them alone, Greema grunted, adjusted the pair of longswords on her hip, raised three fingers into the air, and said, 'The Blade programme runs concurrently to the warlock's – three years, divided into six terms – but with its own unique syllabus. Consider yourself a cadet at a military academy while simultaneously studying at the most prestigious university in Raaya. You will master a weapon, build your strength and resilience, and learn to fight alongside a warlock. You will study the Imperial campaigns and undergo officer training in your second year. You will attend lectures on Jinn theory and demonstrate an intermediate understanding of maayin – Harithian maayin, specifically.'

She let her hand fall. 'For your first year, in term one, your day will be split between swordcraft, practice with your warlock, self-managed training and study, and some battle theory. Term two – the second half of the year – you and your warlock will join a squad and head to Draghal, to the Nathrian border for field exercises. Today, you will meet your warlock, familiarise yourself with their maayin, and fight a practice duel.'

Greema paused. Took a deep breath. Studied the scattered groups of students. 'I heard what the Taemu battalion did during the invasion.'

Kavi's lips tightened into a thin line.

'That experience will serve you well,' Greema said, oblivious to, or choosing to ignore, Kavi's discomfort. 'But do not get complacent. You are not the only one here who fought for Azraaya.' She returned a casual salute from a passing instructor. 'Do you understand why Rathore asked you about sword schools?'

Kavi hesitated. Shook her head.

'Most of your peers have been trained in very specific styles of swordplay called schools – most of them date back to before the Kraelish; some are unique to regions, or families, or tribes, like the Gashani school. Many were developed by individual swordsmen who taught it to earn a living, often exclusively to wealthy nobles. All of them, without exception, have evolved over the centuries with a single, bloody-minded purpose: to master the art of killing.' Greema gazed down at Kavi. 'You have done well to get so far, but make no mistake, you are at an extreme disadvantage.'

Kavi frowned. 'I fought cadets from the Vagola during the Siphon—'

Greema cut her off with a back-handed wave. 'No one worth fighting participates in the Siphon. Only those the Vagola considers expendable.'

She tensed. Caught herself grinding her teeth. 'Ze'aan was expendable?'

'The warlock?' Greema shook her head. 'No, not her. If the archmages had known what she was capable of – no. She hid her ability from her teachers, manipulated them. The girl was a prodigy.'

A prodigy? She was a monster. Ze'aan had been assigned to Kavi's squad for the Siphon – they were meant to protect each other, work together, but instead Ze'aan had waited until everyone on their squad had fallen before revealing the extent of her ability. And then, during the Kraelish assault on Azraaya, Ze'aan had turned traitor, switched sides, and slaughtered her people at the chokepoint.

Why? Kavi had asked her.

I've spent my whole life trying to escape this place, Ze'aan had said. *I used to think there was something wrong with me. That I was the only one who could see its divisions, its obsessions, its rituals that kept everything in its place – the greed and rot at the top, the poverty and desperation at the bottom, the indifference in between ... I searched for others like me, people who didn't belong to either world. But the ones I found I had nothing in common with. They lived with an asphyxiating closedness. Intoxicated with wealth.*

I couldn't stand to be around them. I packed my bags, bought tickets – but then, the week before I was meant to leave, I was forced to test ... Once they learned I was a warlock, I was trapped. I was a mage, and I would serve the Republic. The Vagola would never let me leave. I'd spend the rest of my life in service to the people I hated.

I had nowhere to go, no one to turn to, so I reached out to them, and they offered me a way out. A new life in Kraelin. But I would have to earn it. Kavi could still feel Ze'aan's breath on her face as the warlock whispered in her ear. *I don't belong here, Kavithri, and neither do you. Surrender, and they will let your people live. Fight, stand in my way, and I will not hesitate to move you.*

'Do they know where she is now?' Kavi said, and the venom in her voice drew a sharp glance from Greema.

'No. But they want her back.'

'What will her punishment be? If they find her.'

'Punishment?' Greema said, bemused. 'No, they want her back on our side.'

Blood rushed to Kavi's ears and the berserker in her core hissed and strained at its chains. 'She *betrayed* us. Killed so many.'

'You of all people should know,' Greema said, 'the rules don't apply to someone like her. The girl is too powerful – she's more useful to the Republic fighting for them than she is rotting in a dungeon or beheaded in the bazaar.' She checked the entrance to the courtyard. 'They're running late.'

Kavi bit her tongue. Greema was right, this was how Raaya worked. From its lowest peon all the way up to Councilman Nashik Faria. If you weren't useful, if you weren't wealthy or had no connections to the wealthy, you were not worth their time. It was why Kavi couldn't go to the city guard or the police for help after Sravan's murder.

'Ma'am?' Kavi said, forcing the image of Sravan's slit throat out of her head. 'Rathore said your warlock was an archmage?'

'He did.'

'Are they still alive?'

Greema snorted. 'Oh, yes.'

'So how come you aren't still with them?'

'He got offered a post at the Vagola and retired early,' Greema said. 'You'll meet him soon enough.'

'Did you work together for a long time?'

'Since I graduated.'

'You must be good friends.'

Greema pursed her lips. 'I suppose? We disagreed on an almost daily basis. Came close to killing each other once.'

Kavi jerked her head back. 'But you still stuck around as his Blade? Why?'

'Mutual respect. Ah, they're here.'

Novice warlocks, one for each Blade plus a handful of instructors, streamed into the courtyard. Their badges – flat emerald discs pinned high on their chests – glittered in the sunlight in sharp contrast to the not-quite-here gaze most of them seemed to wear. Unlike her and the other Blade cadets, the novices would spend most of their three years at the Vagola in classrooms and lecture-halls. Training with the Blade cadets was important, but by no means was it a priority.

A warlock at the head of a large group of novices waved at Greema, who raised a hand in response. The man abandoned his students and marched over.

Tall and slender, he had the top of his Kraelish shirt unbuttoned and a thicket of chest hair puffed out of the opening. More hair grew out of his ears, and even more jutted out of his nose where it merged with a bushy moustache.

'Instructor Greema,' he said.

'Archmage Jefore,' Greema replied.

'I haven't seen you since—'

'The dinner at your house two nights ago.'

'Ah, yes,' Jefore said with a grimace. 'Of course, the dinner. '

'How's Radha?'

'She's fine.' Jefore jutted his chin out. 'Why?'

Greema's lips twitched. 'Just asking.'

'Look,' Jefore said, slashing the air for emphasis. 'I don't know what my wife has been telling you behind my back—'

'I haven't heard anything.'

'Good.'

'About the accident.'

His face went red.

And for the first time since Kavi had met her, Greema grinned.

'You—' Jefore flared his nostrils and fought for composure. 'That would have never happened if you hadn't stolen my beedis.'

'Your beedis made the place stink,' Greema said, 'and I wouldn't have taken them if you weren't being such a cantankerous bastard.'

Kavi's eyes shifted between the pair as she tried to keep up. She had so many questions: What accident? What did the beedis have to do with it? What was the relationship between Greema and Jefore's wife? Either way, Greema was goading the warlock and clearly enjoying it.

'Cantankerous—' Jefore said in astonishment.

'—bastard.' Greema finished for him.

Jefore sighed and shifted his attention to Kavi. 'Just the one cadet?' he said. And when Greema didn't respond: 'What's your name?'

'Kavithri.'

He gazed into her eyes; first one, then the other.

'Greema, are there any other Taemu first-years?'

'No.'

'Your cadet has been allocated to the Surin.'

Greema swore in a language Kavi didn't understand.

'Someone had to take him,' Jefore said.

Greema clenched her jaw and looked away.

'Sir?' Kavi cleared her throat. 'What is the—'

'I will speak to you after the pairing is complete,' Jefore said, eyeing the crowd that had now gathered. He exchanged a nod with Greema and returned to his novices.

'Ma'am,' Kavi said, a nameless dread slowly seeping through her skin. 'What's a Surin?'

'Jefore will explain,' Greema said, and hesitated. 'I over-reacted, I apologise. It's nothing to worry about.'

It sure didn't seem like nothing to worry about. But Kavi bobbed her head in acquiescence.

'Cadets! Novices!' A voice boomed through the courtyard. 'Before we begin the pairing, an announcement regarding the annual Blade-lock tournament.'

The source of the voice was a woman, a warlock who stood on the dais and spoke into some sort of voice amplifier.

'Despite what you may have heard,' the warlock said, 'the tournament will still go ahead.'

Kavi scowled. She hadn't heard anything about it not going ahead.

'Preliminary rounds will be held in a couple of weeks and the draw for the first round shall be announced not long after. As usual, only students of the Department of Blades and Warlocks are permitted to participate. We recommend you enter with the Blade or warlock you are paired with, but if you wish to partner with a student from another year, feel free to do so.'

Interesting. But it made no difference to Kavi. The only warlock she knew, Ze'aan, was a mass-murdering psychopath who'd turned traitor and joined the Kraelish. Well, she was now acquainted with Archmage Jefore, but it's not like she could ask him to team up.

'The reward, once again thanks to our generous alumni, will be one hundred thousand rayals, split evenly between the winners. Everyone who takes part will receive a certificate, and applause.'

Kavi froze. There was no way she'd heard that right. 'Ma'am.'

'Yes?' Greema said.

'Is the prize really' – she swallowed – 'one hundred thousand rayals?'

'Oh, yes.'

Eyes bulged skin tingled breath caught in Kavi's thumping chest.

This was it.

This was her way out.

The warlock continued explaining the rules, but Kavi's mind was a pebble in a whirlpool. The prize money, if she won, was something she'd have *earned*. No question. And after what, seven months? Eight? She could buy the rickshaw company back.

She took a series of sharp breaths and forced her fists to unclench.

There was no guarantee that Grishan would keep his word. But she had to try. Had to hope. This was what she needed. She'd start over; do what she'd done with Bithun, back when she'd trained to fight in the Siphon. She'd wake before dawn, when no one needed anything from her, and push her body till it broke. Then she'd heal, using her warped and twisted maayin, and start all over again.

'Now,' the warlock on the dais said. 'We have paired our novices with the cadets we judged best suited to their abilities. You cannot switch partners for the duration of the term. The exception being the tournament, of course. Cadets, please remain with your mentors, your warlocks know who you are, and will come to you.'

Kavi's palms were sweaty again. She wiped the moisture off

them and searched the arena for a warlock who was striding in her direction. Yes, striding. A sign they were confident. Powerful. To win, she needed a competent warlock who could hold their own.

A cadaverous boy came shambling in her direction. Shoulders bowed, as if there were some great weight forcing him down; hands buried in pockets and eyes on the ground before his feet. Each plodding step brought him closer, and Kavi found that she couldn't look away. The boy was the same height as her, but bone-thin with short hair that seemed to curl every which way. A thick scar ran down the middle of his face – from the base of his scalp, down the length of his forehead, between his eyebrows, over his nose, mouth, chin, neck, and disappeared into the buttoned-up collar of his shirt. If she'd seen him on the street and was asked to guess his age, she'd have said thirteen, or twelve; but he was in the Vagola, wearing the warlock's badge, so he had to be sixteen at least.

Entranced and somewhat impressed by the unusual scar, it took her a moment to register the hand he'd extended to her.

A handshake?

His eyes flicked up to her face, then back down to his feet.

Kavi hesitated. His eyes – for just that split-second, he'd recognised her. From where? She'd never seen him before.

Greema cleared her throat.

Kavi slapped her hand into his and squeezed. He'd probably watched her fight in the Siphon or something—

She gasped. A familiar voice simultaneously whispered and roared inside her head.

KAVI. Kavithri.

Drisana.

Close.

Stay close.

What?

To him.

The boy.

She blinked. And she was blind. She screamed, but no sound left her throat. Her ears popped. Pain blossomed inside her chest.

And she could see again.

She hung suspended in the nothingness, in endless pitch-black, a speck in the eye of a Jinn. The dark orb at the Jinn's core dilated like a pupil, and thick, radiant green light curled around its curvature; and while Kavi struggled for air, Harith, the warlock's Jinn, sent its maayin to her. The threads of green light slithered and coiled and intertwined with each other, like snakes, or links in a chain.

She recoiled, shrank from it. This was not her Jinn, this was not her maayin. Hers was the blood-red of Raktha, the cerulean blue of Nilasi. This ... it was *his*, this was the boy's Jinn.

Kavi's chest exploded. She watched as blue and red tendrils of maayin – maayin from her own Jinn, from Nilasi and Raktha – erupted from the cavity in her torso and reached for Harith's threads.

STAY CLOSE.

And she could breathe again. She released the boy's hand as she snapped back to the courtyard.

'Have we met?' Kavi said, mouth dry.

'We – no, never met.' He spoke in a soft voice, almost a mumble, and she needed to lean closer to hear him.

'What's your name?' she asked.

'Azia,' he said, and flinched.

Kavi stepped back. Was she standing too close? 'I'm Kavi,' she said. And just to be safe: 'You've been assigned to me?'

'Just for this year,' he said, bobbing his head in apology.

'Uhm.' She scratched her head. *This* was her warlock? The powerful mage she was supposed to train with and fight alongside for the rest of the year? He looked like he'd keel over if she sneezed at him. 'Thank you?'

He bobbed his head again and shuffled around so he stood at her shoulder.

Kavi chewed the inside of her cheek. This was not what she'd expected. Warlocks were cold, haughty, aloof, unreadable, like Ze'aan.

She squeezed the hilt of her sword. *Why do you want me to stay close to him?*

Silence.

Drisana, why?

Two.

Will save you.

He is.

One.

A sliver of ice expanded and burst inside Kavi's gut. She pressed a hand to her stomach and, out of the corner of her eyes, stared at the boy. *Save me from what?*

'Ah, you found her,' Jefore shouted, striding over.

Azia nodded and mumbled something incomprehensible.

'Good, good.' Jefore slapped the boy on the back and almost sent him flying. 'Now, shall we head to the arena? Which one was it again?'

'I'll lead,' Greema said, and gestured to Azia, who was regaining his balance. 'Walk with me.'

Chapter 7

BLADE

Surin

Greema led them through the building's labyrinthine corridors where the hirsute archmage slowed his pace and gestured for Kavi to do the same.

When he judged they were safely out of earshot, he said, 'So, what do you think of your warlock?'

'Seems nice enough,' she said, and added, 'Archmage.'

'Oh, I'm sure,' he said, flattening his moustache with thumb and forefinger. 'As I was saying earlier, a Surin is a type of warlock. One that is extremely rare.'

Kavi nodded. She'd never read or heard of them.

'You don't see them very often because most are killed during the manifestation.' Jefore raised a hand to forestall her questions. 'Sometimes, typically at the age of twelve, Harith chooses a child and gives them access to a tremendous amount of its maayin. How much? We think the size of their krasna could fill this building.'

Kavi's eyes bulged. Impossible.

'Why? How?' Jefore shrugged. 'We don't know, Harith is the only Jinn that does this. But the initial burst from the connection is so immense, the power so tremendous, that the maayin rips its way out of the child and tears them in half.'

'The Jinn kills its own mage?' Kavi whispered.

'Yes, most do not survive the manifestation. But the rare few that do survive – we've had two in the last sixty years – are scarred for the rest of their lives, and more importantly, the mind of the Surin subconsciously creates what we call an inhibitor. A construct – some say mental, some say in the realm of the Jinn – that prevents them from ever drawing more than a drop of maayin from Harith. Self-preservation, you see?'

'So' – Kavi fought the urge to bite her nails – 'Surin are weaker warlocks?'

'The weakest.'

'And Azia, is—'

'A Surin, yes.'

Fuck.

'We use them as scouts, or sometimes they venture into academia and research,' Jefore said, ignoring her dismay. 'However weak they are, they are still one of us.'

The tournament prize money shrank and sped away into the distance, far out of her reach, and with it, any hope she had of reclaiming the rickshaw company.

'I want you to be extra careful with Azia,' Jefore said, leading her down a winding marble staircase.

'Extra?'

'He has immaculate control of his maayin – partly because of his smaller krasna, but also because he's had private lessons for the last four years, ever since the manifestation.' Jefore sighed, seemed to weigh each word before he said it. 'The boy was severely bullied at school. He has a complicated background, and the scar made everything worse for him. His father told me that he tried wearing a mask, but it changed nothing. So, he just stopped going. With the exception of the Vagola-mandated lessons, he's been a shut-in for at least a year now.'

Kavi cocked her head. 'A complicated background?'

'Ah, it's better if you can get him to tell you himself.' Jefore hopped off the staircase, onto a landing, ducked under an archway, and they stepped into an underground arena similar to the one Kavi had fought in during her training for the Siphon, with tiered seating and bright, artificed lamps that attached to the ceiling. This one was a much larger, cavernous version.

'The scar,' Kavi said. 'Does it go all the way …?' She ran a finger down the length of her sternum.

'From what I've heard.' Jefore nodded. 'But again, ask him.'

Not a chance in Hel.

The sanded field was divided, using white paint, into ten smaller rectangles. At each end of these rectangles sat a pedestal, over which hovered the chicken-sized crystal the combatants would soon aim to destroy. Ten separate arenas where ten separate Blade-lock matches or duels could be held.

'We're in court seven,' Greema said over her shoulder.

'I'll leave them with you,' Jefore said. 'Azia has already been briefed.'

He exchanged a nod with Greema, glanced at Azia with what may have been concern, or pity, and slapped Kavi on the shoulder before turning on his heel and marching back out.

At the edge of each court, standing patiently with a large wooden crate at their feet, was a student – an artificer, based on the thick orange pin on their lapel.

The stocky man by court seven nodded at their approach and undid the clasps on the crate.

'Which one is the cadet?' he said.

Kavi gave him an *are-you-serious?* look and craned her neck to peek inside the crate. Artificed armour. Wooden practice swords.

'They told me to ask,' the artificer muttered, and gestured for Kavi to hand over her sword. 'This will ensure the practice sword matches the weight and dimensions of your weapon.' He unsheathed Drisana and pressed a bronze band onto its blade, squeezed and adjusted until he was satisfied, then repeated the procedure with a wooden sword.

The wooden sword, to Kavi and Azia's amazement – the boy had joined her to watch the artificer work – morphed into a copy of Drisana. The artificer handed it to her, and she tested it: the grip, the swing, the top-heavy blade and the way it urged her forward, all the same.

'Okay?' the artificer asked.

She nodded.

He then fitted her with the armour, which, also to her surprise, was different to what she'd used in the Siphon. As he strapped each component onto her body, he ran a finger along its surface, and the metal moulded itself to fit her perfectly.

'Right or left-handed?' he said, holding up a gauntlet.

'Right,' she said.

'Want shield or not?'

'I can choose?'

'Yes, different gauntlets if you don't use a shield.'

Greema cleared her throat. 'A word with my students, please.'

The artificer inclined his head.

Greema led them away from the man. 'I would recommend *not* using the shield.'

'But we used them in the Siphon,' Kavi said.

'Forget what you did in the Siphon.' Greema gestured for Azia to come closer. 'You need to hear this too. Most Blades don't use the shield – they're more effective without it.'

'But the second maayin release?' Kavi frowned and scratched the back of an ear. Artificed armour was built to absorb a portion of Harithian maayin upon impact, and this maayin could be used offensively by punching one of two buttons on the inside of the armour's gauntlet: the first button discharged the stored maayin from the surface of the entire armour in a small yet powerful explosion – extremely useful in close combat versus multiple enemies; the second, the one Greema was asking her to forsake, released the maayin in a focused, targeted blast from the surface of the shield, which was great against ranged opponents.

'If you know how to use your swords, one maayin release is more than enough.' Greema stuck her tongue in her cheek, glanced at the artificer who was now attending to another student, and lowered her voice. 'It is not good to rely on the shield. The artificers refuse to acknowledge this, but shields are unreliable and have failed us in combat.'

This was news to Kavi. But Greema knew what she was talking about, and Kavi trusted her, so she'd forego the shield. She found them clunky and intrusive, anyway. 'Okay.'

She turned back to the artificer to find him armouring another cadet, who caught Kavi's eye, and smirked.

Kavi's mouth twisted, but she forced it into the semblance of a smile.

Vaisha scoffed and adjusted her chestplate.

'Shield or not?' the artificer asked her.

Vaisha shook her head. 'No need.'

He turned to Kavi. 'What did you decide?'

'Same,' Kavi said.

The artificer reached into the crate and extracted two pairs of identical gauntlets. He flipped them over, pointed to the button embedded under the maayin gauge. 'Only one release.'

He showed it to Vaisha, who nodded; then waved it at Kavi, who said, 'Got it.'

Once they'd both equipped the gauntlets, the artificer shut the crate and laid both wooden swords on top of it.

Vaisha's, Kavi noted, was longer and had a thicker blade.

'The practice swords have been artificed,' he said, and pointed at the edges. 'A powerful hit will stun, a lighter hit – a slash – will just be painful.'

Just?

'The maayin release has also been tempered – smaller radius, less intensity. The Vagola does not wish for any of its students to sustain a serious injury while in combat, so you will fight with these weapons in the tournament and all practice duels. Get used to them.' He gestured for both Vaisha and Kavi to approach. 'Touch it and experience the pain for yourselves.'

Vaisha didn't hesitate. She pressed the flat of one hand on her sword, and snatched it away with a hiss.

That's what you get. You needed to be careful with these things. Kavi gently pressed her index finger onto the— Needles, sharp and searing, jammed their way into her skin and forced her to yank her hand away with a muffled yelp.

The artificer grinned and stepped away from the crate. 'Leave your equipment in the crate when you're done,' he said, and sauntered away to chat with another artificer.

Vaisha picked up her sword with both hands and examined the edge.

Kavi grunted and reached for hers.

'I forgot to mention,' Vaisha said. 'You are not from the tribes, and regardless of how flawed the Gashani school is, you have no right to learn it. The other cadets understand this, and you must, too.' She flexed her wrists, sent her sword slicing through the air in front of Kavi. 'One must stick to what is theirs. You are Taemu, so use the Taemu school, the others are not for you.'

'You just said—' Kavi clenched and unclenched her jaw; forced the air out of her nostrils. Vaisha knew damn well that the Taemu style of swordplay had been wiped out centuries ago. Who the fuck was she supposed to learn it from? Besides,

Vaisha had wanted Kavi to pick Greema as a mentor, right? And she'd happily obliged; but now Vaisha wanted her to *not* learn from Greema? 'Make up your fucking mind.'

'Oh, I have,' Vaisha said, signalling for her warlock, a tall man with patchy stubble, to step onto the court. 'I believe that people, like *rickshaws*, should stay in their lanes. You are born the way you are for a reason. Respect it.'

There was sudden pounding in Kavi's temples, a narrowing of her vision, a heightened awareness of the sweat on her skin and the tightness of the muscle underneath. 'And,' she said, voice dropping dangerously low, 'what reason is that?'

Vaisha smiled. 'Why are dogs, dogs? Pigs, pigs?'

Kavi had met people like Vaisha before: narcissistic psychopaths who tried to shove their worldview onto you, obnoxiously self-assured and confident because a group of imbeciles agreed with every repugnant notion that left their mouth; who told you how to think, what to think, what to be, what to read, how to talk, how to live – it was fucking exhausting. She swallowed through a dry mouth and turned her back on Vaisha.

She'd lost her temper once before in a place like this. She'd allowed the berserker to surface for a single gulp of air and it had gotten her suspended from the Siphon. It wouldn't happen again. Let the woman say what she wanted to say. *Just words. That's all.*

'Relax,' Greema said, tapping Kavi on the wrist.

She'd been clutching the hilt of her sword so hard that her knuckles had turned pale.

'Azia, you know how this works?' Greema gestured to the court, the pedestals, and the crystals.

'The archmage explained,' he said. 'But I've never seen it in person.'

'Each warlock and Blade pair is allocated a crystal; your goal is to destroy the enemy crystal while protecting your own,' Greema said. 'If both crystals are still intact at the end of the ten-minute round, the match is ruled a tie. Warlocks *must* remain behind their crystal at all times and can only be attacked while they are casting. It may not say so in the rules, but the match is essentially over if the warlock ends their cast – not just because their crystal would be without protection, but because it takes most warlocks a couple of hours to replenish their krasna and cast again.'

Greema gave Azia an encouraging nod. 'Go ahead, walk around inside. See what it feels like, test the crystals.'

Azia took a tentative step over the white chalk outline that marked the field of battle.

Kavi flexed her jaw, used the base of her palm to squeeze the tightness out of her neck.

'Breathe,' Greema said. 'If you're not aware of your breath, you are not in the present.' She gazed over Kavi's shoulder at Vaisha and her warlock. 'For today's duel, that is all I want you to focus on. Be present. Keep your mind from drifting into the future or dwelling on the past.'

Kavi managed a couple of slow, deliberate breaths before the image of Sravan's gaping wound flashed through her head and forced her to start over again.

'I know you're fast,' Greema said. 'But speed will not be enough here. Do not fight with preconceived notions of your own prowess.' She tilted her head at Vaisha. 'Your opponent is from the Minari school, this will not be easy.'

It never was. 'You know about this Minari style?'

'*School.* And yes, it's one of the older ones, taught only to nobles and those wealthy enough to afford it.'

Kavi fought the urge to spit. 'So, it's just for the elite?'

'They use a two-handed stance, favour heavier blades, focus

on power and on ending duels with a single blow,' Greema said. She had an edge to her voice that made Kavi straighten. 'Students practise their strikes on cadavers, or on criminals sentenced to death. That's what makes it expensive.'

Because of all the bribes. Kavi's mouth twisted.

'Listen and understand this well,' Greema continued. 'There are only three things a sword can do.' She held up three large fingers in Kavi's face. 'Cut. Stab. Slash. Your opponent will cut. And cut hard. And if that doesn't end the fight, she will retake her stance and look to counter.'

'Yes, ma'am,' Kavi said. This was nothing like Mojan's lessons. The insight, the knowledge – Rathore was right, the other students were all chootias.

'Every strike will have intent. Every movement will have purpose. Find her rhythm, calibrate your speed to disrupt it, and you will win.'

A jolt ran up Kavi's spine. There was still hope. Even if her warlock was the 'weakest', with Greema on her side, she still had a chance. Besides, it was inconceivable that someone like Vaisha, someone who had lived a life of privilege and been handed advantage after advantage, could best her in a battle of wills. The rules were different for Kavi; every mistake she made would be scrutinised, every failure amplified and used as ammunition to argue that the Taemu did not deserve a place at the Vagola. There was so much more at stake for her, and she could not afford to lose.

'Azia,' Greema said, raising her voice. 'You will want to stand at least an arm's length behind the crystal.'

The boy nodded, took up a position a metre or so behind the crystal.

'Ma'am,' Vaisha shouted from across the court. 'We're ready.'

Greema flashed her a thumbs-up.

Kavi slapped her helmet, rolled her shoulders, and walked onto the court.

Chapter 8
BLADE

Duel

'Azia,' Greema said, 'begin.'

Azia raised both hands, palms up, as if he was urging some-one to stand, and froze with his wrists at hip level. The air over both his hands turned translucent, shimmered, and a pair of emerald-green petals, one over each palm, bloomed to life.

Kavi waited. *That's it?* That was all the maayin he could summon? Ze'aan ... Kavi gritted her teeth. Ze'aan was a prodigy, she shouldn't compare Azia to her.

'Listen,' Kavi said, walking up to the frozen warlock, 'I've done this sort of thing before. All you need to do is protect the crystal – use your maayin to keep it safe, intact, and leave the rest to me.'

The boy gazed at her out of the corner of his eyes.

'Good,' Kavi said. 'Let's do this.' She hefted her sword again, steadied her breath, and turned to face their opponents.

Vaisha stood by the white line that marked the halfway point on the field, and beckoned Kavi over.

'My warlock has promised not to interfere,' Vaisha said, craning her neck to look around Kavi. 'Yours, it appears, will make no difference.' She fell into her battle stance: dragged a foot across the sand, bent her knees, raised her sword until both wrists were over her head. '*We* will decide this.'

Kavi took her own stance, the tip of her wooden sword in line with the bridge of her nose, and locked eyes with her opponent.

Vaisha's open stance was an illusion, a ruse to embolden an opponent to make the first move. Perfectly still, but capable of exploding into movement at the slightest provocation. There were no openings; it could adjust to anything Kavi did.

Vaisha watched and waited, her eyes wide, unblinking, and assessing.

Kavi's heart pounded. She licked the sweat off her upper lip. Her breath wavered. She was in the office of the Imperial Rickshaw Company: vomit in her nostrils, vomit clogging her throat, a knee digging into her spine, hands squeezing both sides of her head and forcing her to watch as Sravan's throat was slit. This time it was slower, almost gentle. The blade parted the skin, dark blood trickled down his neck. He choked, gurgled, wheezed. He—

Focus.

Breathe in.

Breathe.

Out.

Vaisha waited. Watched.

Kavi blinked.

Vaisha hammered her right foot down. Twisted her hips, her shoulders. Lips parted to expose bared teeth, eyes widened with fury, and her sword blurred.

Kavi judged the trajectory. Locked her knees. Her wrists. Kept her elbows and shoulders loose to absorb the impact. She could parry to the left, step in with a cut, or a slash.

The swords met with an ear-splitting *crack!* and the blow forced Kavi down to one knee.

Her entire body shook from the impact, and an old memory resurfaced: running skipping giggling through the streets of

Ethuran with a stick in one hand. She jumped over an upturned cart, rounded a sleeping buffalo, and for some asinine reason smacked her stick against the trunk of a large banyan tree. It bounced right off. Her arm *boinnnged* and vibrated and she dropped the stick with a hiss.

This was the same. No pain. Just that jarring feeling. If she took another hit like that, her arms would go completely numb.

Vaisha stepped back into her stance and threw out her right leg.

Get up get-up getup! Kavi grunted. Forced herself upright. Skipped back.

Vaisha predicted the movement. Instead of stomping her foot down, she lunged.

Kavi's eyes bulged. There was no time. She was off-balance. Overpowered. And as much as she hated to admit it, outclassed. She tightened her sword and positioned it into a horizontal block.

Thwack!

Fingers stung. Wrists twisted and throbbed. Her grip loosened, disintegrated, and her sword spun out of her hands.

She stumbled after it, face twisted into a grimace as a bone-deep keening spread through her arms.

Vaisha skipped closer, kicked Kavi in the side, and sent her sprawling in the sand and away from her sword. She raised her practice sword above her head.

Kavi groaned. Lifted a heavy arm to protect her face. This would hurt, but she deserved no less; she'd grown complacent, she'd let events from her life outside the Vagola seep into it. This would be her punishment, then. Her joints and muscles tightened as she braced herself.

Vaisha's eyes flashed with victorious glee, and—

Glass shattered.

Kavi flinched.

'Halt,' Greema shouted, and a burst of applause punctuated the command.

Vaisha froze. She stared, first at Greema, then at Azia. Her mouth twisted into an ugly scowl as she lowered her weapon. 'You understand that *we* are supposed to protect *them*, right?' She turned on her heel, muttered, 'Waste of time,' acknowledged the applause from the spectating students with a wave, and strolled back to her warlock to exchange a congratulatory handshake with him.

At the other end of the court, Azia stood over the shards of their broken crystal. He withdrew his krasna, the petals of maayin evaporated, and he staggered out of his cast.

Kavi shoved herself upright, her sigh of relief cut short as Vaisha's words, the hushed whispers and mangled mumbling of the spectators, and finally the shattered crystal at Azia's feet all added up. He'd destroyed their own crystal to stop the duel.

She'd asked him to defend it, and he'd – the edges of her vision flashed, and heat travelled from her core up through her chest and into her jaw. He didn't trust her. It didn't matter that she'd lost her duel to Vaisha, she'd asked Azia to protect the crystal, and he'd ignored her.

Azia wrung his hands as she strode up to him. 'Are you oka—'

'What the fuck are you doing?' she snarled. 'I asked you to do one thing. One thing. Do you not fucking under—' She clamped her mouth shut as his eyes went wide and he started to tear up.

What the Hel?

Why was he crying?

'Kavi,' Greema said. 'A word.'

Me? This was *her* fault?

Azia turned his back on her, and wiping his face on a sleeve, walked away.

'Kavi,' Greema said again.

'Ma'am.' Kavi lowered her head and walked over.

Greema crossed her arms. 'You think he is weak.'

'I … No, but his maayin—'

'His maayin? Yes. Him?' She studied Kavi in silence, a muscle in her jaw twitching.

Greema was right, his power as a warlock had nothing to do with the sort of person he was. She clenched her jaw. But he shouldn't have intervened. 'Sorry, ma'am.'

'You need to sort this out.'

'I will.'

Greema sighed. 'Is something bothering you?'

If only you knew. But no, she couldn't let one world bleed into the other. She was not a Tivasi enforcer here, she was a Blade. 'No, all good.'

'For as long as you fight with a prejudiced mind and distorted heart,' Greema said, 'you will never fully draw out your ability. Remember this well.'

Kavi bobbed her head.

'You will not survive the year if you fight with only your instincts.' Greema tapped the hilts of her swords. 'Do you know the first thing a Gashani warrior must do after we pass our rites?'

Kavi glanced at Greema's chin. 'Uhm, the tattoo?'

'My swords. A warrior must forge their own weapons so they may understand them well, my master told me.'

'You made them yourself?' Kavi stared at the plain darkwood scabbards; the hilts wrapped in black thread. One weapon was a shortsword; the other, a longsword.

'I can show you my way, if you wish to learn,' Greema said.

Kavi licked her lips. *You have no right to learn it*, Vaisha had said. 'You use both at the same time?'

'Not always.' Greema acknowledged the doubt on Kavi's face with a soft chuckle. 'It's a difficult skill to master, but once you do – in time, if you choose to learn, you will see.'

Drisana was an unwieldy weapon; using it one-handed would be dangerous. Difficult. And since Kavi was heavily right-handed, a weapon in her left hand would be almost useless. She swallowed. But that just meant she'd have to work harder. 'Teach me, please.'

Chapter 9
ENFORCER

Festival

The Taemu sat huddled around simmering pots of congee. They chatted in soft, anxious voices, occasionally casting a glance Kavi's way, as the flames of the cooking fires danced and cast shadows on their exhausted faces.

Kavi peeked into her and Chotu's pot of congee.

'I'm watching it, don't worry,' Chotu said, and nudged her away.

'It burns at the bottom if you don't—'

'I know, Akka,' he said, and bobbed his head at the Taemu. 'They're waiting.'

She had another hour left before she had to report for her shift at the Caterpillar, and Chotu was right, it was time to get this started.

Kavi stood.

The chatter died down and, as one, the Taemu looked up at her.

Her people had, before the massacre at Ethuran, held an annual festival in honour of their fallen. The old songs would be hummed, food would be shared, arrack flasks emptied, and at the end of the night each Taemu would stand and speak for their dead – a few words, or just their names.

Kavi remembered now, and had gathered her people so they could too.

'Amma – my mother, used to know the old songs,' she said, loud enough for everyone to hear. 'Not the words, just the melodies. People would gather at our home, and she would teach them the tunes. They would sit in a circle and my mother would hum the songs to them, and once everyone had learned, they would all hum together.' She paused. 'I don't remember most of these songs.' Maybe one day they would come back to her. 'But there is one that I can teach you.'

Eager nods answered her, along with hushed and awed whispers of, 'Teach us, Akka.'

She took a deep breath, cleared her throat, and hummed the deep, throaty song that once gave her goosebumps. Midway through the song, she made a fist – her fingers still ached from the duel and the training Greema had put her through afterwards, but she forced them into shape – and gently thumped her chest to make her voice wobble, just like Amma and her friends had done.

'So angry,' Chotu whispered when she was done. 'But it's good. It feels good.'

And together – some out of tune, some starting the song earlier than the others – the Taemu began to hum.

Kavi's eyes burned and her vision blurred but she smiled and nodded encouragingly. And when they were done, she said, 'Good. I'll show you again. Listen well.'

They hummed her mother's tune, over and over again, until they were satisfied, and then they began to speak for the dead: children lost at Ethuran, parents killed during the Kraelish assault, siblings beaten to death by gangsters in Azraaya.

'My brother was a simple boy.' A Taemu woman called Dharya, who'd fought with Kavi at the chokepoint, stood and spoke. 'A priest at one of Meshira's temples offered him food. He accepted. That evening, Dolmonda gangsters tied him to a tree, and beat him with iron rods because he had set foot in the *temple*.' She spat the word. 'He was dead when we found him, still tied to the tree, his body – I will never forget what they'd done to his face … his name was Yarid.'

When it was Kavi's turn, she got to her feet and found that the words had dried up. 'Appa, Amma, Kamith, Haibo, Massa, Elisai, Sravan, Hes— Hessal,' she said, faltering as memories of the Taemu elder's death, which Kavi was partly responsible for, came rushing to the surface. 'Hel awaits,' she whispered, and sat back down.

She sensed the mood shift as more and more Taemu spoke. Voices strengthened, heads and chins rose, and defiance clung to every word and gesture made. After they ate, Kavi walked through their little enclave in the slums. Smiled and squeezed shoulders and patted backs. 'We'll make it through this, Akka,' they told her. 'We still have each other, we're strong together.'

She stopped and knelt at the shrine they'd set up for Drisana. Sticks of incense jammed into the heart of a peeled banana burned at the base of the tiny idol. Should she tell them the truth? That Drisana was no goddess. That she was a warrior from a war waged thousands of years ago, a Taemu mage made immortal by a powerful artifact, and that her consciousness now resided in Kavi's sword? And that it could talk to her?

Kavi put her hands together and lowered her head.

No. It gave the Taemu strength and comfort to believe that there was a goddess, who despite everything, was theirs and theirs alone.

Besides, she was still unsure what the sword wanted and why it had shared those visions of Drisana's last stand with her. Kavi shuddered. Even now, months after she'd first experienced them, the sheer scale of the war Drisana had fought in was hard to comprehend.

It is too late for you, sister, Drisana had said to her at the end of the visions. *The corruption has already set in. You may not be the child Raktha is waiting for, but this choice is mine, and mine alone to make.*

Raktha, their Jinn, was waiting for a child. And Drisana had chosen Kavi, presumably against the Jinn's wishes. Why?

'Akka?'

Kavi turned.

Nariga, a tall Taemu with high cheekbones and plaited hair who'd not fought during the assault as she'd been pregnant at the time, reached out and took Kavi's hand. 'Come, Akka, I want you to meet Inaaya.'

'Inaaya?'

'My baby boy.'

Kavi smiled. 'When did you name him?'

'Just this morning.'

Nariga guided Kavi to her hut. Inside, on a bed of burlap sacks, and bundled up in an old sari, was her baby. With one hand supporting his tiny head, and the other wrapped around his body, Nariga carried him to Kavi.

'You want me to hold him?' Kavi said, eyes wide. What if she held him the wrong way and hurt him?

'You must, Akka,' Nariga said. 'He – we wouldn't be alive if it wasn't for you.'

Kavi, as gently as she could, accepted the baby – who barely weighed anything at all – and cradled him in her arms. He was awake, a thumb lodged firmly in his mouth as he watched her with semi-curious eyes. 'I meant to ask,' Kavi said, unable to keep the grin from spreading on her face, 'who is the father?'

'You've not met him,' Nariga said. 'He's Raayan, works in the city. Labourer.'

A Raayan? Maybe there was hope after all. 'Has he come to see the baby?'

'Not yet.'

Kavi glanced up at her.

'He's a good man, Akka,' Nariga said.

I hope he is. Kavi nodded, rocked little Inaaya in her arms, and made silly gurgling noises as she peered into a pair of deep red irises that were so much like her own.

Chapter 10

ENFORCER

The Hamakan

Clouds of grey tamakhu smoke clung to the ceiling. Arrack, rum and the pungent odour of alcohol-tinged belches filled the space underneath and permeated the large open floor where patrons sat on cushioned chairs around dozens of sandalwood tables. The plucked strings of a sitar and the percussion of a tabla accompanied nasal, melancholy vocals that were just loud enough for Kavi to make out the lyrics – *One more chumma aaahhaa, one more night with my darr-linngg Uma . . .*

Waiters zig-zagged between the tables carrying trays heavy with drink and finger-food: smoky chicken tikkas and bite-sized chunks of tandooried lamb pierced with a toothpick so the clients wouldn't have to dirty their precious hands.

All the seating faced a long platform at the other end of the Caterpillar, where men and women available for 'purchase' lounged on enormous red-velvet divans. The women wore sheer saris, some without blouses, and the men sat bare-chested in silk dhotis. They chatted to each other, nursed their drinks, and waited for the Aunty-ji who ran the Caterpillar to beckon them off the platform so they would meet their client and head up into the rooms designated for the transaction to take place.

Bright yellow artificed globes hung over the platform, while duller versions of the same devices lit up the floor; the lighting ensured that the occupants of the divans were on full display, while to them, the clients appeared as dim, foggy, silhouettes.

Kavi stood in an inconspicuous corner beside the bar, where she could take in the entire sordid panorama, and sipped the watered-down, sweet lassi the bartender had been kind enough to bless her with.

She sighed. So here she was, working in a brothel again. An upgrade from her previous stint as a cleaner at the seaside brothel in Bochan, for sure, but it was as if her career had taken two steps forward and three steps back. She winced and set her steel mug down on the counter. Twisted her hips till she heard a crack. Parts of her body still ached from the training Greema had put her through.

First, you must get used to wielding the longsword with one hand, Greema had said. And to that purpose, Kavi had been dispatched to the gymnasium to squeeze some metal contraption to build strength and dexterity in her right hand, then back to the department of Blade and warlocks where Greema watched while she executed a one-handed overhead swing, exactly three hundred times, on a straw practice dummy.

'Oi! What do you mean they're coming back?' A rotund man seated on the table closest to Kavi slapped his friend on the back. 'After what we did to them? No chance.'

Most of the chatter she'd eavesdropped on tonight had either been about the upcoming elections – in which, for the first time in her life, as a student at the Vagola, she was eligible to vote; and vote she would, for Dharvish – or speculation on the Kraelish assault and a potential follow-up invasion.

'Sammi, please, listen to me – Sammi!' The friend shrugged the big man's arm off his shoulder. 'The Kraelish will come back. One hundred per cent, it's just a matter of time.'

'*Time-shime*, now tell me, which one you will choose?' Sammi pointed at the platform, and his friend, who rested his chin on his hand and pouted, considered.

Kavi sighed and took another sip of her lassi. Smacked her lips and wiped her mouth with a sleeve. It was the same kind of crowd as the brothel in Bochan. She'd long ago filed them into four categories:

Category one: men who brought their shy, often more reserved, or sometimes disabled, friends for a taste.

Two: men and women who came and bought company to (temporarily) alleviate a profound and impenetrable loneliness.

Three: rich arseholes with too much money who liked to flaunt it.

And four: inexplicable people like Subbal Reddy, who showed up just for the food and drink and atmosphere. The man had sauntered up to her – thick, leather purse tucked under one arm – not ten minutes after she'd arrived, and asked, 'So, you still fighting in the tournament? Hah? You promised me tickets. I already told my son, so happy that fellow.'

She said, yes, she would still fight, and yes, she would get him the tickets.

'Excellent! Now, tell me, what are your chances of winning? I hear you are not bad, ah?' He leaned closer. 'Any insider tips? You know, for' – a failed wink, a lecherous smile – 'bets.'

'It's not looking good,' she'd said.

'Why?'

She told him she was having trouble with her warlock.

'So change to another one? No problem then? Right?'

'Reddy-sir, you think anyone not assigned to me will want to work with me?' Besides, Drisana wanted her to stay close to the boy, as if the gods damned sword could somehow see the future with all that *He will save you* bullshit. But then again, it was a sentient sword, who knew what it was capable of?

Subbal Reddy made some sympathetic sounds and lied and promised he would place a bet on her in the first round. After that, he sat at a table by himself, ate, drank, admired the merchandise, enjoyed the music, and left.

Applause and cheering from a large, raucous group of clients dragged her attention to a table right by the platform. One of the women had made her choice and was being led by a man to the stairs heading up to the rooms.

Kavi had overheard the Aunty-ji telling the waiters to give that table extra-special attention, so they'd sent over a free plate of biryani. Apparently, the famous poet, Pushpa Kaidal, and her wealthy friends – diplomats, engineers, lawyers, businessmen – were celebrating a birthday.

Curious, Kavi had sidled up to eavesdrop. She'd heard about this poet but had never read her work – the woman had published an 'uplifting' novel in verse about a family of fallen nobility and their rise to prominence.

Kavi had taken one look at her and slunk back to her spot by the bar.

Another case of success being gifted to the already successful. The woman was clearly wealthy, and from the way she talked, had grown up that way. She spoke about the inspiration behind her work: Raayan philosophy, Raayan mythology, Raayan culture, all things she was intensely proud of, because fuck Kavi and the Taemu and the Gashani, because to her, the Raayan philosophy of oppression didn't exist, the mythology in which large swathes of people were robbed of their land didn't apply, and the culture … Kavi made a face.

What did this woman know about life when all she'd lived was privilege? When her entire identity was built on her parents' wealth and connections?

And yet, there she was, speaking with such confidence,

voicing her opinions without fear. Would Kavi be able to live like that one day? Would she ever be deluded enough to nurture such monumental self-importance and hubris that—

Stop.

Just. Stop.

Kavi looked away from the table and into her mug of lassi.

All this was, was jealousy. They had the freedom to speak their minds. They had people to share their thoughts with. They had the money to live their lives the way they wanted.

And she wished she could do the same.

But she needed to accept that it was not for her. Because if she didn't, her bitterness would spill over like it had this morning with Azia. She needed to stop looking at these people and imagining their lives and their luck. She had her path, and they had theirs, and theirs was lined on both sides with gold and friendly faces and free biryani and—

Kavi cursed and sipped her lassi.

A bell dinged behind the bar and the Aunty-ji, who was mingling with the clients and laughing at their not-so-funny jokes, sauntered over. She crouched and narrowed her eyes at an artificed array of lights buried under the counter. 'Taemu, room seventeen. Now,' she said.

'Memsaab.' Kavi gulped down the rest of her lassi, rushed to and up the stairs, took them two at a time, until she arrived on the first floor.

The dimly lit corridor was empty. The only sounds came from the floor below: muffled music, conversation, and the clatter of plates and glasses. But from the rooms themselves? Silence.

The doors and walls had been artificed from the inside to prevent sound from escaping; very expensive, she'd been told, since it required an artificer to visit once a week. It was also what had probably been done to the room the Kraelish had kept her in when they'd taken her prisoner. Kavi shuddered.

The doors in the Caterpillar had no locks or latches, so she steeled herself, twisted the handle to room seventeen, and shoved it open.

'I said I don't want to wear it!' A naked, middle-aged man flung something pale and viscous onto the floor.

Across the room, standing behind a tub filled with soapy water, a man in a silk bathrobe crossed his arms and nodded at Kavi. 'Deal with this, please,' he said.

Kavi stared at the bathrobed man's thick eyebrows. At his upside-down samosa-shaped face; at the bronze studs that pierced his nose and ears; at his long, dark hair and the painful-looking bun it was tied into. She'd never heard an accent like that before. Never seen anyone who looked like this before.

The naked man, who Kavi guessed was the client, brushed his hair back with a flourish. 'I have slept with dozens – hun-dreds – thousands! And I have never worn one, and I will not start now.' He lowered his voice, dropped his eyes, clutched his chest, and said in a voice brimming with passionate sincerity, 'Don't you understand, I want to feel things. I want to feel you.'

Kavi picked up the lambskin sheath the client had discarded (using her thumb and index finger) and waggled it at the naked man. 'You have to wear it, boss. Aunty-ji's rules.'

He huffed and stuck his chest out. 'I am not putting that fucking thing' – he pointed at the skin, then to his semi-erect penis – 'on my dog.'

'Listen, bhai,' Kavi said, still holding the lambskin sheath. 'You either wear this, or—'

The naked man lunged at her.

Fucksake. Kavi sidestepped. Twisted her hips to catch him in a chokehold, changed her mind – what if his *dog* accidentally touched her – and slapped the back of his head instead.

He stumbled into an almirah, cracked his head on its hard-wood surface, and collapsed in a heap.

'Come on,' Kavi said, gathering up his clothes while he groaned and massaged his head. 'Let's go, you're done.'

He swore and hissed at her when she hurled his clothes at him.

'Out. Now.' She brandished her fist in his face and he flinched.

'Fine, fine,' he said, stuffing his feet into a pair of trousers. 'This isn't the only place I can go – fucking Tivasi thugs.'

Once he scrambled into his shirt, she grabbed him by the collar and escorted him down and out through the back entrance.

'You could've had a good night,' she chided him. 'Could've gone home happy and satisfied, but *nooo*, someone is too spoiled, too much of a hero to wear a sheath on his cock.'

'Don't call it a cock,' he mumbled. 'I find it offensive. Please refer to it as—'

'Yes, yes, your dog. Now fuck off.'

She waited while he grumbled and cursed and staggered out of the alleyway, then slammed the back door shut and hurried back up to room seventeen.

The bathrobed man was tidying up the room.

'Is everything – you okay?' she asked.

He smiled. Punched a cushion back into shape. 'It happens now and then – one too many drinks. Thank you for your help.'

The man was obviously not a native speaker. He pronounced each word clearly, and with a slight delay, as if he were rolling them around on his tongue before parting his lips to grace Kavi with these perfect little clouds of sound. She licked her lips. 'Where're you from?'

He looked up, into Kavi's eyes, and held her gaze. 'Hamaka. Have you been?'

She shook her head. He said something about the Hamakan Isles, about how insular they were and how it wasn't surprising that she'd not visited, but that he still liked asking people if they had. She could only stare. Mesmerised by the sound of his voice and the peculiar lilt of his words as her breath slowed, her mouth went dry, and her stomach lurched forward and somersaulted.

A tap on her shoulder forced her to wrench her attention away.

'Taemu,' the bartender said, 'Deva is asking for you.'

She nodded. Turned back to the Hamakan and seared his face into her brain. Every imperfection, every blemish. The almost invisible wisps of hair on his chin, the tiny mole on his upper lip, the mismatched ears – one sharp while the other round. 'What—' She cleared her throat. 'What's your name?'

'Nabosin. And you?'

She wanted to say that it was beautiful. That she'd never heard anything like it before. That she wanted to talk to him some more. To learn about where he came from. To ask him why he was so far from home. What sort of things did he like? What did he not like? Instead, all she said was, 'Thank you.'

She was halfway down the stairs when she cringed and slapped her forehead with a palm. He'd asked her for her name. And she'd ignored him. *Thank you? What?* Stupid stupidstupid.

Downstairs, Deva, unlit beedi jammed into one corner of his mouth and the remnants of his last meal in his thick beard, waited for her by the bar. 'Boss wants to see you,' he said. 'Come.'

Chapter 11
ENFORCER

A Reason to Kill

Into the kitchen, past the bustling cooks and waiters, through a dirt-coloured door, down a creaky staircase and into a narrow passage with brick walls that was lit by a series of ancient-looking artificed globes.

Deva chewed on the tip of his beedi and walked in silence.

Kavi followed.

There was no point asking the man why she had been summoned. He was the kind of person who'd grunt and say, *you'll see*, so she kept her mouth shut and tucked her hands into her pockets.

They eventually arrived at another staircase. This one went up and into an anteroom that led, she assumed, into one of the adjacent buildings. A man, a Tivasi gangster, sat on a stool with his back to a door that filtered the sounds of conversation and laughter and a rapid succession of staccato wooden pings that Kavi found familiar but just couldn't place.

The gangster stood. Saluted.

Deva slapped him on the shoulder. 'You've eaten?'

'Not yet, bhai,' the gangster said.

'Come, I'll get someone to cover.' He gestured to the other door, and the gangster bobbed his head and opened it.

Ah, that's what it was. The *smack-thuds* that echoed through the hall were from half a dozen games of carrom. Gangsters sat slouched over the powdered boards, concentrating (frowning, pouting, sticking their tongues out) as they aimed and flicked the wooden pieces into each other while more gangsters huddled around and watched and cursed and bet on the games.

Hanging on the walls and stacked in the corners were knives, mallets, brass knuckles, hatchets – no military weapons, she noted, nor swords, spears, or shields.

Some of the gangsters had food, some had drink. One of them roared, flipped a carrom board over, and yelled, 'You fuck – illegal move, you fucking cheat.'

His opponent scoffed. Spat. 'Shaddup, you—'

The first gangster lunged, grabbed the other man by the collar, and shoved a handful of chicken biryani along with a drumstick into his mouth. Shouts erupted: *'Dai! Bhai, stop! What fucking clowns, yaar.'* Then curses: *Madarchod bhaenchod bleddy chootia*s and the other gangsters pulled them apart.

'Come,' Deva said.

At the far end of the hall, impervious to the receding ruckus, in a high-back chair covered in worn, dark leather, Grishan sat reading a newspamphlet.

He looked up.

The blood drained from Kavi's face as their eyes met. Sweat burst through the pores on her cold skin.

Deva nudged her, and she stumbled forward.

Why was she so scared? Her mouth twisted. What was wrong with her? Her hate and anger at what he'd done should have trumped everything else. He was just another man. She'd dealt with people like him before.

Her own voice hissed back at her, *No, you fucking haven't.*

Grishan was different. There was something inhuman about him that sent a chill down her spine. Was it because the man was a mage? Was it because of the type of mage she suspected he was?

Biomancer. Her mind recoiled from the notion. Raktha only chose from the Taemu, right?

She swallowed as they walked past the gangsters who were now shaking hands and dusting themselves off.

Grishan stood. Flung the newspamphlet to the side. And tugged his shirt back down into place. 'No need to be nervous,' he said, towering over her. 'You have been doing good work for me. For the Tivasi.'

Kavi failed to hold his gaze, and instead stared at the scars around his neck and – mouth dry and words suddenly sparse and slippery – bobbed her head.

'Come,' he said, turning away. 'I wish to speak to you in private.'

Deva nudged her again, and she followed Grishan through a door behind the large chair. They stepped out into a corridor. Artificed globes on the ceiling. There were no windows. No other doors. The corridor stretched away in both directions until it bent at sharp right angles.

'This way,' Grishan said, and gestured for her to follow.

She fell into step, with Deva in her shadow.

'How are you finding the Vagola?' Grishan asked as he turned the corner.

'Good,' she said, peering around his massive bulk at the door he was walking towards.

He stopped. Turned to face her. 'The other students not giving you trouble?'

'I—' She frowned. How did he manage to sound so genuine? Why was he talking like he'd not ruined her life and killed one of her people? 'No, no trouble,' she said.

'But if there is ...' he said, lips curling ever so slightly and a hint of menace seeping into his voice. 'You are one of us now.'

Not in this lifetime. She bit her tongue. Swallowed. Now was as good a time as any. 'Boss,' she said, smothering a wince. 'The Blade-lock tournament, the prize money. It's earned, yes?'

Grishan's smile widened. 'Of course, and I wish you the best of luck. Now, we have business—' He twisted the door handle and pushed it open. 'Deva, wait here.'

'Boss.' Deva saluted and took up a position beside the door.

Kavi glanced at the bearded gangster as she followed Grishan into the room – Deva refused to meet her eyes and gazed straight ahead as he clenched and unclenched his jaw.

A hand, heavy and powerful, clamped down on her shoulder and urged her through the doorway.

She froze.

The door slammed shut behind her.

The blood drained from her face, her mouth went dry, and she stared, eyes bulging, at the three men and two women on their knees by the wall. Blindfolded. Gagged. Hands tied behind their backs. Thighs strapped together and bound to their ankles to keep them kneeling. They trembled. They whimpered and drooled through their gags. Their heads swivelled at the sound of the door shutting.

Grishan tightened his grip on her shoulder and guided her to the only piece of furniture in the room, a small wooden stool.

'They tried to break into my warehouse to steal *their* swords,' Grishan said as he forced her to sit.

She knew all of them. The two women, Dharya and Haleen, street-sweepers who'd joined the little group that Kavi had trained, who'd fought with her during the Kraelish assault; the men, Tipu, Bundil, and at the far end of the line, Jiboo. She'd warned them not to try anything. Told them what would happen if they did. *Why? Why didn't you listen?* 'Please,' she whispered.

'No, don't beg,' Grishan said. 'It irritates me – it's why I have them gagged.' He stepped away from her. 'You told them to stay away? You warned them?'

She nodded.

'And they disobeyed.' He reached into his pockets and pulled out a small knife similar to the one he'd used on Sravan. 'This will help you keep your people in line.'

'Please—'

'Don't beg.' His voice lost its cadence, and just like the last time, his face changed. The light winked out behind his eyes, his mouth thinned into a straight line, and the skin on his face and neck seemed to stretch and tighten.

Two large strides and he stood facing Dharya. He lifted her chin with a finger and plunged the knife, to its hilt, into her neck. She fell. Choked and writhed on the floor as Grishan stepped over to Haleen, who, although blindfolded, could sense that something was wrong. She screamed under her gag.

'It's okay,' he said, stroking the back of her head. 'It's okay.' Like a doctor reassuring a patient. 'I've done this many times. Relax. It'll only hurt in the beginning.'

He slit her throat.

Kavi couldn't move. Her muscles were too weak. The tightness in her chest made it hard to see. She was, once again, a passenger in a body that wouldn't obey. A slave to a mind that was trapped in the past. She was frozen on her knees in the office of the rickshaw company, forced to watch him kill Sravan; she clutched those same bruised knees to her chest inside a crack in the wall, as she watched them brutalise her mother.

Something warm was squeezed into her hand. She blinked. Peered through the fog at the small knife that sat in her palm.

She looked up at the man who had put it there. His face had changed again. It smiled. 'Go on, try it.' Grishan pointed at Jiboo, the only other Taemu alive in the room. 'It feels different when they're restrained.'

She stared at Grishan's extended arm. At the muscles underneath the scarred skin and the unnatural way they pulsed. If Suman was wrong, if Raktha, after all these years, had chosen Grishan as its first true Biomancer in centuries ... what did it mean? Had Raktha betrayed the Taemu? Had it made a mistake? Bithun had once told her that time was meaningless to the Jinn, that they existed outside the cycles of life and death. Maybe things like logic and reason didn't apply to them either. 'What *are* you?' she heard herself say.

Grishan froze. He studied her in silence. The only sounds in the room: Jiboo's laboured breathing, the patter of blood on the floor, and Kavi's own heartbeat thundering in her ears.

'You noticed?' Grishan said, lowering his arm. 'No one will believe you.'

No, they wouldn't.

'How old do you think I am?' he asked.

Kavi studied the weathered skin on his face, the M-shaped hairline and the patches of grey hair behind it. He looked like he was in his sixties. 'I don't know.'

'I'm thirty-six years old,' he said.

Her eyes widened. It was true. The Biomancer's countervail – accelerated ageing every time they cast – it was all true.

'Ironic, right? That Raktha would choose someone like me,' Grishan said. 'Someone who has brought the Taemu so much suffering.'

She just stared.

'"So rare," they said, after my tests. Ninety-eight per cent of all recorded Biomancers were Taemu, they told me. "You will

99

not be as powerful as a Taemu Biomancer, but the Vagola will still have a use for you.'" He walked over to the door.

Kavi's eyes drifted to crumpled bodies on the floor. 'Why—'

'Why am I not working for the Vagola? Why did they let me leave?' He rapped his knuckles on the door. 'Because everyone who knew the results of my test are dead.'

'Why—' She glanced at Jiboo, who'd started sobbing, and clenched her fists. 'Why are you doing this to us? You don't have to kill—'

The door squealed open, and Deva poked his head in.

'Ah, that is a good question,' Grishan said. 'I have an answer for you, but first—' He gestured for Deva to enter. 'Clear them out, leave the last one.'

Deva glanced at the bodies lying in pools of their own blood and, shoving his index finger and thumb into his mouth, whistled. Anger, so brief that Kavi thought she had imagined it, flashed across his face before it was schooled back to gruff indifference.

Hurried footsteps in the corridor prefaced a trio of gangsters emerging in the doorway.

Deva jerked his head at the bodies, and the men rushed to drag them out of the room.

'Anything else, boss?' Deva said.

'A chair,' Grishan said. He tugged his shirt into place, crossed his arms, and waited.

Once the bodies were removed, the men returned with mops to soak up the blood.

'It always comes back to our childhoods, no?' Grishan said, as the gangsters thumped a chair down in the middle of the room and cleared out. 'Men with violent fathers, who grow up seeing their mothers beaten, who were abused as children, become violent themselves.'

Not always, she wanted to say, but kept her mouth shut.

Deva bobbed his head and shut the door behind him.

Grishan sat. 'Every third person you pass on the street has experienced something truly horrific as a child. The thing is, most of us don't remember. We deny, we ignore. And even if we wanted to share—' He scoffed. 'Everyone wants a world that is safe, manageable, predictable; no one wants to hear something that violates that illusion. So we allow ourselves to forget. But I am different, you see, because I remember *everything.*'

He paused. His eyes lost focus.

Kavi glanced at Jiboo, who'd stopped crying and had cocked his head as he listened to Grishan.

'My parents,' Grishan said, studying a spot over her head, 'were part of a cult dedicated to Raeth, or so they claimed; it could've been to any god, they made up the rules as they went.' His eyebrows twitched. 'They'd strip me. Tie me to a stone altar. Cover their genitals in pig's blood … I'll let you imagine the rest.'

Kavi tasted bile at the back of her throat and her grip on the seat of the stool tightened.

'This would happen three, four times a week, all through the night and the next morning. Every night was a different kind of ordeal, but one thing stayed the same – for the ritual to work, for Raeth to hear their prayers, I had to bleed. So, they cut me.' He rolled up his sleeves and showed her the thin scars that covered his arms. He pointed to the ones on his neck. Then he rolled up the legs of his trousers. 'They would buy me pets, and if I fought or struggled or disobeyed, they would make me watch as they stabbed them to death.'

When Grishan was satisfied with her reaction – face rigid, jaw clenched, unable to blink – he nodded to himself and rearranged his shirt and trousers. 'I hoped that I'd be saved.

Dreamed of it. Someone would come, surely. Just like in the stories.' He tugged on his shirt and leaned closer to Kavi. 'We had a maid, a Taemu, who knew exactly what was happening. I left notes for her, begged her to help me. But all she did was watch. Watch and clean up the mess.'

His face underwent that change again, and Kavi fought the urge to shrink away. 'She left, eventually, I never saw her again. So, when I escaped, I killed the first Taemu I could find.'

Kavi's heartbeat thrashed in her ears. She opened and closed her dry mouth. The maid was a Taemu, no one would have listened to her. Why couldn't he see that?

'And when I killed her, a strange thing happened.' He reclined and Kavi found she could breathe again. 'I had no sense of self. To survive what was happening to me, I'd erased it. But when I killed, it grounded me. I knew where I was, who I was, *what* I was. But there was something else, too, I came close to understanding.

'All my life, I've asked myself, *why?* Why me? Why is this happening to me? Why not someone else? Why do they get everything they want while I suffer? But when I killed her – when I kill now – I feel like I am on the verge of discovering *why*. I can sense it, just out of my grasp. And every death brings me closer.

'It is difficult to take a life,' Grishan said. 'But, if you can see somebody as a *thing*, you can do anything to them, and once I realised that, I was free.' His lips curled into a smile while the upper half of his face remained motionless. 'Does that help you make *sense* of things? Does that make you feel better?'

She stared at the grin on his face, and the uneasy, unsettling knot in her gut tightened. 'You're lying.'

He chuckled. Slapped his thigh. 'What if I told you I had an uneventful childhood? That I was simply curious. Would you believe me? Hmm? No, you wouldn't. You want to be told what is easiest to believe, you want a rationale that fits your worldview, you want a cause for the effect. Well, I just gave you one.'

Some of it was true. It had to be. It made too much sense, it – he was fucking with her head.

When she didn't respond, Grishan gestured to Jiboo, and said, 'I will let this man live, so he can tell the others what happened here. And you, my little enforcer, will participate in a ring-fight.'

Kavi blinked. Formed and forced the words out of her mouth. 'You want me to box?'

'I want you to lose.'

Ah.

Chapter 12
ENFORCER

Amma

'The people of this city don't need a Taemu hero,' Grishan said. 'They need to see you put in your place.'

And you want to make money off me. She glanced at Jiboo, who'd straightened.

'The fight will happen in three weeks. I will have precise instructions for you closer to the date.' He stood, gestured at Jiboo. 'He's all yours,' he said, before walking out of the room.

'Ah, one more thing.' He stopped in the doorway and drummed his fingers on its frame. 'A client has paid us to ensure that his daughter, a cadet named Vaisha, progresses through the tournament at the Vagola.'

'Vaisha?'

'You know her?'

Kavi frowned. Why would *she* need help? 'I know her.'

'Good. I will require your assistance. In return, I can guarantee that there will be no interference in any of your matches in the tournament.'

'And if I have to fight her?'

'I said there will be no interference in *any* of your matches.' Grishan smiled, tugged his shirt into place, and glanced at Jiboo. 'I am a man of my word.'

What the fuck was his *word* worth? She needed more assurances, but Grishan was already walking away.

Jiboo kept his head bowed while Kavi removed his blindfold, undid the restraints on his wrists and legs, and pulled the gag out of his mouth. 'I'm sorry, Akka,' he mumbled.

'Hush.'

His legs had gone numb from the enforced kneeling, so she slung his arm around her shoulders and helped him to his feet.

'I'm sorry, Akka,' he said again.

Kavi clenched her jaw. Was it the festival? Had it emboldened them? No. She'd lost their trust. This was her fault. They would never have disobeyed Hessal.

She walked Jiboo out of the Tivasi den. Past the shops and the inebriated men and women who wandered the streets of the Lantern district. And to a row of rickshaws, at the end of which Ratan was waiting for her.

'What happened?' he asked.

'Later,' she said, guiding Jiboo into the backseat.

'I'm sorry, Akka,' Jiboo said, over and over again, as they drove back to the slums.

Kavi looked away; watched the city blur as Ratan accelerated through it. She didn't trust herself to speak. Her life, her people's future, and everything she'd dreamed it would be, was unravelling in front of her eyes. The tournament now seemed like the only way out, and she was scared, not for herself, but for them.

Chotu was waiting for her at their hut when she returned, eyes wide with concern. He'd heard about what had happened. Everyone had.

'Akka—'

'Chotu,' she said, collapsing on her sleeping mat. 'Can you get me more agoma?'

He studied her in silence, then reached for his crutch and levered himself upright. 'Come with me.'

It didn't seem fair to ask him to go by himself, and a small part of her was curious as to where he was acquiring the drug from. 'Where?' she said, groaning as she got back on her feet.

'Beyond the slums – but not far, we can walk.'

And walk they did: past huts and tents and the occasional cooking fire where congee boiled and simmered under the patient, watchful eyes of hungry men and women.

The thunk of Chotu's crutch punctuated the crunch of their feet on the dirt path as they wound their way out of the slums in an otherwise peaceful and silent night.

Kavi focused on the sound. Ignored the soft *squelch* of Grishan's knife plunging into Dharya's throat; the gurgling, the loud ragged breaths that—

She squeezed her temples, massaged her eyes, and sighed.

'This way,' Chotu said, turning right on the dilapidated street that marked the outskirts of the slums with its overflowing gutters and mounds of rubbish that a group of urchins assiduously picked through while stray dogs waited their turn.

'I tried to warn them,' he said, softly.

'So did I.'

They crossed the street, stepped over a massive cat that glared at them, and entered a narrow gully where they had to walk in single file.

'How did you find this place?' Kavi asked.

Chotu's shoulders tightened. He glanced back at her. 'My friends told me about it.'

He had friends now? 'How did you meet them?'

'What?'

'Your friends.'

'Wait here, Akka,' he said, stopping outside a two-storey

building. 'I won't be long.' He knocked on the door. Waited. Answered, 'It's me', to a muffled, 'Who?', and disappeared into the building when the door was pulled open and quickly slammed shut.

Kavi dropped to her haunches, rested her elbows on her knees, and stared at the chipped and faded blue paint on the building's walls. Chotu obviously cared about her, respected her, loved her even, in an endearingly protective sort of way, but godsdammit was it a struggle to talk to him sometimes.

He barely ever spoke, and when he did, he never said more than a few words at a time. It had taken days for him to share what had happened to Appa and Kamith.

'They're dead.'

'Yes, I know, how?'

He'd lowered his eyes and limped away. Returned a few hours later. 'Bled to death.'

'Both of them?'

He'd nodded.

'How?'

He'd shaken his head and retreated into himself. When he was ready, he would then share the next little detail.

And despite her best efforts, all her jokes and wisecracks, he never smiled.

Then again, there wasn't much to smile about these days. But still, just once, she wanted to see what it looked like on his face.

The door creaked open, and was quickly slammed shut after Chotu stepped out with a small tin in one hand.

Kavi's knees cracked as she stood. 'How much was it?'

'Don't worry,' he said, and hesitated. 'Are you sure you want it?'

Was she? No, but it helped her escape, and it was only for the time being. 'It's fine,' she said, and he passed her the tin.

She shook it, felt and heard the discs clatter around inside. There was enough here for weeks.

'Chotu.'

'Akka?'

'I—' *don't want to go back. I don't want the others to look at me.* 'Do you want to stop by the chaiwallah?'

'Can,' he said, without a *Why?* Or a *How come?* and he led the way back out of the gully and further down the street.

The chaiwallah was a roadside stall where a hairy, skinny man in a banyan sat on a stool under a lantern that hung from a wooden pole. He attended to a large pot of masala tea simmering over a coal fire.

'Two, uncle,' Kavi said. No one knew the man's name; everyone just called him uncle. He, in turn, treated everyone with the same mute indifference.

Uncle pocketed the rayals she handed him and scooped the sweet-spicy-smelling tea into a pair of small glasses.

Chotu blew over the rim of his glass until the froth on top cleared, and took a tentative sip. 'Want to sit?' He pointed at the footpath next to the tea stall.

'Okay.'

A steam-rickshaw rattled past, a group of labourers lumbered back home to the slums, and a herd of buffalo buffled down the road while their herder puffed away on a beedi and encouraged them onward with an exhausted, 'Ousss, ouss.'

'Did he make you watch?' Chotu asked, while he watched the animals saunter away.

'Chotu …'

His lips trembled. 'He's a monster.'

'I'm sorry.'

He shook his head. Looked away from her and wiped his eyes on his sleeve.

She stared into her half-empty glass of tea. *It'll be fine, we'll be okay, we'll make it through this just like we have everything else* – all she had for him were white lies, and she would not disrespect him with them.

'Akka,' he said, once both glasses were empty.

'Hmm?

'Can you tell me about Amma?'

She blinked. 'Amma?' That's right, he was too young to remember. 'What do you want to know?'

'Anything.'

Kavi leaned forward to rest her elbows on her knees. 'She was tall.' Or at least she'd seemed that way. 'Her eyes were like ours.' *Not Appa's.* 'She was pretty, not like—' *Me.*

'What else?' Chotu stared at her, eyes wide and attentive.

'She was proud of who she was, and she wanted us to feel that way, too. She had a loud, strong voice, and she could be stern and strict – I was always more scared of her than Appa. She never beat us, not like he did, but Kamith and I were terrified of her scolding us. Somehow, it felt worse.'

He nodded for her to continue.

'She would worry about us, talk to Appa about what sort of lives we'd lead, the type of people we'd grow up to be.' Kavi set her glass aside, shuffled closer to Chotu, and wrapped an arm around his shoulder. 'She would've been proud of you.'

'I wish I could remember her,' he said, and leaned into Kavi, ever so slightly, but it was enough to instigate a small explosion of warmth in her chest.

*

Chotu waited for her to settle on her sleeping mat before blowing out the dia lamp.

The agoma had already entered her bloodstream. The roof of the hut disintegrated into specks of dust that the wind picked up and blew away.

Kavi sought out the makra head.

Her toes sank into the soft, warm ash of the Deadlands. The stars winked out, and the sky transformed into a cloudless, deep cobalt. A gentle breeze ruffled her hair as she walked to the metal wreck jutting out of the plain, and into the odd envelope of safety and comfort it projected. She sighed as the events of the day and the ugly emotions that accompanied them withered and fell—

Kavithri.

She froze. *Drisana?*

Step back.

Metal groaned. Ash swirled and eddied around the makra head.

Step back.

The makra head twitched, cracked, and the torn metal twisted and wound itself back into place.

Thunder rolled across the Deadlands as the makra head rose from the ash to reveal a neck.

Please.

She stepped back.

The world around her metamorphosed again. The Deadlands shrank, the sunlight dimmed and faded into a soft yellow, the sand beneath her feet disappeared and was replaced with ice-cold metal that crept and grew and rose on all sides to seal her away in a cocoon.

She was naked. But the body didn't belong to her. It was stronger. Lighter. There was an ache in her abdomen that she'd never felt before; a pressure under her knees, above her elbows, her sternum, and between her eyebrows that—

Kavi stared at the discs implanted in the powerful body. Touched the one between her eyebrows.

Vectors, they're called.

The discs?

Yes.

What is happening?

The drug in your blood
has opened
conduits,
allowed more of my consciousness
inside.

Is this one of your visions?

No, a memory.

A jolt, a sudden weightlessness, and Kavi was lifted off her feet. *Where am I?*

Inside Gayathri.
The pilot's pod
of my makra.

Long, thick needles extended from the walls, plunged into the vectors on her body, and Kavi screamed and convulsed as agony seared its way into her limbs, her chest, her forehead. Maayin – Drisana's maayin, so different from Kavi's own – was suddenly siphoned away into the makra.

Open your eyes.

Kavi obeyed.

She hovered in a sky the colour of vermilion, high over a range of mountains arrayed with colours and trees she'd never seen before. Her body had changed again. She *was* the makra now.

Vertigo-laced nausea slammed into her. Made her head swim. She flailed.

Relax.
The makra will respond
to your emotions.
Breathe.
Kavi shut her eyes, steadied her breath. *Why are you showing me this?*
I want you
to learn.
Why?
Because one day,
you will need to fight, Drisana said.

And in her clipped speech, in her patient, soothing voice, she taught Kavi how to pilot a makra.

She showed Kavi how to control the flow of maayin in the makra. To send bursts of it out from the soles of Gayathri's feet, from the base of her palms, from the ports on her spine. She taught Kavi to walk, to run, to use these bursts of maayin to initiate dramatic shifts in direction. She encouraged Kavi to experiment. To jump and twist and see how far she could push the makra. She made Kavi detach and swing the heavy, twin swords on Gayathri's back.

Now, Drisana whispered, *defeat them*.

Defeat who?

A trio of makra, all with the same insectoid heads reminiscent of the Kraelish makra that had breached the walls of Azraaya, tore their way out of the mountains and came bounding at her with weapons drawn.

Kavi stood her ground, hefted the unwieldy swords. This wasn't real. She couldn't get hurt here. Right?

You will still
feel pain.
She groaned, clenched her teeth, and swung at the first

enemy makra that came into range. It slipped under her strike with ease and plunged its sword into Kavi's torso.

Kavi screamed. The enemy makra winked out of existence, and the pain subsided.

Again, Drisana said. And the trio tore their way out of the mountains and came bounding at her.

Over and over again, the Harithian makra, as Drisana referred to them, stabbed and pummelled and ripped her makra to pieces until finally, exhausted and beaten half senseless, she begged Drisana to stop.

Clumsy, Drisana said,
but you will
improve.

Chapter 13
BLADE

Courage

'No training this session,' Greema said. 'I want you both to go somewhere – not in the department, go outside, find a quiet place, and talk.'

Kavi glanced at Azia, who had both hands tucked into his pockets while he searched the ground between his feet.

She sighed, which drew a sharp glance from Greema.

'Problem, cadet?'

'No, ma'am,' Kavi said and snapped a salute. 'Is the next session still swordcraft?'

Greema nodded. 'I will see you back here.' And turned her back on them and walked away.

Scattered around the indoor arena were other cadet and novice duos. Some sat around their mentor and listened to them talk strategy, some duelled, others practised for the tournament – cadets donned artificed armour and had their novices batter them with maayin.

'Let's go,' Kavi said. She'd much rather be practising, but Greema was right, if they were to stand any sort of chance in the tournament, she needed to talk to the boy. And not just that. *You have field exercises in the second term,* Greema had said. *If you don't sort this out now, things will not go well for you both.*

Azia followed her in silence. Out into the long corridor and up the staircase that led them out of the bloated-looking building. She scratched a spot on the back of her neck – where she'd pressed the agoma disc the previous night – as she walked. It was disorienting, to be back at ground level, on her own feet, after piloting a makra.

Why? She'd asked Drisana again. *Why're you teaching me?* And all the sword would say was:

Because one day,
you will need to fight.

Drisana knew something about what was to come and was preparing her for it.

Kavi might have to pilot a real makra one day.

But why? And against whom? The Kraelish? Would there be another war on the same scale as the one from Drisana's visions? And where would she even find a makra? She tsked. If only she could have a real conversation with Drisana instead of the cryptic, clipped exchanges she was now used to.

After Drisana was done with her, she'd gone back to the beach and called for Tsubu, the stray dog she'd adopted into Bithun's household in Bochan, and the dog had come, tail wagging tongue dangling, and laid his head in her lap – something the real Tsubu would never do – and allowed her to pet him while she breathed in the peace and silence.

She hoped he was doing okay. And Bithun, too.

As soon as she'd woken, the world had crashed right back down on her – Grishan's knife, the blindfolded Taemu who died as the mobster's blade plunged into their necks or sliced across them; the utter helplessness as her mind travelled to places she didn't want it to and her insubordinate body succumbed to fear and sat locked in place while Grishan killed her people. And then there were the things he'd told her about himself.

He's just a man. She repeated the lie, over and over again, and it didn't change a thing.

'Where to?' Azia mumbled as they exited the building.

Somewhere quiet, Greema had suggested. 'The lake with Meshira's shrine. You know it?'

He nodded, and they set out.

Meshira's shrine was halfway into the peacock-blue lake that sat on the fringes of the Artificers' College. The only way to reach it was over a submerged marble platform, where the water came up to your ankles so your feet were washed clean by the time you set foot on the shrine.

Kavi found a park bench overlooking the lake and shrine and sat. She waited for Azia to settle down, then said, 'All good?'

He glanced at her, looked away and studied a group of students rolling up their trousers and hitching up their skirts as they walked across to the shrine. 'Yes, all good.'

It clearly wasn't; the boy was moping. She frowned. Or maybe not. Maybe that was just his face.

She caught herself staring at the scar that ran down the middle of his face – something he'd noticed as well. His lips tightened and he seemed to sink even more into himself.

Kavi wrenched her eyes away. *Stupid.* She needed to get him talking. 'What do you like to eat?'

He blinked. Cast an uncertain glance at her. 'What?'

'You know, your favourite foods.'

'Oh.' He fidgeted with the green warlock's badge on his shirt. 'I eat what my father cooks.'

'Lucky,' she said. 'Is he a cook?'

'No, he's—' He hesitated. 'No one's told you?'

'About?'

'About me.'

She gestured to her face; her *eyes*. 'You think anyone tells me *any*thing?'

His chin twitched, and he nodded.

Was that a smile? That might have been a smile. 'So, what does your father do?' she asked.

'He doesn't work,' Azia said. 'We live off my stipend.'

Kavi's brows shot up. The novices got a stipend?

'He – my father's family used to be nobles,' Azia said, straightening defensively. 'They've struggled since Raaya's independence.'

She had nothing to say to that – nothing *aloud*, at least – and they lapsed into silence.

'I saw you,' Azia said, finally. 'Once before.'

'Oh? In the Siphon?'

He shook his head. 'I didn't go to watch. It was – do you remember the Kraelish attack?'

How could she forget? 'What about it?'

'We hid, Father and I, in our house,' Azia said. 'But the Kraelish soldiers, they were going house by house, dragging people out – we were scared. They were getting close. But then' – he swallowed – 'you were there.'

I was?

'You, a group of Taemu and other men and women with weapons.' His eyes shone as he described the wave of fear that washed over the Kraelish as Kavi and the Taemu battalion smashed into and through their lines. 'It was chaos. But I could *see* you. You fought under a dark-red banner, and everyone rallied around you. You never wavered. Never hesitated. You saved me and my father and so many others on that street.'

Kavi fought to keep her lips from trembling. That was a lifetime ago. Now ... She puffed out her cheeks. 'I'm glad you both made it through.'

He bobbed his head. His chin and mouth twitched as he smiled in that peculiar way of his.

'So, you've been in Azraaya all your life?' she said, desperate to change the topic.

He stiffened, cast a sharp glance in her direction. 'No.' And wrung his hands. 'I'm from the coal mines outside Meriyachal.'

Kavi frowned. 'You lived in a village *near* the mines?'

He shook his head. 'The mines. My—' He hesitated at the confusion on her face. Muttered something under his breath, and said again, 'My biological parents, they used to work in a coal mine. We lived at the site – I went to school while they worked.' He swallowed. 'There was an underground fire one day, and both of them died. After that the boss sent me into the tunnels.'

Oh, Hel. 'I'm sorry.'

He shrugged. 'Some days were okay. Some days it hurt to breathe and there was a pain in my back' – he slouched to mimic being weighed down by something heavy, and tapped the top of his head – 'the roof of some tunnels were low, so it was difficult.'

It wasn't hard for Kavi to see herself in his place. Alone. Scared. Life in the hands of callous, cold-eyed adults. She nodded as an uncomfortable lump rose up her throat.

'Then one day, a couple from the city came. They washed me, gave me food and clothes, and brought me here.' He stared at the shimmering surface of the lake with a faraway look on his face. 'People mock them for being fallen nobles, but Mother and Father adopted me and gave me a new life.'

Mother and Father, not Amma and Appa. Those words, she guessed, were reserved for the parents who died in the coal mine. 'They sound like good people,' Kavi said.

He glanced at her. 'And you? What about your parents?'

A lie formed on her tongue – *I don't remember my mother, she died when I was young, and my father lives in another city* – but she caught herself. What was the point? Deep down, she wanted to trust Azia. He'd been honest with her, and now it was her turn.

So, she told him. About how her mother died at Ethuran. How her father sold her for pocket change. And how she'd found Chotu and learned what happened to Appa and Khagan.

Azia lowered his head. 'It's not fair, is it?'

'It is, for some,' Kavi said. *But not for us.*

'Father has struggled a lot since Mother passed, and I want to help. I want to repay him.' He stared at his palms. 'I practise every day, I know I can control my maayin better than any of the other novices, but I'm weak, and—'

'I don't think you're weak.'

He faltered.

All the bitterness, all the negative thoughts and emotions, everything that had happened to her: she was not being herself. Greema was right. She had to apologise, she had to make things right. Her desperate situation was not his concern, and neither was her desire to win the tournament. 'I'm sorry about the other day.'

He waved it off. 'No, it's okay.'

'You're one of the bravest people I've ever met,' Kavi said, and she meant it. She was a fool for assuming he was weak. The boy had seen and been through things that the other students at the Vagola could never imagine. 'No one expects anything from us, but if we work together, I think we can surprise them.' She stood. Extended her hand. 'Should we give it a shot?'

'The tournament?'

She nodded. 'But only if you want to.'

He fidgeted with his badge. Smoothed out the creases on

his trousers. Took a deep breath, and stood. Gently placed his hand in hers. 'Okay.'

She squeezed and pumped. 'Warlock.'

He squeezed back. 'Blade.'

They walked back to the department of mages and warlocks, half the way in comfortable silence, the other half spent talking about Blade-lock strategy. Azia had this ridiculous idea that he could hide a petal of maayin in her armour. 'The other warlock will be so used to attacking our crystal that they will not see it coming.'

'Impossible,' she said. No one had that sort of control. He'd have to be focused on not just defending their crystal, but also watching how and where she moved so he could maintain and move the maayin hidden in her armour. A lapse of concentration and it would either disintegrate or tear through her body.

'Kavithri—'

'Just Kavi.'

'I can do it, Kavi, we can practise.'

She gave him a dubious side-eye, but agreed to try it out.

He left her to attend a lecture on Jinn theory and power dynamics: 'Apparently, the power of an individual mage is inversely proportional to how many total active mages a Jinn has. So the fewer mages a Jinn chooses, the more powerful those mages are, and vice versa,' he said, when she asked what that was, and then promised to explain more later when she pressed him. 'It's just a theory, but the evidence for it is astounding.'

Kavi waved goodbye, cursed the fact that she couldn't study as a mage, then dragged her feet to the armoury to collect Drisana.

'Number 72,' the man behind the counter said, more to himself than to her, as he passed her the sword.

'I hope you're happy,' she said under her breath as she

collected her weapon. 'I'll be staying close to the boy, like you wanted.'

The sword hummed its approval.

When ready
I can bond
You both.

Kavi froze. Her grip on the hilt tightened. She fought to keep a straight face as the armoury attendant stared at her.

'Something else?' he asked.

'No,' she said, voice hoarse, mouth dry, and turned around and strode to the staircase that led down to the arena.

You can bond us? Like the warlocks and Blades before the Retreat?

A pulse of confirmation.

Raeth's translucent balls. That meant Azia could ... what? Move around while he cast? And her? She'd have to take the brunt of his countervail. Would she get stronger? Faster? What would actually happen? Wait.

I thought you couldn't affect the world.

The bond is
not in this world.
Where the Jinn dwell,
you will link.
He will
replace me.

Kavi missed a step and latched onto the banister to steady herself. That was the most the sword had ever said in one go. And what was this *replace* nonsense? Drisana?

Only one
can hear
my voice.

What the Hel? So if she bonded with Azia she'd lose her connection to the sword? She clenched her jaw.

Is that what you mean?

Drisana hummed in agreement.

Then I don't want it.

The sword remained silent.

She tsked. Either way, bonding with Azia would only draw more attention to her. 'Not worth it,' she muttered as she stepped into the arena.

Chapter 14
BLADE

Mentor

Several duels were in progress. One, in particular, had drawn a crowd. Rathore stood, wooden longsword held with both hands, mouth screwed up in concentration, sweat dripping off his chin, as he faced Greema and her practice swords.

Kavi rushed to join the audience. Nudged her way to the front. And stared, unblinking, Drisana's revelation forgotten, as Greema *moved*.

She'd expected brute force, but what she found was a dancer.

The swords, like twin fangs, one long, one short, flashed at Rathore.

He fended them off, took a step back.

Greema glided closer. Switched stances. Went from holding both swords at hip level to shortsword over her head and longsword pointed at Rathore's nose. She struck again.

Thunk-thunk!

Then she was holding the swords extended and parallel to each other.

Kavi's mouth hung open. It was as if she was watching a zobhanatyam performance. The way Greema fought was serene. Fluid. Mesmerising.

Rathore stepped in.

Greema responded. Feinted with the shortsword, feinted with the longsword.

And when Rathore retreated, she surged forward, twisted her hips, and the longsword blurred as she hammered it into his side before he could react.

Rathore grunted. Raised a hand and doubled over gasping for air. 'You promised to take it easy,' he said, when he could finally speak.

Greema frowned. 'When did I say that?'

'Dammit, Greema.' Rathore spat as he gestured for the students to disperse. His eyes landed on Kavi, who was still staring at Greema with unashamed awe. 'Your cadet is here – how much did you see?'

'Um.' Kavi checked to ensure the man was addressing her – he was. 'Just the end.'

He cocked his head at Greema. 'Think you can fight like her?'

No. She swallowed. 'I—'

'Your cadets are waiting,' Greema said.

Rathore tsked and waved her off. 'Well?' he asked Kavi again.

What did he expect her to say? Yes? 'I will try my best, sir.'

He snorted, but the answer seemed to satisfy him. He nodded at Greema and, clutching his side, joined the group of men and women waiting for him.

'Kavithri,' Greema said. 'Did you deal with it?'

Kavi blinked. It? *Ah.* 'We found some common ground.'

'Good.' She beckoned Kavi closer and held out her wooden longsword. 'Set your sword aside. Use this from now on.'

The practice sword was weightier than Drisana, but had the same top-heavy feel to it. Her muscles strained as she hefted and held it out one-handed.

'Before we begin,' Greema said, 'I would like you to answer a question.'

'Ma'am?'

'Training in the Gashani school is gruelling – more so than any of the other schools.' Greema spoke with a quiet intensity that made Kavi stand straighter. 'So, I want to understand: what do you *want*, Kavithri?'

Kavi fought the urge to scratch the itch at the back of her neck. What *did* she want?

'I want to hear you say it. I want to hear your *resolve*.'

It had been so simple once. Get into the Vagola, use the Venator, find her family. Now, the future was this vague, amorphous destination, and – she ground her teeth – it frustrated her.

She wanted to get the rickshaw company back. She wanted to leave her brother and her people in a better place. She wanted to protect—

She winced as a pang of guilt sunk its fangs into her heart. Did her fear of Grishan trump her desire to regain the rickshaw company? Did it? She checked, looked past the horror, the grief, the rage, the berserker chained within her, and found that she didn't just want it, she burned for it. She'd do anything to get the company back. Her fingernails dug painfully into her palms as she clenched her fists. Anything to win the tournament.

'There is something,' Kavi said. 'But it's just a dream.'

'The reason we call them dreams, Kavithri, is because they're difficult to turn into a reality.' Greema placed a heavy hand on her shoulder and squeezed. 'But that is why we work so hard for them.'

Kavi looked up at her mentor. Her vision blurred. A part of her wanted to crumple and tell Greema all about the rickshaw company, the Tivasi, and to ask for her help; the other half snorted and said, *Go, run away, let her sort out your problems. Go, coward.*

'I want to be stronger,' she said in a hoarse whisper. 'I want to protect what is mine. I want to *win*.'

Greema took a step back. Studied her in silence for several heartbeats. And nodded. 'Raise your sword.'

Kavi obeyed. Lifted it one-handed while she kept her empty hand clenched at her side.

'Stay still, and point the tip at my nose – no, do not use your wrist, you will put too much strain on it. Use your little finger to control the sword.'

Kavi loosened her bottom finger, and the tip of the sword, on account of its own weight, dropped down to Greema's chest. She tightened it, and the tip curved back up.

Oh. She studied her grip on the hilt. Why didn't she think of this before? She'd need to practise, but this made the sword so much easier to manoeuvre; not to mention the power she could generate with such a slight movement. This changed everything. This – her stomach clenched, and she hesitated.

'Ma'am,' Kavi said, 'are you – am I allowed to use the Gashani school?'

Greema blinked. Considered. Then gazed out over Kavi's head at the students scattered around the arena. 'There is this belief that one should stick to the school they inherit,' she said. 'That to study one that is not *yours* is somehow wrong; that to do so would open it up to corruption.'

Kavi lowered the sword. Bit the inside of her cheek.

'Stay on your path, they will tell you. Know your place. Be mediocre, take no risks, learn what is tried and tested, do what pleases those above you.' Greema's mouth twisted. 'These people can go fuck themselves.'

Kavi jerked her head back at the venom in Greema's voice.

'My master once told me that abandoning your uniqueness is the same as dying.' Greema bent and picked up Drisana, frowned at the threads wrapped around its hilt. 'Kavithri, I will not ask you to fight like me. I want you to take what I teach you and make it your own.'

The tension seeped out of Kavi's muscles, and she relaxed. Yes, how could she have forgotten, Greema's opinion was the only one that mattered.

'Maybe you could even start your own school one day,' Greema said, a hint of a smile on her lips.

As if. *I'll be dead in six and a half years, ma'am.* Kavi chuckled. 'Maybe.'

'I'm not' going to ask how you got this' – Greema tapped Drisana with her index finger – 'but I hope you know that this is a Taemu swordmaster's weapon.'

Kavi froze. How did she know?

'The guard, the hilt, the length of the blade.' Greema tapped each part as she called it out, nodding to herself. 'It probably has a shorter twin out there, somewhere.'

What? 'Ma'am?'

'Taemu longswords are meant to be used in combination with shortswords,' Greema said, and almost reverently, drew Drisana. The blade left its scabbard with a soft *shing*. 'Much of the Gashani school comes from the lost Taemu art of the sword. Our elders believe that it was the Taemu who put swords in our hands and taught us to fight.' She glanced at Kavi over the edge of the blade. 'What I just told you, it remains between us.'

Goosebumps rippled down Kavi's forearms and up her neck. She swallowed. Her people had once fought with two swords.

And now, so would she.

Chapter 15
BLADE

The Gashani School

The draw for the tournament was scheduled to happen in two weeks' time, and Kavi and Azia's first match, depending on whether they drew into the prelims or straight into one of the hundred-and-twenty-eight first-round matches, could happen on the same day, or on the day following. Until then, Kavi trained.

First, Greema showed her the stances. The same ones she'd used against Rathore. Stance one: both wrists level with hips.

Stance two: both arms extended to the opponent.

Stance three: shortsword overhead, longsword pointed at the opponent.

And stance four: a wide stance where she spread her arms out like she was challenging someone to hit her.

'These are just guidelines,' Greema said, 'a framework for you to build and create your own style.'

She tied a shortsword to Kavi's left hand and made her memorise each of the basic stances. Then came the padded wooden post with splotches of black ink strategically splattered across its surface.

Kavi circled the post, and when Greema yelled *Strike!* she aimed and struck the ink-targets with both swords. When Greema said *Switch!* she changed stances and continued circling.

'You are not empty,' Greema said every time Kavi made a mistake. 'When you're empty – when you're not thinking about anything – that's when you start to truly pay attention to yourself. To your senses. To the weapons in your hands. Start again.'

After a while Kavi entered this fugue state where her arms and legs took over. She became what Greema wanted: empty. Her body reacted to *Strike!* and *Switch!* and nothing else mattered.

Then Greema started teaching her between the calls.

Things like: 'The longsword is versatile, it can be used in any situation, but the shortsword is superior in confined spaces.'

Or, 'Always try to fight with the sun at your back or behind your right shoulder.'

And, 'Always aim for the face.'

She told Kavi that while the Gashani school was effective in duels, most of the techniques were meant for fighting multiple opponents. 'When faced with several enemies, use the broad stance. Fling your arms out to both sides. Deal with your enemies in order. Be aware of everything and never stop moving. You stop, you die. If you can, herd them to a place where they are forced to come at you one at a time. No counterattacks. Aim to end it with one blow, do not exchange. Remember this well.'

When Kavi's arms sagged and she was at her limit, Greema would make her stretch, then sit her down cross-legged with a canteen of water in her hands, while she spoke.

'Do not stick to one stance. Switch as needed. You are empty, fluid. No thought, no form.'

'Never, ever, get attached to your weapon. If you need to relinquish it to win a battle, be prepared to do so.'

'You must always be in control. If an enemy attacks, it is because you want them to. To master this, your body must learn the rhythms – striking, the interval in between, the counter-attack cadences.'

And Kavi's personal favourite, which Greema repeated at least once a day, was, 'You must *see* without moving your eyes.' After which Kavi would open her eyes as wide as possible to try to observe people in her periphery, until Greema told her she was overdoing it and to knock it off.

At the end of every lesson Greema would nod, look Kavi dead in the eye, and say, 'Remember this well.'

And Kavi did. She repeated each word in her head and filed everything away.

When Greema left at the end of their allocated hours, Kavi threw herself into the exercises Bithun had taught her – push-ups, sit-ups, crunches, weights, sprints – and she broke and rebuilt her body. Salora funded Kavi's countervails and paid for Ratan to remain on a retainer. He'd wait in his rickshaw with the rats concealed under his backseat, and Kavi would limp over, heal, catch up on the latest gossip, and head back into the Vagola.

After a week, she and Greema began to spar. Two-minute rounds where Kavi defended strike after bone-rattling strike, until her arms went numb, the swords tripled in weight, and she was left on the verge of passing out from exhaustion.

Greema fought with an intensity that left Kavi drained. She now understood how Rathore had felt when he'd had his arse handed to him.

When she wasn't learning to dual wield or training to strengthen her body, she worked with Azia. She tested his range, which was mediocre, but enough to span a Blade-lock court. His control, however, was immaculate, and like he promised, he could maintain a petal of maayin concealed within her armour while she moved. And his power ... not so great, he struggled to fill the gauge on her armour. He would occasionally surprise her with the speed of his projectiles and the velocity at which they changed direction, but when they hit her, they lacked the weight to do any serious damage.

Neither Azia nor Greema asked her about her life outside the Vagola, and she never spoke about it.

She stood guard at the Caterpillar in the evenings, collected payments on the weekends, waited for news on Grishan's boxing match, and at night, when she pressed another disc of agoma into the back of her neck and left the gates to her subconscious unlocked, Drisana and Gayathri were there waiting for her.

*

'It's here,' Azia said, waving a folded piece of paper as he walked into the arena.

'Finally,' Kavi muttered, groaning as she stretched her shoulder until it cracked.

Azia bobbed his head at Greema and presented the paper to her with both hands.

'That's okay,' Greema said, bemused. 'Read it to us.'

'Kavi.' He turned to her, excitement in his eyes. 'We dodged the prelims.'

She let her arm fall. 'You're joking.' Luck going her way? Unheard of.

'Not joking.' He showed her the draw, two long rows of names with lines connecting each bracket, and pointed. 'Down here.' *First-years: Azia/Kavithri vs. First-years: Nithya/Rogul.*

First-years. More luck. What was going on?

'Should we use the Plan here?' Azia asked. The Plan being the hidden-maayin-surprise-attack on the crystal he'd come up with.

'No, we should save that for a difficult match-up.' Kavi ran

131

her finger up the brackets. 'We could run into third-years in the later rounds.'

'We – you think we'll make it into the later rounds without using the Plan?'

She tsked. 'Have some faith, man.'

He shrugged, scratched his head. 'So, what *is* the plan for the first round?'

Kavi pursed her lips. She had a plan. It was risky. It lacked subtlety. But no one would expect it and she was confident she could pull it off. She told him.

His eyes bulged. 'You could get hurt really badly.'

Greema cleared her throat. 'The novice is right, it's dangerous.'

'I know, ma'am,' Kavi said. Greema had told her, and Kavi had agreed, that she was not ready to use the Gashani school, and until she was, the only way they'd progress in the tournament was by taking risks.

'Are you sure?' Azia asked, the concern apparent in his voice and on his face.

Kavi slapped him on the back. 'What? You worried about me?'

'Yes,' he said, utterly sincere, and it caught her off-guard.

She lowered her eyes. Now she had to contend with not one, but two teenagers concerned about her wellbeing? Her lips parted, but the words, *Do you trust me?* died on her tongue. That was what she'd said to Elisai. Brave, loyal, kind, Elisai, who'd lost her entire family at Ethuran, who'd stood and fought with Kavi at the chokepoint, and who'd died when Ze'aan's maayin had punched a hole in her skull. Kavi clamped her mouth shut. She would never ask that of someone again. 'I can take the hits,' she said instead. 'I've handled far worse.'

Azia studied her in silence. Lips a thin line. Eyes large and worried.

'Novice,' Greema said after several heartbeats had passed. 'I must train my cadet, you can speak to her later.'

'Sorry, ma'am.' He bobbed his head and glanced at Kavi. 'Are you free after practice?'

'Yes, why?'

'Father has invited you to join us for dinner.'

Kavi's eyes bulged. 'Hah? Why?'

'He wants to meet you.'

She swallowed. 'Can it be an early dinner?' The Aunty-ji at the Caterpillar would not be pleased if she showed up late for her shift.

'Sure,' Azia said, smiling. 'I'll see you then.'

'Yes, bye.' She stood scratching the back of her head as he walked away.

'Kavithri,' Greema said once he'd left. 'Focus. We spar now.'

*

Kavi wiped her mouth and passed the empty water canteen back to Greema, who sat cross-legged at her side. She reclined against the wall that circled the empty arena and watched the last few students trickle out.

'Tomorrow,' Greema said softly, 'do not hesitate.'

Kavi nodded. Sighed and rested her head on the wall. The last few weeks had been calm. Peaceful. All that would end tomorrow. She glanced at Greema, who sat perfectly straight and still, and when she was sure the woman wasn't looking, stared at the dark fangs tattooed on her chin, down each side of her mouth.

'Ma'am,' Kavi said, 'may I ask you a question?'

'Ask,' Greema said, without looking at her.

Kavi licked her lips. 'The tattoos – your rites of passage? What *are* they?'

Greema studied her without expression until she squirmed.

'I'm sorry, I didn't mean to—'

'The Culling, we call it,' Greema said. 'It began after the Raayan kings forced us off our land and into the hills and mountains.' She collected a handful of dirt and let it crumble between her fingers. 'There wasn't enough food for all the tribes to survive the winter. Fights broke out. Many died. So, the elders, they decided that since we were going to fight each other anyway, that they would choose how.

'They organised battles between the tribes until a quarter of our number were killed – were *culled* – and there was no longer a shortage of food.' She dusted the dirt stuck to her palm off on her thigh. 'In the decade that followed, until we learned how to survive in those new conditions, the Culling was held annually to reduce the burden and keep things fair.

'Now, every year, when our children come of age, we arm them with wooden swords and send them to fight those of the other tribes. We do it to remember our ancestors, to remember what they endured. A rite of passage, like you said. My mother and father fought in the Culling, so did my grandparents and their grandparents. Some still die, but not many. Those who run or hide are tattooed with a single fang and shunned for cowardice. Those who survive the night are given both fangs and are welcomed to adulthood.'

'And what if they go somewhere else and get a second fang tattooed?' Kavi asked.

'Changes nothing. They are still cowards, and the tribes will not forget their names and faces.'

It wasn't fair. A person's entire life should not hinge on a single night of violence. Kavi crossed her arms. If she could, she'd find all these single-fanged outcasts and tell them that there was nothing wrong with them. Nothing wrong with being afraid. She understood the desperation the Gashani must have felt all those centuries ago, but it did not justify the lives they ruined today.

But hey, who was she to judge? 'Thank you for sharing,' she said.

Greema nodded, and they sat in companionable silence as Kavi imagined herself charging a horde of Gashani with her practice sword. If half of them were like Greema, she'd be lucky to make it out alive.

'I have a nephew,' Greema eventually said. 'My brother's son. His Culling is next year.' She paused, then sighed and shook her head. 'He's never shown any interest in swords, or in our way of fighting – he's learned it because he's had to, but if he had a choice … *Aunty*, he told me, *I want to go to the university in Azraaya, I want to be a surgeon.* I promised him then that if he worked at his swordplay and made it through the Culling, I would pay for him to study at the university and he could live with me in Azraaya.'

'That's why you took this job at the Vagola?'

'This job is safe. Its secure,' Greema said, and turned to face Kavi. 'Tomorrow, when you fight in the tournament, you must remain focused. The first round was always the worst for me. Every year I'd make the same mistakes. Misread the opponent. Struggle to remain empty.' She stood and stretched her back. 'But survive the first round' – *crack-crack-crack* – 'and it gets easier.'

*

Azia's father was waiting at the door of their house, a two-storey beige and white bungalow that had no doubt seen better days. He was a fragile-looking man, with deep-set eyes and thinning hair that he'd oiled back on his head, accentuating his skeletal appearance.

'Kavithri,' he said, shaking her hand and studying – she assumed – the peculiar colour of her irises. 'So nice to finally speak to you.'

'Thank you for inviting me, sahib,' she said with a respectful bob of the head.

He smiled at the honorific and gestured for her to enter his home. 'Come, the food is ready, Azia mentioned you were in a hurry.'

She slipped out of her chappals and left them at the threshold. 'Sorry for the inconvenience, sahib.'

'Not at all.' He led her to a room with a sink where they washed and dried their hands, then guided her to a small dining room. 'Sit, please.' Three steel thalis had been arranged on the table, along with three mugs, a pitcher of water, a serving dish heaped with fragrant basmati rice, and a smaller plate covered with sliced cucumber, red onion, and topped with a slice of lime.

'You too, Azia,' the sahib said and ducked into the kitchen.

'Mutton curry,' Azia said, taking the seat next to hers. 'It's a recipe that's been in my father's family for generations. Takes hours to cook.'

My father's family. Not *our* family. Kavi nodded as she took in the worn and faded furnishings, the dull artificed lamp that hung from the ceiling, and dust that clung to a portrait on the far wall – an oil painting of a middle-aged woman with thick worry-lines and a dour mouth.

The sahib emerged from the kitchen with a heavy, steaming

pot that he carefully positioned – with some effort – in the middle of the table, within reach of all three diners.

Kavi flared her nostrils. Gods, that smelled good. Tangy, so it had to be tomato based. What else? Green chillis? That earthy, nutty scent had to be fresh coriander. Also pepper, cloves – and then there was the meat itself. She swallowed a sudden efflux of saliva.

They took turns scooping rice onto their plates, then ladled the curry on top and added slices of cucumber and onion on the side. Kavi waited for the sahib to take the first bite before shoving a piece of mutton into her mouth. It melted. She stared at Azia, wide-eyed.

He chuckled. The sahib smiled. 'I'm glad you like it,' he said. 'There's more rice in the kitchen so please don't be shy.'

Kavi bobbed her head, her mouth already full with another bite.

They ate in comfortable silence, and when they were done, Kavi insisted on washing the plates. 'Please, sahib,' Kavi said, 'it's the least I can do.'

In the kitchen, while she used the running-splashing water to smother a series of burps, the sahib and Azia heated and poured out three cups of tea.

'Did Azia tell you,' the sahib said, when they returned to the table with their tea, 'about the first time we saw you?'

Kavi blew over the rim of her cup. 'He did.'

'I've never seen anything like it,' the sahib said, a faraway look in his eyes. 'We owe you, and the ones who fought with you that day, our lives.'

Kavi shuffled in her chair. How was she supposed to respond to that? *You're welcome? Don't mention it?* She acknowledged his gratitude with another head bob.

He asked her about herself: where she was from, what she did before the Vagola, how she'd learned to fight.

She told him the truth: Bochan, a railway porter, a sahib called Bithun had helped her.

He treated her like an equal, speculated on the Kraelish motives for the invasion ('to scare us into re-drafting the trade agreement'), discussed the upcoming election for the Azraayan seat on the Council and the rising popularity of the upstart young politico, Dharvish. He told her stories from Azia's childhood: the stray dog he used to feed who kept returning to the house and annoying his mother ('I like dogs, too', Kavi said, and told them about Tsubu), the time Azia got lost in the bazaar and was found helping out at the gulab-jamun stand ('You should open a restaurant and sell that mutton curry,' she said, 'Azia can wait tables.' 'Shut up, Kavi,' Azia mumbled with an embarrassed smile while the sahib snorted), and when it was time for her to leave, he walked her to the door, sent Azia back inside to bring her a container-full of rice and mutton curry, and rested a hand on her shoulder.

'Kavithri,' he said, 'may I ask you a question?'

'Sahib?'

'Do students get injured? During the tournament, I mean.'

'They – it can happen, yes.'

He clenched and unclenched his jaw, averted his eyes, and said, 'Azia respects you – talks about you all the time; calls you his friend. He's never had that before.' He hesitated, then turned back to gaze at her with a vulnerability in his eyes that threw her off-balance. 'Keep him safe, please.'

Kavi studied the man's tired, earnest face. And nodded. 'I will, sahib. You have my word.'

Chapter 16

BLADE

Tournament

'You know what the odds are for your match?' Subbal Reddy asked.

Kavi tightened the strap on her shield until it dug into her forearm. She glanced at Subbal Reddy. The inexplicable man had shown up in her locker room and decided that now, minutes before her first-round match, was the time to have a conversation. 'What are the odds?'

'Five-to-one for you and the skinny boy win,' he said, almost bouncing with excitement.

'Isn't that bad?'

'I placed a five-hundred rayal bet on you.'

Oh, Gods. 'I'm flattered, Reddy-sir. But—'

'No buts, only guts.'

She snorted before she could stop herself and he flashed her a thumbs-up with an *I-made-you-laugh* satisfied smile on his face.

'How did you get in here, anyway?' Kavi asked.

'I said I was a relative of a contestant.'

'And they believed you?'

Reddy winked. 'Gave security one-time-use coupon for dead body disposal.'

Why would anyone even want such a coupon? Kavi shook her head and ran another check on her armour. There was already a

139

sheen of sweat on her face, and the tightness in her chest forced
her to take shallow breaths which made her light-headed and—

Breathe.

She stopped fidgeting with her chestplate.

Breathe.

Last night, as she was escorting an inebriated client out of
the Caterpillar, Deva had come up behind her, and said, 'Five
nights from now. Be here on time. I'll be your second.'

The ring-fight was happening, as she knew it would, but
having it confirmed had made it real. *Later, think about it later.*
One thing at a time.

'I need to be alone now, Reddy-sir,' she said, 'to concentrate.'

'Good luck,' he said, voice and expression uncharacteristically
sombre, before he tucked his purse under his arm and walked
out the door.

She waited until his footsteps faded away and reached into
her pocket. Grishan had given her an artifact, a tiny obsidian
cube half the size of her thumb, that he claimed would alter the
balance and weight of a previously artificed object. The object in
this instance being Vaisha's opponent's sword.

It will make a difference, not enough to raise suspicion, but enough
to give our client an advantage, Grishan had said.

Vaisha's first-round opponents were a pair of third-years –
maybe she could've won without the weapon-tampering, but
they'd never know, because earlier Kavi had snuck into the
third-years' locker room and followed Grishan's instructions.

Her mouth twisted as she gently placed the cube inside her
locker and slammed it shut. *Bring it back in one piece, it's ex-*
pensive, he'd said. *Damage the artifact and I'll take it out of your*
wages.

She checked her equipment again; tightened the strap on her

shield, tugged and slapped the various pieces of armour, and strode out of the locker room.

'Kavi,' a familiar voice said as she shut the door behind her, 'how're you feeling?'

'Nervous,' Kavi said, and acknowledged Salora's presence with a polite head bob. 'What're you doing here?'

The artificer uncrossed her arms and pushed herself off the wall. 'I had a meeting at the Artificers' College – thought I'd swing by and wish you luck. Walk with me to the arena.'

'How're things at Artificed Hydraulics?' Kavi said, falling into step.

Salora glanced at her. Hesitated. 'Chotu has been doing well,' she said.

'That's—' *not what I asked* '—good to know.'

'He has a mind for numbers – your brother would've excelled at the university.'

'Could he apply?'

Salora shook her head. 'He didn't attend school or pass the certified exams – *I know*,' she said when Kavi opened her mouth to protest, 'he never had the opportunity to. I'm sorry.'

Kavi looked away; forced a breath through the tightness in her chest. What would happen to Chotu when she was gone? When her remaining six years were up? The future that she'd worked so hard to create – the rickshaw company, the agreement with the military – had all but evaporated, and the uncertainty, the fact that she wouldn't be around to protect him, scared her.

'I have a feeling,' Salora said with a reassuring smile, 'that he'll be just fine.'

'Could he work for you? As an artificer's clerk or a secretary?'

Again, that hesitation. 'Things are ... *difficult* right now.'

Kavi frowned. 'What do you mean?'

'I – there are some incredibly stupid people running this

country,' Salora said with scowl. 'Bureaucrats who hide behind outdated procedures and process, unqualified officials who've landed their jobs through connections, politicos who are pawns for the wealthy, councillors driven by greed and self-interest – do people really think that a man who has hoarded millions of rayals really cares about the average Raayan? How do they fall for it? How—' She puffed out her cheeks, breathed in deep, and slowly exhaled. 'I'm sorry, they will not allow me to hire a Taemu in any official capacity.'

Kavi stared at Salora, this was the first time she'd seen the (usually composed) artificer this agitated.

'Sorry,' Salora whispered.

'That's okay,' Kavi said as they turned into a tunnel that led to the arena.

'I'm making things sound worse than they are,' Salora said, forcing a smile. 'Talks with the Nathrians are going well – there are even joint field exercises planned for you next term. Who would've thought, four years ago, that we'd be here today?'

Nathria and Raaya had fought over the disputed western border for decades. The Nathrians claimed the land was theirs, that the Kraelish had given it to the Raayans through cartographical error. Raaya disagreed; argued that the lands beyond the mountain range called Gashan's Teeth had historically been ruled by their kings and queens. After a particularly bloody skirmish four years ago the two nations had finally sat down at the negotiating table and signed an armistice. No one really knew how long it would last, but Salora was right, these joint military exercises were a good sign.

Salora stopped at the entrance to the arena. 'Good luck out there.'

'Thank you,' Kavi said.

The artificer gave her a grim nod and walked back down the tunnel.

Outside, in the arena, Azia waited for her at their allocated court. He gave her a nervous, twitchy nod and turned his attention back to the match currently underway. The arena had been rearranged into four courts so simultaneous matches could take place, and a pair of third-years were facing off in the far court – emerald-green maayin whizzed around at dazzling speeds while swords clashed in the middle.

Kavi tsked and looked away. For some reason watching the duel made the jittery feeling in her stomach worse. Instead, she observed her and Azia's own opponents, who stood at the other end of the court: a novice with long, braided hair and all the traditional Raayan piercings – both ears and in one nostril – and a stocky Blade who, like Kavi, carried a shield and longsword.

The duo paid Kavi and Azia no attention. They were busy chatting to a small crowd gathered around them: family and friends, from the snippets of conversation she caught.

Kavi's mouth twisted of its own accord, and she tasted bile at the back of her throat. She was a child again, standing on the footpath at a traffic intersection in Dyarabad; given a stolen baby – who was fast asleep with her head on Kavi's shoulder – by the boss of the Chutti-Mohan beggar gang to boost her quota of alms. The traffic hawaldar raised a hand, halted the stream of traffic and Kavi pinched the baby's arm hard enough to make her cry as she sprinted to the nearest steam-rickshaw. 'Please,' she said, gesturing to the bawling baby.

The driver shook his head and shooed her away. The passengers ignored her and continued chatting to each other. 'Please,' she said again, making the empty-stomach-eating-food gesture this time. They ignored her, giggled at a joke, adjusted their dresses.

'Please.' *Look at me*, she wanted to scream. Her mouth curled as a wave of hatred crashed down on her. *Why won't you look at me?* But they never stopped talking. Never acknowledged her presence. Every sentence that came out of their mouths was an *I* or a *My*: I like, I want, I think, I need, My house, My husband, My father, My son, My—

The hawaldar waved traffic through and the rickshaw sputtered and rattled away. Kavi staggered back to the footpath where she hushed and rocked the baby as she muttered 'Sorry, sorry.'

That was who the novice, the cadets, and their entourage reminded her of: the passengers in the steam-rickshaw. Well-adapted people with supportive families who'd experienced a far different childhood than she had; who lived a cosy, neutered version of life, like in all those stories where no one fucked, no one swore, and death was the same as falling asleep. They seemed so secure, so confident. They would never really *see* her or others like her – not just the Taemu, but anyone who had something missing inside them. Like Azia, or Chotu, or Greema, or, as much as it galled her to admit, Grishan.

Did they know what it felt like? If she explained, would they understand?

No, how could they? If she told them about Grishan, they'd laugh, say she was making things up, no one would do that to their own child, they'd say, because nothing in their lives would've given them any indication of what life outside of their—

Kavi bit the inside of her cheek. But was she any better? Standing here, *judging*, so full of bitterness and so eager to hate. She thunked her sword against her shield as a cold anger, different from the searing rage that was the berserker, settled at the bottom of her stomach and washed the jitters away.

Whatever it takes. She cracked her neck. This was her way out. She would win, or she would end this day as a corpse with a late-night booking at the municipal crematorium.

'Okay? Kavi?' Azia said.

'I'm good, you?'

He shrugged. Absent-mindedly massaged a portion of the scar on his forehead. 'Nervous. A bit.'

'You'll be fine once we start.' She inclined her head at their opponents. 'Your father didn't come to watch?'

'He doesn't like violence.'

Fair enough.

The audience gasped as a cadet went down – knee twisted at an odd angle, armour around it cracked as blood seeped through; his warlock hammered him with pellets of maayin to saturate the armour and he swung his shield around to reach for the release.

His fingers never reached it. A projectile knocked his hand away and the opposing Blade jammed his sword down on his shield-arm. A crystal shattered, and the match was called.

'Used too much maayin to help her Blade,' Azia muttered.

Kavi agreed. 'Difficult choice to make. What would you do?'

His mouth twitched, and he glanced at her. 'The same thing.'

'Even if it meant we lost?'

'It's just a game.'

That's right, to him this was just a game. 'If there's a chance we could win, even if I'm hurt, I want you to take it.'

'It means so much to you?'

'Right now, winning the tournament is the only thing that matters to me.'

'Why?'

'I – if we win it, I'll tell you,' she said.

He shoved his hands into his pockets and looked away.

'It'll make sense, I promise.'

He sighed but gave her a reluctant nod.

'Match twenty-seven,' an instructor shouted. 'First-years, Azia-Kavithri versus first-years, Nithya-Rogul.'

Azia turned to her; his jaw set with grim determination. 'I trust you.'

'I—' *won't let you down?* She couldn't bring herself to say it. 'Thank you,' she said instead, and they walked onto the court.

Azia took up a position behind their crystal, and Kavi stood behind the halfway line, shield raised to eye level, while she waited for this Rogul to saunter over.

She forced herself to take a series of slow breaths and tried to ease some of the tension out of her muscles. Azia knew what he was doing; his pool of maayin, his krasna, it was tiny, but his control over it was astonishing. He could deflect anything thrown at their crystal. All she had to do was stick to the plan.

Both Kavi and her opponent wielded wooden swords artificed to either stun or inflict some serious but non-lethal pain, depending on the impact. The shields were also modified: the artificers added an inhibitor to stunt the power of the release. No one, it seemed, wanted dead students.

The instructor who'd made the announcement raised a metal baton, checked that the combatants were watching, and brought it down. The crystals hummed, a faint orange light emanated from each core, and they began to rotate on their axes.

Both warlocks went into their cast. Kavi didn't need to turn around – maybe it was because of how much they'd practised, but she sensed Azia's krasna manifest itself.

At the other end of the court, the enemy warlock summoned an orb of maayin roughly the size of a small melon.

Not another Ze'aan then, which suited Kavi just fine.

Pellet-sized projectiles shot past as Kavi stepped forward.

Some thunked into Rogul's back and he shouted a garbled battle-cry and charged her.

Kavi whispered an *Aadhier Taemu* and sprinted at the man, building her own momentum. She clenched her jaw, braced for the collision, but was brought up short when Rogul ducked and dived to the side. *What the Hel?* In his place, hovering at chest height, was a rapidly rotating orb of maayin that pulsed, once, twice, and shot out at her.

It slammed into her shield. She grunted, her heels scuffed the dirt, and she stumbled.

Rogul dashed past.

Kavi found her footing, cursed – of course they'd have a plan too, they were going straight for Azia – and raced to catch up with the man. Her calves burned. Her heart pounded. It was over if he knocked Azia out of his cast. There would be no protection for the crystal, and all her hopes of buying back the rickshaw company would be smashed to pieces.

Rogul's back continued to recede away from her. He was too fast. But Azia – eyes wide with fear, face coated with sweat – remained in his cast. His pebbles of maayin flitted around the crystal, knocking away the enemy warlock's maayin and keeping the match alive.

He trusted her. *Good.* She flipped her sword, held it like a javelin, aimed, and hurled it at Rogul's feet.

It caught. And he fell – arms flailing, ankles painfully knocking against each other – with a strangled cry.

Kavi rushed over, bent to retrieve her sword, and grunted as Rogul's heavy boot crashed into her chin.

Lights exploded. Her vision swam. But she remained on her feet and, shuffling around Rogul, positioned herself between him and Azia. She caught her breath, had a moment to brace herself before Rogul shot upright, spat at her feet, and charged her again.

Shields collided with a deafening crash. Kavi's world narrowed and shrank to the sweaty, heaving man and his shield and his sword as it came hurtling down at her.

She blocked. Fended off his strikes. And inch by inch, pushed him back into his half of the court, and within range of his warlock.

Close enough. She planted her feet. Counted her breath and found her rhythm.

There are three ways to parry, Greema's voice said in her ears. *One. Deflect their weapon over your right shoulder by thrusting your sword at his left eye.* Kavi jabbed with her sword. A short, sharp motion that sent it snapping at Rogul's eye.

It caught his sword, knocked it over her shoulder while her blade clipped the side of his helmet.

Rogul hissed. Took a step back.

Kavi followed. *Stick to him.* Nothing else mattered if she couldn't stick to him.

Rogul slashed at her.

Two. Thrust at the eye, but follow through to nick their neck. She held her thrust for a heartbeat to match the timing – *now* – and punched her sword at his face. It deflected his blade away, narrowly missed his forehead, but caught him on the collar when she yanked it down at his neck.

He roared and shield-slammed her away.

Her ankles and calves strained as she bounced right back.

They exchanged blows. Rogul tried to shove her away. She growled and stuck to him. *Stop pushing me away, you bastard.*

He hissed with frustration and reached for the release on his shield-arm.

Already? She'd barely noticed how much maayin his warlock

had pumped into his armour. It was earlier than she'd expected, but it was what she'd been waiting for.

She tucked her tongue in, gritted her teeth, ducked her head behind the shield and planted her feet.

Dhoom! The blast of maayin from his shield hit her point blank, and everything turned white as the taste of metal filled her mouth. Then came the keening in her bones and a powerful ache in her chest, stomach, and abdomen.

Colour slowly returned; she squinted at the gauge on the inside of her shield-arm.

Half-full.

Just as she'd hoped.

She knew the modified release mechanism wouldn't kill, like she'd seen it do during her training for the Siphon, and she'd gambled that it wouldn't knock her out either. She coughed. Her mouth filled with fluid, and she spat it out. Blood, and something else.

Artificed armour was not as efficient against re-used maayin – the kind her opponent had just blasted her with – she'd read that in one of the academic journals at the library. And the armour didn't seamlessly protect her entire body, so she was bound to take some damage at close range. But she was prepared for this.

Rogul was staring at her, eyes wide with surprise.

She took a step forward, stumbled into him; he shoved her away with his shield, lashed out with his sword, and—

Her body reacted. Her left arm, her shield-arm, which she'd drilled into wielding a shortsword, flung itself up and out. She was vaguely aware of what she'd just done – her mind and body still scrambling to re-align – as her shield met Rogul's sword halfway through its downswing with just the right momentum, timing, placement, and power. It was perfect. It was the third parry Greema had taught her.

Thud.

Rogul's sword bounced back up off her shield. Threw him off-balance.

At the same time, the nerves in Kavi's limbs burst to life. Her vision cleared, her purpose reasserted itself, and the strength returned to her core. She spun on her heel, brought her sword around, leaned into it and put every ounce of strength into her swing.

It slammed into Rogul's un-shielded midriff, and he doubled over gasping for air.

Not yet. She raised her sword and slashed down at his wrist.

It connected, sent his arm snapping back and forced him to drop his sword.

Not yet. She stepped in and head-butted him.

Their helmets collided. He staggered back but found his footing. Over Rogul's shoulder, his warlock's maayin flashed as they sent a row of shimmering green pellets hurtling at his back. *Here it comes.* She shoulder-barged him off his feet and raised her shield.

Thunk-thunk-thunk.

Her gauge was now full.

She surged forward at the opposing warlock.

Their eyes met. Blood pounded in Kavi's ears as her lips curled into a bloody grin at the fear and hesitation in the warlock's eyes.

Kavi stopped, rocked back on her heels, and aimed her shield at Rogul's warlock.

The air shimmered as the warlock pulled all her maayin back to create a defensive shield around herself, leaving the crystal exposed.

Kavi switched targets – *got you, bhaenchod* – and punched the release.

Dhoom.

The blast of maayin from her shield shattered the crystal into pieces.

She ripped the helmet off her head and sucked in huge gulps of air. Runnels of sweat crawled down the sides of her face, collected at her chin, and dripped to the ground. It was over.

They'd done it.

The adrenaline faded, the pain returned, and she swayed on her feet. But Azia was there. He linked his arm in hers, struggled with her weight, but kept her standing.

One day, she'd walk out of these duels on her own two feet. *One day.*

'Well done,' she said in a hoarse whisper.

'You need a healer,' Azia said in response.

'Have my own. You know where the rickshaw stand is?'

He grunted.

'Thank you.'

Another grunt.

The 'friends and family' of their opponents converged on the court; they fussed over Rogul and his novice, offered condolences at the loss, and blocked Kavi's and Azia's way out.

'Move,' Kavi said, with no indication in her voice that it was a request.

A woman paled and clutched her friend's hand. The friend's eyes widened with outrage. 'You—'

'*Move.*'

They moved.

'You okay?' she said, squeezing Azia's shoulder as they walked through.

He looked away from her. His chin trembled. 'You're a Blade, right?'

'Uhm – what do you mean?'

'Your job,' he said, voice cracking, 'is to protect your warlock, right?'

'Yes, yes, it is.'

'How can you protect your warlock,' he said, 'if you're hurt so badly?'

She stopped. Gods, but he had a good heart. Too good for this line of work. 'I'm sorry.' She pulled him closer. 'I won't do that again.'

'You promise?' he said, slowly turning to look up at her, tears welling in his eyes and trickling down his scarred, open, and honest face.

'I—' *can heal myself*, she wanted to say, *so no one else needs to get hurt except me. Not you.* Not Chotu or the Taemu. Just her. That's how she'd protect them; that's how she could win this tournament. She felt her ribs tighten as a whisper of doubt wound its way around her chest. She was this badly injured after just one match – and what if winning the tournament meant Azia had to, at some stage, get hurt. What would she do then?

'Kavi?'

She swallowed, averted her eyes, and said, 'I promise.'

END OF PART ONE

INTERLUDE - I

Ze'aan

My father, who was Kraelish, told me stories about the Empire: how it was nothing like the classist Raayan society we lived in, how everyone was equal under the emperor. *It is a country with real history and culture,* he'd said. *Raaya was far better off under Kraelish rule. The Empire brought it peace, gave it structure.*

His stories captivated me. Captured my dreams. I'd imagined the capital, Balthour, as this great city filled with splendour and dazzle, with centuries of culture and art around every corner, with history in every structure.

But it was just another city.

The buildings lacked the manically colourful facades of those in Raaya, but were older and taller. Many, more than I could count, were museums or galleries stocked with artifacts, trinkets, tokens, and spoils from the Empire's former colonies – one particularly grotesque exhibit that I was urged to visit featured a collection of human pelts, taken from the bodies of Raayan freedom fighters who were flayed alive.

The streets were always damp, some in perpetual shadow, and there were pamphlets strewn everywhere. Propaganda for Kraelin's latest act of aggression on the subcontinent. *The Empire will reclaim its history!* one pamphlet proclaimed, under a charcoal impression of the emperor's haughty profile. *Kraelin's return to glory!* another one said under the same imperious profile.

After my first week in the city, I grew to despise this profile. The fucking thing was everywhere: on the money, on the faces of buildings, on pedestals in shops, in restaurants, at train stations, on umbrellas, on gloves and hats – the Kraelish clung to their emperor like he was a life raft that kept them afloat in a storm.

There was, however, a faction in the capital, a group who had spoken out against the remilitarisation of the Empire. They'd gone quiet now, after a string of mock trials and subsequent executions, but rumour had spread: some of the most powerful people in Kraelin were anti-royalists. No one knew who they were, or how many, but they existed.

Then there were Raeth's priests. I found them around every other corner; they sat cross-legged in front of their shrines and blessed pedestrians who stopped for a prayer. The priests underwent a ritual that supposedly allowed them to see their god – and, to ensure that it was the last thing they ever saw, they cut their own eyes out.

It made my skin crawl.

Almost a year ago, while I was a second-year novice at the Vagola, I'd reached out to the Kraelish ambassador in Azraaya. I left a note at his office; told him my father was Kraelish, and that I'd like to speak.

He ignored me.

I left another note the next day with the exact same message. That time, I mentioned I was a warlock. He met me that evening.

I told him I wanted out. He said the college of mages in Balthour would welcome me with open arms, but they would first need to see if I was capable.

I showed them how capable I was in the Siphon, and I proved my loyalty during the assault on the city.

The college of mages in Balthour, as promised, found me a place among their ranks. They made me a junior warlock, assigned me to a senior warlock, and asked me to attend to him. A kind of apprenticeship, not unlike what the Vagola did with their Blades and mentors.

The senior warlock I was assigned to, a man in his late forties with a repugnant comb-over, dismissed me. Told me to explore the city, to learn its unspoken rules, and that he would send for me when he needed me.

They gave me a room on the second floor of a dormitory for warlocks and artificers. It had a bed, a table, an almirah, and a single window through which I had the pleasure of observing a large oak tree's branches and leaves.

The other mages treated me as an outcast, and the novices kept their distance. Everyone else I encountered – shopkeepers, waiters, coachmen – were superficially happy to see me, but I sensed no warmth from them.

The dormitory was rigorously guarded, at least on the outside. Once I endured all the checks and searches I had to undergo to enter and leave the compound, I was free to go wherever I pleased.

I spent my days in a daze while I waited for the senior warlock to summon me. I ate without pleasure. I read books that I forgot as soon as I flipped the last page. I wandered through the city like a ghost without a haunt. It was cold. It was wet. And I was adrift.

At night, when sleep eluded me, or the nightmares – in which Kavithri and the Taemu I killed forced me into a corner, latched onto my arms and legs, and pulled and pulled – startled me awake, I would take the stairs up to the top floor and spend hours exploring and studying the array of items in the college repository. Artifacts from before the Retreat – the mysterious few centuries following the collapse of the First Empire from which no recorded history remained – whose purpose remained a mystery, sat on shelves or in display cases. There were paintings of forgotten battles, iridescent pieces of metal (with a note claiming they were material from another world), ink-stained pages with shapes and words I'd never encountered before.

And then there was the First Mage's eye. It hung suspended in an artifact – a glass box with silver edges – that had survived the Retreat, and which preserved the eyeball in the exact state it had been in when Kraelin, the mage who'd discovered the Jinn and after whom the Empire was named, had lost it. I spent hours – mesmerised, unnerved – staring at its dark pupil and the ocean-blue iris that surrounded it, and trying to imagine the sort of world it had seen.

And then, finally, four months after the assault on Azraaya, almost a month after I arrived in Balthour, Senior Warlock Ackerman sent for me.

Meet me at the entrance of the dormitory his note read.

'Ze'aan,' he said. 'You will follow me on my rounds today – make yourself known to the staff.'

'The staff?'

He hopped up the stairs and through the coach door and made an impatient gesture for me to follow.

We travelled in silence.

Through the coach window, the plumes of smoke from the city's factories got closer and larger, and a metallic odour that reminded me of the scent of blood slowly infused the air. We passed through half a dozen checkpoints, where soldiers peeked inside the coach, rifled through the trunk at the back, and waved us on.

The coach dipped, sped up as it rolled down an incline. The grey, overcast sunlight winked out and was replaced by the harsh yellow of artificed globes that lined the sides of a tunnel.

'Stay close, don't speak,' Ackerman said as the vehicle came to a halt. 'If there is something you need to know, I will share it with you.'

I followed him into a large chamber filled with long, bluish-gold cylinders, then through to a hallway lined with doorless rooms where the same bluish-gold cylinders were affixed via cable to incapacitated men or women strapped to gurneys.

The Kraelish were drawing blood and storing it in these cylinders.

'Move,' Ackerman said, and I stepped aside to allow a gurney to be wheeled past.

The man on the gurney – the man *strapped* to the gurney – looked up at me as they passed. It was only for a heartbeat, but it was enough.

His eyes were empty, glazed over, and if they hadn't flicked up to meet mine, I would've assumed he was dead.

I knew where I was. I was in the blood banks.

The man's irises were red. The man was a Taemu, like all the others here.

'We force them to test when they turn sixteen,' Ackerman said. 'If they fail, we dispose of them. If they pass, if they're chosen by a Jinn and are able to draw its maayin – it alters their blood, and we take it from them.'

Why? I wanted to ask, but I kept my lips sealed.

'You understand what a vector is?' Ackerman asked.

I shook my head. I'd heard the soldiers refer to the six discs on the Kraelish makra as vectors, but I had no idea what they were.

'Material not from this world. We recently learned that with the right catalyst – a Taemu mage's blood – it can power a makra,' Ackerman said as they stepped into another hallway. 'Their blood acts as a conduit, allows our mages to interact with the vectors, and through them, the makra.'

My mouth had gone dry, and I was sweating.

'You're wondering how we use the blood, right?'

I inclined my head.

'Transfusions. We give the blood to our warlocks, and our warlocks pilot the makra.'

So *this* was why the makra – the metal behemoths used to breach the walls of Azraaya – had been used so sparingly. Within a day, or maybe even a few hours, the warlock's own blood would contaminate the transfused blood and reduce its effectiveness. I wiped the sweat off my forehead. How many Taemu were living here? How many had they *disposed* of over the years? It was repulsive, grotesque, nauseating.

I lowered my eyes as another gurney rolled past. I had no right to judge the Kraelish, I was as selfishly monstrous as they were.

Ackerman pointed me out to staff as we walked past, said I was, 'the Junior Warlock who will take over my rounds'.

We went from hallway to chamber to corridor. Through an administrative office packed with desks and ledgers where the air smelled of musty old paper. And into a large warehouse where stack after stack of thick, dark material – if I wasn't imagining things – seemed to absorb the light from the artificed globes.

'Vectors,' Ackerman announced.

Yes, I know. I clenched my jaw and nodded. When the Kraelish left the subcontinent they had also left behind stockpiles in the 'First City' – the labyrinthine, underground tunnels that were remnants of the ancient metropolis Azraaya had been built over. But now they knew what to use that alien material for, and they had used their assault on Azraaya as a distraction to retrieve it. They'd succeeded, and now had enough vectors to power the fleet of makra they were assembling to launch a full-scale invasion of the subcontinent. The emperor's dream of reclaiming Kraelin's lost territories would soon turn into a reality.

'Senior Warlock Ackerman!' A woman, dishevelled and reeking of tamakhu, came running through the stacks. 'Did you get my letter?'

Ackerman's left eye twitched. 'Artificer Janell,' he said. 'What can I do for you?'

'The letter,' the woman persisted. 'Did you read it?'

'I'm afraid I haven't—'

'Listen, the artifice – the blueprints His Majesty sent us – it works,' Artificer Janell said, eyes bulging.

'That's great—'

She grabbed him by the shoulders and shook him. 'No, no, it's not. I used it, I felt – I felt something. The Chain must not be fixed, Ackerman. What if there's someone – *something* out there? What if it comes through?'

Ackerman peeled her fingers off his shoulders. 'Artificer—'

'The people must be informed. They *must* know.'

'Tomorrow.' Ackerman smiled and patted her on the shoulder. 'Tomorrow I will talk to the emperor in person, and I shall relay your concerns.'

The next morning, Artificer Janell, along with seven others, were tried and executed for treason.

And to ensure that an over-zealous daughter or grandson or even a resentful second cousin would not seek revenge, the families of the 'traitors' – a total of eighty-seven men, women, and children – were also executed.

Whatever this *thing* was that the emperor had the artificers working on, it was clear that dissension would not be tolerated.

Not long after, Ackerman was dispatched to the Imperial

palace on some secretive mission, and I was asked to conduct what he called 'the rounds' on his behalf – I'd check in at the administrative offices at the warehouse, make my presence as Ackerman's representative known, ensure that the Vectors were all accounted for, that the artificers were hard at work, and that the blood banks were running smoothly. But with each day, and with each visit, the sight of the Taemu, broken, treated and disposed of like objects, their lifeforce used as fuel, began to chip away at me.

It shouldn't have, and it wouldn't have, if I'd never met her.

The nightmares got worse. On some nights, after my visit to the repository, I would lie in bed, afraid to sleep, and watch the branches of the oak tree outside my window till the sun came up.

I'd always been lonely, even in Raaya. But this was a different kind of loneliness. I'd uprooted myself. Stripped myself of my defences and exposed myself to a world that barely understood me.

But then again, should a monster deserve understanding?

Once, when I was a girl, during a family gathering, my mother pulled me aside – I still remember her fingers digging into my arm – and she told me, 'You have a cruel smile, Ze'aan, it's making them uncomfortable. Try not to smile so much.'

I lay on my back, in the darkness of my room, and curled my lips.

When was the last time I'd smiled without thinking of my mother?

With Kavithri.

I could still hear the girl's sobbing, still feel the shock that ran through my body as her sobs turned into a roar. The shrieks of the Kraelish soldiers that died on her blade. The mocking laughter as she chased them down. And her face: covered in blood, the veins standing on her forehead and neck; and her eyes: accusing, furious, unforgiving.

I'd taken so much from her, caused her so much pain. And she'd helped me, unwittingly, to discover this new person within myself. A person I would never get to share with anyone, or with her.

The only thing that had mattered was leaving Raaya. The desire had suffocated me. Funnelled my thoughts. My hate for my country of birth – for its rigid hierarchy and inequality and injustice, its greed, corruption, nepotism, and bile-inducing obsession with wealth, beauty and appearance – fuelled by my father's stories and his resentment of the place, had made me blind to everything and everyone else. I'd needed to leave so I could breathe.

I was a fool.

I shut my eyes, ignored the tears that oozed out of them, and hugged my knees to my chest.

I'm sorry, Kavithri. I'm so sorry.

Part Two

Chapter 17
ENFORCER

Dharvish

'Why did the Kraelish invade? Hah?' Naadan the bookseller pulled a comb out of his pocket and, with one hand bracing the side of his head, combed his hair. 'Simple. It was a trial run. The chootia wanted to test our defences to see how far they could get. Why else would they withdraw so easily? Why else did those monsters, those *makra*, just stand outside the walls and watch? I tell you, Collector-memsaab, they're coming back, and next time, they will flatten the city.' He sliced the air with his comb. 'Flatten!'

Kavi – who sat on a stool by the door, chin propped up in the base of one palm – sighed and nodded. There were no Vagola lessons or tournament matches on the weekend, and her ring-fight was another three days away, so she was on collector (extortion) duty for the Tivasi, which she'd already completed, and was now killing time in the bookshop until the Caterpillar opened for business.

'What do you think?' Naadan.

'Makes no difference to us,' she muttered and sighed again.

'Dai,' Naadan said, peering at her. 'Why so sulk? Ah?'

Why? She'd learned, over the last few days, that, 'The Taemu are struggling to find work. No one will hire us. Even the jobs we used to do – they won't take us back.' Some, like Nariga, had even returned to begging.

Naadan threw a conspiratorial glance over his shoulder and leaned over the counter. 'You want to know why?'

Kavi sat up. 'Tell me.'

'The gangs,' he said, dropping his voice to whisper. 'Tivasi and Dolmonda – mostly Tivasi, they've threatened us, told us not to hire Taemu or they will ruin our businesses.'

Her eyes bulged. Blood pounded in her ears and she deliberately, slowly, arranged her clenched fists in her lap. They were a tumour at the heart of this city, these gangs, and while they continued to pump poison into its veins, her people would struggle to have a future in it.

Across the street, the doors to the Caterpillar thudded open, and Deva, trailed by a dozen Tivasi goons and dragging a heavy-looking mallet, strode toward the bookshop.

Kavi stood. Stepped out to meet them.

'We have a job,' Deva said and held the mallet out to her.

She hesitated. 'What kind of job?'

'Boss wants you to use this,' he said, and forced the mallet into her hands. Once it was securely in her grip, he reached into his shirt pocket, extracted a semi-crushed beedi, and waited for one of his men to light it for him. He took a long drag and gestured for her and the Tivasi gangsters to follow as he set off down the road.

'Do you know who Nashik Faria is?' he asked as Kavi fell into step.

The councillor who'd signed and approved the document that gave Grishan the rickshaw company. She nodded.

'There is a politico running for Faria's spot on the Council,' Deva said. 'A man called Dharvish.' He flicked his beedi, sent ash tumbling into a gutter. 'We will encourage him to withdraw.'

*

Women screamed, glass shattered, a man pleaded and begged as he was dragged out of his home.

Kavi stood in the street, white-knuckle grip on the mallet, surrounded by a large crowd of onlookers. *Wait here*, Deva had told her, *I'll bring him out. Boss wants you to use the mallet on his legs.* The spectators gave her a wide berth while they whispered and stared and pointed.

Off to the side, Tivasi gangsters made a small hill out of Dharvish's campaign materials – his pamphlets and badges and banners and flags – doused it in kerosene and set it on fire.

'Please, my family,' Dharvish pleaded and batted at the powerful hand dragging him by the hair.

Deva spat and adjusted his grip on the smaller man's thick head of hair. 'Bring them, they need to see,' Deva ordered one of the Tivasi, who hurried into the house and returned with a woman and little girl: Dharvish's wife and daughter.

'Please, leave them, they—' Dharvish managed before Deva grabbed him by the collar and shoved him at Kavi's feet.

Dharvish's wife was sobbing, clutching her daughter's face to her stomach and gibbering as she tried to force her way to her husband. The Tivasi gangster slapped her. Once. Twice. And she whimpered and fell silent.

'Why?' Dharvish squeezed Kavi's ankles and gazed up at her with tears running down his bruised face. 'Why? I only tried to help. Why are you doing this?'

I have no choice, she wanted to tell him, *you don't know what he's like. I have to obey.* Her lips trembled, and she tried to step away, but he would not let go.

Deva kicked him in the side and sent him sprawling. He

gestured for Kavi to come closer. 'Face them when you do it,' he said, cocking his head at the crowd.

Kavi nodded. She understood what Grishan wanted.

'Hold him down,' Deva said, and two other gangsters punched and kicked Dharvish until he was still and they could restrain him.

Deva sat on his haunches and patted Dharvish on the cheek. 'You have one day to withdraw from the elections, bhai.' He pointed at Dharvish's wife and daughter. 'Or we will return, and do to them, what the' – he raised his voice – '*Taemu* is about to do to you.' He stood and backed away. 'Proceed.'

Kavi's hands shook as she raised the mallet over her shoulder. Her cheeks and neck burned with shame, but she gritted her teeth – *I have no choice.* Her vision blurred as she sensed the hate and anger from the crowd. She flinched as the fear on Dharvish's face twisted into outright revulsion. But she swung the mallet.

It connected with a sickening *crunch!* Dharvish gasped in pain and spasmed, his wife screamed and begged for Kavi to stop.

She shattered one knee, then the next, and along with them smashed to pieces any residual goodwill the people of Azraaya may have still had for the Taemu.

Chapter 18
ENFORCER

Round One

Kavi took a drag. The tamakhu was of a variety she'd never tried before. Smooth. Barely any friction as it slithered down her throat. She licked her lips – cloves, the sweet aftertaste of fennel, and something else she couldn't identify – and exhaled. The grey stream of smoke billowed until it escaped the awning and was obliterated by the rain.

It was a quiet night, by Lantern district standards. A steam-rickshaw splashed past. An early-bird client glanced her way and stepped into the Caterpillar. Rain continued to clatter on the rooftops.

Kavi took another drag.

She'd spent the morning training with Azia. Their next match was against another first-year duo, and the Plan – concealed-maayin-surprise-attack – was to remain in their back pockets. They'd racked their brains, tried to think of a different strategy, but, as Subbal Reddy liked to say, *Nothing is coming*.

Speaking of Reddy – she flicked the butt of the beedi and sent ash spinning to the ground – she had him to thank for the expensive tamakhu between her fingers.

He had been leaving the Caterpillar just as she arrived to start her shift, and had asked her to join him outside for a smoke.

'I heard about the ring-fight,' he'd said with a grin. 'I'll be placing another bet on you.'

She winced, and said, 'Don't.'

'Hah? Why not?'

'Reddy-sir ...' She stared at him, then cracked her neck in the direction of the brothel.

'Ah.' His humour evaporated, and he took an expansive pull on his beedi.

They stood in silence, watching the rain and smoking, until he finally flung his beedi to the ground, crushed it underfoot, and re-tucked his purse under an arm. 'The things they make you do ... you deserve better,' he'd said, and walked away before she could respond, one hand raised in farewell.

Don't we all. She took a step back as the rain worsened and splashed onto her feet.

Last night, the father of Nariga's baby boy, the Raayan labourer she'd told Kavi about, had come to visit. He'd held Inaaya up to the light of a streetlamp, and Kavi's mouth had tightened at the disappointment on his face as he noted the deep red irises in his son's eyes. He'd dropped the baby in Nariga's lap and left without saying a word.

'It feels like we're going backwards,' Chotu had said.

Kavi sighed and switched to holding the beedi with her index finger and thumb. The only time she got to spend with her brother was at the end of the day, when both of them were exhausted, and she was slowly discovering that Chotu was not all that he seemed.

He'd brought her rats for tonight's ring-fight; said Ratan would keep them in his rickshaw for her.

She'd not asked him where he was getting the money for the rats, or for the agoma she used every night. His body language told her he didn't want her to, and she respected that. Instead, she'd asked Ratan.

He'd given her a sharp glance, then said, 'He's part of a small smuggling business.'

'A *what*?'

'Don't ask me how, but from what I hear, he knows what he's doing – he's good with numbers, apparently.'

'What do they smuggle?'

'Arrack, pepper, rum, this and that.'

She flicked her beedi into the rain, sent it spinning out into the street where it went out with a soft hiss. Chotu should've told her. There was nothing to hide from her. In fact, hearing about what he was up to, it made her proud.

Proud, but sad.

Her face sagged. She was empty and heavy at the same time. It was hard to stand straight, to keep her shoulders from slouching. She tucked her hands into her armpits and stared at the ripples in a puddle of rainwater.

She could just stop. Leave everything behind and run. Her hands shook, and she squeezed her armpits down on them. *No.*

This compulsion that lived inside her, this need to do what – in her eyes – was right and good, that had gotten her into so much trouble in the past, would never allow her to do it. She could never abandon her brother and her people. It made her feel small that she'd even thought about it. And it made her feel so lonely.

She closed her eyes, breathed in the earthy scent kicked up by the steady pitter-patter of the rain, and let her body shudder as she searched for that old, lost feeling of being loved, of being safe, that only her mother had ever evoked in her.

What would you do, Amma?

'It's time,' Deva said, standing in the doorway.

She ignored him.

'You remember what you need to do?'

'Go down in the second round,' she said, softly. 'Take a beating in the first, go down in the second.'

*

Deva left her in a dingy little room attached to the back of the abandoned warehouse where the ring-fights took place. It had a wooden stool, a sink, a cracked and rusted mirror, and was lit by a single dia lamp.

She changed into the training shirt and trousers she'd brought with her from Bochan; the same clothes she'd worn the last time she'd fought in a ring. The bandages, however, she needed help with. She nudged the door open and gestured for Deva, who stood outside, probably to keep her from running away, to help her with them.

'I don't know how,' he said.

'I'll show you.'

She sat on the stool while he unfolded the long strip of fabric.

'Around my wrists first.'

He nodded.

'Then the knuckles.' The base of her palms, between each finger, and then back around again.

Deva did as she asked, expressionless, efficient; if touching a Taemu bothered him, he didn't show it.

'How much longer?' she asked, once he finished and had stepped back out of the room. The warehouse, based on the noise – people shouting, laughing, the rumble of conversation that echoed in the large, contained space – must almost be full.

He cocked his head, listening. 'Come.'

They took the back entrance and emerged behind a kiosk

selling arrack and chicken 65 – a drinking snack that had seen a recent boom in popularity. Chicken chunks marinated with garam masala and other spice powders; deep fried, cooled, then tossed in hot oil with curry leaves, dried red chillies, and garlic. Why did it have 65 in its name? Speculation was rife: maybe the cook who invented it was sixty-five years old; maybe it was the sixty-fifth item on the menu of the restaurant that first served it; maybe the chickens were sixty-five days old when they were slaughtered. No one knew, and the mystery added to its appeal. Kavi had sampled some at the Caterpillar and fully approved of the hype – it smelled incredible and tasted even better.

'Special discount if you buy both,' a man behind the counter was telling a customer.

'Bhai, just arrack—'

'Wokay.' The man raised his voice for the cook. 'One chicken 65 and one arrack!' He turned back to the bewildered customer who was being jostled by the men and women behind him to hurry up. 'Twenty-five rayals.'

'But—'

'Bhaenchod, just pay and go!' someone yelled from the back. 'Bleddy chootia holding up the line.'

The dejected man paid and accepted a chit with his order number on it.

'Next!'

Large artificed globes hung from the high ceiling and bathed the packed warehouse in brilliant yellow. Kavi tracked her shadow as it followed Deva's heels to the edge of the ring.

'Is he here?' she asked.

'No,' Deva said. He knew exactly who she was referring to. 'But he's watching.'

What the fuck did that even mean?

Deva pulled a stool out from under the ring and thumped it down in a corner. 'Let's go.'

She puffed out her cheeks. Slammed her fists together – why? She wasn't going to use them today. She tsked and slid under the rope Deva held down with his foot.

'Boss wanted you to see,' he said when she stood, and pointed to a section of the crowd.

Kavi followed the line of his finger to a cluster of gangsters, and her mouth went dry. Ice-cold tendrils of fear unfurled in her stomach and twisted their way down to her knees.

The gangsters surrounded a group of Taemu. Boxed them in and left them no choice but to stand and watch what would happen in the ring. They stared at her with wide, terrified eyes.

It was a threat. It was what she expected from him. *Disobey me*, she heard Grishan whisper in her head, *and see what happens to your people.*

Her chest heaved as she took shallow breath after shallow breath. It'd be fine. She didn't intend to disobey him, anyway. They'd be fine.

Her opponent stepped into the ring, but she barely paid him any attention. She was starting to see dark spots. They moved when she moved her eyes. Not good.

'Sit,' Deva said, and with a hand on her shoulder, urged her down onto the stool. 'Are you scared?'

She refused to look at him.

'Makkur is the current champion,' he said. 'Good fighter, hasn't lost yet.'

'Because all his matches are fixed?' Kavi muttered.

Deva shrugged. 'You know the rules? Each round—'

'I've fought before.'

He inclined his head in an unexpected gesture of respect. 'Remember, second round.'

Her opponent – this so-called champion, Makkur, a clean-shaven Raayan man with a powerful upper body and a hairy chest – sat on his stool and glared at her from across the ring. She blinked. 'Does he know?'

Deva paused. Glanced at Makkur. 'I'm not sure. Open.' He positioned the gumshield in front of her face and pushed it in when she opened her mouth.

She clenched her jaw and sank her teeth into it.

'Good luck,' he said, and stepped out of the ring.

With what? Her knees trembled as she stood. The referee – a thin, sweaty man in a white baniyan that clung to his torso – gestured for both fighters to join him in the middle of the ring.

Kavi couldn't remember walking up to him, but yet there she was, right in front of his face. He said something, Makkur nodded. He looked at her, waited. She nodded.

The lights, the sinuous movement of the spectators in her periphery, the excitement that clung to the air, so many jeering and hooting at her, like human vultures, waiting to see her lose so they could pick apart what was left – the bell rang, and she went blind.

Time lost its coherence. Turned into a confusion of noise and helplessness and fear – not for herself, but for the Taemu huddled and herded into the corner of the warehouse. Her legs were stone. Her lungs felt like they were filled with water. She was drowning. Her hands, of their own accord, covered her head as she sank into the turtle-like defence Bithun had taught her.

Makkur threw a tentative jab, and when she didn't react, punched through her guard and *crunch*, connected with her mouth.

Her head snapped back. But the pain was not immediate. It hovered over her for a heartbeat before sinking into her muscles and bones.

She flung out a half-hearted jab of her own.

He dodged with ease. Didn't even bother to move his feet, just swayed out of the way, and went to work on her body: liver blows and hook after powerful hook banged into her ribs as she was forced back into a corner.

Then he really began to hit her: left-right combos to the jaw that made her head swim.

She tried to shove him away, catch her breath, but he just slipped past her arms and hammered more hooks into her kidneys.

She wanted to throw up. She wanted to breathe without it hurting. Her eyes watered and blood clogged a nostril – she wheezed and forced it out, tasted it as it slithered in between her lips and coated the inside of her mouth. *It's fine, I'm okay.* As long as she was the only one getting hurt, she would endure.

The bell rang, and she stumbled out of the corner.

'Wrong way, Taemu,' the referee said, and shoved her back into her corner.

Hands on her shoulders urged her to sit. They massaged her jaw until she spat out the gumshield. 'Water?' Deva asked.

Kavi squeezed her eyes shut. Opened them. Bright white spots flickered, shifted, and exploded into Deva's bearded face.

'Water?' he said again.

A nod.

She spat first, then drank.

He had nothing else to say, and for some reason, she was grateful for his silence.

It would be over soon – she'd done the hard part; she'd taken a beating and remained standing. Now, all she had to do was give in to the exhaustion.

Makkur came bounding out of his corner as soon as the bell rang.

A series of body blows sent her stumbling to the ropes where she flailed and tried to regain her balance – *What's his problem? Relax, bhai, you're going to win anyway* – when a jaw-breaking uppercut caught her on the chin.

Her body instantly severed ties with her mind. She stiffened, her legs gave out, and she crumpled. There was no need for her to pretend.

A moment of spinning disorientation, colours and lights merged and stretched, an ache in her jaw crept up into her temples and jammed itself into her skull, and then she was drifting above herself. She dispassionately watched as Makkur kicked her, first in her ribcage, then in the head, before the referee pushed him away and the darkness that'd been coalescing on the edges of her vision converged and blacked everything out.

Chapter *19*
ENFORCER

This Place, It's Mine

Kavi stared at her battered face in the mirror: welts under both her eyes; black-blue bruises on her cheeks and chin; congealed blood in and around her right ear; swollen lips. She gently prodded a welt and hissed when it sent searing needles of pain into her sinuses.

'Are you dressed?' Deva said from outside the makeshift locker room.

'Come in,' Kavi said.

The door squealed as he pushed it open. 'Here.' Deva placed a small wad of banknotes on the empty stool. 'For the healer.'

'The Taemu—'

'They're safe. He – we let them go after the fight.'

She sighed and some of the tension left her muscles.

'Return to the Caterpillar for the rest of your shift,' he said, and left before she could respond.

They wouldn't give her a day off even after a beating like that? She pocketed the money and limped outside. Bleddy gangsters.

Ratan was waiting for her around the corner. He sat in the front seat of his steam-rickshaw, newspamphlet in his lap, watching her as she approached.

'They're saying you couldn't even throw a punch,' he muttered as she slipped into the backseat.

'Does it matter?' She reached for the rat boxes stowed behind the seat and called her *maayin*. Shimmering blue threads – visible only to her – ripped their way out of her body and slithered into the boxes to *take* from the animals.

'People are talking, saying you and the Taemu never fought the Kraelish, that it was all a lie.'

Grishan's doing, no doubt. 'It's what he wants.'

'Frustrating,' Ratan said, pumping the lever to start the rickshaw. 'Home?'

'No, they want me to finish my shift.'

He spat. 'Bleddy gangsters.'

She whispered a *Thank you* and *Forgive me* to each rat she killed, and when she was done, she stowed the boxes back behind the seat and settled in to watch the city speed past. A city that, if what Ratan said was true, was unsurprisingly eager to forget what the Taemu had sacrificed for it.

She fought to keep the tightness out of her jaw, to keep her brows from furrowing and her mouth from twisting. *Breathe.* She swallowed. Unclenched her fists. *Breathe.*

She hadn't fought the Kraelish for a reputation, none of them had; they'd done it to save themselves, to save their homes. But still, it irked her how easily the city seemed to turn against them. Maybe Grishan was right, maybe the city didn't need Taemu heroes. She looked down at her trembling palms, at the angry veins that stood on the insides of her wrists. She should've let this fucking place burn.

*

Kavithri Taemu, congratulations, and they'd hand her the Bladelock tournament trophy along with a fat wad of cash. Applause, envy on the faces of the losers, she'd flash a proud Greema a

179

thumbs-up, shake hands with Azia, and be on her way to buy back the Imperial Rickshaw Company. The Taemu would be rickshaw drivers again, and she could—

'Oye, Taemu, deal with that,' the Aunty-ji said, smashing her daydream to pieces.

A client, clearly drunk, was trying to leave, but kept stumbling into tables and chairs, knocking them over.

'Okay, bhai, let's go,' she said, helping him up.

'I did nothing wrong,' the man said, slurring his words.

'Sure, sure, now come.' She guided him to the door. 'How're you getting home?'

'Home?' He looked at her with big, wide eyes that started to tear up. 'I have no home.'

That makes two of us. 'How come?'

'My wife kicked me out.'

'Just say sorry,' she said, and hailed a cycle-rickshaw. 'Whatever it is, I'm sure she'll forgive you.'

'You think so?'

'Of course, now tell the driver your address.' She waited till he settled into the rickshaw, where he continued to babble about his wife's fury and how it was not his fault that someone called Pucchamma had seduced him.

'Come back here if he doesn't pay,' she told the rickshaw driver as he slowly pedalled away with his inebriated cargo.

Back inside, despite the late hour, the Caterpillar still thrummed with lecherous energy. Sitar, tabla and vocalist serenaded the floor as clients continued to make their choices and the beautiful, elegant men and women on the divans stood, took them by the hand and led them upstairs.

Wary glances were thrown Kavi's way as she wiped sweaty palms on her trousers and walked up to where the Aunty-ji watched the floor with unconcealed disinterest. Dharvish had withdrawn from the elections, and word had spread of what a Taemu enforcer working for the Tivasi had done to him.

'Memsaab,' Kavi said. 'I'll go up and check if everything is okay?'

The woman nodded without looking at Kavi, and she took off up the stairs. Straight to Nabosin's room.

The door was open. She stopped, adjusted her clothing, brushed her hair back. She just wanted to talk to him, there was nothing wrong with that; with everything else that was going on, why shouldn't she be allowed a little self-indulgence?

She poked her head in. The room was empty – ah, not quite, Nabosin was in the huge bathtub built into the floor, scrubbing it on his hands and knees. She cleared her throat. His head snapped up.

'Hello,' she said, and waved. Why was she waving? She clenched her fist and swung the arm back down to her side. And why was it so hard to say his name out loud?

'Ah, Kavithri,' Nabosin said, and carefully set one foot out of the tub.

She rushed over and held out a hand to support him.

'Thank you,' he said, bemused. 'Can I help you with something?'

'Yes – no, I just came to chat.' She smiled. 'Quiet night downstairs.'

He chuckled and rolled his trousers back down to his ankles when he was free of the tub. 'What would you like to chat about?'

'I wanted to ask—' Yes, what *did* she plan to talk to him about? This was as far as she'd thought things out. 'Uhm, what did you do in Hamaka? Was it the same as here?'

'No.' He strolled over to a side-table with a large jug on it and filled a couple of steel mugs with salted nimbu-pani. He offered her one and walked over to a window where he pushed the thick curtains open.

Kavi joined him, sipped her drink, relished the tangy, lime-flavoured beverage. The window overlooked the entrance to the Caterpillar, and beyond it the rows of shops she collected protection money from.

'I was a student at the college of medicine,' Nabosin said, watching traffic crawl on the street below.

'What kind of medicine?'

'The mind.'

'A mind doctor?' Kavi said with a frown. Was that an actual thing?

'Yes,' he said with a smile, 'you can call it that.'

'So how—'

'Look.' He pointed. 'The chickens are here.'

The chickens? She craned her neck, and yes, a small group of chickens had gathered outside the shops.

He started talking about how a shopkeeper had bought the chickens, kept them in a shed at the back, and then later had adopted a dog. Since the two parties were incompatible, he had then released the chickens. The birds wandered the Lantern district, but every night, without fail, would return to the shop and refuse to leave till they were fed.

While he spoke, Kavi stared. She vaguely registered what he was saying, nodded when she felt it was appropriate and chuckled when he paused. But it was clear he was deflecting; he didn't want to explain how he went from student in the Hamakan Isles to prostitute in Azraaya. Kavi didn't care. Her mouth was dry, her skin tingled, her stomach somersaulted, and for some bizarre reason, she began to imagine them together – clammy with sweat, hair plastered to their heads, bodies slapping sucking sticking.

'Funny, no?'

She blinked. Oh, what the Hel? 'Yes,' she swallowed and smiled.

A bolder woman would've said, *Dai, I like you, enough small talk, you like me too or what?* Could she say that? She hesitated. He probably didn't fully understand what she was. Not many Taemu lived in the Hamakan Isles anymore, and she'd heard that the prejudice that existed on the subcontinent had never really caught on there. But he was in Raaya now, and he was bound to find out. And then? He'd be repulsed. *A Taemu? Pining after me?* He'd gag. *Disgusting.*

Yes, she should leave him alone. This was stupid. This was …

But she couldn't help it. Her arm, as if of its own volition, moved, and her fingers, with an almost imperceptible tremble, tapped him on the shoulder.

How did these things even work? Did she just come out and tell him what she thought of him? That would be creepy. And unsettling. There had to be another way. Another—

'Tea,' she said. It was how Elisai got them to spend time alone.

'Sorry?' He glanced at the mugs in their hands. 'There is tea at the—'

'Do you want to drink some tea with me?' Kavi said, and retreated into her head where she cringed and screamed in embarrassment. What was she doing?

Genuine surprise flickered across his face. And he smiled again, this time with a hint of amusement in the angle of his lips. 'Forgive me, Kavithri, I have to return to work.'

There. He's not interested. Walk away. Walk. Away. 'After work?'

'After?' He faltered. 'I – I'm sorry, I do not have that luxury.' He bobbed his head and walked to the side-table, set his mug down and rolled up his trousers before stepping back into the tub.

She'd tried. It hurt, but she'd tried. She could move on. She didn't deserve love anyway, someone like her. Besides, what she wanted belonged in books and plays and stories. It was not real. It was not for her.

But still, *it would have been nice*. If it was him, she could tell, even though they'd barely exchanged a dozen words, that it would've been nice. She swallowed the lump in her throat, pinched her lips tight to keep them from trembling, and—

Nabosin stopped. He turned, studied the expression on her face, then blasted her with his smile.

Kavi's breath caught. Her heartbeat quickened. And she couldn't help it, she smiled back.

'I would be happy to chat with you whenever you are working,' he said.

'I'd like that,' Kavi said. It wasn't what she wanted, but it would have to do. Whatever this was, it had taken root and would not let go; and if conversation in the Caterpillar, where he worked and fucked men and women who felt nothing for him was all he could offer, then that would be enough for her. She kept the smile on her face, fought off the hollow sense of dejection and disappointment that threatened to drag it down, and left the room.

She was halfway down the stairs and teetering over the precipice of a pit of thick, cloying self-pity, when she glanced down at her hands. Dammit, she'd brought the mug with her.

Go back and return it? She tsked. No, snap out of it. She could just leave it at the bar.

Downstairs, at the bar, she found Naadan, the bookseller from across the street, deep in discussion with the bartender.

'I liked it,' the bartender said as he wiped a mug clean.

'No, no – listen, yaar.' Naadan slapped the counter. 'The first half of the novel? Boring. Written like the author is ticking things off a list – hero goes here, does this, sees this, talks to this arsehole and that bastard – you can tell the bloody bhaenchod planned the whole thing out and hated writing it. Then, the hero, the fucking hero, this so-called doctor who is supposed to be an intellectual giant – guess what? He. Never. Uses. His brains. All the chootia does is get angry and shout at people and expect them to obey him. Then the romance' – he slapped his forehead – 'Meshira have mercy, I felt nothing, the fucking characters felt nothing, but still, love at first sight.' He bobbled his head, mouth upturned with disgust.

Kavi left the mug on the counter and rested her elbow next to it. This book was clearly no Tsubumani – those novels were achingly relatable, written for people like her by someone who knew what it was like to live in the gutter – but she might ask Naadan if he could lend her a copy. She needed a distraction, and this sounded like one of those inoffensive books that she could read and forget.

'I tell you,' Naadan continued, 'this chootia has no idea how real people behave. He does not understand – has never had to struggle for anything in his life. You can tell – no, no, be honest, you can tell. It makes me sick.' He stuck his tongue out and pretended to gag, caught sight of Kavi, standing there with mug in hand, and stood. 'Oh, Collector-memsaab, I've been waiting for you, come with me.'

'What's going on?' Kavi said as he led her out of the Caterpillar by the crook of her elbow.

'Ruckus is going on,' Naadan said, checking the street for traffic before crossing. 'Dolmondas have come to Chella's shop, want him to pay.'

'Dolmondas? But this is not their turf.'

'Exactly.'

A crowd had gathered around Chella's footwear shop. Kavi and Naadan shoved their way through.

Chappals and juttis, once neatly arranged on the display shelves, were strewn across the floor, and the Dolmondas, five men in the signature blue lungis of the gang, surrounded Chella, a middle-aged man with a potbelly, and his wife, a woman with greying hair and a large mole on her face. Both crouched in a corner, terrified, pleading; Chella shielded his wife as a gangster tried to land a kick and missed.

'Dai,' the kicking gangster said, 'pay up. Full interest, or—'

'Bhai, please.' Chella put both his hands together as he begged. 'You said we had till the end *ooof!*'

The gangster landed the kick this time. 'You pay when we tell you to.'

Naadan nudged Kavi in the side. 'Collector-memsaab, help him, please.'

Kavi nodded. Gently pushed him back into the crowd, and stepped out.

A gangster noticed her and made a clicking sound with his mouth to get the others' attention.

The kicking gangster, who was obviously in charge, turned to face her. 'The fuck do you want?'

'Let them go.' The words just came. No thought behind them.

The man cocked his head. 'Let him go?' He snorted and returned to the cowering Chella and wife. 'Get rid of her.'

The four other men converged on Kavi.

'Dai, isn't she the Taemu from the ring-fight?'

'Hmm? Oh, yes, it's her!'

'Chootia Taemu couldn't even block properly.'

'*Let them go?* Stupid bitch.'

One of them shoved her and forced her to take a step back. 'Let them go,' she said again, as if those were the only words she knew.

They laughed.

They shoved her again.

One of them slapped her. Spun her head around and stung her cheek with the force of the blow.

'Let them go.'

A hand was on her face. Palm smothering her mouth, fingers digging into her cheeks as it squeezed and tried to push her away.

It reeked.

The hand reeked of tamakhu and stale piss and of all the ways the Dolmondas had hurt those she loved: Haibo, who they tortured and left for dead; Chotu, whose leg they took and whose life they'd made miserable; all the Taemu they'd bullied and beaten. It reeked. It fucking reeked.

'What is wrong with her—' He never saw the punch coming. A vicious right hook that crunched into his ribs, blew him off his feet and into the wall. *Crack-thud*. He fell in a heap, unconscious.

Kavi spat. Wiped the stink off her face with the back of her hand. Raised both fists to eye level. Rolled one shoulder, then the other, and stepped up to the closest gangster.

His eyes widened as a sharp one-two, a jab into a straight, shattered his nose and splattered his clothes with blood. He reeled. But she didn't let him fall. She shifted her weight and threw a liver-blow that knocked the man into the path of another astonished gangster and sent them both stumbling to the ground.

That's three. She squared up to the next gangster, who'd drawn a sickle of all things, and rushed her with a howl.

She sidestepped. Punched him in the neck. Skipped back to the third gangster, who was getting to his feet, and stomped down on his knee.

He clutched the knee, cried out in pain, and stayed on the floor.

Blood pounded in Kavi's ears, her heart thrashed against her chest, and the berserker strained against its chains. A shriek built and filled the base of her throat as it tried to force its way out, but she clamped her jaw shut and kept it inside. *I don't need you for this.*

Two left standing. Leave the boss for last.

She feinted, threw a series of compact jabs at the sickle gangster – *hiss-jab*, just like Bithun taught her – until he collapsed, his face a smashed mess, her knuckles covered in blood, and she turned to face the boss.

He stared at her, wide-eyed, a layer of sweat on his face, hands trembling.

She stepped in his direction.

He backed away.

And just like that, it was over.

'Remember this well,' Kavi said, surprised at how steady her voice was. 'This place, it's mine. These people, they're under my protection.' She lowered her fists. 'Do you understand?'

He swallowed, his eyes flickered to his men, and he nodded.

'Take your men and go, and never come back.'

In the hushed silence that followed, the Dolmondas picked themselves up, moaned and groaned and cast glances at Kavi, who stood, arms crossed, glaring at the gangsters until they left.

She turned to a relieved Chella and hissed at him. 'Why the fuck would you borrow money from them? You know this is Tivasi turf—'

Chella scrambled forward on his knees and latched onto her

ankles. 'Please, Collector-memsaab, you take so much, we had to borrow – please.'

Kavi leaned over and gently urged his fingers off her feet. 'Tell me, next time,' she said. 'We can work something out.'

He bobbed his head, wiped the tears off his face. 'Thank you, Collector-memsaab.'

She nodded. Exchanged another one with Naadan. And walked through the gap in the crowd.

'Akka,' someone whispered.

Kavi stopped. Searched the faces staring at her – no, she must've imagined it, there were no Taemu here, no one who'd called her Akka – before heading back to the Caterpillar.

Her eyes went straight to the entrance, where Nabosin stood, watching her, still as a statue, under the light of a gas lamp.

She bobbed her head as she strode past, and froze when he tapped her wrist.

'Your hands,' he said.

Kavi looked down at her bloodied knuckles, at the pale white of a shattered tooth that protruded between them.

Her eyebrows rose as he gently lifted her hands up into the light and frowned at them. 'Come with me,' he said, and taking her by the wrist, he led her into the Caterpillar, past a bemused bartender, up the stairs, and back into his room.

'Sit, please.' Nabosin gestured to the bed.

What the Hel? Had he changed his mind about her? She sat, stared at his back as he rifled through an almirah. But this was too fast, *at least have some tea with me first before you—*

He turned back to her with a small box filled with bandages, towels, ointments, and a pair of scissors.

Ah. She sheepishly studied the floor as he used a damp towel to clean her fists.

'You can fight,' he said, switching hands.

She glanced at him, swallowed, and glanced away. His face was so close. Too close. It made her ears burn. 'It's why they gave me this job,' she mumbled.

'I'm going to pull it out,' he said.

'What?'

He pointed to the broken incisor buried between her knuckles.

'Thanks – go ahead,' she said.

He nodded. Pouted with concentration as he extracted the tooth from her hand.

Gods, he was being so gentle, so kind to her. Someone who looked like him had no right to behave this way. How was she supposed to feel now?

He glanced up at her when she didn't flinch, and dropped the tooth into the bloodstained towel he'd used to clean her knuckles. 'I heard about the ring-fight.'

She sighed. 'Did you?'

'Did the boss force you to lose?'

The pungent ointment he massaged into her bruised knuckles forced her to wrinkle her nose. 'Yes,' she said.

'Were you scared?'

'Very.'

'Did it hurt?'

'A lot.'

He nodded and wrapped the soft, clean bandages around her knuckles.

Why was she letting him do this? She didn't need bandages and ointments; she could stop by a gutter on the way home and find a rat to heal herself with.

But there was this *pull* she sensed from him; hooks that had latched onto her, made her stupid, and planted this need in her to be close to him. To do whatever she could to spend another heartbeat in his presence.

It made no sense. It was inexplicable. But it was real.

He examined her neatly wrapped knuckles and, satisfied with his handiwork, stood. 'Don't lose hope, Kavithri.'

'Kavi,' she said.

He smiled. 'You can call me Nabo.'

Chapter 20
BLADE

The Plan

She put the beating and humiliation at Makkur's hands behind her – it rankled, but there was nothing she could do about it now. She set Nabo's rejection aside – well, not really. Every time she walked past a chaiwallah now she cringed and sped up; all she'd done was ruin tea for herself. Anyway, the Blade-lock tournament resumed, and it gave her a much-needed respite from her life outside the Vagola.

First up, they faced off against another first-year duo in round two.

Their opponents were cautious – the cadet hesitated before using his maayin release, the novice focused more on Azia than on saturating her cadet's armour. Kavi fought with a shield again, but her left arm and wrist were stronger now, and she used her shield as if it were another weapon: she parried with it and slashed and swung, and inch by inch she pushed her opponent back until eventually he left an opening and she *thunked* her sword into his armoured ankles and sent him stumbling. While he flailed, she skipped over him, reversed the grip on her sword, aimed, and flung it like a javelin at the crystal. The result:

First-years: Azia/Kavithri *beat* First-years: Deol/Rubashatri. After that, round three.

They were up against a vastly more experienced third-year duo who'd made it to the quarterfinals last year, according to Rathore, who'd dropped in during one of their practice sessions and had offered the unsolicited piece of information. Both Azia and Kavi agreed: it was time to pull the Plan out of their back pockets and slam it down on the table.

Neither of their opponents noticed the petal of maayin Azia threaded through the gap in Kavi's armour to hover just under her chestplate. But the Blade she faced was strong; he fought with a heavy tulwar and each time he slammed it down on her shield it felt like he would slice right through.

She gritted her teeth and withstood his attacks; focused on manoeuvring into place so her novice could do his job – which meant forcing her opponent out of the way so Azia could see the crystal, and positioning herself so that there was nothing between her and the crystal.

So she waited, patiently blocked and dodged and drew her opponent off to one side and as he launched into another over-head strike, ducked under his swing and lunged forward.

'Now!' she yelled. Azia did the rest. The result: First-years: Azia/Kavithri *beat* Third-years: Rohana/Wirath.

No interference had been required for Vaisha's second-round match, where she'd fought another first-year duo, but she was up against third-years in the third round, and Grishan had tasked Kavi with more weapon tampering.

This time, however, he'd instructed her to use the cube on Vaisha's sword. *It will increase the severity of the pain inflicted upon contact,* he'd said.

She'd done as he'd instructed.

Vaisha and her novice won. Her opponent collapsed upon being struck by her weapon – foaming at the mouth and convulsing while Vaisha looked on in bewilderment – and had to be stretchered away.

Another casualty of the Tivasi. Only this time, Kavi was an accessory, and it made her want to drag her nails across her face. She hated herself for being a part of it; hated Grishan for forcing her to do it.

I don't have a choice, she'd repeated to herself, over and over again until she believed it. All she could do now was hope that Grishan would keep his word and ensure that the next round would be free of interference.

*

You need to be fit as well, novice, Greema had said. *The field exercises are being held on the Nathrian border this year, with Nathrian cadets and soldiers.* She turned and spat. *A thoroughly unpleasant lot. They will not go easy on you just because you're a warlock.* So now here Azia was, jogging at Kavi's side on the pavement that ringed the campus lake. Or at least, he was trying to. Azia's mouth hung open as he gasped for air, his arms and legs rose only the barest fraction for him to take the next step. Sweat soaked his clothes and dripped a consistent tattoo as it hit the ground between his feet.

'You don't need to do so much on the first day,' Kavi said, giving up all pretence – she'd been fake-jogging, pumping her arms and legs but not going anywhere – and slowing to a walk.

He glanced at her, mouth hanging open, and with a grunt, slowly, excruciatingly, raised an arm to give her a thumbs-up.

She tsked. 'Stubborn.'

His mouth twitched as he tried to grin.

Kavi resumed her fake-jogging.

Their next match, round four, or the round of sixteen, was

against a pair of first-years they'd faced before, on their very first day at the Vagola: Vaisha and Pragan.

'Why does she bother you so much?' Azia had asked when Kavi had made a face at the other cadet's name, and she'd struggled to articulate the roiling dislike she felt for the woman. She hated the love Vaisha got for saying things that, at their core, were just another form of hate and exclusion; she hated that she couldn't *say* anything back to Vaisha; she hated that there would be no comeuppance for – for what, exactly? Weapon tampering? Vaisha wasn't even aware it was being done. Getting under a Taemu's skin? That wasn't a crime, but still, it chafed and made her grind her teeth. How was she supposed to explain that to Azia without sounding completely deranged?

'Is it because she beat you?' he asked while she floundered, which offered her a way out.

'Yes, that's exactly it.'

'Don't worry, things will be different this time.'

They better be. There was already so much at stake, but then this morning Ratan had passed her a sealed envelope on the rickshaw ride to the Vagola. Inside was a letter from Bithun. He was coming to Azraaya, and he wanted to see her.

There isn't much time left, he'd written, cryptically. Time left for what? For her? Unless she met her end in a fiery steam-rickshaw accident, which was entirely possible, given the way Ratan drove the damned vehicle, she still had a good six years left, so what was he talking about?

Either way, she was ecstatic that he was coming. Bithun had connections and wealth, and if anyone could outthink Grishan, it was him. And if she wanted to show him that his investment in her was not a waste, she'd have to make it to the semifinals of the tournament, and then she'd have to tell Reddy, *Sorry, sir, but I have a friend attending, I need to rescind one of your tickets.*

The demand for tickets had spiked since round three, and from round four onwards it was mandatory for Council members to attend, which meant a more elevated section of society would jostle for seats in the arena.

'You. Go. Ahead,' Azia said, gasping for air after each word.

'Sure?' Ever since the meal with his father they'd met on an almost daily basis; either to eat (nibble, in his case) together at the canteen or just to chat and discuss strategy. She'd developed a genuine affection for her complicated young warlock.

He nodded, waved her onward, and she took off. The wind whistled past her ears and lifted her hair off her scalp, cooled the sweat on her face and neck as she finally stretched and pushed her muscles.

The steady thudding of her feet on the pavement and the consistent rhythm of her breathing forced everything else from her mind. It left her to contend with the single, shrivelled-up notion she'd left ignored and unconsidered ever since the start of the tournament: if all the councillors *had* to be present from round four onwards – Kavi stopped, rested hands on knees as she caught her breath – then wouldn't Councilman Faria, the man who'd instigated the massacre at Ethuran and whose backing had allowed Grishan to usurp the rickshaw company, be there too?

He would. He fucking would. And she'd have to pretend like it meant nothing to her.

Chapter 21

BLADE

A Quiver Full of Rage

'You're ready,' Greema said.

Kavi stared at the wooden shortsword held out to her. She'd been getting better, faster, more accurate with her strikes and able to manoeuvre both swords independently – her sessions with Drisana, when she fought with the makra's enormous twin swords, had also helped her improve. But ready? No, she didn't feel ready. 'I – you sure?'

Greema took Kavi's hand and closed her fingers around the grip. 'Remember your training. Now come, your warlock is waiting.'

The miniature artificed globe that lit the locker room flickered and Kavi smothered a flinch. This was not the same locker room as the ring-fight. She only had to look around: it was bigger, cleaner, nicer, and there were at least three people – four if she counted Reddy's son – who actually wanted her to win. She paused. The Taemu at the fight would've wanted her to win. She hadn't had a choice then. Now, however …

She stood. Ran one last check on her armour – each piece was fastened tight and sat comfortably, where it was meant to – and latched both her swords to the clasps on her back so that the hilts stuck out over each shoulder.

They found Azia in the corridor, fidgeting and muttering to

himself as he picked at the long-healed scar on his face. He breathed a soft sigh of relief as she walked up to him. 'We need to hurry, there's a line – the councillors want to meet all of us.'

'Meet?' Kavi said, fighting to keep the alarm from her voice.

'Yes – shake hands, hi-hello-good-luck, you know,' he said, and gestured for her to speed up.

Shake hands? Good luck? The tightness in her chest made it hard to breathe, and she had to force her heavy feet to keep moving.

'Hurry, Kavi,' Azia said.

Outside, barely a few steps into the buzzing arena, a line of uniformed novices and armoured cadets slowly wound its way to and away from a row of distinguished-looking men and women.

Kavi swallowed. Gazed up at the crowd. From where she stood, every seat was taken and they'd even arranged for hawkers to roam the aisles and scream their wares: *Masala bonda! Potato bonda! Onion pakora! Nimbu-pani! Fresh – no discounts, bhai, why so cheap? All Fresh! Take it and go!*

Off to one side, in a cordoned-off section of the audience, a group of empty seats were covered with plush rugs and marked V.I.P. *Very Incompetent Politico*, she could hear Massa scoff and swear, *Bloody bhaenchods*. That's where the councillors would sit once they were done greeting the students.

They joined the line. Azia retreated to his safe place – both hands in pockets, shoulders slouched, head bowed – and Kavi, just so she didn't have to look at the councillors until she absolutely had to, continued to observe the crowd.

The simultaneous matches had ended with the last round. Now every eye in the arena would focus solely on the combatants: on her and Azia, on Vaisha and Pragan.

The first councillor, an elderly man with a wispy moustache, shook her hands and said, 'All the best, may Raaya always prevail,' without really looking at her. He moved on to Azia, to whom he said the exact same thing.

The next one, a middle-aged woman with hennaed palms, had the same dead eyes that looked at Kavi without really seeing her. She used words repeated so often that they'd been sapped dry of meaning: 'Good luck, you are Raaya's future.'

Next.

And again, and again. None of them introduced themselves, so she had no idea which one was Nashik Faria. Maybe that was for the best. After all, what the Hel was she going to do about it, anyway?

'You must be Kavithri,' a councillor said, and the voice locked her feet in place and sent a trail of ice shooting up her spine.

She stared at the councilman's chest with bulging eyes as he reached out and shook her hand. She tried to breathe, but an invisible dagger had plunged into her throat and sealed her windpipe shut. She tried to swallow, but there was nothing, the moisture in her mouth had evaporated.

The councilman squeezed and released her hand. 'Nashik Faria, pleasure to finally meet you.'

He usually wore short sleeves, but today they were buttoned up to his wrists. Still, she could make out a thin, pale scar just under his palm. There would be more under his shirt, running all the way up both arms, overlapping, criss-crossing. She wrenched her eyes off his wrist and, dreading what she'd inevitably find staring back at her, gazed up at his face and at the haphazard and inconsistent ageing of his skin.

Grishan smiled.

And she wanted to run.

'Novice Azia,' he said, turning to shake Azia's hand while Kavi stood frozen. 'Fight well.'

Kavi took in the buttoned-up collar and the thick shawl Grishan wore around his neck. Her heart thrashed in her chest as she reached for disparate threads and tied them together. This was why she never saw Grishan out in public. Always behind closed doors, always surrounded by the Tivasi. And it was why the *councilman* was so rarely seen – *some sort of bone disease*, Solara had said. That too was a lie.

Azia tapped her on the shoulder, concern obvious on his face.

'It's fine, go first,' she said, voice hoarse and strained as the ramifications of who Grishan really was hammered its way into her skull and her fear began to, piece by piece, transform into a smouldering, palpitating rage.

She locked eyes with Grishan and, for the first time, didn't flinch. 'Were you at Ethuran that day?'

'I was.'

Hands twitched. Muscles strained. And the berserker called. It was him. *He* was why it happened.

Grishan moved closer, leaned in and placed a hand on her shoulder; a perfectly amiable gesture from afar, but they couldn't *see* the subtle change in his face, couldn't feel the pressure of his fingers digging into Kavi's shoulders through the gaps in her armour. 'A person can be many things, Kavithri, be made up of many parts.' He lowered his voice. 'I hear your friend from Bochan is travelling to Azraaya. I will keep a close eye on him for you. Good luck with your match.'

Kavi's mouth twisted as Grishan turned his back on her and walked away to join his colleagues in the V.I.P. seats.

Did they know? Did they know what he was? What he'd done?

Of course they did. That was why they sat where they sat. That was how it worked. The kind and good lived their lives and worked to keep a roof over their heads and feed their families.

The evil conquered and built kingdoms to rule; and if you were one of those rare, good people who spoke up, who had the courage to point out evil and shout? Then the evil, devoid of conscience and guilt, would not hesitate to brutalise, pillage, rape, and murder until the good learned to shut the fuck up and go back to work.

It's what Kavi was doing now, as she staggered down to the court to fight in a game she'd invested so much into while her world, once filled with shades of grey, disintegrated into unmarred black and white. A part of her objected to it, but she shut it down; it was convenient to simplify. It made things easier. Everything that had happened to her could be traced back to him. All those years she'd spent alone, standing on the outside and watching as girls her age played and went to school and made friends and met lovers. If Grishan had never brought his hate to Ethuran, Amma would still be alive, her father and brother would still be alive. The Taemu would still have a home.

A spike of pain in her temples forced her to unclench her jaw.

But the way things were, the threats he made and the power he exerted over the city, meant she couldn't do a thing about it. She was helpless.

For now.

She would find a way. She had six years left, and if it meant she had to wait till the very last day of her life, even if it was to return just a fraction of the pain and misery he'd inflicted on the Taemu, she would find a way.

I promise, Amma. I will make him suffer.

But for now, all she had was a quiver full of rage without a target to aim it at.

'So, you decided not to listen.'

Kavi's head snapped around.

Vaisha glanced at the hilts sticking out over Kavi's shoulders. 'I told you the Gashani school is not for you. You are not—'

Kavi stopped listening. She stared at Vaisha's mouth as it moved.

Why? Why do you care so much? What makes you think you can tell me what to do? The heat in her core, that had built and built and threatened to overflow, fizzed out into her limbs, to the tips of her fingers and toes. The berserker sensed the weakening of its chains and howled with glee.

'—your positions!' the announcer yelled from a distance, and Kavi forced her feet onto the court. She stopped, turned around to check, through a crimson haze that was closing in from all sides, that Azia was in place, and she drew her swords.

She rocked back on her heels. Memories of the Kraelish assault on the city flashed through her mind – fighting with Elisai on one side, Sravan on the other. Sravan, who'd fought, just like his ancestors, with two swords. Sravan, who'd died on his knees, throat slit, mocked as he bled out while she watched, paralysed.

Her hands trembled, her grips on the swords loosened. She was not worthy. She didn't deserve to fight like the swordmasters. Maybe Vaisha was right. If it wasn't for her Jinn, for her corrupt maayin, she wouldn't—

'Fight!'

Vaisha drew her longsword and advanced, mouth curled into a scowl of disdain as her eyes flicked between Kavi's twin blades.

Stop it. Stop looking at me like that, you're the one who's wrong.

Kavi let her swords slip out of her hands and fall to the ground. Vaisha was everything that was wrong with this place. Its rigid insistence for people to stay who they were, its reluctance for anyone to assimilate, its blind adherence to an inviable past – always telling her what to do, always thinking it was right, that just because it had a voice that its opinions mattered more and that it could force it on her with no consequences.

No more.

Time lost its meaning. There was no present, no past, no future, only her rage. The berserker was her destiny, and today, she would not run from it.

One by one, the chains snapped. A thin film covered the inside of her mouth and her tongue as her lips parted—

Vaisha lunged.

The Berserker caught the sword – grinned as the bones in her palm cracked – and used her free hand to rip the helmet off Vaisha's head and expose her stunned face.

Crack. The Berserker's fist connected with Vaisha's temple.

Crunch. The Berserker's helmet smashed into her regal face.

Vaisha staggered back, eyes rolled up into her skull, blood covering her fractured face. She moaned, and blinded by pain, searched the air for her bearings.

The Berserker flung the sword aside. Snarled and launched herself at the cadet.

Vaisha's teeth crunched together as they collided, and she sliced the tip of her tongue clean off as the back of her head smashed into the ground. The Berserker straddled Vaisha, and her fists rose and fell. Rose and fell.

The arena was silent except for the *whack-smack-splat* of the punches. Blood splattered both sets of armour as the Berserker's knuckles twisted and cracked and bled, and Vaisha's face lost its shape and turned into a pink, white, and dark-red mess of gore.

The Berserker's grin widened. *You will never talk to Kavi that way again. You will never—*

A green orb of maayin smashed into the Berserker's chest and threw her off Vaisha.

She scowled at the novice who'd attacked her.

The man paled, dropped his krasna, and backed away.

Wait your turn. The Berserker got to her feet, took a step in Vaisha's direction and was hammered by powerful blasts of maayin that spun her around like a ragdoll.

Her knees collapsed, and she fell as men and women in military uniforms rushed onto the court.

The Berserker called for Nilasi. For the blue threads of maayin that would use them as a countervail and fix her.

No. Enough.

But—

That's enough.

Kavi wrenched her way back to the surface as the Berserker fought and scrapped for another heartbeat of freedom. But Kavi's rage was spent, its target lay unmoving, comatose, maybe even dead, and all she had left now was a hollow regret.

She let them restrain her. Let the announcer peer down at her with fear in his eyes as he announced their disqualification and told her she would have to go in front of a Vagola-instated disciplinary committee.

As they carry-dragged her away, as her hopes of regaining the Imperial Rickshaw Company crumbled into dirt, she searched the court for Azia, and when she found him, all she could do was look away.

The horror on his face, the disappointment in his eyes – her vision blurred, and her throat clogged up with shame. *I'm sorry.* She could only hope that after this he'd still want to speak to her.

Chapter 22

ENFORCER

The Caterpillar

Glasses clinked. Chairs scraped the floor. A waiter repeated a client's order. The sitar player tuned his instrument and sent a warbling echo through the wide-open floor of the Caterpillar.

Kavi sighed in the corner beside the bar. Scratched the back of her neck then crossed her arms. She was almost done with her shift, and the knot in her belly and the dullness in her chest had still not dissipated.

They'd given her a hundred rayals, despite what she'd done, for making it to the fourth round. Combatants got injured all the time, they'd said, but never to this extent, and never so violently and with such obvious disregard for the rules and objectives of the tournament. 'Were you even trying to get to the enemy crystal? Was this some sort of grudge?'

She had no answer. *I'm sorry*, was all she said.

'You will stand before the disciplinary committee early next week. We will notify you. Until then, you may attend all classes except the ones with the novices.'

No interactions with Vaisha were permitted, not even for an apology – she was being attended to by healers and was alive. Beyond that, 'You will find out during your hearing.'

And Azia? Nowhere to be found. After she healed herself in Ratan's rickshaw, she'd gone looking for him and ran into

Greema, who, instead of berating her, like she'd expected, had given her look of utter disappointment, and said, 'You forgot everything I taught you.'

I'm sorry, ma'am.

'You told me you wanted to win.'

She had nothing to say to that.

'Well, if you wanted to scare them, I think you succeeded. I will see you in class tomorrow.'

No, she wasn't trying to scare them. She'd not even been thinking. Her half-a-minute interaction with Grishan/Nashik – were either of those even his real name? – had left her reeling, slackened her control over her berserker, and Vaisha had tipped her over the edge.

Either way, she was lucky they'd not immediately expelled her – maybe it was because she'd had her helmet on throughout and no one, besides Vaisha and her novice, had gotten a good look at the berserker's face. But who knew? This committee could end up throwing her out, anyway.

She sighed, for the hundredth time that evening, and glanced at the raised platform, where Nabosin sat chatting with one of the other men. He wore a deep-blue silk robe today, open at the neck so that it exposed his sternum and chest. They'd not spoken since her confession – Kavi frowned. Was it a confession? All she'd done was ask him to meet her for tea outside the Caterpillar.

A waiter walked past with a tray loaded with tandooried shrimp and forced her to shuffle back.

'Sorry,' she muttered, and turned around to rest her elbows on the counter. She caught a reflection of herself in one of the newly installed mirrors behind the bar and flinched.

There were bags under her eyes. Her hair was a mess. There

were food stains on her collar. She looked so weak. Deficient. And ugly.

'Such a beautiful man.' A woman, a client seated at the table closest to Kavi, twirled her hair with a finger and smiled at her friend. 'So exotic, I tell you, and the massage he gives you before—'

'Shut up, you,' her friend said with a giggle, then leaned closer. 'Which one?'

'The foreign-wallah.' She pointed at Nabo. 'With the piercings.'

Kavi's ribs tightened, and she lurched forward as a pair of invisible hooks plunged into her gut, and pulled.

Stop it. He's not yours. He's not—

She whirled around, searched the floor for the Aunty-ji – *there*, chatting to a group by the divans.

She wanted him, but was afraid of him; she so desperately wanted to feel him, but she was also afraid of his touch.

Enough, she was done being confused and uncertain. This was the only way it could ever happen – all she had to do was look in the mirror. Besides, she had nothing left to lose: the rickshaw company was beyond her reach, her future at the Vagola was uncertain. So fuck it.

She waited for the Aunty-ji to finish her conversation, and as the woman turned to leave, stepped into her path. 'Memsaab, can I end my shift? Please.'

The Aunty-ji raised a manicured eyebrow.

'I'd like to …' Kavi glanced at Nabo, caught him watching her, and immediately looked away.

The Aunty-ji followed the line of her glance, and her mouth opened with a silent *Ah*. 'Taemu,' she said, 'are you sure?' She paused, watched Kavi squirm. 'Nothing is ever as good as you imagine.'

Kavi bobbed her head. 'Please.'

'Fine,' she said with a sigh. 'You have the money?'

'Hundred rayals.'

'That will get you an hour.'

'Thank you, memsaab.'

The Aunty-ji collected the cash, turned, snapped her fingers at Nabo, and patted Kavi on the shoulder. 'One hour.'

Surprise flashed across his face. He stood, adjusted his robe, walked over to Kavi, and held his hand out to her.

Kavi wiped the sweat off her palms, swallowed – *this is not a mistake this-is-not-a-mistake* – and placed her hand in his.

Her blood jumped at his touch.

'This way,' he said, like she didn't know exactly where they were headed, and holding her clammy hand, led her upstairs.

Still, when she arrived at his room, it was not what she expected.

They had placed translucent shades over the lamps to dim the light, and it painted the walls and furniture in soft red. The scent of jasmine, infused into the oil of the dia lamps, drifted out of the room and into her flaring nostrils as she hesitated on the threshold. Was this really okay? Was she being selfish?

Nabo stopped, studied her with impassive eyes while she averted her own.

The only thing she had to look forward to now was the day she'd hurt Grishan. While she was certain that she'd make it happen, the how and the when were still a blurry silhouette on the horizon – she tightened her grip on Nabo's hand – and until then, there was *nothing* wrong with her chasing something as meaningless as the erotic. Selfish, yes, but so what? She wanted this. She wanted to feel something that wasn't grief or fear or anger. And she *needed* it to be him.

'Sorry,' she muttered, and stepped inside.

He guided her to an empty corner of the room, released her hand, strolled over to the bathtub, and spun the taps open. Water gushed from the faucets and a layer of steam rose to hover over the tub.

Kavi scratched the back of her neck with her fingernails. Artificed piping? Or maybe an artificed water tank, it had to be. She'd not seen anyone heating a giant pot of water over a furnace.

She fidgeted with her collar as Nabo kicked open a collapsible table and arranged it in the middle of the room. After that, he pulled the bedcovers off the bed, fluffed up the pillows, patted down the sheets – all this without saying a word to her – and once he was satisfied, took her by the hand again, and led her around a wooden partition where, on a square of black marble flooring with a small drain on one side, sat a bucket of water, a gilded steel pail, and a bar of soap.

He handed her an unusually fluffy towel.

She clutched it to her chest.

'You must wash,' he said.

Gods, the towel was soft. She dug her fingers into it and stared at him.

'It's one of our rules.'

Ah, right. She bobbed her head.

He nodded and left her to it.

She flung her clothes over the partition and tested the water. *Warm.* Smelled the soap. *Rose-scented.* And reached for the pail.

She paused. Shuddered as a tingling surged through her body, all the way from her scalp to the tips of her toes. She was naked, and he was just there, on the other side, still in his clothes. Kavi swallowed. Filled the pail with water and splashed it over her shoulders. She sighed at the warmth, bent, emptied another pail, and reached for the soap.

The last thing she wanted was more unexpected embarrassment, so this would have to be the most meticulous wash she'd ever subjected herself to.

Once she was done, she dried herself with the exquisite towel, wrapped it around her chest, and peeked around the partition.

She blinked. Her clothes had been folded and arranged in a neat pile by the door; the collapsible table now had a thin mattress or some sort of blanket on top; and next to the table, sitting on a hollow pedestal over a dia lamp, was a bowl of oil.

Nabo, still in his robe, spun the taps around, stopped the flow of water, and emptied a sachet of something white and granular into the tub. 'Massage first,' he said, without looking at her. 'Then bathe and wash off the oils. After that we will retire to the bed.'

'More rules?' Kavi said before she could stop herself.

Nabo paused. 'No, it's an arrangement that my clients enjoy.' He glided over to – what the fuck was wrong with her, *glided?* She tsked. What was he? A flying fish?

He patted the massage table. 'Lie face-down, please – without the towel.'

Kavi froze. Hesitated with a thumb tucked into the folds of the towel, and Nabo inclined his head – was that amusement on his lips? A smile? – and turned to face away from her.

Out of courtesy, and because of how respectfully he'd treated her cheap clothes, she untucked and folded her towel into a neat square, made sure each end was aligned, and left it on the floor. It was damp, and used, and it would go in the big basket the cleaners would bring around after she was done, but what the Hel, it made her feel good to do it.

Exposed, self-conscious, and with a sudden awareness of how utterly ridiculous all this was, she climbed onto the table and lay face-down, on her stomach, head cradled on the back of her hands, skin alive with goosebumps, and sighed as the thin mattress moulded itself to her body.

She heard the rustle of his robe falling to the ground. Watched him dip his fingers in the bowl of oil. Her heart drummed against the table; her breath turned shallow. *It's fine. I'm fine.* She was in control here. She could end this any time she wanted. She unclenched her fists. Forced herself to take long, slow breaths. *I'm fine.*

His fingers touched the skin on her back, and all pretence of serenity disintegrated.

She stiffened. Her eyes widened. She squirmed, and her confused body of its own accord shied away from his touch.

'You want to stop?'

'I—' Her voice was hoarse, raw. She cleared her throat. 'I've never done this before.'

He placed his palms flat over her spine and gently leaned into them. 'This is meant to help you relax. If it isn't—'

'No.' She set her jaw. 'Continue, please.'

She forced herself to hold still, and with each thunderous heartbeat, as he pushed and squeezed and nudged, the tension oozed from her muscles, the rhythm and repetition calmed her cartwheeling mind, and she relaxed.

His palms were soft, worn smooth by the many massages he'd given. He was gentle. He applied just the right amount of pressure; lingered in just the right places.

She held her breath as he finished with her back and his hands circled her legs – he started at her ankles, and inch by inch, wound his way up until there was nothing left except the warmth in between and she gasped and twitched as the back of his hands, and his knuckles, gently kissed, then slowly, inexorably, dragged their way up the curve of her – *slow down, keep them there*, but the words died on the tip of her tongue as he started again, back at her ankles, up her calves, her thighs, and she couldn't help it, her lips parted, and a low moan escaped her throat.

He stopped. His hands left her body, and the table creaked as he joined her on it, a knee on either side of her hips.

The Hel? She turned her head to one side – out of the corner of her eye, Nabo emptied the rest of the oil onto her back, set the bowl aside, and rested both forearms on the small of her back.

She grunted in surprise as she felt his weight, his breath, as he slowly slid his forearms up and down the length of her body.

The air whooshed out of her lungs and she shuddered as another layer of tension was released. His weight made her aware of her own body. It made her feel *safe*. All her emotions – the anger and bitterness, the despair and grief, the helplessness and hopelessness, the envy and hate – seeped out of her pores. Her skin came alive; was sensitive to temperature and touch like never before. Each breath she took was an assault on her senses: coconut, jasmine, the pungent detergent used on the mattress; and running through everything like a nerve on fire, him.

His breath: tinged with spices from the tea he'd been sipping – cinnamon, cloves, anise, cardamom. His skin – she twisted her neck to breathe him in as he slid over her: lavender scented soap, and underneath, the faint musk of his sweat.

She curled her toes as warmth filled her core and radiated out into her limbs. It rippled across her skin and left more goosebumps in its wake. The soft linen that covered his crotch failed to disguise the hardness underneath, and she twisted her hips into him, shuddering again at the rush of blood – he was attracted to her, he had to be, otherwise it wouldn't feel that way, right?

The idea was intoxicating. It gave her courage. Made her run her hands down the outside of his thighs, and—

He sat up. Eased his arms off her back. And got off the table.

So fast? Dammit, she was just starting to feel comfortable.

He used a towel to wipe the oil off the soles of her feet, then folded the towel and arranged it in front of the tub.

'Please,' he said, and gestured to the gently swirling steam over the water in the tub.

Kavi turned away and forced herself upright on weak wrists. She covered her chest with a forearm and her – she frowned. He'd already been more intimate with her than anyone else in her entire life; why was she so concerned about her modesty now? She let her arms fall to her sides and walked over to the tub.

Her stomach fluttered as she tested the water with her toes – not too hot, she could handle it – and brimming with anticipation, one foot on the precipice of turning thoughts into deeds, she sank into the water with a sigh.

She rested her head against its marble rim, and through the steam, with eyes narrowed to slits, she unabashedly followed Nabo as he arranged more towels around the tub, slipped out of his last piece of clothing, and joined her in the warm water.

He eased himself into the other half of the tub. Stretched his legs out to either side of Kavi's hips and watched her with an unreadable expression on his face.

Kavi sat up, shuffled closer until they were an arm's width apart, and knees jutting out above the surface of the water, ran both hands down the inside of his thighs, searching, until she found what she was looking for.

Breathless, she traced his rigid outline with her fingers while her eyes remained locked on his face.

He didn't react.

She went higher. Let one hand rest on his stomach while the other played and explored.

His abdominal muscles tensed and went rigid.

She paused. Was this part exceptionally sensitive? Was she hurting him? She eased her fingers off the head, and instead pushed against it with her palm, then slowly circled it, thumb and forefinger eventually turning into a fist that she gently tightened and squeezed – she sucked in a breath as she felt him harden and throb and she shivered as his fingers trailed down her legs, along the grooves of her groin; lights dimmed as her eyes, almost involuntarily, rolled up into her head and her brows tightened, her heavy skull tilted back, and her hips forced their way closer to—

She blinked. Refocused. Looked at his face again. At his eyes. Clear. Placid. Empty.

The thunder in her chest subsided. There was no pleasure on his face, no passion in his movements. She was just another client. He would do his job. He would fuck her, then forget her. She was not his friend. She was barely his lover.

Kavi jerked herself away. Water splashed and sent miniature tidal waves up and down the tub as she shot upright and, one leg at a time, stepped out of the tub and rushed to where she'd left her towel.

I can't do this. Not when he looked at her like that. Not with those eyes.

'You still have thirty minutes left,' Nabo said, in the same dispassionate voice he'd used all evening.

Kavi's lips trembled. She fought back the tears as she dressed. *You know what?* 'Fuck you,' she said, and reached for the door.

She caught a glimpse of his face as she stepped through the door, and the obvious hurt on it almost made her hesitate. But she was committed now, and a part of her was glad she'd hurt him. It was mean and petty and cruel, but she was glad. *Now you know what it feels like.*

She slammed the door behind her.

Chapter 23
ENFORCER

Appa

She was halfway down the stairs when a startling moment of clarity – the kind she'd only experienced in the aftermath of a poor decision – brought her to a halt. Nabo was not working at the Caterpillar of his own free will. He was as trapped as she was, if not worse. And what he did, his *job*, was not easy. Far from it. She couldn't imagine the toll it took on him. And then she'd shown up out of the blue with her infatuation and her *Do you want to drink some tea with me?*, he'd still been nothing but polite and respectful, and now …

Gods, he probably thought she was a real chootia.

And he'd have been right if he did.

'Collector-memsaab!'

Chella, the shoe-seller she'd helped the other day, stood by the entrance to the Caterpillar and bounced from foot to foot as he wrung his hands.

The Dolmondas again? 'What happened?'

'They came back.' he said, and dug a handkerchief out of his pockets to wipe the thick layer of sweat off his forehead. 'Different goondas this time, they brought weapons.'

She tsked. Ushered him out of the brothel. 'Where's your wife?'

'My wife?' He repeated with a frown, then shook his head. 'No, no, they came for Naadan this time, not us.'

A spike of panic rammed its way into her spine, and she sped up. She'd developed a fondness for the curmudgeonly bookseller. He treated her fairly, let her borrow his books for free, and, for some reason, was always happy to see her. 'Why? What do they want with him?'

Chella bobbled his head as he tried to keep up with her and said, mouth upturned, 'Don't know, Collector-memsaab. They just came.'

She barged into the bookshop with her fists clenched. If they'd hurt him – she froze. Her eyes bulged. Her stomach sank. And her mouth worked as her mind struggled to piece together the disparate images and sounds that assailed her.

A gaggle of Dolmonda gangsters stood in one corner: they chatted, they smoked, they chuckled and rifled through Naadan's books.

In the opposite corner, behind the counter, a small girl – seven, maybe eight – sat with feet drawn into her chest. Her entire body shook as she sobbed and sniffled and choked and repeated, 'Appa, Appa, Appa.'

And between them, from a noose looped around a beam in the ceiling, hung Naadan. The girl's Appa. He had both hands inside the noose; face turning purple as he struggled to breathe. His legs – *Drisana have mercy*, his legs. Twisted, swollen, and broken.

She rushed to him, wrapped both hands under his shattered knees, and pushed him up. She grunted as the muscles in her neck and arms strained under his weight.

Naadan gasped, and he sucked in a huge gulp of air.

'It's her,' a gangster said.

'This is the one? You sure?'

'Madarchod, why were they so scared?'

'Chootias, all.'

'Dai, bring my chain.'

'And my lathi.'

Footsteps rushed out of the shop.

Kavi frantically searched the shop for something to support Naadan. A chair. A stool. Something. She caught his daughter's eyes. 'Chair,' Kavi said.

Naadan's daughter stared back at her with wild, confused eyes. 'Ch—'

Footsteps rushed back into the shop.

'Hide,' she said, and reeled as she heard her mother say that same word to her. *Hide.* She pushed Kavi into the crack in the wall. *Hide, Kavi.* Knees scraped and bled. Screams filled her ears. Amma turned to face her murderers.

'Hide,' Kavi whispered to the girl, but she wouldn't move.

The gangsters walked around her and into sight.

Ack-thoo!

She flinched as a blob of saliva hit her on the forehead. Grunted as the first blow, a lathi strike to her lower back, made her stumble.

She recovered, planted her feet and tightened her grip on Naadan's knees.

What was the plan? Wait for help? No, she couldn't rely on anyone here. So then what? Release Naadan so she could fight?

Out of the question.

A finger lifted her chin. 'See this?' A man said, and he held a broken cycle chain in front of her face. Dried blood and strands of hair, some with scalp still attached, were stuck between the links of the chain.

The muscles in her torso spasmed, and she tucked her head in. This would hurt. A lot. But not as much as Naadan dying.

Once the gangster was satisfied that she'd *seen*, he took a step back, wrapped the chain around his knuckles, and hammered his fist into her jaw. After that, she lost the ability to tell who or what was hitting her.

Pinpricks of light danced around her vision. Her mouth filled with the taste of metal. Her head swung from one side to the other. But she would not let go.

Fire in both temples. Agony in her back, her hips, the bones in her legs. Her wrists had gone numb after a sharp crack. But she would not let go.

Spittle flew from between her lips. The more they hit her, the stronger her resolve grew. She would not lose another one. If he died, she died.

Through her blindness, through the pain, a familiar voice whispered inside her head, **Use your Jinn**.

Drisana. Her sword was back in her hut, in the slums, but it felt her pain.

Call Nilasi.

No, not in front of the girl.

The blows stopped.

Panting. Muffled cursing. Sobbing in the corner.

Shouts from outside. More cursing. A scuffle, then silence.

The sound of her own ragged breaths filled her ears as her vision began to clear. She squeezed her eyes shut, opened them. Spat the blood collected in her mouth as the world swam and spun and her knees buckled.

An arm wrapped itself around her shoulders and held her upright.

'Why?' A gruff voice said. A voice she should recognise. 'Why do you put up with this, Akka?'

Kavi blinked. Slowly turned her head and stared at Deva's bearded face.

He shouted over his shoulder. 'Get him down.'

Tivasi men came rushing into the shop as Deva gently undid her grip around Naadan's knees. 'He's safe, we'll take care of him,' he said.

They found that chair she so desperately wanted. They undid the noose around Naadan's neck and carried him out of the shop while his daughter held his hand and wept. And when they were alone in the shop, Deva looked at her wounds, and said, 'You won't need a healer, right?'

Kavi fought to keep a straight face. 'What do you …' The words died, and she stared, slack-jawed, as Deva rolled up a sleeve and showed her a dark-red band tattooed high on his arm.

'You could kill us all,' he said. 'Why do you not fight?'

She swayed as a wave of dizziness slammed into her. *He fought with us?* When? She didn't remember—

'I joined you after the railway station tunnel collapsed.'

One of the Raayans she'd saved.

'I was there at the chokepoint. I've seen you fight.'

Kavi lowered her head. Stopped fighting the tears and let them spill out and down her cheeks. 'My people, he'll kill them.'

Deva nodded, turned to leave, and paused in the doorway. 'When you're ready, we'll be waiting.'

We? 'What do you—' But he was already gone.

What do you mean we?

Chapter 24
BLADE

Replaced

Vice Chancellor Farah Duggal flipped a page, picked up a pen, and scratched something off in her ledger.

'The committee have decided,' she said. 'You will not be allocated a warlock for the remainder of the year. You will not be permitted to attend the field exercises at Draghal. And you will not be allowed to enter next year's tournament.'

That's all? Kavi stood, arms clasped behind her back, spine as straight as she could make it, and stared straight over the woman's head, just like Greema had instructed her to. The rest of the committee, a pair of serious-looking men in warlock's robes, sat behind the large desk on either side of Farrah Duggal, and glared at her.

'Cadet Vaisha has been permanently disfigured, but is otherwise fit and will continue her training.' Duggal slammed the ledger shut. 'I hope you realise how fortunate you are. *Mentors* have vouched for you, have said that you will be an asset to the Vagola, to the Republic.'

Kavi remained silent. *Don't speak unless they ask you a question,* Greema had said. And besides, she had nothing to say. Next year's tournament was too far in the future for her to worry about, and she couldn't have gone to the border for the field exercises even if she'd wanted to – Grishan had made it clear that she was not to leave the city. The only thing that really stung, was the 'no warlock' punishment.

'Do you wish to comment on our decision?' Duggal asked.

She might as well ask. 'What will happen to Novice Azia?'

'The novice has been reassigned to a new cadet; you need not concern yourself with him. Anything else?'

He refused to talk to her. *Sorry, I have class*, he'd say and walk away. She'd apologised and tried to explain what happened. *Sorry, I'm late for practice*, he'd say and turn his back on her. It rankled, it made her cheeks burn and her stomach clench, but there was nothing she could do about it. She'd got him disqualified – worse, she'd scared him, made him feel like he couldn't trust her. But then again, he wasn't talking to her, so she had no clue what had upset him the most. There was only so much she could do before it turned into outright harassment.

'No, ma'am, nothing else,' Kavi said through a painful lump in her throat.

Duggal exchanged nods with the men on either side and gestured to the door. 'Dismissed. Do this again, and we will have no choice but to expel you.'

*

'So no suspension or expulsion?' Greema asked. She sat on a large wooden stool in a corner of the armoury – where she'd asked Kavi to meet her after the 'sentencing' – longsword in her lap as she cleaned and polished the blade.

'No, ma'am. But I will not be allowed to participate in next year's tournament, or attend the field exercises in Draghal, or work with a warlock—'

'But you will remain a cadet at the Vagola.'

'Yes.'

Greema grunted, set the sword aside, picked up another, and polished it in silence.

'Ma'am—'

'You're the first person that I've taught the Gashani school to,' Greema said. 'Many asked, over the years. I turned them all down. None of them were fit to inherit our way of fighting. But you – *this one here*, I thought to myself, *this one, has the spirit of a swordmaster*.'

Kavi winced.

'Have I made a mistake?' Greema asked, looking up at Kavi.

'No,' Kavi whispered, and lowered her eyes.

Greema sighed. Reached for a box of thread and began replacing the grips of her swords. She ignored Kavi while she worked, unspooling and spooling the thread with precise, practised motions.

'I … will you stop training me?' Kavi said, a quiver in her voice.

'No. But we will take a break – you can resume your training after your colleagues return from the field exercises. That should give you enough time to find your meaning again,' Greema said.

My meaning? Kavi's lips trembled, but she stifled her shame and frustration, saluted Greema, and backed out of the armoury.

Outside, she succumbed to her weak knees and dropped to her haunches, gasping as she sucked in great gulps of air. Her vision blurred but she blinked and dabbed at her eyes until it cleared. Somehow this, out of everything, hurt the most. She could handle the punishment the Vagola had meted out, weather the cold shoulder Azia was giving her – he would eventually come around, the boy was incapable of holding a grudge – but Greema's disappointment?

Kavi took a shuddering breath and lurched back to her feet. She had the rest of the day to herself, and there was a book

– *The Retreat and Life Before It, Collected Essays* – being held for her at the library, so she might as well make use of it. She might not be a student in the same capacity as the novices were, but her status as a Blade cadet gave her access to the Vagola's library: the largest collection of books and scrolls at the most renowned university on the subcontinent; and she intended to take full advantage of it. Outside of battle theory and a basic understanding of Harithian maayin, no further study was required of first-year cadets this term, and having already satisfied Greema with her knowledge on both topics she was now free to indulge her curiosity.

An overcast sky along with the dull, grey buildings and unfriendly faces of students – who quickened their pace as they walked past her – gave the campus an aura of dreary hostility. The promise of rain, on the other hand, and the earthy scent that accompanied it, helped to somewhat improve her mood.

The Vagola's library was a large, flamevine-covered structure with a dozen stairs leading up to the entrance. She took them two at a time but was forced to wait while a rotund guard checked her cadet's badge.

'Bhai, you see me almost every week, what is this?' she said, making a face.

He squinted harder at the badge. Sighed, handed it back, and waved her through. 'Just trying to do my job,' he muttered. 'Some chootia have a problem with everything.'

She rolled her eyes, walked to the 'On Hold' counter with hands in her pockets, looked around for the missing librarian, and froze.

Azia, with a large tome under each arm, was shambling out of the main library.

'Hey!' She waved and rushed over to him.

He stopped, flinched, and continued on his way.

Kavi blocked his path. Gave him a tentative smile. 'How're you doing?'

'Good,' he said, without meeting her eyes.

'And your father?'

'He's fine.'

'I—'

'I'm late for class, sorry,' he said, and stepped around her.

Kavi's mouth thinned into a straight line. How much longer was he going to be this way? She'd already apologised. Why – she clenched her jaw. Fine, if he wanted to be left alone, if he wanted to end their friendship over someone like Vaisha, then so be it. Fuck him.

'You have a book on hold?' The librarian, back from wherever he'd absconded to, asked her at the counter.

She collected the book, found a quiet spot inside the library, and sat slumped over the desk as she flipped through the pages without reading any of them.

It was fine, she was fine. It was better this way. She had bigger things to worry about. *Remember why you're here.* Just her presence at the Vagola meant there was still hope for her people. Since its inception, no Taemu had ever been accepted as a student at the Vagola. It was considered ridiculous for her people to even try. She was the first, and if she had her way, she'd be the first of many.

She was setting an example – poorly, at the moment, but still. She was showing the younger Taemu it could be done. That they too could make it to the Vagola one day. And despite everything, she'd turned a dream into reality: she'd earned her place here. She *belonged* here.

She sighed and flipped back to the first page of her book. Besides, she still had a friend, and he'd be in Azraaya soon.

If anyone could see a way out for her and the Taemu, it was Bithun. Everything would be okay once he was here.

*

She didn't actively seek Azia out anymore, and by the end of the week, like all the other first-year warlocks, he disappeared from campus. Unlike the cadets, the novices had an end-of-term exam to sit, so classes were suspended to give them more time to study. Cadets, meanwhile, were given the option to work during the warlock exams and the term break that followed, and Salora signed Kavi up as a bodyguard.

She spent her mornings reading in Salora's office (while the woman worked in an *artificer's-only* section of the building); her afternoons stuffing her face with food from the Artificed Hydraulics canteen and chatting with Chotu, who continued his lessons with Salora after lunch; and her evenings at the Vagola: in the gymnasium, jogging, or browsing the stacks in the library. Her nights, however, remained exactly the same. Escorting spent drunkards out of the Caterpillar, threatening rowdy clients, breaking up fights, and avoiding eye contact with Nabo, who, thankfully, made no attempt to speak to her either.

But when she went on her rounds to collect for the Tivasi, the shopkeepers, without exception, treated her with respect. A chair or a stool would be pulled out, she'd be urged to sit, offered a tea, or even a *Shoulder massage, Collector-memsaab?* No, thank you, she'd say. She was done with massages, never again.

Naadan had healed up. His neck now had a scar circling it, but otherwise the man was back to ranting and complaining about the state of Raayan publishing; and to thank her for saving him, he allowed her to pick three novels of her choice, *All yours, no need to bring back, my gift.* Except for the pornographic ones, of course, those were his money-makers.

Back in her hut, her stash of agoma waited for her. Chotu made a non-committal remark about the growing redness at the back of her neck and the short-term memory loss that affected regular users of the artificed drug. She promised she'd stop using it soon, that it was just for the time being.

What she didn't share with him was that she'd noticed the missing hours – chunks of the day that, try as she might, she just could not remember. Memory, it appeared, was not something her maayin could heal or recover.

Eventually, the day of the semifinals of the Blade-lock tournament arrived – which, of course, she was barred from attending – and she slipped into her best salwar-kameez, tidied up her hair, then fidgeted in the back of Ratan's steam-rickshaw as it sputtered and rattled down to Artificed Hydraulics.

Bithun's train was scheduled to arrive in the late afternoon, and she planned to be there at the station – with Salora as a third wheel, the artificer had insisted – to pick him up.

Chapter 25
BLADE

7D

She'd shown up at Salora's office early, just to be safe – the Chimabali Express was not due for another couple of hours – and had caught the artificer with one foot out the door.

'Are you ever going to tell me where you go every day?' Kavi asked.

Salora hesitated, clearly in a rush, but also conflicted.

Oh? This was new, maybe today was the day. She twisted the screws. 'You know you can trust me, right? Massa did.'

Salora swore and ducked back into the office. 'Here.' She flung a long, blue coat at Kavi, and keys jangling, locked the door. 'Wear it.'

Kavi slipped her arms into the coat. 'What's this for?'

'So you don't stand out,' Salora said, and strode down the corridor, past Kavi, to the staircase.

They wound their way down into the underbelly of Artificed Hydraulics, using the same route they'd taken to the chamber holding the Venator; and that sense of familiarity that infused Kavi's senses every time she was in or around the building grew stronger.

Salora hopped off the staircase and hurried into a long, dark corridor labelled *7D*. She ran her fingers along the wall and a series of artificed tubes in the ceiling burst into bright yellow light.

Kavi fell into step. Questions died on her lips as images from Drisana's war flashed and screeched through her head: mountains of metal colliding, human beings torn to pieces on battlefields the size of continents, toxic maayin spreading through the Chain and decimating worlds and the people on them. The sound of Raktha's voice as the Jinn spoke to Drisana, *You will have the power to bring a god to his knees. Draw.*

She cocked her head. This wasn't the first time she'd experienced these visions with such clarity. The day she'd found Chotu, when Solara had brought her down here to use the Venator, it had happened then, too. Kavi licked her lips. What was *really* down here?

Salora stopped at a dead end: a flat, shiny wall built entirely out of steel with a white 7D painted on it. She punched the base of her palm into the 7 and, with a groan and hiss, the wall slid open to reveal a small platform. Salora stepped onto it and gestured for Kavi to join her.

'What is this?' Kavi poked her head inside, craned her neck to peer at the pitch-black darkness above. There was no ceiling.

Salora grabbed her by the wrist and yanked her inside. 'Our transport,' she said, and slapped a bronze disc on the wall.

The floor juddered and Kavi – eyes bulging at a vertigo-laced spike of alarm – latched onto Salora's arm.

'Relax.' Salora patted Kavi's hand as the platform slowly sank down into the square-shaped tunnel.

'What the Hel is this?'

'It takes us down into the First City,' Salora said.

'The tunnels?'

'Not where we're going,' Salora said. 'But yes, it's all linked.'

Some said that an underground people now lived in these

ruins; others argued that it was all underwater; a chaiwallah had once told her that the Kraelish used it to smuggle spies into the city; her personal favourite was that it was merely an entry point to a vast labyrinth that led even deeper under the surface. She shuddered.

Minutes passed and Kavi sheepishly released her grip on Salora's arm. She cleared her throat and rearranged the coat. The strange falling-but-not-falling sensation was now just an after-thought. 'How much longer?'

The platform squealed and ground to a halt, and the *door* hissed open.

Salora stepped out, Kavi followed, and froze.

Sounds – the *thunk-thuds* and screech of metalwork, the hum of conversation, the echo of an occasional shout – all faded into the background. One thing and one thing only dominated the cavernous space. The people were merely ants scurrying at its feet and climbing up its sides on scaffolding and platforms.

A makra. Here, right in front of her. Any moment now, she half-expected it to come alive and swat them all off him.

Kavi blinked. *Him?*

'Stay close and don't speak,' Salora said, taking off in the direction of the makra's right foot.

It felt right, to think of the makra that way. Everything about him – the strange, dull red metal making up his body, worn and chipped and scratched across his surface, the sharp angles of his arms and legs, his boxlike head with the elongated ...

'Kavithri, come on.'

No, it can't be. It couldn't be the same – a wave of dizziness crashed down on her and she swayed. Stumbled. Dropped to her haunches and tore her eyes away from the makra. Water. She needed water. Her mouth was dry, swallowing did nothing, she stuck and unstuck her tongue from the roof of her mouth.

So thirsty. Hungry. Her feet hurt. The blisters on her soles had bled and burned. She'd done what Amma had asked her to, she'd walked straight to – Amma? No, Appa had told her to.

'Kavithri?' Salora snapped her fingers in front of Kavi's face.

'Where did you find it?' Kavi muttered as she got to her feet. It was the same. The head, it was the same one. The same hollow, metal box she'd mistaken for a hut in the Deadlands. The empty eye sockets were now filled with something dark and glassy, the front of the face, that had been ripped open, had been welded shut.

Goosebumps rippled down the skin on Kavi's neck. *It was the same.*

'What?'

'The makra, where did you find it?'

'Some parts were in the tunnels; some were sold to us by scavenger crews.' Salora paused. Narrowed her eyes. 'Is something wrong?'

Kavi shook her head and immediately regretted it. 'I'm okay, sorry.'

Salora studied her for several heartbeats, lips pursed, eyes stern and unreadable, and nodded. Kavi wrenched her eyes off the makra and fell into step behind the artificer. Her head swivelled as she counted the massive tunnels – *seven* – that punctured the cavern; and in each of these tunnels: railway tracks that trailed away into the opaque darkness. Her heart thudded in her chest as a fear of the unknown clashed with her need to know – *what else is down here?*

'Wait here,' Salora said, stopping at a tent not too far from the makra's right foot. 'I won't be long.'

Kavi tucked her hands into the coat's ample pockets and craned her neck to gaze up at the makra. Beneath the awe, the menace, was that same nostalgia and familiarity.

But he was different from both the Kraelish makra and those from Drisana's war. This one was missing the six discs – the vectors, Drisana had called them – that the makra and their mages from the war had been embedded with; and that wrongness she'd sensed from the Kraelish makra was also absent. In fact, with this one, she had this urge to get closer, to feel the metal, almost like she was attracted to—

Drisana, can you hear me?

The sword hummed inside her head. It had felt alive ever since she'd set foot in the cavern.

She swallowed. *Will I be able to pilot this makra?*

The humming stopped. The sword assessed. And whispered in Kavi's head,

Not as he is,

but if fixed,

Yes.

You know how to fix him?

Another pause. Hesitation.

I am

Unsure.

Is it the missing discs? The vectors?

Unsure. Accompanied by a pulse of puzzlement. **He is,**

Different.

Kavi frowned. If she set aside the absence of vectors, the body of the makra looked identical to the others, to Gayathri.

She squinted. Took a step closer. And stared in horrified fascination, one hand tugging on her earlobe, at the flesh-like material that overlaid the makra's ankles, knees, hips – on all its joints. The texture of muscle but with a complete lack of colour; it throbbed and writhed and spasmed like it was alive.

But it wasn't. She'd seen it before; in a decrepit park where so many men and women had perished.

'I'm done,' Salora said.

Kavi pointed at the makra's ankle. 'How did you do this?'

The artificer stepped closer, stood shoulder-to-shoulder with Kavi. 'Necromancy.'

Of course, what else could it be?

'Massa worked on the wrists.'

Kavi started. 'He *did*?'

'The Vagola didn't give him a choice.'

Her brows shot up. 'The Vagola are involved with—' She gestured at the makra and the enormous cavern they stood in.

'Kavithri,' Salora said with a tired sigh, 'if there is maayin involved, the Vagola are involved.'

'But … they knew what he was?'

'Of course they did. The Vagola controls the tests, you think they wouldn't know that he passed them?'

So many secrets. If Massa was alive, with time, would he have shared them with her? 'How long has it been down here?'

'Almost a year.'

Kavi's brows shot up. 'Why didn't you use it when the Kraelish attacked?'

'We already had the material, but our allies only recently shared the information – the designs, the schema – to assemble the makra.'

'Allies?'

'The Fumeshis and Hamakans.'

Kavi frowned. 'And Nathria?'

'Still on the fence.'

What was there to be on the fence about? 'Why won't they commit? I thought we'd resolved things with them.'

'To all appearances, yes,' Salora said. 'But they're still negotiating for territory on our side of the border; still adamant that it belongs to them.'

'Does it?'

'Does it matter?'

'I suppose not,' Kavi said. 'Do you trust them?'

'I don't, but the people who make the decisions do, and all we can do is obey.' She sighed. 'The Kraelish are not done with Raaya, and we're desperate for allies.'

'How many makra do we have? Including this one,' Kavi asked.

'Just us? One. Along with our allies, three.'

'And the Kraelish?'

'Intelligence says at least a dozen, and with the material to build more.'

Well, fuck. 'Why – what do you think the Kraelish want?

'Conquest?' Salora said with shrug. 'That's what they *want* us to think, anyway. The only thing we know for certain is that war is coming to the subcontinent, and the makra will decide the outcome.'

Kavi scratched her chin. There was something Jarard, the Kraelish mage who'd tortured and experimented on her, had said to her before one of his sessions. *We left something behind. Material from the Deadlands whose value we didn't fully understand back then. There are stockpiles buried all across Raaya – the biggest right here in Azraaya – and now that we know how to use them, we want them back.* 'Was anything ... stolen during the attack?'

Salora froze. 'How did you know that?'

Kavi told her.

'Vectors,' Salora said with a sigh. 'Material that can be used to power a makra. Your captor was referring to vector stockpiles we didn't even know were in the city.' She pointed at the Raayan makra's head, chest, and legs. 'The Kraelish shape them into discs and embed them in their makra.'

Kavi pretended like this was new information to her. 'So, what's wrong with our makra?'

Salora paused. Cocked her head. 'What makes you think something is wrong with it?'

'Oh, uhm.' The truth would sound ridiculous. 'It wouldn't be sitting here otherwise?'

'The Fumeshi schema – the makra they've developed, it's different from the Kraelish. They claim that only *their* artificers can complete the design, and want us to send the makra to them, along with pilots to train.' She gestured to the swarm of men and women working on the makra. 'Our Council were not particularly fond of the idea, and so here we are, trying to figure out what's missing.'

They didn't trust each other, these so-called allies. 'And will you?'

'Not a chance in Hel,' Salora said.

Kavi scoffed. 'So we'll have to send hi— send *it* to them.'

'There are people on the Council already thinking of ways they could profit off it.' Salora tilted her head at the makra. 'Others who don't trust our allies and argue that we don't need them. Many who even want the Vagola stripped of its power – they want to turn it into a tool used by the Council, instead of the independent institution it is now. We're better off sending it to them.'

'Where?'

She considered. 'If I tell you, no more questions.'

'Okay.'

'Ethuran.'

'Ethu—' Kavi's eyes widened. Her skin tingled as blood rushed to her head. Ethuran? Her home? It was supposed to be a ruin. Everyone said it was a ruin. 'Wha—'

'No more questions,' Salora said. 'Now, come, we should leave if we want to be at the station on time.'

*

Porters hustled from one end of the platform to another. Hawkers cleared their throats, prepared their vocal cords for the shouts they would soon emit. Beggars watched with tired gazes as passengers sat on their luggage and fanned themselves with newspamphlets.

Kavi stood on the platform with Salora – who'd rebuffed all her attempts at extricating information about Ethuran – and fought the urge to pace. She popped her collar and blew air down her chest. Why was she so jumpy? It was only Bithun, there was nothing to be nervous about. Her lips tightened. What if he was disappointed with her? When he learned of everything she'd lost.

She tsked. Crossed her arms. No, he wasn't like that. If anything, he might have some ideas on how to improve things.

The stationmaster, a tall woman who chewed and spat tama-khu, raised a whistle to her stained lips, and blew. A shrill *phwweet* cut through the hubbub of the platform and from the distance, as if it had heard the whistle, the Chimabali Express responded with a whistle of its own.

Kavi's feet moved of their own accord; took her to where the largest cluster of porters waited, which would be where the first-class compartments usually stopped.

The train burst past, the artificed cylinder that was the engine shimmered with bright orange maayin, and her eyes skipped from cabin to cabin filled with tired faces – some smiled, some pulled out suitcases, some, with their children, waved at people on the platform.

A prolonged hiss. A loud creak. A thud, and the locomotive came to a halt.

Porters leaped onto the train, and hawkers screamed into the windows. Kavi took a step back, searched the windows for Bithun's bald head as a wave of humanity washed past her.

She cocked her head: was that a dog's bark?

There, again, a deep *grrwoof!* that you'd find threatening if you weren't familiar with it. Kavi jostled toward the barking – an unexpected warmth in her chest, her limbs alive yet weightless – as her lips curled into a smile.

She found him at the entrance to a first-class compartment, blocking the way with his considerable bulk.

Their eyes met. He froze. His head titled one way, then the other, his ears flopped, he barked again, and – tail wagging – came bounding over to her.

Kavi dropped to her knees and wrapped Tsubu up in a hug. The dog wriggled and twisted and for the first time in what felt like forever, through a mouthful of fur, she laughed. 'Stop fighting it.'

But the bastard just wouldn't stop squirming. He alternated between licking her face and barking into her ears. She laughed again. Where was all this love when she was in Bochan? 'Did you miss me?'

'He sulked for weeks after you left.'

She looked up, and standing in the doorway, with a cane in one hand, was Bithun. 'Sahib—'

Her smile faltered. What the Hel? Why did he look like that? 'How was the journey?'

Tanool, Bithun's imperious Kraelish-style butler, joined him in the doorway, and helped the sahib disembark.

Kavi stared. Bithun's hands and wrists, once so powerful and full of life, were now just bone. The skin on them was dry and scabbed – she could tell he'd been picking at them. And the rest of his body was the same: caved-in chest that shook as he wheezed with each breath, scrawny shoulders that made his shirt look too big, and his face …

Her vision blurred, and she fought to keep the sound of her heart breaking from her voice. 'What happened?'

He passed Tanool his cane, coughed into his handkerchief, and held his other hand out to her. 'It's good to see you again, Kavithri.'

She released Tsubu and shook his hand. So frail. He'd become so frail. The skin on his face had sunk, it clung to his skull, made his cheekbones jut out and his eye sockets more prominent. 'You too, sahib.'

But still, he smiled at her. 'Help me walk.'

She offered her arm, and he rested a hand on the inside of her elbow.

'Salora?' he said, peering at the artificer.

'Jarayas, welcome to Azraaya.'

He inclined his head and urged Kavi forward.

'The healers—' He fell into a coughing fit; used his handkerchief again when he was done. 'Sorry.'

She shook her head. Didn't trust herself to speak. There was blood on the handkerchief, some still on his lips.

'The healers think I have a month left, at most,' he said.

The knots in her gut tightened. Her lips trembled, and she widened her eyes to keep the tears from spilling over.

He squeezed her arm. 'It's okay, Kavi.'

She choked back a sob.

'Hel awaits us all,' Bithun whispered, and wiped the tears off her cheeks with his thumb.

Chapter 26
ENFORCER

Bloodhound

The Blade-lock tournament petered out to a one-sided final – or so she'd heard from an ecstatic Subbal Reddy – where a third-year duo walloped a pair of second-years and took home the prize money.

Azia, his new Blade (whoever the Hel they were), and the first-years packed their things and boarded a train headed to Draghal, a fortress town at the southernmost tip of Gashan's Teeth, the mountain range home to Greema's people and the first in a series of military settlements on the disputed Raaya-Nathria border.

Kavi, meanwhile, spent every moment she could steal with Bithun. She introduced Chotu to him. She showed him Drisana. She told him everything that had happened since she'd left Bochan.

Bithun wept with her when he heard about Hessal, about Massa, about Elisai and Sravan. He clenched his fists and shook with fury when he learned who and what Grishan was. He told her not to lose hope. That she would find a way. That he would do whatever he could to help.

On quiet afternoons, after his nap, he'd tell her stories from his childhood – about his father, strict, reticent, and unyielding; his mother, easily manipulated and with a heart of gold;

his time in Kraelin – boxing in the capital, Balthour; the way he adapted to being shorter; the matches he lost and learned from; the victories he slowly accumulated and the respect he earned. How he met his wife; the birth of his daughter, Freya; and the mistakes he made and everything that led up to her suicide.

Kavi let him speak, didn't mention that Salora had already shared the story, and when he hung his head in shame, she told him it was in the past, that he was a good man.

Every day, when the healers came to grant him a few hours of relief, she'd rouse him with an 'Up, sahib,' help him sit, then watch over him while the mages went to work. He'd feel better for an hour or two before returning to his weakened state.

It's his heart, they told her. *It is struggling to pump blood.* Why? *Because his blood is toxic, thick, and heavy. It is systematically poisoning his organs. The pain, although he doesn't show it, must be astounding.*

Every day, after Tanool helped him wash, Kavi would carry him to a chair facing a window, unzip a leather case that they'd brought from Bochan, and arrange its contents on a table: a small square mirror, a metal bowl, a bar of white soap, a straight razor, a shaving brush, a small glass bottle, and a towel.

She'd watched Tanool do it for him, and she'd learned.

She wrapped the cloth around Bithun's neck, wet the shaving brush, and ran it across the surface of the soap. She then pressed it into the metal bowl, where she made circles with it until a small mound of white foam built up. Then she lathered up his face, picked up the razor, gently drew his sagging skin tight, and ran the blade across it. Once she was done, she used the towel to wipe his face, splashed some of the sweet-smelling clear liquid from the glass bottle on her palms, and gently patted them on his cheeks.

And when she said, 'Done,' Bithun smiled at her, revealed a mouthful of crumbling teeth and dark, bloody gums, and whispered, 'Thank you.'

She had watched one parent die. Learned of the other's execution second-hand. But she had never, like so many children, nursed either to the fringes of Hel.

That soul-eroding need, that desperate desire to help someone you love, to ease their pain and comfort them while being fully aware that you will never be able to, was not new to her. Even so, it took its toll. She worried about him when she was away. Planned her day around him. And when she couldn't cope with being away anymore, she brought her sleeping mat to the house Salora had rented for Bithun, told Tanool to get some sleep, and kept watch over Bithun from her place on the floor.

She began to inadvertently wean herself off the agoma – she needed to be alert if Bithun needed her. So she tossed and turned as her body cleansed itself of the drug. In its place came temple-crushing headaches, chills, and aches in the strangest places – her armpits, behind her ears, her lower back, and her knees. She bore with it, and a few nights later, she found herself alone with only her nightmares, which, oddly enough, were no longer as intense.

Bithun would wake every couple of hours and need to be helped to the toilet. He refused her help, initially, but when he tried to stand and fell back onto the bed, he grudgingly allowed her to wrap an arm around his shoulders to take his weight while he wheezed and shuffled along.

It got harder for him to eat. Air trapped in his belly would cause it to swell, painfully, and during mealtimes she'd wait with a bowl of soup while he tried to burp. When he was successful, he'd nod, and she'd feed the soup to him, using his handkerchief afterwards to wipe his mouth.

Eventually, three weeks after he arrived in Azraaya, Bithun lost the ability to speak, and they arranged for a small slate and piece of chalk for him to communicate with.

His spirit never wavered. After she helped him shave, he'd still write, 'Thank you', and he'd still smile his shattered smile at her, and the light in his eyes would force her to smile back.

'I'm not afraid,' Bithun wrote. 'I'm ready.'

*

The lawyer – a jowly man with a sharp, receding hairline – cleared his throat, glanced at Kavi, and read, 'The remaining half of the estate is to be liquidated and ownership of any and all monies transferred to one Kavithri Taemu, adopted daughter of Sree Jarayas Bithun.'

Kavi started. Fumbled the empty jug of water she was carrying to the kitchen to refill. '*What?*'

Bithun smiled. Dismissed the lawyer with a wave and reached for his slate. 'Had to adopt,' he wrote. 'Was only way to make it legal.'

'You already—' He had already asked if he could adopt her, said he wanted to leave her some money and that it would make things easier. She'd agreed. It made no difference to her. She couldn't use it to buy back the rickshaw company because it wasn't *earned*. But half? She turned to Tanool – the other half was going to him, with instructions that he share the inheritance with the rest of the staff in Bochan. Tanool gave her a grim nod and escorted the lawyer out.

Bithun scrubbed the slate clean and wrote. 'Tanool knows. He will help set up an account for you at Merthali bank.'

'It's too much,' she said, setting the jug down. 'Isn't there someone else—'

He squeezed her arm. Wrote on his slate. 'You will use it.'

'For what?'

He ignored her, scrubbed the slate clean, and wrote, 'You're like me, Kavi. To stand inside a ring. To hit and get hit. Something is wrong with us.' Scrub. Dust. He wrote, 'Something primal in us has not been extinguished. Like it has in everyone else.' Scrub. Dust. 'You know what happens when you hurt a wild animal?'

'They bite?'

He nodded, wrote, struck something off and wrote again. 'You're stubborn. Relentless. ~~Once you set your mind to~~ Once you have a scent, you will not let go. Like a bloodhound.'

Scrub, dust. He held the slate tight over his stomach, and the powder from the chalk gathered on his shirt as he wrote. When he was done, he squeezed her arm again, and turned the slate so she could read: 'He does not understand you, Kavithri. He will underestimate and underestimate, and he will not see you coming.'

He. Grishan. Her lips tightened. Bithun had too much faith in her. But she nodded. She would find a way to use the money. 'Thank you,' she said. *For everything.*

He set the slate and chalk aside and smiled.

Two weeks later, in the middle of the night, while Tsubu barked in the garden downstairs and steam-rickshaws hissed and sputtered down the street outside, Bithun shot upright in his bed, coughed up dark – almost black – blood, while more came pouring out of his nostrils as he gasped and struggled to breathe.

Kavi rushed to his side, screamed for Tanool.

Bithun knocked the pitcher of water over as he frantically searched for his slate and chalk. Kavi passed it to him. Helped steady his shaking hands as he wrote three tremulous, incomplete words on the slate: 'Sta wit m.'

Stay with me. 'Till the end,' she whispered.

He managed a nod before he doubled over and vomited into his lap, a mixture of blood and bile and thick clumps of pink.

Footsteps approached the room at a run, then more lamps were lit.

Kavi sat on the bed, cradled Bithun in her arms; his feather-light head in the crook of her elbow; their eyes locked together. Tears trapped in the wrinkles on his battered face. He spasmed. Shuddered. More blood gushed out of his mouth and nose, a stain slowly spread on the sheet beneath his hips and thighs. But he never looked away. Never wavered. Even when the light behind his eyes dimmed and the sound of her own sobs filled her ears and her vision blurred. *You take the punches and you do not flinch,* his eyes said to her. He was showing her how to die. Even now he was teaching her.

She nodded. Pulled her sleeve up and used it to wipe the blood off his face. She caressed the sunken cheeks she had shaved earlier that day.

His lips and chin were still smeared dark-red. So, she wiped his mouth again.

And again.

And again.

'Kavi,' Tanool said softly. 'Stop, he's gone.'

He was more of a father to her than her own had ever been.

No more pain, or suffering. Rest now, sahib. She pushed his eyelids shut with trembling hands, kissed his cold forehead, and hugged him to her chest as she wept.

Chapter 27
ENFORCER

Gas Lamps and Crushed Beedis

'I will need you for a fight,' Grishan said, using a handkerchief to wipe the sweat from his scarred neck. He reclined in his large chair in the Tivasi den and crossed his legs. 'This one will be bigger – you'd be surprised by the number of people who want to see a Taemu put in their place.'

No, she wouldn't.

'And how much they'd pay to see it. I've secured a more exclusive venue. And on the night, we can expect a more, shall we say, sophisticated clientele.' He smiled and tucked his handkerchief into a shirt pocket. 'The fight will take place the day after tomorrow – these guests are important, so I want you to put on your best performance.'

Kavi stared at the unevenly aged skin on his face, at the eyes that could change in a heartbeat, and averted her gaze. It unsettled her, *he* unsettled her, and the knowledge of who he really was made his presence even more unbearable.

'Drag it out,' he said. 'Three rounds this time. Make them think your opponent earned it. Can you do that?'

'Yes, boss.'

'Good.' He sighed and nodded to himself. 'I heard about your acquaintance from Bochan.'

Kill him, the berserker whispered. *Kill him now, don't let him say Bithun's name.* Kavi tightened her lips, kept her eyes on the ground.

'Did he suffer?' Grishan said.

'No.'

'It was quick, then?'

'Yes.'

'He must've been terrified – no family, no friends, he came all the way up here to die.'

'He wasn't scared.' *And he wasn't alone.*

Grishan snorted.

The muscles in her jaw, in her neck, twitched as they were pulled taut. Her hands, which were clasped behind her back, trembled. Her eyes, of their own accord, climbed their way up Grishan's feet, his torso, and settled on his face.

She didn't flinch when he held her gaze. Didn't relent when his smile widened.

'He wasn't scared,' Kavi said again.

'Sure,' he said, and scoffed. 'By the way, you need not concern yourself with Vaisha's father.'

Kavi frowned. *Should* she be concerned?

'His daughter progressed to the next round – that she was no longer able to participate is not our problem.' He leaned forward. 'Besides, he knows you're one of mine. Consider the matter resolved.'

It hadn't even occurred to her that Vaisha's father, now a disgruntled Tivasi client, might be out for revenge. She nodded.

He grunted. Cocked his head and studied her in silence.

Kavi lowered her gaze to the scars on Grishan's arms and the powerful muscle underneath. 'Was there anything else?' she asked.

'You're special, Kavithri.'

She looked up.

'You're one of the only people alive who know what I am.' He paused. 'Have you told anyone that I'm a mage?' He said in that dispassionate voice he used when he killed.

'No, boss.'

'Do you want to know why I keep you alive?'

'No, boss.'

'I like watching you struggle.'

Kavi kept her face expressionless while inside the berserker's voice got louder. *Kill. Him.* 'Was there anything else?' she asked again.

'Aren't you curious?'

'About?'

Grishan tapped his forearm. 'Biomancy.'

Kavi glanced over her shoulder. Except for a couple of games of carrom, the den was empty. The gangsters there were too engrossed in their game to pay them any attention.

'I won't hurt you,' Grishan said. 'It's been years since I could talk to someone about it.' He gestured for her to approach the chair and, despite everything, her curiosity got the better of her.

The muscles in his forearm pulsed, contracted; his arm blurred, and before she could react, he'd latched on to her collar.

Her eyes bulged, she tried to pull away, but his arm wouldn't budge.

He released her and pointed to his wrist and forearm. 'Rakthan maayin is always in a Biomancer's blood,' Grishan said. 'All I did was redirect the flow, command more of it into my forearm and wrist, to alter its density. The results – well, you've seen the results a few times now.'

'How much?' Kavi said, softly.

'How much what?'

'How much did that take from you?'

'Ah.' He reclined again. The smile slipped off his face and his eyes turned cold. He flicked his fingers, gesturing for her to get out. 'I will send word about the fight. You may return to the Caterpillar.'

The Caterpillar hummed with its usual hedonistic energy. Kavi stood by the bar – arms crossed, eyes surveying the clientele; to all appearances alert and ready to live up to her reputation as a no-nonsense Tivasi enforcer.

Inside, however, she was drained. She'd lost her purpose after her disqualification from the tournament, then found a temporary one in caring for Bithun, and now? She was adrift again. Empty. Alone.

Her throat was raw, her eyes were dry, her eyelids heavy. Her stomach hurt – she had no appetite, she'd skipped breakfast and lunch; and her mind returned, over and over again, to Bithun's cremation.

His body had been wrapped up in white cloth, his eyes closed, his nostrils plugged with cotton. A priest from one of Meshira's temples mumbled his gibberish and rubbed holy oils on Bithun's forehead, before the body was carried away to the artificed incinerator.

It was all so rushed, but they'd had no choice. The crematorium was fully booked, and this was the only appointment available. If they waited till the next available slot, *It will be really bad, memsaab*, the manager said, *body will decompose and—*

Okay, we'll do it today, Salora told him.

Kavi had held herself together, done whatever Tanool and Salora had needed her to do. She'd already shed her tears at his deathbed, and the last thing she wanted to do was cause a scene. But the sight of the cotton in Bithun's nostrils smashed her composure to pieces. She lost control of her facial muscles.

Her chest and shoulders and arms shook. The tears would not stop, and she'd lost track of time.

A client slammed his drink down on the table and spat. 'We should've never trusted them!'

The others on his table agreed. 'Bloody bhaenchods – first the Kraelish, now this.'

That's right. News of a border skirmish had reached the city: the Nathrians, under the guise of a joint exercise, had launched an attack on Draghal. Reinforcements had already left Azraaya, with more scheduled to depart over the next couple of days.

Kavi's reaction to the news had been muted, given the circumstances, but she hoped Azia was okay. She was worried, yes, but also emotionally exhausted and trapped. There was nothing she could do for him; Grishan had forbidden her from leaving the city. Not that her presence on the border would change anything.

'Taemu,' the Aunty-ji said from behind the bar, 'room seventeen. Quick.'

'Memsaab.' Kavi bobbed her head and took off up the stairs. *Seventeen.* Nabo's room.

She shoved the door open. 'What's—'

Nabo lunged at her, ducked under her arms and hid behind her back. 'She's lost her mind,' he hissed.

Kavi glanced at him over her shoulder. Nabo had one hand pressed down on a bleeding shoulder, and his neck was covered in bite-marks.

Lurching out of the bathtub, clearly drunk, was a woman with long black hair, a large mole on her chin, and blood all over her mouth. 'Give him,' she said.

'Hah?' Kavi's lip curled into a snarl. 'What's wrong with her?'

'She says she wants to eat me,' Nabo said, peeking at the woman over Kavi's shoulder.

'He's delicious,' the woman whispered and licked her lips.

He sure is, but, 'That doesn't mean you can eat him, you wretch.' Kavi grabbed a towel, flung it at the woman, and tackled her to the ground.

The woman howled and flailed as Kavi bundled her up in the towel and dragged her out of the room. 'I'll be back for her clothes,' she said, and Nabo gave her an exhausted nod.

She left the crazed client sobbing and throwing up in the bathroom below and returned to find Nabo sitting on the bed with his bandages and ointments, wincing as he struggled to clean the wound on his shoulder.

Kavi clenched her jaw. Stomped up to him. And snatched the towel away. 'Look that way,' she said, before examining the wound.

'I can do it myself,' he said, reaching for the towel.

She nudged his hand away – the woman had almost bitten a chunk out of his shoulder – and gently dabbed and wiped the blood clear.

He lowered his head, surrendered, and remained silent as she cleaned and dressed his wound.

Kavi avoided meeting his eyes and took her time: gently massaged the ointment around the teeth marks, measured and cut the bandages, checked his neck to see if the skin was broken there, and finally, when she was done, she sat by his side, and said, softly, 'I'm sorry.'

He glanced at her and averted his eyes.

'I—' She wanted to explain, wanted to confide and share everything that had happened to her. But what if it scared him? If he knew about all the violence and horror in her life it would just make things worse. 'I just wanted to be close to you.'

'Why? We don't even know each other,' he said. 'You don't know anything about me.'

He was right. She didn't. All she knew was that he was kind and gentle and he weighed every word before he spoke and he never complained and he made her heart race and stomach flutter and when she was around him the longing in her chest vanished. 'So, tell me.'

'Will you do the same?'

'I—' She wanted to. So badly. 'It's difficult.'

He shrugged. Then hissed and nursed his shoulder.

Kavi stood. Wiped her sweaty palms on her trousers. It wasn't just Bithun or Massa or her, everyone was terminal. *We're all dying, and life would be so much easier if we acted like it.*

'I like you, Nabo, I really do,' she said. 'When I'm with you I feel like my heart could explode, and it makes me do foolish things.' She swallowed and stepped away from the bed. 'You don't need to respond, I just wanted you to know.' She picked up the woman's clothes, glanced at Nabo, who sat perfectly still, facing away from her, and walked out of the room.

The woman (the aspiring cannibal) seemed to have come to her senses, and she gratefully accepted her clothes before profusely apologising to the Aunty-ji, who threatened her with *consequences* if she damaged the merchandise again.

Kavi trudged back to her vantage point by the bar, relieved and at the same time terrified about what she'd just said to Nabo. Grumbling to herself, she returned to her observation of the Caterpillar's clientele.

Conversation ebbed and flowed, food and drink travelled across the floor on trays, men and women went up and came back down the stairs. All was peaceful, until a glass shattered and an ayah was dispatched to clean up the mess. Kavi watched the girl sweep the shards into a bucket as the—

She started as a man brushed past her and, ever so briefly, squeezed her hand. 'Dai, what—'

Nabo turned, met her eyes for a heartbeat, and walked away. He'd left a piece of folded paper in her hand.

'I'll be outside,' she said to the bartender, who gave her a distracted nod.

She threaded her way to the entrance and walked out into a warm, humid night. On the other side of the road, a queue snaked its way to a mobile kebab stand and groups of people walked from shop to shop as they hunted for a deal. Naadan poked his head out of the bookshop and waved at her.

She waved back, rifled through her pockets, and found a crushed beedi. She used Massa's artificed matchstick to light up; the tamakhu dulled her nerves, and she took another drag before stepping under the light of a gas lamp and unfolding the paper.

She blinked. Frowned. And read it again:

Meet me at the Chokai hawker centre at midday tomorrow.

Chapter 28
ENFORCER

Pav Bhaji

The call for volunteers had gone out overnight.

The Raayan military was stretched thin – they'd increased their presence on the northern and western borders to prepare for a Kraelish invasion, and now did not have enough troops to send to the eastern border, where they'd assumed they were safe. Woodblock prints plastered all over the Chokai hawker centre asked for anyone with combat experience, anyone who had fought the Kraelish, to join the reinforcements being sent to Draghal.

The Chokai hawker centre was a large, square courtyard with food and drink vendors on the perimeter and an open-air seating area in the middle. Kavi wandered through, hands in her pockets, hair brushed and neatly arranged, salwar-kameez clean and ironed, soul exhausted but body well rested. She'd caved and taken a disc of agoma last night. Chotu had given her a disapproving (albeit concerned) glance as he blew out the dia lamp; but how else was she supposed to sleep?

Drisana had come calling, like she always did when Kavi was in the agoma dream, but Kavi had turned her away. *Not tonight*, she'd said, and remained by the disembodied makra head in the Deadlands.

She tsked. Stepped over a toppled garbage bin and set out on another circuit of the hawker centre. Nabo had not said where exactly he wanted to meet, so she'd shown up early and was now carrying out a thorough inspection of each food stall.

The Nathrians were all anyone could talk about: *Are you going to Draghal?* No, I have a wife and small baby. *You?* No, I have to take care of my amma, she's old now. *What about you?* I have things to do. *What things?* Private things, chootia, mind your business!

Variants of the same conversation played out on almost every table she walked past. The good citizens of Azraaya, it seemed, were not keen on dropping everything and taking a train to the border to get stabbed in the face.

'Kavi.'

She turned to the source of the familiar voice.

'Have you been waiting long?' Nabo said.

And despite everything, her stomach fluttered, her heart leaped up into her throat, and she forced out a hoarse, 'Just got here.'

He smiled. 'Are you hungry?'

'No – yes.' The pav bhaji did look and smell really good.

Nabo pointed to an empty table by a sugarcane juice stand. 'Meet you there?'

She nodded, and he wandered off.

It was strange to see him in a shirt and trousers. Even stranger to see him outside of the Caterpillar. He stopped outside a biryani stand, studied the menu with a fist under his chin, then moved on to the next vendor.

Kavi sighed, joined the line outside the pav bhaji stand, and craned her neck to watch the cook mash the spiced potatoes and chickpeas on a large griddle; he shovelled the mixture to one side then plonked a dollop of ghee in the middle into which he pressed two thick chunks of bread. He swirled them around till they were brown and crisp at the bottom then transferred everything: the spicy mashed potatoes and chickpeas; the ghee-toasted bread; to a plate, and added a handful of chopped onions and a slice of lime. Then he started again.

Kavi paid, collected her plate, and strolled over to Nabo, who was already waiting at their table with a bowl of sambhar-soaked idlis. 'Are you waiting for me to start eating?' she asked as she sat.

'I—'

A menu was slapped down on their table and the culprit, a youth with an incongruously thick moustache, cleared his throat and said, 'Order please.'

Kavi glanced at the menu – a list of sugarcane flavoured beverages – and shook her head. 'I don't want. Do you?' She still couldn't bring herself to say Nabo's name out loud.

Nabo shook his head. And the waiter tsked. 'Cannot sit here if you don't order drink.'

This fucking guy. 'Dai—'

'It's okay.' Nabo pointed to the iced option. 'We'll take two.'

The youth bobbled his head and walked away, and they ate in silence until the drinks arrived. Kavi sipped the sweet, foamy beverage. 'How's your shoulder?'

Nabo lifted the bowl to his lips and slurped up the last of the sambhar. He wiped his mouth, set the bowl aside, and reached for his drink. 'You asked me to *tell* you, last night. Do you still—'

'Yes.'

He nodded, pursed his lips, a gesture she found maddeningly alluring, and said, 'My plan, ever since I set foot in Azraaya, was to complete my contract and go home. I promised myself that I would not form any bonds or have any entanglements that might keep me here.'

I'm an entanglement? She fought to keep a straight face as a rush of warmth circled the grief embedded in her chest and spread, slowly, through the rest of her body. *Is this what it feels like to be flattered?*

Nabo smiled and looked away.

'You—' She frowned. *Wait.* 'What do you mean by contract?'

He hesitated. Sighed. 'In Hamaka, when a person is in debt, they can indenture their children to help pay it off.'

Ah, Hel.

'The Tivasi bought my contract.'

'Can't you just run?'

'Hamakan officials check in, from time to time, to ensure I am fulfilling the terms of the contract. If I was missing, they would imprison my mother.'

Kavi swallowed the bitter tang at the back of her mouth. The Hamakans were not so different from the Raayans after all. They too had built a structure to preserve the people at the top at the expense of the rest – the desperation of one generation used to hobble the next and ensure that everyone stayed in their place. 'How long have you been here?'

'In Azraaya? Two years. Before that, I was in Fumesh for three.'

'And how much longer?'

'Three more years.'

Eight years for a crime he didn't commit. She tapped her fingers on the table. Chewed her lip and scratched the back of her neck. Her account at the Merthali bank would be ready in another day or so; she could offer to buy out his contract and get him out of the Caterpillar. How much would it cost? *Doesn't matter.* What was important was if he would let her do something like that.

'Your turn,' Nabo said.

Kavi stared at the table and its worn and scratched surface.

'Did something happen?' he said. 'You look sad – more than usual, I mean, and we haven't spoken in a while, not since ...' He sighed and swirled the sugarcane juice around in his glass.

The temptation to tell him *everything* slammed into her like a rickshaw full of schoolboys. She faltered. Caught herself. No, it would be too much. It would scare him away. 'I lost a friend recently, someone who was like a father to me,' she said, and gritted her teeth as her vision blurred. *I will not cry in front of him.* She tightened her lips. Took a deep, expansive breath, and composed herself. 'He died in my arms. I could do nothing for him.'

'I'm sorry,' Nabo said, softly.

Kavi nodded. She didn't trust herself to speak without bursting into tears.

'But there is something else, no?'

She met his eyes. His kind, earnest eyes, and she caved. It all came spilling out: Sravan, Grishan and the fear he instilled in her, the things he'd taken from her, the anger and the helplessness. Her hate and her bitterness. What she'd done to Vaisha during the tournament, how she'd lost Azia's trust.

She wiped her eyes on a sleeve. 'I'm sorry.'

He shuffled closer. 'You have someone who cares for you? Who listens to you?'

What a strange question. 'Yes—' Haibo, Bithun, Massa, Hessal. All gone. All dead. She shook her head and averted her eyes. 'No. I did, once.'

'You have a brother, yes?'

'How did you – I can't, I have to take care of him.'

'But these people you once had, they saw something in you that made them care. You were worth their attention and kindness. Do you remember what that felt like?'

Safe. She'd felt safe around them. She could trust them and they in turn had trusted her. She glanced at Nabo. It was the same with him. 'It feels like you care too.'

He blinked. Hesitated. His eyebrows twitched and furrowed, and an expanse of emotion flashed across his face before it mellowed back down as whatever internal debate he was having found its resolution. 'I do,' he said, and licked his lips. 'In Hamaka I would make a formal application to court you—'

'No need.' Kavi raised both hands in alarm. What did he think she was? A post office? 'You don't need to apply, we can *court*,' she said, slightly giddy.

He sipped his sugarcane juice, set the glass down, and sighed. 'May I speak honestly?'

Kavi bobbed her head.

'It is not my place to tell you how to live your life, but—' He clenched and unclenched his jaw. 'May I give you some advice?'

'Can,' she said.

'First, promise me that if things ever get too much, you will come and talk to me.'

She smiled.

'And the agoma – I saw the marks that night,' he said, after she sat back defensively. 'You don't need it. Please, Kavi, you don't need it.' He waited till she accepted the statement with a nod. 'And I feel like there are some things you have not shared with me. Things that perhaps even you have not fully acknowledged or ever said out loud.'

'Is this your mind doctor training?' she asked, crossing her arms.

He ignored her. 'But until you say these things, and have someone – have *me* – understand and acknowledge them, you will not begin to heal. You will remain at war with yourself.'

She looked away again. Her lips trembled, and she shook her head. No, there was no point in—

He reached out across the table and slipped his hand into hers. The smooth, warm webbing between his thumb and index finger squeezed into her own as he pulled her closer. 'Say it, Kavi.'

'It's – are you sure?' *Sure you want to hear this? That you'll still want to sit here with me when I'm done?*

'Yes.'

She nodded, chewed the inside of her cheek, and said, 'I couldn't help my mother, I was just a girl – I watched as she was murdered. My father hated me, wanted nothing to do with me, but I still loved him.' Each word she uttered was accompanied by this strange feeling of weightlessness that grew as she continued speaking. 'I am responsible for the deaths of my friends – Hessal, Elisai, Haibo, Sravan, and so many Taemu. When I was captured by the Kraelish and tortured – I gave up. I did things I'm ashamed of.'

'It was not your fault,' he whispered.

'There is no one else at fault – it was me, Nabo.'

'No. *No.*' His voice grew stronger. 'None of it was down to you. There must be someone else.'

Someone else? Someone else responsible for her mother's death? For her father and her brother's? For Sravan? For the massacre at Ethuran? For everything that had happened since … her mouth twisted. Yes, there *was* someone else. Someone who had single-handedly caused the Taemu more pain and suffering than anyone else on the subcontinent; who'd instigated the massacre at Ethuran; who'd stolen the rickshaw company and their future; who'd lied and killed and poisoned minds against them. She tightened her grip on his hand. *Grishan.*

'Now, tell me,' he said. 'What do you want?'

'I have six years left to live,' Kavi said, 'and in that time, I want to do everything I can to make things better for my people.'

He didn't flinch or hesitate or question it. 'Then you know what you have to do.'

There were still people alive whom she cared about; and who cared about her. She'd found her brother, Chotu. She'd met Azia, she'd made a friend. She'd yearned for so long to have someone like Nabo in her life, and here he was sitting across from her. She'd given her people hope and belief before Grishan snatched it all away, but still they called her *Akka*, big sister, still they had faith in her. Even if this entire city, with its corruption and prejudice and disdain, was against her, even if this country she *belonged* to hated her, she wasn't alone. She had people to protect. And to protect them, to move forward, she had stop blaming herself for what had happened. The girl who hid and watched as they brutalised and murdered her mother at Ethuran; the woman who remained on her knees as Grishan slit her friend's throat, she needed to forgive them both.

He brought her hand up to his lips, kissed her knuckles, and just like that, the pressure in her temples, the weight on her chest that had been growing lighter, disappeared.

'Thank you,' she said, and got to her feet.

He released her hand. Stood. Gazed at her with a question in his eyes.

She leaned in, hesitated – what the fuck was she scared off? – and kissed him on the cheek.

He blushed.

Really? They'd committed, what Raeth's priests would call *unspeakable acts* together, and this was what made him blush?

'There is something I have to do,' she said, unable to keep

the smile from her lips. 'A warlock I promised to protect is in Draghal.'

His chin quivered, but he smiled back. 'Can I get you to make another promise?'

She cocked her head.

'Come back alive?'

'Only if you promise to have some tea with me.'

He chuckled. 'You can choose the chaiwallah.'

'I know a guy,' she said, reaching for his hand.

He met her halfway. Intertwined his fingers in hers. 'Kavi?'

'Hmm?'

'Why do you only have six years left to live?'

She traced the lines on his palm with her thumb. 'I'll tell you when I'm back.'

*

Chotu's eyebrows shot up as she handed him the agoma tin. 'You don't need?'

'No,' Kavi said, wrapping him up in a hug. 'You know where to go if you need something?'

He hugged her back, tighter. 'Salora.'

'And?'

'Ratan.'

She puffed out her cheeks and stepped back. 'How's your little gang?'

He started. Fidgeted with the metal tin. Sheepishly glanced at her and grinned. 'Fine. We're expanding.'

'Make sure you don't get caught.'

'Akka, please, we're not amateurs.'

'Still, be careful,' she said, as she picked up her sword from its spot in the corner. 'And keep an eye on the others.'

'Of course.'

She stopped in the doorway. 'I'll see you when I'm back.'

He nodded, and said, without a flicker of doubt on his face, 'I'll be waiting.'

Outside, Ratan sat in his steam-rickshaw, picking his teeth with a toothpick; and in the backseat, puffing away on a beedi while he stared at nothing with glazed eyes, was Deva.

Kavi cocked her head in surprise. 'What're you doing here?'

'Boss wants to see you.'

Kavi gestured for him to vacate the steam-rickshaw, and once he was clear, shoved her bag and sword into the backseat. 'I'm volunteering for the reinforcements to Draghal,' she said.

'Grishan told you not to leave the city. The fight's been booked. He won't be happy when he—'

'I'm going.'

Deva flicked his beedi, sent ash spiralling down the street. 'Has anyone told you what he did to the old Tivasi boss?'

There was an old boss? 'No.'

'I worked for him for sixteen years before Grishan took over,' Deva said. 'We found him and his family – wife, two children – in the office. They'd been stabbed, over and over again, so many wounds you couldn't count, and then he decapitated them, neatly arranged their heads between their legs.'

Her lips thinned into a straight line, and she turned and spat. 'I'll *deal* with him when I'm back.'

Deva stared at her. Took another long, slow drag and nodded.

'Let's go,' she said, hopping into the steam-rickshaw.

'Boss.' Ratan tipped his flatcap, and pumped the ignition lever until the engine roared to life.

END OF PART TWO

INTERLUDE - II

Ze'aan

Leaves rustled, branches groaned, and raindrops pitter-pattered against my window.

The rain here was different. Neither heavy nor a drizzle, it spat and sprayed and went on for days. It lacked that earthy scent that accompanied the rain in Raaya, the scent that always made me stop and take a deep breath.

The streetlamps cast shadows on my ceiling – gently swaying leaves and branches that morphed from intricate latticework to ominous shapes and faces. The newspamphlets said the Raayans were panicking, that the attack on Azraaya had left them reeling and they now wanted to renegotiate the trade agreement with Kraelin.

Did they?

I pulled the blanket up to my chin and flipped onto my side, away from the window.

Kavithri would be a cadet at the Vagola by now; she would've been assigned a first-year novice. Whoever it was, I hoped they were treating her well.

I flung the blanket away and sat up. There would be no sleep for me tonight. I gulped down a glass of water, slipped my arms into a robe, and as was habit now whenever sleep eluded me, I went up to the repository and looked for the First Mage's eye.

It was in the same spot it always was, in the middle of the repository, suspended inside the silver-edged glass box. I had since learned that the eye, nerves and all, was still functional. That time itself was frozen inside the glass artifact.

'I come here to visit the eye as well,' a voice said.

I started, slapped one hand over my chest and searched for the source.

A man stepped out of the corner, flanked by another heavily armoured man and a cloaked woman – clearly a warlock and Blade. The man gestured, and the pair stopped while he walked up to me.

He carried a golden sceptre mounted with a dark orb, and his face – his face …

My eyes went wide. Pinpricks of ice crawled through my gut, expanded into my chest.

I'd seen his face before. How could I not? It was everywhere.

I dropped to one knee, lowered my head. 'Your Majesty,' I whispered.

'Stand.'

I obeyed.

The emperor gazed out at the repository. 'So much lost, so much we still don't understand,' he said, more to himself than to me. 'Did you know, before the Retreat, mages could make one request – a wish if, you will – of their Jinn? And if it was within their power, the Jinn would grant it. The Retreat itself was said to be the result of one such wish.'

'I was not aware,' I said, and when the Blade in the corner cocked his head, I added, 'Your Majesty.'

'Would you like to see something?' the emperor asked, and leaned closer, eyes wide and head cocked, like a child eager to share a new discovery. 'Something that will help you *understand* why we must unite the continent under our banner?' He spun the dark orb off the top of his sceptre and offered it to me.

An even darker eye had been stencilled into the orb, and he pointed at it. 'Made entirely out of vectors, to give us a glimpse.'

'Of what?' And why did he need me to *understand*?

The Blade in the corner bristled, but the emperor was unfazed. 'There are worlds out there, don't you want to see?' He reached out, took my hand, and before I could react, pressed my index finger into the eye.

My body locked itself in place. Harith's maayin seared its way into my chest. But instead of expanding out into the world as my krasna, it funnelled itself into the orb. It had triggered a cast. Called my Jinn for me and was consuming my maayin.

That shouldn't have been possible.

The repository disappeared. Shards, shattered links of something so vast it dwarfed even the Jinn, flickered in and out of existence.

'It's called the Chain,' the emperor's voice said, from somewhere faraway.

A sparkle. A flash. And I could sense them, four other worlds in addition to ours, that this Chain had once connected.

There was life on these worlds, and a different kind of nature – pure, unhindered, and devoid of humanity – flourished on three worlds, but on the fourth. On—

'Harith, the world is called Harith,' the emperor said.

The same as my Jinn. Why?

My vision twisted, dilated, and I hurtled down towards Harith. I tore past spires that punctured the atmosphere and plunged through the darkness that surrounded the world. There was humanity here, but it was overshadowed by the inhuman.

Something shimmered in the darkness, and a head turned to gaze up at the sky. At me. I tasted bile at the back of my throat.

The air caught in my chest. Fear – cold, jagged, unlike anything I'd experienced before, raced through my body.

It was a man, alone, at the base of a colossal spire, with something sharp and jagged implanted in his spine. A surge of maayin shot through this thing on his back, and he reached out to—

I snapped back to the repository, gagged and retched on my hands and knees.

The orb squealed as the emperor spun back onto the sceptre.

'It may take another millennium, or two, but the Chain is re-linking.' He stepped back from the mess I'd made on the floor. 'But we now have in our possession an artifact that will allow us to exert a level of control over the Chain – to accelerate the re-linking, if we so desire.'

My body wanted to contort, to twist and curl into a ball to protect itself from the horror. But I wiped my mouth and staggered to my feet. This was what the artificer at the blood banks had warned against.

'What awaits on Harith is beyond horrific, and to face it, we need to be united, we need to take them by surprise. We need *all* our makra.'

Makra? A question I'd been too afraid to ask Ackerman came tumbling out of my mouth. 'Why won't you ask the Taemu to help? Why keep them captive and use them the way you're doing?'

'We tried. The first thing they did was try and rescue the others. They cannot see beyond themselves.'

'But what you're doing to them ...' It was sickening, repugnant, evil.

'The Taemu were savages,' he hissed. 'Did you know that before a battle, they would cut out the heart of a child and pass it around so each fighter could ingest a portion? They believed it made them invincible.' His mouth twisted. 'We brought a stop to it; we gave them civilisation. No. This is the only way we can fight the monsters on Harith.'

It still didn't make sense. His motives still rang false in my ears. 'There is time to prepare,' I said. 'Millennia, so why—'

'Ze'aan,' the emperor said, 'the only path to peace is through war. My ancestors have proved this—' He cocked his head, as if he was listening to something, and nodded. 'When the Chain re-links, the Jinn will regain their sentience. They will return to what they once were: entities a thousand times more powerful than what they are today, and this power will be shared by their mages.'

But that meant mages everywhere, not just in Kraelin, would become stronger. 'How does that benefit—'

He raised a finger to silence me. 'I wasn't finished.'

I lowered my head in apology.

'We have a god on our side,' he said, and paused to let the statement hang between us. 'And with his help, once the re-linking is complete, while the Jinn are still recovering, while they flounder and grapple with their re-discovered awareness, while they are at their *weakest* … ' He smiled. 'If I control the Jinn, I control who they *choose*.'

My breath caught, and I backed away from him.

'Good,' he said, 'you understand what that means.'

A future where only Kraelin had mages.

'These four other worlds were once inhabited,' the emperor said with a faraway look in his eyes. 'There are things abandoned on them – resources, artifacts of unspeakable complexity and grandeur … ' He smiled to himself again. 'Would you believe me if I told you they created an artifact that could make a mage immortal?'

Is that what it was all about? He wanted to become a mage

and use this impossible artifact to extend his life? Surely not, he wouldn't risk the lives of millions for—

I swallowed. He would. He fucking would.

'The Nathrians have already agreed to join us. The Fumeshis remain uncooperative – they have a fleet of makra, different from ours, but we will take them. The Raayans will be dealt with, along with the rest of the continent.'

The hubris was astounding. This man genuinely believed he could make decisions on behalf of the entire world. 'Why are you sharing this with me?' I asked.

'You understand what we use the blood banks for, you've seen our vectors, our makra, and now you know what is out there.' He flicked his wrist, gestured for me to approach.

He lifted my chin with one finger and forced me to look him in the eye. 'Ze'aan, you're young, but your krasna is larger, more powerful than many archmages'. You will make a fine pilot.'

I recoiled. Opened my mouth to speak, but the emperor was already walking away. *This* was why they'd agreed to help me defect? Not because my father was Kraelish, or because of what I'd done for them during the assault on Azraaya, but because I could pilot a makra?

I was back on my hands and knees. Shaking, struggling for air as my heart threatened to pulverise its way out of my ribcage. I was wrong about this place; wrong about everything. What had been simmering in Kraelin was far worse than anything I could've imagined.

And the Taemu they kept captive, the Taemu whose blood would be pumped into my veins for me to pilot their makra ...

No.

No.

I had hurt them enough. I would not be a part of this.
I had to get out.

Part Three

Chapter 29

BLADE

The Sisters

Two bespectacled men in clean, creaseless military uniforms sat behind a desk and watched Kavi approach. Behind them, across the railway platform, a train hissed and rumbled as railway porters and soldiers dragged and loaded it with large wooden crates – provisions, or weapons, Kavi guessed.

She saluted the men behind the desk. 'I'd like to volunteer.'

They glanced at each other, and the man on the right said, 'Where did you get that sword?'

'It was a gift.'

'We only want people with combat experience.'

'I know how to use it,' she said.

He scoffed. 'Sure you do, now get—'

'Officer cadets,' a man shouted, and the two men shot upright.

They snapped crisp salutes and said as one, 'Sir!'

Brigadier Thordali – clean-shaven, straight-backed, epaulettes on his shoulders – ignored them as he strode over to the desk. 'Is it just you, Captain?' he asked Kavi.

Kavi cleared her throat to mask her surprise and gave the brigadier a stoic nod.

'Assign this one to me,' he said.

'Sir, I don't think she has—'

The brigadier's wide, furious eyes shut the man up, and he bobbed his head and scribbled in a ledger.

'This way, Captain,' the Thordali said, gesturing for her to follow.

'The battalion doesn't exist anymore, I'm not a captain,' she said, hurrying to catch up to him.

'You are to me.' He grabbed a handrail and yanked himself into a buzzing train compartment. 'Lieutenant Mehta, this one's in your squad.'

'Yes, sir!' Mehta, an immaculately groomed man with a shiny gold wristwatch, saluted. He glanced at Kavi and failed to keep the confusion from his face.

Brigadier Thordali gave her a firm, one-pump handshake. 'I really am sorry that things didn't work out.'

'It's not your fault.'

The lieutenant's eye twitched at her casual tone, but Thordali gave her a respectful nod. 'Glad you could join us, Captain,' he said. 'The lieutenant will outfit you with armour and ensure you're fed. We leave in an hour.' And with that, he turned on his heel and strode into the adjoining compartment.

'This way,' Lieutenant Mehta said. 'You can sit with the sisters.'

She followed him down the aisle – past rows of face-to-face seats where soldiers played cards, read novels, sipped from flasks, smoked beedis, stared out the window, sharpened their weapons, arm-wrestled, snacked, or, like the sisters, napped.

'We will be travelling to the Ghotal cantonment where we will unload and bivouac for the night,' Mehta said. 'The train will return to Azraaya with our wounded while we march to Draghal – two days, if conditions are good.'

'March? Sir?'

'The Nathrians damaged the railway tracks before falling

back to Draghal, and they're still being fixed.' Mehta clapped his hands.

The sister with a longsword in her lap opened her eyes and glanced at Mehta. 'Oye, he's here.'

'Hah?' This sister's head was shaved clean.

All three sisters were tall and muscular, but the woman by the window was the biggest of the three, at least as large as Greema. 'Which one?' she said with her eyes still shut.

Longsword-sister looked Mehta up and down. 'The posh one.'

Mehta bristled. 'Now look—'

'And he's brought a Taemu with a sword,' she said, ignoring him.

The bald sister grunted. 'Hah?'

'She will be part of our squad,' Mehta said, and walked away with a disgusted look on his face.

The longsword-sister pointed to herself. 'Mozhi.' To the bald sister. 'Bola. And by the window, Hazeen. We're the Gandalkar sisters, everyone just calls us the sisters.'

'Kavithri, you can call me Kavi.'

'Oye, move, let her sit.' Mozhi nudged Bola, and the sour-faced woman grudgingly put her feet down.

Kavi sat facing Bola with Mozhi at her side and studied the three women.

'You're wondering if we're actually sisters,' Hazeen said, from over by the window.

The only thing these three had in common was their robust physique. 'Are you?'

'We're half-sisters. Our mothers were Raayan,' Hazeen said.

'Our father was Gashani,' Mozhi added.

'And that chootia can go die,' Bola finished, and all three of them turned and pretend spat: *thu, thu, thu.*

Kavi frowned. So they all had the same father? A Gashani? But they didn't have the tattoos on their mouths, and — she glanced at the weapons: longsword-shield, broadsword-shield, longsword-shield — none of them carried two swords like Greema. 'You don't use the Gashani school?' she said, and immediately regretted it.

Bola's face turned even more sour. Mozhi shuffled and glared out the window. Hazeen clenched her jaw till it made an audible crack.

Kavi winced. She'd clearly touched a nerve. 'I'm sorry—'

'The tribes won't acknowledge us,' Hazeen said.

'And they refuse to teach us,' Mozhi added.

'So fuck them, we fight our own way,' Bola finished with a petulant pout and the others nodded in agreement.

Is this how they always spoke? Like a three-headed—

'What about you?'

'What's your story?'

'Hah?'

Yes, it was. She'd need to get used to this. 'I'm a cadet at the Vagola.'

Three pairs of eyes simultaneously widened.

'Really?'

'They let a Taemu in?'

'Bhaenchod, don't lie.'

Kavi grinned despite herself. 'I'm not lying, look.' She showed them her Vagola badge.

The sisters took turns ogling at it. Hazeen frowned when it was her turn. 'Shouldn't you be with your novice?'

'Ah, yes, there is a story there,' Kavi said.

'We love stories,' Mozhi said, shuffling closer.

'And it's a long train ride,' Hazeen added.

'So come, talk,' Bola finished.

Why not? What did she have to lose? So, she told them about Azia, about the Blade-lock tournament, about how she lost her composure when she met the man responsible for the massacre at Ethuran; about the disqualification and how Azia was reassigned to another cadet. And by the time she was done the train was chugging rhythmically through the outskirts of the city.

'Harsh,' Mozhi said, patting her on the shoulder. 'So, this Azia doesn't even know or care that you're coming.'

'Well—'

'I know it, that feeling,' Mozhi continued with a faraway look in her eye. 'That feeling when you think you're becoming friends with someone, but they're just being polite, and you don't know that, so you drop everything to spend time with them, but all you are to them is an acquaintance? And that moment when you realise the truth? Heartbreaking, it will keep you cringing for years. I sympathise, I truly do.'

'That's not—' *Ah, fuck it.* 'Thank you.'

'Your meals,' Lieutenant Mehta said, dropping a stack of banana-leaf-wrapped packages into Bola's lap.

She hissed. Cast an angry glance at the lieutenant – who'd already moved on – before passing each of them a package.

'Let me share some wisdom with you, Kavi,' Bola said as she unwrapped the banana leaf and inspected the rice, dal, stir-fried bitter gourd, and deep-fried chicken inside.

'Must you?' Mozhi said, before mouthing, *Ignore her,* to Kavi.

Hazeen mumbled something unintelligible and began shovelling food into her mouth.

Bola looked Kavi dead in the eye, and said, 'If you want to know if someone is stupid or not, look at what they spend their money on.' She picked up a drumstick and bit into it. 'You see them spend thousands on a watch you could buy in the Lantern district for ten rayals, just because it gives them status?' She jabbed the half-eaten drumstick at Lieutenant Mehta's back. 'That there is one dumb motherfucker trying his best not to appear like a dumb motherfucker.'

'Bola!' Mozhi hissed.

'We told you not to use that word,' Hazeen said through a mouthful of food.

'I embrace the swearings from all cultures,' Bola said and gave Kavi an encouraging nod. 'I learned it from a Kraelishman. You should try, it feels good to say.'

'Maybe later.'

Mozhi grimaced. 'I just don't like it.'

'So close your ears,' Bola said.

Mozhi set her food aside and bared her teeth. 'You want to fight?'

Bola raised a placating hand. 'Let me eat first.'

The sisters didn't end up in a physical altercation. Instead, Bola pulled out a pack of playing cards and each of them took turns shuffling the deck – they offered Kavi an opportunity to shuffle out of courtesy, but she declined – before they settled in for a tense and prolonged game of Ganjifa.

Kavi played a couple of hands, lost most of her money, and sat out the rest. She fidgeted with the grip of her sword and let her eyes lose focus as she stared out the window. The train sped past paddy fields and tapioca farms and eventually plunged into pitch-black darkness punctuated by a drowsy cantonment or station where they stopped to pick up more reinforcements. She tried to sleep, but instead found her mind skipping and spinning, like a stone flung across a still pond, from one thought to the next.

If what Raeth's priests said was true, Bithun's soul would be somewhere in Hel, wandering as it shed its memories and scars to prepare for its rebirth. Would he find his wife and daughter? If they were still waiting, maybe, but they wouldn't know who he was. They could be right next to each other and not know. Gods, that was heartbreaking.

And what about Nabo? He'd asked her to *Come back alive,* but his eyes and face had said, *Come back to me.*

Or was she reading too much into things? Either way, what did they mean to each other now? Were they lovers? She swallowed. No, that didn't make sense, they were just friends who had done some incredibly intimate things together. Right? No, that wasn't it either. She tsked. Now was not the time to worry about this. There was a reason she was sitting in this train, listening to these women argue about a card game.

Was Azia still alive? Was he hurt? She didn't—

He's alive.

Her hands snapped tight around the hilt of the sword. *Are you sure? How do you know?*

I would know
if he died.

She swallowed. Glanced at the sisters who were busy squabbling over the legitimacy of the last hand.

Drisana, you remember what you said about the bond?

It pulsed a sensation that reminded Kavi of someone cocking an eyebrow.

Is there no other way?

To bond?

She started to nod but caught herself. *Yes.*

I cannot coexist
with another
mind.

Kavi bit the inside of her cheek.

You can,
but I can't.
What does that mean?
I will be
pushed out.
I have no
choice.
What do you mean 'You can, but I can't?' Drisana?
It hummed for her to be patient.
You will understand
when it is
time.

Chapter 30

BLADE

Khichdi

The train groaned to a halt with a loud screech and startled Kavi awake. She rubbed bleary eyes and flinched as the artificed globes on the ceiling flickered to life.

Lieutenant Mehta walked down the aisle, nudging soldiers awake and yelling at them to begin unloading. Outside, on a bustling platform, men and women in military uniform lugged trunks and pushed box-laden trolleys, all under a large yellow-and-black sign that read, *Ghotal Cantt.*

Bola wiped a trail of saliva off her chin and yawned. 'Wa's going on?'

'We're here,' Kavi said.

She joined the three sisters as they yanked-dragged four heavy trunks out from under the seats and carried them out onto the platform.

'Armour, shields, and ancillary weapons,' Hazeen explained, rapping her knuckles on a trunk.

A clerk assigned them a trolley and they loaded the four trunks onto it. Mehta, clutching a wooden clipboard and a pencil, arrived not long after.

'Sisters and Taemu,' Mehta said, striking something off his clipboard. 'Tent 352, lot 17.'

The Ghotal cantonment consisted of the train station, a

large, rectangular red-brick building, and a row of small blocky houses that Bola pointed out had been commandeered for the officers. 'One day, I will sleep in there,' she said.

Mozhi snorted. 'Keep dreaming,'

The rest of Ghotal was a sea of tents and lanterns and cooking fires. In the distance, a long column of yellow lights – lanterns of soldiers and the wounded returning from Draghal – bobbed and flickered as it snaked its way into the cantonment.

They parked the trolley outside a makeshift armoury, found their tent, and sat huddled around a lantern while Hazeen went to collect their dinner. Mozhi and Bola seemed content to wait in silence, while Kavi let her mind drift. Chotu should be asleep by now. Nabo would be cleaning his 'office' before the Caterpillar closed for the night. Hopefully his clients hadn't given him too much trouble. And Azia ... she sighed as Hazeen returned with four bananas, four steel spoons, and a small pot of khichdi.

'No achar?' Bola asked, peering inside the pot, while Hazeen passed Kavi a spoon and a banana.

'You think this is a hotel?' Mozhi said, reaching for her spoon.

'I told you we should bring our own,' Bola muttered.

The lantern was replaced by the pot of mashed rice and lentils, and Kavi and the sisters sat knee-to-knee around and ate straight out of the pot.

'So, Kavi,' Mozhi said between mouthfuls, 'how're you feeling?'

'About?'

'Heading into your first battle.'

Kavi shook her head, chewed and swallowed. 'It's not my first.'

The sisters paused, exchanged glances, and stared at her.

'What?'

'You've been in battle before?' Mozhi asked.

She told them about the Siphon, about leading her Taemu against the Kraelish and their stand at the chokepoint.

'You have more experience than our bloody lieutenant,' Mozhi said.

'They should let you lead a squad,' Hazeen added.

'Better than that donkey, Mehta.'

Kavi chuckled. 'What about you three?'

'We were all stationed at Dyarabad during the Kraelish attack,' Mozhi said. 'Went there straight after we graduated from the military academy – none of us have fought in a real battle.'

Kavi stifled a burp, set her spoon aside, and peeled her banana. 'So, how're you feeling?

'We've trained for years,' Mozhi said, 'we know how to fight.'

'But?' Kavi said, reading the uncertainty on Mozhi's face.

'It's—'

'Nerves,' Hazeen said and gently squeezed her sister's shoulder. 'It's just nerves.'

Bola grunted. 'It's what happens when you think too much.' She licked her spoon clean and pointed it at Mozhi. 'You always have this problem.'

Mozhi tsked and made a face. 'Shaddup, I don't want to hear it from *you*.'

'Me? Was I the one who stayed in bed and cried and sulked for' – she shoved three fingers in Mozhi's face – '*three* days after that arsehole cheated on her? *Oh! I'm so sad. Oh! my love has betrayed—*'

Mozhi lunged at Bola and wrestled her to the ground.

'Not my banana, you wretch!' Bola yelled, curling into a shell around her banana while Mozhi tussled with her to get to the fruit.

Kavi glanced at Hazeen, who was picking her teeth and watching her sisters. 'They're always like this?' she asked.

Hazeen grinned. 'You'll get used to it.'

They finally agreed to a temporary truce when Bola promised to never bring up that 'cheating bastard' again, and it wasn't long before she was sharing more unsolicited nuggets of wisdom with Kavi, gems like:

'Listen, Kavi, when you start naming places and buildings and what-not after politicos who are still alive, who are *still* in power, then there is something deeply wrong with your country.'

Kavi had responded with, 'Naming anything after a politico is a chootia idea anyway.' The notion that something could be named after Grishan made her skin crawl.

Bola guffawed, reached over and slapped her on the shoulder. 'I like you, I will share more wisdom.'

'That's okay—'

'Listen to this.' She cleared her throat. 'Any philosophy derived from religion is *in-her-ently* flawed and can get cunted straight into the sun.'

'Meshira have mercy, where did you hear that?' Hazeen muttered.

Mozhi groaned. 'How is that even relevant – stop using words that you don't know how to use.'

'Shaddup, I speak how I want—'

The ground shuddered with the *dhoom!* of an explosion and Kavi and the sisters scrambled out of the tent.

Men and women sprinted past, screams and cries filled the air. 'What's going on?' Hazeen shouted at a man who was directing soldiers toward the station.

'Nathrian attack,' he shouted back. 'They're trying to get to the station and the train.'

'The train is still here?' Hazeen said.

'Wounded are still boarding – get to the armoury, now.'

Kavi grabbed her sword and joined the sisters as they rushed to the makeshift armoury. Hazeen led them straight to the trolley with their trunks. She hurled them onto the ground, unclasped them, and flung open the lids.

'I thought they were being held at Draghal,' Mozhi said as she snapped and buckled her greaves.

Hazeen just shook her head. 'Ask questions later.'

Kavi rummaged through the trunks until she found a set of armour that would fit her. *Drisana, is he okay?*

He is alive.

Good. She gritted her teeth and steadied her breath as the familiar rush of adrenaline that preceded a battle coursed through her body. Her heart thumped against her ribcage, her fingertips tingled, her muscles yearned for a release.

When she was done adjusting her armour, she beckoned Mozhi – who was watching her with wide, anxious eyes – closer. She tugged on the straps of Mozhi's armour, tested the clasps, and ensured that it was secure. 'Stay close to me, okay?' Kavi said, under her breath.

Mozhi nodded.

'Let's go,' Hazeen said, and tossed Kavi a shield.

They ran in single file; followed the directions officers yelled at them until they arrived at an area several hundred feet east of the station where a pitched battle was underway.

A full moon lit up the battlefield and gave the soldiers clashing and dying on it an unnervingly spectral appearance. Spikes of emerald-green maayin whizzed overhead in both directions. Injured and wounded were dragged or stretchered away. Screams, commands, and the discharge of artificed weapons made it hard to hear—

'Join the second rank,' an officer yelled in their faces and shoved them along. 'Second rank!'

'Yes, sir!' Bola shouted back, then turned to Kavi. 'Where the fuck is the second rank?'

'Behind the frontlines – there.' Kavi pointed to a row of soldiers slowly trudging forward with shields raised.

Kavi used her shield to shove her way into the second rank. Soldiers on both sides gave way as the sisters joined her – Bola and Mozhi on flanks, Hazeen on Mozhi's right.

'Steady,' Kavi said as Mozhi stumbled over a severed leg. 'Don't lose your footing.'

'Yes, ma'am,' Mozhi said, eyes locked on the fast-approaching frontline and the bloody, sharp-edged chaos in it.

Bola glanced at the severed leg and snorted. 'Don't lose your footing, nice one.'

Hazeen hissed at her. 'Not now, Bola.'

'Halt!' The cry went up at the other end of the line and was repeated until everyone came to a stop.

'Now what?' Bola said.

Kavi glanced at her. Was the woman grinning? No, just the shadows and moonlight. 'Now, we wait,' she said.

'Wait for wha—'

'Lock shields!' Kavi screamed as the Nathrians smashed through the frontline, stabbed and stomped and tore their way into the second rank.

Mozhi and Bola slammed the sides of their shields into Kavi's.

'Hold!' Someone shouted over and over again.

She'd fought this way before at the Siphon, side by side with the other cadets who'd all fallen until Ze'aan—

She clenched her jaw. *This is not the Siphon. Ze'aan isn't here.* It would be different this time. The sisters would live, she would make sure of it. And then she would find her warlock, and bring him home to his father, just as she'd promised.

'Hold!'

She tightened her grip on her sword, dug her heels in – 'Aadhier Taemu,' she whispered – and added her voice to a roar that crescendoed as the lines met with a thundering crash.

Chapter 31
BLADE

To Lathun

'Next,' the healer said, and made an exhausted gesture for Kavi to step up.

'I'm fine, just scratches,' she said, and urged Bola forward instead.

The healer shrugged and turned to Bola. 'Where are you hurt?'

Mehta's squad had been instructed to gather outside the medical tents for treatment followed by debriefing from the esteemed lieutenant himself.

'She's pretending,' Mozhi said, shaking her head at Bola, who was showing the healer a mole on her shoulder.

'Leave her.' Hazeen smiled. 'She fought well last night, and so did you.'

Mozhi's anxiety had vanished when the lines collided. Her sword had been a blur, whipping out to slice and plunge into necks and faces with sharp, fluid movements. Bola, on Kavi's other flank, had fought with unrefined brute force. Her strikes cracked helmets. Shattered faces and bones as she bludgeoned the Nathrians until they finally retreated.

Not once had Kavi been threatened on the flanks. If anything, she'd struggled to keep up with the relentless, frenetic rhythm the sisters had fought with. *Protect them*? She scoffed. They'd protected her.

'Are you sure you don't need a healer?' Mozhi said, studying the gash on Kavi's cheek. A Nathrian spear had sliced it open. 'That looks painful.'

'I saw a surgeon earlier.' Snuck into the tent and used his antiseptic on all her cuts and wounds. 'Also, I don't want to trouble the healers.' She didn't want them to discover she was a mage. She'd considered healing herself – the healers had brought along countervails; cartloads of rats and other poor creatures – but had decided against it. Easier to explain away some borrowed antiseptic than her impossible ability if they caught her in the act.

She sighed and raised a hand to shield her face from the sun. In the adjacent tent, bodies of the Raayan dead had been arranged in neat rows, their faces covered with torn pieces of cloth, and Brigadier Thordali – with an attendant at his side – walked down the rows, stopped at the foot of each body, and nodded as his attendant read something from a clipboard.

Some of the bodies, Kavi knew, would be missing ears. The Nathrians took them as trophies.

'Oh, here comes Mehta,' Mozhi said and cocked her head at the lieutenant.

Lieutenant Mehta trudged up to his squad, steel whistle in his mouth, sweat beading on his forehead and ruining his otherwise immaculate appearance. He blew into the whistle – a shrill note that forced the squad to snap to attention – before spitting it out and letting it dangle from the cord around his neck. 'Line up!'

Bola thanked the bemused healer and rushed back to Kavi's side.

'The Nathrian objective,' Mehta said, 'was to damage either the tracks leading back to Azraaya or the train itself. Thanks to your efforts and sacrifices, they failed.' He clasped his arms behind his back and stuck his chest out. 'But Draghal is lost. For the last two days, our brothers and sisters have fought a tactical withdrawal – they have been chased and in turn have harangued the enemy all the way to the fortress at Lathun. They are out of supplies, exhausted, and at the end of their tether.'

'Who uses words like harangued and tether?' Bola mumbled and was instantly shushed by Mozhi.

The lieutenant either didn't hear or chose to ignore the sisters. 'As per the last scouting report, the Nathrians have yet to attack the fortress – they might be waiting for the cowards from last night to rejoin their ranks. Rest up and eat while you can, we march for Lathun in two hours.'

*

The glare of the rising sun forced Kavi to squint as plumes of smoke rose from within the walls of a fortress that squatted on a small hill.

'Is that Lathun?' Kavi asked.

Bola nodded. 'It is.'

They had marched through the night, alongside a steady column of wounded soldiers – lying on bullock carts or being stretched by medical staff – headed in the opposite direction, back to Ghotal. It had been a constant reminder of what awaited them at Lathun.

Two shrill bursts from Mehta's whistle and the squad switched from a fast walk into a jog. The early morning air, pungent with smoke and the burnt-milk stench of artificed machinery, stung Kavi's nostrils as she jogged with the rest of the squad. There was still dew on the patchy grass that littered the plain leading up to Lathun, and Mehta shouted a warning to 'watch your step'.

Troops that had arrived earlier had set up palisades on both sides of the hill, presumably to keep the Nathrians from surrounding or flanking the fort, and the *dhoom-dhoom-dhoom* of artificed weapons, the screams and shouts in the distance, and the sense of urgency the lieutenant was attempting to inject into the squad could only mean one thing. The Nathrians had attacked the fortress.

Drisana, is he here?

The sword pulsed a confirmation, and the breath caught in Kavi's throat.

Mehta led the squad to the palisades and yelled garbled encouragement that was lost in the cacophony of panting, stomping boots, and the pounding of blood in her ears.

A large chunk of the reinforcements split away and made a beeline for the partially open gate at the back of the fortress, through which came columns of stretchered and injured soldiers all headed for the train.

She tensed. Breathed through a tightness in her ribcage.

Is he with them? Drisana, where is he?

She sensed the sword pause, and a claustrophobic thought, alien and at the same time familiar, shoved its way into the back of her head. She flinched, stumbled, and found her footing again as a tunnel opened up in her mind; a tunnel that blocked out all the noise and smells and violence and led her straight to—

Azia, he was inside the fort. By the east wall. He was not moving.

Is he hurt?

He is alive.

If you get closer,
I can initiate
the bond.

No. Not if it meant she would lose Drisana. She would find a way to save him without needing the bond. Kavi gritted her teeth. Glanced at the sisters – *fuck it* – and broke away from Mehta's squad.

'Kavi!' one of the sisters yelled, but she ignored them and burst into a sprint. It felt good to have them on her side; she liked being a part of their little group. But she had to do this alone.

Her knees and ankles strained under the weight of her armour as she cut across the plain and joined the back of a squad rushing to enter Lathun. A soldier reeking of vomit glanced her way, but his empty eyes looked right through her.

She slowed to a jog, lowered her head, panted, coughed, caught her breath, and as soon as she set foot inside the fort turned on her heels and sprinted again, past row after row of wooden barricades where soldiers screamed at her to 'Stop!'.

She ignored them and barrelled down a pothole-ridden street, into the burnt ruins of a home, and back out onto another street where she ran face-first into a large group of panicked Raayan soldiers heading in the opposite direction. Away from where she was headed. Away from Azia.

She grabbed a woman's arm as she rushed past. 'What's going on? Hey, what's—'

The woman snatched her arm away and shouted, 'Nathrians, run!'

Kavi stood stock-still as they streamed past her, their armour battered and stained black, cuts and gashes on their faces and necks, hands bereft of weapons – discarded, she assumed, in the panic to escape.

She tried to swallow, but her mouth had gone dry. She reached for her sword, fumbled, and tried again.

He's alive, Drisana whispered. **Go**.

Her hands shook as she drew her sword. Her breath came in

short, sharp gasps as she crossed the street, and stepped into a dilapidated alleyway.

The sun winked out of existence. The air grew damp, turgid with the stench of vegetable refuse and stale urine. How many Nathrians was she up against?

Enough to send an entire squad running.

The footsteps of the enemy got closer, their shouts louder. There was no time to find a way around them. There was no … Kavi stared.

Jutting out of the bricks in the wall of the alleyway was a sword.

You have no right to learn it, Vaisha hissed in her ear.

Kavi yanked the shortsword out of the wall.

You are not empty, Greema said, voice heavy with disappointment.

The sword's grip was damp with blood and sweat, its blade chipped and cracked, but it would do.

When you go to that place you go to, you're fast — faster than all of them, Ze'aan whispered.

Kavi's mouth twisted and she shoved Ze'ann's dispassionate voice out of her head. All she had to do was be *empty*, right? She could do that; she could clear her thoughts and allow her instincts to take over.

She clenched her toes.

Steadied her breath.

And searched for its rhythm.

Her jaw went slack, and a trail of saliva dribbled down the corner of her mouth. The children in the Chutti-Mohan beggar crew used to make fun of her for this. Every time the boss taught her new sums and tested her, she'd have to concentrate so hard that she'd forget what her face was doing. *Brainless oaf,* they called her.

'No thought, no form,' she muttered. 'No thought, no form.' All that mattered were the words she repeated to herself. The sounds they made inside her head, the shapes her lips made and the way her tongue moved as she said them.

The Nathrians came barrelling into the alleyway, whooping and yelling with the exhilaration of a battle already won, hungry for the wounded prey they chased.

No thought. No form.

Her body moved of its own accord, her heels ground themselves into the dirt, and her arms arranged the swords into the third stance:

Shortsword overhead, longsword pointed at her opponents.

Chapter 32
BLADE

Swordmaster

The first Nathrian she killed stared at her with wide, confused eyes as his lifeblood seeped through the severed carotid in his neck. The next attempted a half-hearted sword-strike and died gurgling on her own blood.

Their bloodlust was spent, their minds were on the spoils, and Kavi had found the emptiness she sought.

She slashed with her long sword, stabbed with the short. She *saw* without moving her eyes. In the emptiness, unhindered by emotion and thought, she found in each heartbeat the most rational movement.

She switched stances; threw out both arms and used the narrow alleyway to herd them in and force them to come at her one at a time.

No thought, no form.

She infected them with doubt, with fear.

Every strike had intent. Every strike was powerful. And every strike resulted in another Nathrian falling; sometimes in silence, sometimes screaming and clutching a fatal wound.

Never stop moving, Greema said. *You stop, you die.*

Yes, ma'am.

She didn't wait for them. She instigated. She controlled the rhythm.

She slammed Drisana into an armpit. Tried to pull it back out, but it wouldn't budge. *Never get attached to your weapon. Keep an open mind and adapt.*

Kavi snarled and released the hilt. Shoved the man back into his colleagues who flailed and tumbled to the ground. More Nathrians came bounding at her.

She kicked her heels and dodged away. Extended an open palm to her sword – the berserker had done it at the choke-point, so why couldn't she? – and called to it. *Drisana.*

It hummed with delight and – *shing!* – flew out of the tangle of limbs, hilt-first at Kavi.

She waited until the last second, and as it zoomed past, snapped her fingers around the hilt and used its momentum to drag her out of the path of a flung spear.

She hissed. That had been a mistake. It left her open to an attack from the flanks.

A pair of soldiers lunged. At the same time, a man shouted something that made the rest of the Nathrians collectively duck.

A dissonant shriek of panic threatened to obliterate Kavi's emptiness as – over the heads of the genuflecting Nathrians – an artificed musket was levelled at her head.

There was nowhere to run. She was trapped. She was—

She exhaled, let the panic ooze out of her skin.

No thought, no form.

She ignored the soldiers rushing her from the sides, narrowed her focus to the musket, to the muzzle, the barrel, to just the finger on the trigger.

Not yet.

It twitched.

Not yet.

It curled.

Not yet.

And pulled.

She dropped to her knees. Swung Drisana down at the empty space in front of her head.

Dhoom – the sword thrummed; a spike of agony shot up her quivering wrist – *kling! Splat-splat.*

The soldiers on either side of Kavi dropped as halves of the slug exploded through their neck and head.

Kavi stood. Flipped the shortsword into the air in front of her. Took a step back, gritted her teeth, forced every ounce of strength she could summon into her legs, and hammered the sole of her boot into the pommel of the sword.

It shot out, tip first, its shape a silver blur, and buried itself in the musketeer's throat with a wet *squelch.*

He gaped at her as blood squirted from the wound and he fell to his knees, his face frozen in a rictus of pain and surprise.

The Nathrians gasped, muttered, stepped back.

Once panic and confusion sets in, you've won.

From somewhere behind her, three familiar voices cut through the hushed awe:

'Meshira have mercy.'

'A swordmaster.'

'How?'

Kavi glanced at the astonished sisters who stood at the entrance to the alleyway, weapons lowered, staring at her.

I don't have time for this.

She bent, wrenched a sword out of a dead soldier's hands, and advanced on the Nathrians.

'Move,' she said, her voice a hoarse whisper, but with enough menace in it to force a dozen soldiers to retreat.

'Hold!' An order went up from behind the terrified Nathrians. And again: 'Hold, or you will be tried as deserters!'

Kavi scowled. Spat.

The threat had its effect on the soldiers. They were more cautious now. Less likely to cut and run.

But it made no difference. She wiped the drool off her chin with the back of her hand. Azia was close. He was still alive.

She sucked in a lungful of air, whispered, 'Aadhier Taemu', and charged.

She never reached the Nathrians, because the sisters got to them first.

Three howling, roaring, metal-clad boulders hurtled past her and crashed into the enemy soldiers. Weapons flashed, limbs were severed, bodies were crushed underfoot as Hazeen, Mozhi, and Bola smashed their way through and out of the alleyway.

Kavi dashed past the carnage they left in their wake.

She slowed. Caught Mozhi's eye.

An understanding passed between them, and Mozhi said, 'Go. We'll hold them.'

Thank you. Kavi nodded and burst into a sprint. Past a row of charred, wooden barricades, down a ruined street – *east*, she had to go east – took a left, and arrived at the gates to a large parade ground.

The field was littered with bodies. Raayans in khaki military uniform, mostly, but civilians too. Clusters of Nathrians stood around and smoked and chatted, while at the far end a row of men and women – Raayan warlocks, based on their robes – knelt with their hands bound behind their backs. A Nathrian walked up to the first woman in the line, pressed an artificed pistol into the back of her head, and *dhoom!* pulled the trigger.

Her head burst into a red mist of gore that hovered and dissipated as the body fell.

Kavi swallowed her nausea; ignored the wave of dizziness that slammed into the back of her skull. She stumbled onto the field, searched the row of warlocks awaiting their execution, and found him.

He was at the end of the line, kneeling in the dirt. Shoulders slumped, hands bound, shivering despite the heat as he stared at the ground.

A growled 'What the fuck?' snapped Kavi's head around. A mailed fist, tipped with something sharp, hammered into the side of her neck, clipped her jaw, and sent her sprawling to the ground.

Nathians, standing on both sides of the gate, stubbed out their beedis and hefted their weapons.

Careless. How could she have been so careless? She flexed her jaw – winced as daggers of pain shot up her temples – and tried to prop herself up on her elbows.

Rough hands grabbed her by the back of her neck. Her shoulders. Her arms.

They kicked and stomped on her wrists till she released her swords. They ripped her helmet off, and the same mailed fist cracked into the back of her exposed head. Her forehead collided with the ground. Her vision swam as bright spots exploded and darkness collected on the edges. Warm blood trickled down both sides of her ears. She struggled to get free – he was just there, so close – and gasped as the sharp end of a sword plunged into her back, between the gaps in her armour.

'Stop squirming,' a voice said, and the sword was withdrawn.

Someone grabbed her by the hair and pulled her head back. She moaned as the agony in her back spread.

'A Taemu! Lucky-lucky,' a man said. And one at a time – as her back arched and spasms wracked her body, as her jaw and mouth quivered, as tears came spilling out of her eyes and searing agony burrowed into both sides of her head – he sliced her ears off.

The Nathrians laughed and added her ears to a long string filled with more they'd taken from other people.

She could still sense him, there across the field. Scared. Alone. *I'm coming, Azia.* And half-blind with pain, she dragged herself in his direction.

'Stupid bitch doesn't know when she's dead,' a muffled voice said through the keening in her head.

They kicked her.

She twisted. Grunted. Continued to crawl to her warlock.

'Deshpande, give me the pistol,' a gruff voice said. 'Let's see how much she can take.'

Dhoom!

The slug tore through her left foot and ankle and turned it into bloody mush. She choked on a sob, clenched her fists as the pain threatened to obliterate her awareness—

'Kavi!'

She lifted her head. Through a blur of pain and tears and rapidly fading vision, Azia struggled against his bonds, shuffled forward on his knees, and screamed, tears running down his scarred face. 'Kavi!'

He was the last warlock alive. The executioner raised his pistol, aimed.

She reached one trembling hand out to him. *I'm sorry, Drisana. I tried to do this on my own, I tried – I'm sorry, I can't let him die.*

Do it.

Bond us.

The pain vanished. The keening in her ears subsided. The sky caught fire. The corpses on the field sank into the ground and were replaced by shattered chunks of metal that spanned from horizon to horizon.

Kavi stood, whole, uninjured, and stared. She was no longer

in Lathun. Or Raaya, or anywhere in her world. Her consciousness had been wrenched out of its battered body and transported to this ... *place.*

Nothing moved, or breathed, the air was still and odourless, and beneath her feet – she blinked, knelt and ran her fingers across its worn and chipped surface – was the gigantic neck of a makra.

Gayathri, Drisana's makra. She was in a memory?

Chapter 33

BLADE

The Bond

It lay on its back with its head torn open – its wolf-like jaws a twisted mess. Its chest was battered and broken, an arm was missing, and at the other end, hovering over its massive feet, was an emerald-green orb the size of a small mountain.

A soft rustle, a gentle touch on her shoulder, and Kavi – mouth dry, eyes wide – turned and gazed up at Drisana.

At her mismatched eyes – one with a blood-red iris, the other pitch-black. At her dark brown skin, so like Kavi's own; at the strange clothes she wore – a piece of dull, blue cloth that acted as both shirt and trousers. She was tall. Taller than any Taemu Kavi had ever seen.

'Kavithri,' Drisana said, in a voice that was simultaneously powerful and gentle.

Kavi reached out and touched the back of Drisana's hand. 'You're real?'

She smiled. 'In this place? Yes.'

Her words were strange, her language was alien, but nevertheless, Kavi understood. 'Where is *this place*? Another memory?'

'Walk with me,' Drisana said, stepping onto the makra's chest. 'This is not a memory. We are in the Jinn's realm – inside a fragment of the Chain that our engineers preserved within your sword.' She turned and smiled at Kavi. 'This is my home.'

The hair on the back of Kavi's neck stood as she fell into step beside Drisana. 'How— why couldn't we talk like this earlier?'

'You can only come here once.'

Kavi licked her lips. Chose to ignore the ramifications of that statement. 'You must be lonely here.'

'Not since I found you,' Drisana said, softly. 'There is never a quiet moment in your head.'

'Sorry.'

Drisana waved it off.

'I'm sorry for leaving you,' Kavi said.

'Don't be, I would be disappointed if you chose otherwise.'

Kavi gestured to the motionless carnage they were surrounded by. 'How long ago was this?'

'I'm not sure. Feels like yesterday to me.' She paused. 'Time works differently here, it's why I'm still alive.'

Kavi had so many questions, but she sensed they were running out of time. 'Where are we going?'

Drisana pointed a long, slender finger at the massive green orb.

'Is that …' It was smaller, but it resembled a Jinn she'd seen in the abyss. 'Harith?'

'No,' Drisana said with a chuckle. 'That, Kavi, is your warlock's krasna.'

Kavi's jaw dropped. She stared – knees locked, eyes bulging – at the orb that hung over them. A warlock's power was measured by the size of their krasna, by the pool of maayin at their disposal. When they opened themselves to Harith and went into their cast, they drew from this pool, channelled the maayin into existence to shape and control. Until now, Ze'aan's had been the largest krasna she'd ever encountered. But Ze'ann's krasna was a grain of sand compared to this one. 'That's impossible.'

'Yes, which is why he can't draw it out. It would kill him.' Drisana stopped. Waited for Kavi to find her feet again and catch up. 'But, after you bond with him, you will pay his price, become his countervail, and he will draw it out into your world.'

Kavi's lips tightened. 'You can see the future?'

'No.' Drisana frowned. 'But sometimes, the past, present, and future, they feel like the same thing. Feel like they're happening at the same time. You understand?'

'Not really – you said he would save me.'

'He will.' There wasn't a shred of doubt in her voice.

'This feels like *I'm* saving *him*,' Kavi said as they hopped onto the makra's right leg.

'You are.'

'But—'

'He will have his chance.'

Kavi nodded. 'You said there was one more who would save me. Who did you mean?'

Drisana smiled again, but this time, there was sadness in her unfathomable eyes.

'It's not time?' Kavi asked.

'No.' Her melancholy now infected her voice. 'Submerged truths only surface when it is time.'

Kavi sighed. Cocked her head at the enormous orb of maayin. 'How are we able to see his krasna?'

'This fragment we are inside once belonged to a link in the Chain that connected Raktha to Harith – that linked our Jinn, what this world calls the Biomancers' Jinn, to your warlock's Jinn.' She drew a circle in the air, pausing at even intervals as she positioned the Jinn and their worlds within the Chain. 'Harith, Raktha, Nilasi, Zubhra, Kolacin. And among them, it was the connection – the *bond*, between Harith and Raktha that was the strongest. The Gates between the two worlds exhibited the least resistance; the maayin from the two Jinn were symbiotic. None of the others had the relationship that Rakhta and Harith did.

'Which was why, when the contamination spread, when Raeth corrupted Harith's maayin, it spread to Raktha first. We were the first to fall.' She gestured to the desolation that surrounded them. 'All the Transplants – artifacts like your sword – were created using fragments from the same link in the Chain that once connected Raktha to Harith, and it is through these links, through the Transplants and the consciousness that resides within them, through someone – *something* – like me, that Blades and warlocks, those chosen by Harith and Raktha, can be *bonded.*'

Kavi frowned. 'So the bonded Blades and warlocks from before the Retreat – you know what the Retreat is, right?'

Drisana smiled.

Of course she did. 'So those Blades, if they were chosen by Raktha, they had to be …'

'Biomancers, or Rakthan hybrids, like you.'

Kavi's mouth went dry. But that meant …

'Taemu, yes. Most of them were Taemu.'

Her jaw dropped. If that was true, then that meant that the Taemu, who everyone believed were 'discovered', uprooted, and brought to the Raayan subcontinent *after* the Retreat, had once had a presence in pre-Retreat Kraelin. The Taemu had been the Empire's Blades. Why did no one know about this? 'Why—'

A shudder ran through the makra beneath her feet, and the world – the sky, the flames that roiled in its clouds, the carnage that stretched into the horizon – flickered.

'We don't have much time,' Drisana said. 'It won't let you stay here for much longer.'

'What won't?'

'The Chain.'

Kavi cocked her head. Checked over her shoulder. 'It's alive?'

'In its own way, yes.'

They stopped. The orb, Azia's krasna, hovered directly overhead and sent shivers down Kavi's spine.

Drisana reached out, took Kavi's hand, and squeezed. 'This is goodbye, Kavithri.'

Kavi fumbled for words. There were so many questions she still wanted to ask. 'Why did you pick me?' She whispered.

Drisana smiled. 'Because you remind me of myself.'

Kavi's lips trembled, and she took a slow, shuddering breath. 'Thank you, for everything.'

A shiver ran through the enormous krasna, and it slowly began to fall.

Drisana squeezed Kavi's hand again and held it up so that her fingers were within touching distance of the shimmering maayin. 'Find him, sister.'

'I—' Her fingertips grazed the surface of Azia's krasna, and the world, once again, vanished into nothing.

She floundered in the abyss, fought to orient herself, searched for something to cling onto.

Find him, Drisana's voice whispered.

She sensed a pressure in the corner of her mind. A roiling, seething bundle of emotion that was not hers. She reached for it, and instead of slipping through her grasp, it reached out to her.

Kavi?

I'm here, Azia.

Kavi, I'm scared.

There's nothing to be scared of.

What is happening? What is this place? I can't see. I — I can't feel anything.

Will you trust me?

There was a pause. Then, *You came for me? All the way to Lathun?*

I made a promise.

I trust you, Kavi.

Then let me in.

Hearts thundered, blood pounded, and with a sensation like fingers interlocking, he did.

Tidal waves of emotion and memory crashed down on her. She spluttered, choked, but did not drown.

They clung to each other as all his insecurities and fear, his courage, his dreams, seeped into her; and all her rage and grief, her drive and bone-headed refusal to give up, rushed into him.

She watched him struggle for air as he crawled in the mines, as he mourned his amma and appa. She was there when his adoptive parents wrapped him up in blankets and brought him to Azraaya. She screamed with him when Harith tore its way through his body. She stood with him as the older children in the city stripped him naked so they could check if the scar went all the way down his body. He shook, quietly wept as they lifted his hands to *look*.

And she knew that he too was in her memories. Watching her mother's death. Walking past the mangled bodies in Ethuran. Huddled in a corner of the beggar cart as they took her away after her father sold her for a handful of rayals.

She clung to him even tighter. What if she scared him again? What if he rejected her? Refused to bond with her?

Kavi, his voice said, *stop fighting it.*

I— She was fighting it? Yes, she was, not him.

You don't have to do this alone. It's okay, I understand now.

You do?

He didn't need to answer; she sensed his acceptance. All her flaws, her mistakes, he took it all, and it changed nothing. He trusted her, and he was asking her to do the same. He was asking her to complete the bond.

She stopped resisting. Lowered barriers she didn't even know she'd erected. And opened herself to him, made herself utterly vulnerable.

Threads of green, Harithian maayin slithered and wound themselves around her and Azia. Binding them tighter, tighter, and tighter—

—until the air exploded outward with a loud *whumph!* and she was back writhing on the ground in Lathun.

Chapter 34
BLADE

Scatter

Around her, the Nathrians who'd been blown off their feet slowly stood, dusted themselves off and, bewildered, stared at the source of the explosion.

Kavi unwound her mutilated body and gazed across the field.

Azia, still on his knees, but with particles of shimmering green suspended in the air around him, stared right back at her.

'Do it,' she said.

There's so many, he said in her head, from a place once inhabited by Drisana.

She gritted her teeth and shoved herself to her knees. Ze'ann's words, once said to her among the dead and dying cadets of the Siphon, whittled their way into her head: *They wouldn't have thought twice about saving you.* It chafed, but it was true.

They were going to execute you, she said.

A pause. He agreed. *But I will hurt you,* he said.

You know what I can do. It will not kill me.

Azia stood. Stumbled, regained his balance, and with hands still bound behind his back, began limping in her direction. He ignored the Nathrians around him. He kept his eyes on her. Even when they closed in, even when they raised their weapons.

She sensed him reach for his krasna, felt him hesitate – *I'll be fine,* she said.

They both knew that was a lie, but he nodded and wrenched his maayin into existence.

She had a moment to prepare. She lunged at a distracted Nathrian, tackled him to the ground, and—

The weight hit her first. Forced her jaws shut with enough force to shatter teeth. Her body locked itself in place. Pressure burst in her chest and spread outward, turned her flesh into stone, her bones into iron, made it hard to breathe, to move. Then came the fire, white-hot and searing – it roared through her blood as she convulsed and her heart pounded and threatened to bludgeon its way out of her chest.

Another louder, more concussive explosion with Azia in the epicentre *boomed!* through the parade ground.

Kavi called for Nilasi, and the blue threads of maayin sprouted across her entire body. They writhed, vibrated, and waited for her command.

Take.

They latched onto the Nathrian under her, and *took.*

He screamed.

She stared into his wide, panicked eyes, unlocked her jaw, and screamed back as even as she healed, the skin on her face and body hissed and burned itself away as Azia used her as a countervail.

At the same time, the skin on the spasming Nathrian's face, on his body, melted away as her maayin reshaped it for her. His ears withered away; hers grew back. His foot disintegrated; hers reformed.

Kavi panted, gagged as the stench of burnt skin and hair filled her nostrils and hit the back of her throat. She grunted as she tried to lift her head. So this was the warlock's countervail: the incredible, paralysing weight, the fire in her blood and veins; she'd experienced this once before, when she'd been strapped into the artifice used for the first test in Bochan. But this was so much worse.

I'm sorry, Azia said, *I took too much.* And before she could respond, he cut his krasna in half.

The pressure on Kavi eased, the fire in her body diminished. She could move her head, but the rest of her body remained locked in place and her skin continued to burn away.

There are three women somewhere behind me, she said. *Don't hurt them.*

I won't.

Around her, the Nathrians stood with mouths open, gawking as emerald-green petals coalesced out of nothing and hovered in the air. They spanned the entire field, shimmered in the sunlight, and gently floated down between the astounded men and women.

Kavi felt more than heard the word Azia whispered. The simple command he gave his maayin.

Scatter.

The petals froze in mid-air. Kavi held her breath, the Nathrians muttered and – *whoosh!* – the petals burst across the field and through the shocked soldiers.

They swirled and spun through bodies and limbs. Through screaming mouths and bulging eyes. The petals hissed and lost substance as Nathrian after Nathrian fell, clutching their wounds.

And through this storm, this whirlwind of death, Azia limped towards her. Head bowed, shoulders trembling. He was aware of every single petal of maayin. Aware of everyone they touched. He didn't need to look. He didn't *want* to look. He just knew.

When the petals fizzed away to nothing and the survivors struggled to their feet, he clenched his jaw, squeezed his eyes shut, took a harsh, ragged breath, and gave his maayin another command.

Return.

Gasps punctuated the screams and moans as the last Nathrians fell, choking on their own blood, as Azia pulled from their lungs the particles of maayin he'd let them breathe. On their chests, dark-red pinpricks grew like ink blots, merging with each other into one large, wet stain.

He dismissed his krasna, sent it back to the Jinn's realm, and Kavi sighed with relief as the pain lifted and Nilasi healed the last of her damage.

Azia was crying – tears on his cheeks, snot under his nose; great coughing sobs that made his chest jump. 'So many,' he said aloud. 'I killed so many, Kavi.'

She groaned and forced herself upright. *Don't look,* she said inside his head. And out loud. 'They would have killed us.'

He nodded. Kept on limping to her.

They were within touching distance when his knees gave out, his eyes rolled up into his head, and he passed out.

Kavi rushed to him. Caught him before he hit the ground. He was okay, she could sense it. He was just exhausted.

She sighed and undid the binds still tied around his wrists. Brushed the hair out of his eyes. He was too kind, too gentle for this.

'Oye, Kavi!'

'She's alive.'

'Did you see those green things? They sliced right through—'

Mozhi's eyes widened as she took in the massacre.

Hazeen muttered a quiet prayer to Meshira.

And Bola walked up to Kavi, trying her best to appear nonchalant. 'You did this?'

Kavi bobbed her head at Azia. 'My warlock.'

'Is he dead?' Bola asked.

'He's resting.'

Bola nodded, took a deep, expansive breath, and cleared her throat. 'We have a request. The three of us.'

Hazeen and Mozhi joined her. 'Yes, we want to ask you something.'

'Something important.'

Kavi used her sleeve to wipe the tears and snot off Azia's face. 'Go on.'

'We want you to teach us,' Hazeen said.

'The Gashani school you used,' Mozhi added.

'We want to be your disciples.'

Disciples? Oh, Gods. 'No.'

'You're the only one who can teach us, Kavi.'

'Please.'

'Master!'

Fucksake. 'Can you help me with him?' she said, gesturing at Azia.

While Kavi crouched, the sisters helped Azia onto her back; slung his arms on both sides of her neck, rested his head on her shoulder, and slipped his feet into the loops she made with her elbows.

So light. She needed to make sure the boy ate more. 'Okay, thank you,' she said, and stood.

'Was that a yes?'

'Sounded like it.'

'Thank you for accepting me as your disciple, master.'

Kavi tsked. 'Stop it, I'm not your master.'

'If we're your disciples.'

'Then you must be our master.'

'Everyone knows that.'

Kavi sighed and started back down the way she'd come. The three disciples – *godsdammit* – the three sisters, followed while she carried the most powerful mage on the subcontinent out of Lathun.

Chapter 35
ENFORCER

Inaaya

'Azia, let me share some wisdom with you,' Bola said, leaning forward to gaze intently at the bemused warlock. 'Reflect, but don't regret. Regret never pushes you forward, it only leaves you trapped in the past.'

Azia scratched the scar on his chin and gave Bola a thoughtful nod.

'Hey, that actually makes sense,' Mozhi said.

Hazeen agreed. 'Not bad.'

'Very wise, Bola,' Kavi added.

The bald woman shrugged like it was of no consequence.

A judder ran through the cabin and the train slowed to a crawl as it entered a residential area. Kavi rested her head against the grilled window, gaze skimming past Azraaya's buildings and tenements, whose colourful facades were eerily muted in the light of the setting sun. She fidgeted with the threads on her sword's hilt. Drisana was still in there, but it no longer spoke to her.

Mozhi sighed and propped one foot up on the seat. 'Shame we couldn't stop at Meriyachal, the hot springs there are supposed to be great. Especially if you're recovering from a battle.'

'One day,' Hazeen said.

'Let me share more wisdom with you.'

Mozhi made a face. 'How much more—'

'Shhh.' Bola cleared her throat. 'Memories of places are really memories of people you went there with.'

'Oh,' Mozhi muttered, and the three of them, with Azia, contemplated that in silence while Kavi let the warm, humid, air caress her face and hair. Bola was right with that one. Her memories of Bochan were now memories of Haibo, Zofan, and Bithun.

Azia nudged her with his elbow. *Why're you sad?* he said inside her head.

She smiled at him. *Thinking of my friends from Bochan.*

He nodded. *They were good friends.*

They were.

'It's strange,' he said out loud. 'Talking like that.'

Kavi glanced at the sisters, who were busy making dinner plans.

'Ranganath's for biryani?' Hazeen asked.

'What about the Chokai hawker centre?'

'Pfft, the real good stuff is in the Lantern district.'

Kavi turned back to Azia. 'You'll get used to it.'

'Let's talk normally,' he said, 'unless we really can't.'

Okay.

He frowned and pouted.

Kavi chuckled.

They couldn't hear each other's thoughts, thankfully, but she was aware of his emotional state. Right now, he was determined, reflective; the horror of what he'd done – and what he could do – remained, but he was choosing to be hopeful.

At Lathun, they'd joined the line of injured soldiers waiting to be treated, and while the sisters had their wounds tended to, Kavi took Azia to Brigadier Thordali, and confessed that this passed-out, slip of a boy was her warlock: *He's only a first-year, sir, already hurt and not fit for the front lines.* The brigadier commandeered a bullock cart heading to the Ghotal cantonment for them, and Kavi had bundled the sisters in with her.

They'd learned, just as the train began its journey back to Azraaya, that the Nathrians had withdrawn. Heavy losses at Lathun — Kavi and the sisters exchanged glances and stared at Azia, who had still been passed out — combined with rapidly disintegrating supply lines, caused in no small part by the sudden arrival of allied Hamakan troops from the sea, had left the Nathrians no choice but to retreat.

The three sisters promised to keep Azia's power a secret. But only if Kavi confirmed that they were, in fact, her disciples — which, much to their elation, she reluctantly did.

Bola had accosted her earlier, in the corridor outside their cabin, and insisted that Kavi begin her training in the Gashani school. 'At least give me some theory, please!'

Kavi had obliged, and immediately regretted it. 'In powerful winds,' she'd said, mimicking Greema's sombre tone of voice, 'trees fall, branches break, but grass bends, and when it's over, gets back up.'

Bola made a face. 'I'm grass?'

'That's not—'

'I think I'm more like the wind.'

'—what I'm trying to say.'

Bola tsked. 'You may be a swordmaster, but you still have much to learn.'

The lessons were now indefinitely postponed.

'I was thinking,' Kavi said, glancing at Azia, 'if you use less than half, say, a quarter of your krasna' — the fire and pressure might still be there, but — 'I should be able to move.'

Azia nodded. 'I think so too, but a quarter is still a lot.' He shuffled closer. 'Earlier, when I went to the bathroom, I tried casting.'

Kavi cocked her head to the side. 'I didn't feel anything.'

'I know, I only drew out a little, just this much' – he held his hand apart, and Kavi's eyebrows rose: the size of a rickshaw tyre – 'and I could move as I cast. Also, I could send it away, and channel a different section of my krasna. I didn't need to wait to cast again, like I used to. Like all the other warlocks have to.'

'That—'

'Should be impossible,' he said, eyes wide with wonder.

'—is incredible.'

'But it makes sense that you didn't feel much,' he said. 'How strong – according to Jinn theory, how badly a warlock is affected by their countervail is directly proportional to how much krasna is drawn out. So, if I just use a small section of it, because my krasna is … '

'Enormous?'

He scratched the back of his head. 'What I'm trying to say is that even though I'm channelling *a lot* of maayin, compared to what I can actually do, it's only—'

'A drop of water in a bucket,' Kavi said. 'I understand. I know how it feels when you draw more out.' It had literally burned the skin off her body.

'What about you?' he said. 'Do you feel different since we bonded?'

Things were brighter – more detailed than they once were. Smells were more intense. Tastes were more complex. She felt lighter, stronger, faster. 'A little, yes.' And she could tell, instantly, if someone was a mage.

*

'Is that him?' Chotu said, looking Azia up and down while porters and passengers trudged past on the platform.

Kavi patted Azia on the back. 'Azia, meet Chotu, my—'

'Brother, yes.' Azia bobbed his head and extended a hand. 'I'm the warlock.'

Chotu shook his hand, distracted by the three women looming behind Kavi. 'Who're they?'

'They're my ...' She grimaced. 'Friends.'

'We're her disciples,' Bola said.

Chotu blinked. 'Her what?'

'*Dee-sai-pills.*' Bola repeated.

'Dee *what?*'

'Okay, that's enough.' Kavi waved them along. 'These are the Gandalkar sisters. This is my brother. Now, let's go.'

'We're going home first,' Mozhi said, putting an arm around Azia's neck. 'This one lives in the area, so we're taking him with us.'

You're okay with that? Kavi asked him.

He flashed her a sheepish thumbs-up as he tried to wriggle out from under Mozhi's arm.

'Where do we find you?' Hazeen asked.

She told them where her hut was in the slums. 'If I'm not there, I'll either be at the Vagola, or the Caterpillar.'

'The Caterpillar? Like the brothel?' Hazeen said, a flicker of surprise on her face.

'Yes.'

Bola gasped. 'No – really?'

'Shuddup, you,' Kavi said with a loud tsk. 'I'm a bouncer – and besides, there's nothing wrong with working there.'

She waited till Azia and the sisters spluttered away in a steam-rickshaw – the poor boy had to sit in Bola's lap because there was no space – then joined Chotu as they searched for Ratan's rickshaw.

'How did you know I'd be on that train?' Kavi said, as they spotted Ratan's flatcap and waved at him.

'We heard the train from Lathun was returning, so we came, just in case.'

Kavi linked her arm through his. 'Thank you.'

He gave her a serious nod, and said, 'I knew you were coming back.'

Ratan tipped his cap and slipped into the driver's seat. 'Welcome back, boss. Where to? Home?'

She hurled her bag into the backseat, helped Chotu climb inside, then sat and arranged her sword between her knees. 'Caterpillar, first,' she said. Nabo would want to know she was safe—

She tsked. Why lie to herself? She wanted to see him, there was no need to make excuses. She wanted to see him, so she would go see him. After that, she'd return to the hut and eat, rest, and plan.

'Tanool and Tsubu are still here,' Chotu said, hanging on to the rail as Ratan rolled through a pothole. 'They want to say goodbye before they go back to Bochan.'

Kavi smiled at him. In such a short time, while she'd been busy with her life at the Vagola and her work for the Tivasi, he'd gone from barely speaking and avoiding eye contact to this new, more confident version of himself.

'Akka?'

'I'll go see them after my shift tonight,' she said, and frowned as Azia's emotions spiked – a strange mixture of relief tinged with melancholy. Was he not happy to be home?

All okay? she asked him. Could they talk to each other re-gardless of distance?

Yes, he responded. *You seem excited?*

She blinked. It was true. The closer they got to the Caterpillar and Nabo, the faster and louder her heartbeat got.

Is it a lover?

So not all their memories had been shared.

I'm going to beat you up.

You came all the way to save me, no chance.

She sighed.

I – was that what Nabo was to her? *– kind of, yes.*

You're not sure?

It's weird, she said, *until recently I thought he had no interest in me, but that changed.*

Azia went silent. The rickshaw rattled to a halt at a traffic stop. *What does it feel like?* he asked. *To be in love.*

She stifled her surprise, but not enough, apparently.

I'm sorry, he said, clearly afraid that he'd offended her, *it's okay if you don't want to share.*

He knew so much about her, and besides, she was learning how to confide in the people she trusted.

It's hard to describe, she said.

Try, please.

She chewed her lower lip. *It's – my eyes follow him whenever he's around. I hate working for the Tivasi, but I look forward to going there because I know I will see him. And when I speak to him, I get nervous; butterflies in my stomach, fingertips tingling. I obsess over what to say – sometimes I feel like running away mid-sentence.*

You want to be around him, and also run away from him? Sounds complicated, Azia said.

You'll understand one day.

Have you seen my face? he said, with something resembling a scoff. *This scar – I'm ugly.*

Don't say that, she said, with more venom than she intended, then softened her tone. *Trust me, there is someone out there who will love you for what you are.*

Taken aback. Unsure, he sent her an abashed, *Thanks.*

You're welcome. Now leave me alone.

Nabo was waiting outside the Caterpillar. He spotted the rickshaw and came bounding out to them.

'Nabo—' Her smile faded, punched through by a spike of alarm. There was fear in his eyes, on his face. 'What's wrong?'

'Grishan,' he said, pausing to catch his breath. 'He knows you're back.'

She stepped out of the rickshaw, placed a hand on his shoulder. 'It's okay, I don't—'

'No, Kavi, he's angry – been angry since he learned you'd left the city.' He glanced at Chotu and Ratan. 'He took his men and left for the slums.'

Her eyes bulged, and the blood drained from her face. 'I have to go.'

'I know,' Nabo said, and squeezed her wrist.

'Ratan—'

'I heard, get in.'

She was halfway into the vehicle when he twisted the accelerator – Chotu yanked her the rest of the way inside and she held on for dear life as Ratan pushed the steam-rickshaw to its limits. It hissed, spluttered, rattled; the tires shrieked as it skidded through an intersection – other drivers cursed and yelled at him to slow down.

She glanced at Chotu, at his white-knuckled grip on the guardrail. She wanted to reassure him, tell him it would be okay, but her mouth was dry, and she lacked the conviction.

Kavi? What's wrong? Azia said inside her head.

Listen, Kavi said. *Whatever happens, whatever you sense from me, stay where you are, until I tell you otherwise.*

What's going on? Azia replied.

Azia, promise me.

I promise, now tell me.

Grishan, he's headed to the slums. Kavi cursed internally. She'd thought she'd have more time.

We can fight him.

No, you can't, she said. *I don't want you involved.*

You've seen what I can do.

This is not your fight.

He fell silent. She'd wounded him. *I trust you,* she said, *you know* that.

Yes.

So, trust me back, she said. *When I want you to fight, you will know.*

That reassured him. **Stay safe,** he said.

I will. And just to see if she could, with nothing but the force of her will, she tried to shut him out of her head.

His presence receded to this vague entity on the other side of the city. His emotions faded to a muffled echo. And she knew, if she tried to speak to him, that she would be nothing more than a whisper.

Not what she'd imagined, but it would do.

The steam-rickshaw screeched to a halt as it ran out of road on the outskirts of the slums. Kavi hopped out. Burst into a sprint.

But she was too late.

The forty-odd Taemu, all of them, had been gathered up and forced to kneel in a tight huddle. Tivasi gangsters surrounded them, shoved them down if they tried to stand, slapped the back of their heads if they spoke.

Grishan stood outside her and Chotu's hut. He peered inside, wrinkled his nose, and tugged his shirt down.

'Boss,' a gangster said, and cocked his head at her.

'Ah, Kavithri.' Grishan strode over to the group of huddled Taemu, and beckoned her over. 'Come.'

Her feet were heavy as sacks of rice, but she obeyed.

'Come, I won't hurt you,' Grishan said, smiling, and as soon as she was within touching distance, he grabbed her by the back of the neck – hard enough to make her hiss with pain – and muscled her down to her knees.

'I am in a good mood today,' he said. 'So no one will die. But you must be punished for your disobedience.' He snapped his fingers, and a dozen gangsters, all smoking beedis and carrying large, rusted canisters, stepped forward, spread out, and began emptying a blue, oily, pungent liquid onto the walls of the Taemu huts.

Kavi flared her nostrils. Kerosene.

She tried to stand. Grishan tightened his powerful grip on the back of her neck, and she gasped and flexed her jaw.

'You've cost me money,' he said. 'The venue, the people who paid to attend – you made me look like a fool. Now you will remain on your knees, and watch.'

Chotu and Ratan staggered out of the gully that led to the huts, and a trio of gangsters hiked up their trousers, spat, and swaggered over to them. They snatched Chotu's crutch and sent him stumbling.

'Please,' Kavi said, 'don't hurt him. His leg – please don't make him kneel.'

'Bring the brother,' Grishan said to his men. Then to Kavi: 'he can stand and watch.'

She tried to catch Chotu's eye as they returned his crutch and escorted him to her side, but he was too focused on the men dousing the huts with kerosene.

One by one, the gangsters flung the empty canisters into the huts and turned to face Grishan.

'Light them up,' he said, as cries went up among the Taemu.

'Please!' and 'This is all we have—' and 'Our food—' and 'Our clothes—'

Stop, Kavi wanted to shout, *he doesn't like to hear begging, it could set him off, he could do so much worse.*

She felt him twitch. 'Shut them up,' he said in a low, dangerous voice.

The Tivasi walked through the kneeling Taemu, kicked and slapped and cursed until they were silent again.

The gangsters who'd been ordered to *Light them up*, nodded to each other, and flicked their beedis at the huts.

It started with a hiss and turned into a roar.

The thatched roofs crackled and burned. Fires jumped from hut to hut. Walls collapsed and crashed to the ground. Fumes and smoke rose into the sky in dark, angry plumes as the exhausted, distraught Taemu knelt and watched their homes burn.

'You should be pleased I'm not killing anyone,' Grishan said.

The heat stung Kavi's nostrils. Her scalp crawled and prickled. Her lips twisted, curled back, and exposed her grinding teeth.

'Inaaya!'

Standing at the entrance to the gully Chotu and Ratan had stepped out of, with a sack of rubbish slung over one shoulder, was Nariga.

'Inaaya!' she screamed, and dropping her sack, ran at a burning hut.

'Hold her back,' Grishan said. 'Let her watch, too.'

Inaaya? Kavi's eyebrows's twitched. *Inaaya?* Her baby boy. Nariga's five-month-old baby boy was still in their hut.

Nariga thrashed as a pair of gangsters grabbed her by the waist and dragged her away from the fire.

'My baby,' she cried. 'My boy is inside!' She bit one of the men on the forearm and he growled and punched her in the temple. She barely flinched. She struggled and kicked, wept and screamed, and when they continued to drag her away, she began to wail and slap her own forehead. Over and over again. *Smack. Smack. Smack.*

Kavi tried to twist out of Grishan's grip, but it would not give.

'I said watch,' he said. 'Or would you like her to join the baby?'

She stopped fighting and stared at Nariga's burning hut.

The heat from the flames; the pungent scent of burnt wood and straw; Nariga's despondent cries and pleas – Kavi seared it into her soul. And in the pit of her stomach, the berserker thrashed and shrieked and begged and gibbered to be let out.

Soon.

It foamed at the mouth, strained at its chains, and subsided. She was not lying; it would get its chance.

Soon.

Grishan made them watch until there was nothing left of their homes but smouldering, charred heaps. And when he was satisfied, he released her. 'You will fight in a match tonight. This time, you will drag it out, make it last five rounds.' He gestured to his men, and the gangsters followed him into the gully.

Kavi stood on unsteady feet and staggered over to Nariga, who was struggling to breathe from how hard she sobbed. Spittle flew and hung from her chin, her mouth opened and closed. She slapped her own chest. Slapped her head again.

Kavi caught her wrists. Forced them down and wrapped her arms around the woman.

Spittle and tears covered Nariga's face as she screamed herself hoarse. And when she could no longer scream, she hit Kavi. Slapped her face, her arms, her shoulders.

Kavi held her tighter. Embraced her until there was nothing left but soft, gentle sobs.

'I'm sorry,' Kavi said.

'For what? Can you bring him back? Can you bring my baby back?'

'No.'

'Have you ever had children?'

'No.'

Nariga wiped her face on her forearm. 'I want to tear that man to pieces,' she whispered, her body trembling with rage. 'Rip him limb from limb. I want to make him suffer.'

'I can do that for you.'

Nariga looked up at Kavi. Peered into her eyes, studied her face, and nodded, satisfied with whatever it was she found. 'Then make sure you do, Akka. Make sure you do.'

Chapter 36
ENFORCER

Round Two

Deva unfurled the bandages. Pressed one end into the back of her wrist, held it tight with a finger, and wrapped it around her palm.

Kavi blinked. He remembered how to do it.

The legs of the stool she was seated on were uneven, and it clunked as she shifted her weight: up and down, up and down. Through the thin, corrugated iron walls of the 'dressing' room, the shouts and curses of the crowd in the warehouse, where a fight was currently underway, rose and fell.

'Stay still,' Deva said.

Kavi stopped. Spread her fingers so he could wrap the bandage between them. 'Who am I fighting?'

'Same as last time, Makkur.'

The so-called champion of Azraaya. She flexed her fingers and offered him her other hand. A roar went up from the warehouse. A knock-out, probably.

'You know what he did?' she asked. There was only one *He* that mattered to them.

Deva shrugged. 'I warned you.'

'You did.' She cracked her neck, one way, then the other. 'Will you help me?'

He paused with the bandage halfway around the base of her palm. 'When?'

'Tonight.'

The muscles in his jaw worked, but he didn't give her an answer.

He wrapped the rest of her hand in silence, and when he was done, he reached into his shirt pocket and pulled out a pack of beedis. He slapped the base, slipped one out, and held it in front of Kavi's mouth.

She leaned forward and took it between her lips.

The match caught on the first strike, and he lit her beedi before firing one up for himself.

He stood. The door squealed as he nudged it open.

Kavi stared at the tip of her burning beedi. At the grey smoke that twisted and curled into the ceiling.

Sweat beaded on her forehead, her face, her chest. But somehow, she was cold. Numb. The flames that had burned her people's homes still danced in her periphery; Nariga's cries still echoed in her ears; the back of her neck still ached from where Grishan's fingers had dug in.

It was as if her mind had, of its own volition, sectioned off the raw, visceral, reaction to what had happened – to allow her to think. But she could tell that it was a temporary reprieve; those emotions would not disappear, and she would, eventually, need to face them, or find a way to release them.

She took a shallow drag, reclined and rested her head on the wall as she exhaled.

Deva paused in the doorway, waited until she looked at him, and nodded. 'It's time.'

They used the same back entrance as last time, emerged behind the arrack and chicken 65 kiosk, and elbowed and shouldered their way to the ring. The crowd was as rambunctious as her last fight, but the atmosphere was different: faces were strained, voices had a dangerous edge to them.

'Conscriptions,' Deva shouted into her ear.

'What?'

'The Council announced military conscriptions.'

Ah, that would do it.

She climbed the portable wooden stairs up to the ring. Ducked between the ropes and found her footing on the blood-stained mat.

Deva hefted himself up behind her. 'Mouth guard,' he said, and offered her the gumshield.

She bit down on it and he snatched his fingers away.

'Easy,' he said, as cries of *Makkur!* and *Makkur, bhai!* and *Makkur, kill her!* filled the air.

Kavi ignored her slowly approaching opponent; turned away from him and searched the crowd for her people.

She found Chotu, standing with his crutch under one arm as he watched her with clear, fearless eyes. He rolled up his sleeve and patted the tattooed band on his shoulder.

Aadhier Taemu. She nodded.

Next to him – she stepped closer to the ropes – with his face pinched and his lips tightened to a straight line, was Nabo. He tried to smile, and faltered.

You don't need to smile. You're here, that's enough.

She found Azia, who stood between the three sisters with his arms crossed, and chin dipped as he tried not to look at her. He was upset that she'd blocked him out, and was sulking. Still, *Don't get hurt*, he said inside her head. She nodded.

And Ratan, who tipped his hat and waved Massa's beedi case and artificed matchstick combo at her. She'd asked him to hold on to it. *Keep them safe.* She nodded.

And finally, in the corner, boxed in by Tivasi gangsters and forced to stand and watch the forthcoming humiliation, were a dozen Taemu. A reminder and a threat, like last time, of what would happen if she disobeyed Grishan's instructions.

This time, however, the faces of the Taemu – lit by the harsh yellow of artificed globes – were different. Doubt replaced with purpose. Fear replaced by fury. And in the middle of the group, Nariga stood and glared at Kavi with bloodshot eyes filled with grief and rage.

Grishan had taken the rickshaw company from them. He'd killed their family and friends, burned their homes. What else could he do? What else was there to be afraid of now? Death? No, that would just bring an end to their suffering.

Blood pounded in her ears, muscles tensed in anticipation of violence, and Kavi *understood*, in a dazzling moment of clarity, what she meant to her people:

She was the aggression they couldn't show.

The violence they could never return.

She was their hope of vengeance.

Kavi rolled her shoulders, threw a sharp practice jab at the air in front of her face, and turned to face Makkur.

The referee checked her bandages, her mouthguard, went over the rules with her and Makkur – neither of them were listening. Makkur thumped his fists together and stared her down. He'd already beaten her once. He was confident. He thought he knew the extent of her abilities.

Kavi raised her fists until she made a bridge under her eyes; dropped into the stance Bithun taught her.

The referee cleared out of the way, and *ding!*

Makkur stepped in with a monstrous right hook.

She twisted, took it on her biceps. Shuffled to the side with the force of the blow and kept her guard up.

Makkur walked up, no fear of her hitting back in his eyes – he knew, the bhaenchod *knew* the fight was fixed – and threw an uppercut that blew through her guard. She hissed as his knuckles grazed past her forehead and scraped the skin off it.

Okay, fine, have it your way. She dropped her guard, switched to a side-on stance with both fists hanging at her sides, and searched for her rhythm.

Babump

She was not trapped. She was not stuck.

Ba-bump

She could see the choices, the paths she could take.

Ba. Bump

And she made her decision.

Makkur hesitated, as if he sensed that something was off, but he shook it off and closed in.

Kavi dodged under a punch but stayed where she was, bouncing on her toes. *Come.* There was something she needed to show them all.

Makkur threw a compact one-two.

She head-slipped the jab, parried the straight, feinted with a jab of her own, and with an explosive burst of speed, skipped around him.

He swivelled to track her movement. His head was still spinning around when she lunged, and *aim-hiss*, whipped Bithun's flicker jab into his mouth.

The cheers of the spectators faltered. Makkur frowned, flexed his jaw and refocused on her. He raised his guard. Lumbered over to her, and threw a tentative *What are you doing? You're supposed to let me hit you* jab.

Kavi countered. Snapped his head around with a textbook right straight.

Makkur stumbled. Flailed. And regained his balance.

The warehouse was silent now, except for Makkur's loud, ragged breaths and the scuff of Kavi's feet kicking the mat.

She stopped bouncing on her toes, walked up to Makkur, and planted her feet. *You're an in-fighter right?* She beckoned him closer with both hands. *Come, champion.*

A thin trail of blood leaked from his right nostril and the veins on his neck stood out as he shook with unconcealed rage. This was not how the night was meant to turn out; he was not supposed to be the one humiliated.

Is that what you're thinking? She shuffled even closer. *Come.*

He roared, sent spittle flying in her face, and sent punch after punch at her head.

She blocked, parried, twisted and swayed around them, but refused to move back.

And when he ran out of breath, when he stood gasping for air with one arm on the top rope – as she'd expected him to after such a reckless assault – she used her left arm to aim for his jaw, took her time with it, and hammered her fist into his face.

His head snapped back with a sickening crunch. Blood splattered into the audience. And Makkur toppled back onto the ropes, which bounced him right back into her.

She caught him, forced him back upright, exulted in the fear on his face, in his eyes. Good. *Good. Now you've learned.* She glanced at her corner, where once, almost a year ago, Bithun had stood, white-knuckled with tears in his eyes, and urged her to fight back against hawaldar Bhagu.

Bloodhound, he'd called her. Maybe he was right. She drew her right arm back, and crunched a hook into Makkur's kidneys.

The strength went out of his already weak legs and he collapsed with his head on her shoulder.

Her mouth twisted, she placed the base of one bandaged palm on the side of his face, and shoved him away. He slid down her shoulder and *thump*, fell flat on the mat.

The referee flung his arms in the air, the bell *ding-ding-dinged*, but she'd already walked away, searching for her Taemu.

The Tivasi gangsters were herding them out of the warehouse.

Nariga caught her eye as they shoved her out. The grief, the rage, were still in her eyes, but they were joined by a fierce pride that sent wisps of warmth crawling through Kavi's cold, numb body.

Grishan would hurt them, but he wouldn't kill them unless she was there to watch. They were safe for now.

She strode to her corner, and Deva held the ropes apart for her.

She ducked through, skipped down the stairs, and the crowd parted for her as she walked back to her derelict dressing room.

Azia, she said through the bond, *I need you to pass a message to Chotu.*

Go on, he replied.

Tell him to bring everyone who wants to fight to the Caterpillar.

Okay.

You go with him, take Hazeen and Mozhi.

No, I'm staying with you.

A woman held the door to the back entrance open for Kavi and she stepped through.

Fine, she said, *bring Bola and Nabo and meet me at the back of the warehouse.*

'The boss will want to see you,' Deva said, at her back.

'Tell him I'm coming.' While Grishan was alive, while the Tivasi ruled the undercity, her people had no future. She sat on her stool inside the tiny room and held her hands out to him. 'But I won't be alone.'

He glanced at her face, and the beard around his mouth twitched as he unwrapped her bloody bandages. 'You were never alone.'

Chapter 37
ENFORCER

Brawl

Bola slapped all her pockets and glanced at Kavi with puppy-dog eyes. 'I'm out of beedis.'

Kavi, with her last beedi halfway to her lips, paused, muttered, '*You have much to learn*, she says. Now she wants my beedis.' She lit her beedi with Massa's artificed matchstick and took a drag. 'I'm out, too,' she said with a smirk, and waited for a cycle-rickshaw to creak past before crossing the street to the Caterpillar.

Bola tsked and followed.

Azia, hands tucked into his pockets, eyes darting everywhere, hurried to keep up. Once he was safely across the street he stopped and gaped at the wide, four-storeyed, innocuous-looking building. 'That's a brothel?' he asked Nabo.

'Oh, yes.'

'And you work there?'

'I do.'

'Like how Kavi does?'

'Not quite.'

Kavi cleared her throat. Gestured to a gloomy gas lamp. 'We'll wait here.'

Foot traffic was steady, like it usually was at this time of the night. The shops were all open and brightly lit – Naadan was having a sale: buy any book and a get free deck of pornographic playing cards (imported from Kraelin and featuring art prints of Kraelish ladies in various stages of undress); a paani-puri stall was surrounded by hungry customers; the queue for the tandoori and kebab stand snaked around the corner; and punters continued to walk in and out of the Caterpillar.

'So, what do you do?' Azia asked again. The boy had never set foot in the Lantern district before – Kavi could sense his curiosity and fascination with the place – and had been plaguing Nabo with questions. Azia had taken an instant liking to the Hamakan. She suspected he was leeching off her own powerful feelings for Nabo, shared through the bond, but it didn't bother her.

'I am a prostitute,' Nabo said.

Azia blushed and looked away.

'He is also the master's concubine,' Bola added.

Kavi sighed. 'You're using the wrong words again – and stop calling me *master* in front of other people.'

'Sure, master.'

Nabo chuckled, shuffled closer until their shoulders touched. 'I like your friends.'

She smiled at him; took in his nervous eyes and the anxious set of his mouth. *Don't worry*, she wanted to say, but the words failed her. Instead, she reached for his hand, intertwined her fingers with his, and left it there.

The collective crunch of footsteps and the hum of chatter dragged her attention away from Nabo.

Her people were here.

Chotu led them down the street – Mozhi and Hazeen at each shoulder – face grim, eyes daring passersby to question their presence. Her brother was looking for a fight, and so were the rest of the Taemu.

All of them were there: Jiboo and his friends, the older men and women, the children – the youngest of whom was tied to her mother's chest with a bedsheet. And all of them either wore the red armband or had rolled up their sleeves to expose the tattoo.

A spike of fear jabbed its way into her heart: Was she leading them to their deaths? Was this a—

Nabo squeezed her trembling hand.

She swallowed. No, this was how it had to be. They had to be here. They had to be *seen*.

'Akka,' Chotu said, and the word was echoed by the other Taemu.

Nabo released Kavi's hand and stepped away.

She cast a questioning glance at him.

'A leader shows no weakness,' he said, softly.

Her eyebrows twitched. 'You're not—'

'Akka,' Chotu said again, and Kavi turned to find him ushering half a dozen gangly boys – older teenagers from the looks of it – in front of her. One wore spectacles, one had a horrible case of acne, one had an inexplicable eyepatch (he lifted it to get the gunk out of the corner of a perfectly functioning eye), one had a ponytail with flowers in it, and one carried a notepad in the crook of his elbow.

'Who are these' – she was going to say fools, but changed her mind – 'men?'

'These are my friends. They want to fight with us.' Chotu puffed his chest out. 'They want to help.'

Ah, his smuggling gang. She crushed her half-smoked beedi underfoot – to Bola's audible dismay – and, one by one, shook their hands. 'Thank you for taking care of my brother,' she said.

They muttered something about how it was no trouble, how Chotu was the one taking care of *them*; a couple of them even called her *Akka*.

When she was done, she gazed out at her ragged army, and the sight filled her chest with a melancholic sense of pride. 'I—'

A chorus of ear-splitting rickshaw honks pierced the air, and all heads swivelled toward the sound.

Kavi stared, mouth agape, as a horde of steam-rickshaws rattled and sputtered their way to the Caterpillar. They blocked off the street, filled the air with their fumes, drove up on the footpath and sent pedestrians scattering.

In the lead rickshaw, sharing the driver's seat with Ratan and hanging halfway out of the vehicle, was Subbal Reddy. The rickshaw hissed and came to a halt by Kavi's feet.

Subbal Reddy hopped out, tucked his purse under one arm, and waved. 'Kavithri!'

'What's *he* doing here?' Chotu said.

Reddy pointed to the rickshaw. 'I bring gifts.'

Kavi, Chotu, and the sisters peered inside the rickshaw.

The backseat was piled with spanners, pliers, hammers, drain-pipes, metal rods, bits and pieces of rickshaws, and an assortment of implements that could be used as—

'Weapons,' Chotu said.

'Don't be shy,' Reddy shouted to the Taemu. 'Take whatever you want.'

Kavi walked over to Reddy while the others swarmed the rickshaw. 'Why?' she asked.

Reddy reached under the back seat and pulled out a broken cycle chain. 'You like to use your fists right?' He placed the chain in her hands.

'What—'

'Boss,' Ratan said, and tipped his hat. 'When the other drivers heard what Grishan did – they wanted to help.'

She blinked. He was wearing the city's rickshaw driver

uniform – an unbuttoned khaki shirt with a white banyan underneath. She'd never seen him wear it before. 'The drivers?'

Ratan pointed at the Taemu, at Jiboo and the others who'd briefly driven for the rickshaw company; they were laughing and chatting with the khaki-clad drivers of all the steam-rickshaws that now filled the street.

It seemed that they'd forged a few bonds of their own.

'They want to fight too?' Kavi asked.

Ratan nodded.

She turned to Subbal Reddy, who was lighting up a beedi with hands cupped around it. 'You too, Reddy-sir?'

'Hmm?' He waved the smoke away from his face. 'Meshira, no. I'm just here to deliver the weapons.' He frowned and cocked his head at the sisters who – equipped with hammer, rod, and wrench – were standing protectively around Kavi. 'Who're they?'

'Who are *you*?'

'Do we have a problem?'

'Hah?'

Oh, Gods. Kavi waved the sisters away from Reddy. 'I'll explain later.'

'Kavithri,' Reddy said, re-tucking his purse into his armpit. 'When you're done, if you need any bodies disposed of, I can give you a discount.'

He was not joking. 'I'll keep that in mind,' she said.

'Good, now send that bhaenchod' – he spat – 'to Hel.' And with that, he turned and walked away through the narrow gaps between the rickshaws.

Kavi hefted the cycle chain, how was she supposed to …

Ah, that's right. She'd seen the Dolmonda gangster use it. She placed one end in her palm, wrapped the rest of the chain around her knuckles, and clenched her fist.

This would do nicely.

A hush fell over the group, and all eyes – the Taemu, the rickshaw drivers, her brother and his gang, the sisters, Nabo and Azia – watched Kavi stride to the entrance of the Caterpillar.

They don't need to fight, Azia said inside her head. *None of them need to get hurt. I can take care of this.*

Thank you, she said, and meant it. *But I have to do this. They have to see me do this. And they need to fight.*

If it gets too dangerous, I will intervene.

Her brows rose at the quiet confidence she sensed in him. *If I don't bring him down myself,* she said, *then there is no meaning to this. Protect my brother and his friends, and keep Nabo safe.*

I will, I promise.

'Akka, where's your sword?' Chotu asked, examining the cycle chain around her fist.

'No need,' she said. *There is only one man I intend to kill, and I will not waste my sword on him.* She mastered the fluttering in her chest, clenched her jaw, and reached for the door handle.

'Wait!'

Kavi froze.

Bola swaggered up to the door, and gently pushed her aside. 'We go first, test things out, then you can come.'

Hazeen and Mozhi joined her. The sisters nodded at Kavi, whispered to each other, then collectively took a step back, and kicked the door down.

The wood crunched and exploded and the sisters barged their way inside.

Shouts, screams; plates and utensils clattered; glasses shattered. The sister's voices:

'Meshira have mercy on your soul.'

'Shhh, go to sleep.'

'Motherfucker.'

Kavi peeked inside.

Hazeen had kicked a gangster halfway over the counter of the bar.

Mozhi had another in a chokehold.

And Bola was stealing an unconscious man's beedis.

Clients and staff rushed for the back door. Musicians protected their instruments – carried their tablas and sitars over their heads – and yelled at people to hurry up. The Aunty-ji was running up the stairs to the first floor.

The door to the kitchen burst open, and gangsters armed with knives, mallets, brass knuckles, and hatchets came streaming through.

Kavi tightened the chain around her fist and stepped inside.

A woman with a hatchet screamed and charged her, raising the weapon over her head before swinging it at Kavi's face.

Chink! The hatchet bounced off Kavi's chain-wrapped fist.

The woman swung again. *Chink!* Kavi punched it out of the air again.

Around her, the Taemu and the rickshaw drivers charged in, collided with the outraged gangsters, and then the brawl was well and truly underway. Chairs and tables went flying. Bottles were shattered, windows were broken, mothers were sworn on, fathers were cursed at, accusations of incest were exchanged. Bones fractured and teeth cracked as violence filled the once-alluring ground floor of the Caterpillar.

Hatchet-lady persisted. She swung at Kavi over and over again, and her frustration grew as Kavi deflected each swing with sharper and sharper punches.

Enough. Kavi stepped in, grabbed the woman's collar, and smashed the top of her head into the woman's face.

The hatchet slipped out of the woman's fingers, and she collapsed, her nose a bloody mush.

Kavi shoved her away, tried to wipe the blood out of her eyes, and stumbled.

You promised, the berserker shrieked, its rage surging through Kavi's veins.

Not yet. She fought to regain control of her body, to see through the haze of red and the blood in her eyes.

Her neck whipped to the side as she was tackled to the ground. She floundered. Flinched as fists rained down on her.

Not yet.

Her fingers found purchase on her assailant's hair, and she pulled with one hand and punched with the other. *Crack. Crunch. Splat.*

The weight slipped off her body and she scrambled to her knees; dabbed and wiped at her eyes until she could see again.

She was under a table. What the fuck was she doing under a table?

A gangster tripped over a chair and fell. He groaned, started to rise, and did a double take.

They stared at each other.

Kavi lunged. Wrestled herself around him and guided his forehead into the unsuspecting knee of another gangster.

Crunch. The man on the ground went limp.

'Madarchod!' The gangster with the busted knee yelled. Something heavy and metallic connected with Kavi's left cheek – sent needles of pain shooting under her eye socket – and knocked her flat on her arse.

You know how I win fights? Massa said.

How, boss?

I aim for the gonads. One hundred per cent success rate.

She punched the gangster in the crotch.

'*Oof.*' He toppled, frozen, with both hands clutching his balls.

Kavi stood. Kicked a table and sent it sliding into a gangster's back. Punched another in the stomach. Snatched his mallet from him, and hurled it at a woman attacking a rickshaw driver.

She re-oriented herself, searched for the kitchen.

There.

The passageway that led to the Tivasi den was in there.

She steeled herself. Adjusted the chain around her knuckles, and dived into the brawl.

Chapter 38
Boss-1

The chain around her fist was covered with blood. The right side of her face was bruised and swollen. There were cuts and slices on her arms and back. Her chest and shoulders heaved with each breath.

It was all catching up to her: the sleepless nights at Bithun's side, Ghotal, Lathun, forging the bond with Azia. Her limbs were heavy, her movements – at least to her – seemed sluggish. But she was almost there. *Almost.*

She gathered up the blood, phlegm, and shattered pieces of teeth in her mouth and spat. Thirty? No, at least fifty Tivasi gangsters stood between her and the Caterpillar's kitchen. On her side, the Taemu and the rickshaw drivers were making use of the unspoken, yet mutually agreed upon, intermission in the brawl to drag the wounded away. Nabo was among them, propping up a Taemu with a broken leg. The sisters sat on their haunches, panting and glaring at the gangsters. And Azia – she cast a glance over her shoulder – stood in the doorway with Chotu, who for some reason had a large burlap sack at his feet.

Azia stared at her. His jaw set, his mouth a thin line, the hair that usually covered his forehead brushed aside to expose the jagged scar running down his face.

What? she asked.

He didn't respond. Continued to stare at her. But she sensed an emotion pulse through the bond, one that was achingly familiar to her but unusual for him: anger.

Why?

I'm waiting.

For?

There's too many of them. You can't win.

She grimaced and spat again. He was right, they were outnumbered, so what? They— she blinked, stared at a rickshaw driver who was shaking an unconscious Taemu: 'Lenga, wake up,' he said, and shook the Taemu, who had a large, bloody wound on his head, again. 'Wake up, please.'

Kavi stumbled, her vision swam, and the punctured and broken bodies of the Taemu from the chokepoint rose to meet her.

Bola's powerful hands held her upright. 'Kavi?'

She'd blamed Ze'aan for the dead that day, but Ze'aan hadn't led the Taemu into the chokepoint. Kavi had. And she was doing it again. It was a mistake to involve them, she should've done this alone, she—

Kavi, her mother's voice whispered. *Look.*

Amma. Her lips trembled, the strength oozed out of her knees. *Amma, I can't do this again.*

Look at them, Kavi, her mother said. *Look.*

She wiped her face with the inside of an elbow and gazed into Bola's concerned eyes. At Mozhi and Hazeen's sweaty, worried faces. At the bloodied and battered Taemu who'd stepped up and formed a protective barrier between her and the gangsters.

You know what our greatest strength is? Amma had once asked, while Kavi sat in her lap and squirmed while she massaged coconut oil into Kavi's scalp. 'The swordmasters?'

'No.'

'Our courage?'

'No.'

'That we always stick together?'

'No.'

'Then what, Amma?'

Her mother kissed the top of her head and said, *Our greatest strength, Kavi, is our willingness to die for each other.*

Hessal, Elisai, the Taemu at the chokepoint, her mother – they'd all made a choice. They'd all put themselves in harm's way for someone they cared about, and had died for it; and if she could go back and give them the opportunity to choose again, she knew, without a shadow of a doubt, that every single one of them would make the same choice.

Kavi forced herself upright.

This need to protect, this responsibility to ensure their safety, it wasn't a one-way street, it had never been. That wasn't how friendship or family or love worked. The respect she had for the sisters was mutual. The fierce love she had for her brother was reciprocated. Her desperate desire to ensure her people's survival was shared. She could rely on them the way they relied on her. She was not alone.

'Fall back,' she said.

'Akka?' The Taemu exchanged puzzled glances but stood their ground.

'Trust me. Fall back.'

They obeyed, reluctantly backed away from the gangsters.

'You three as well,' Kavi said.

The sisters nodded and stepped back, leaving Kavi alone to face the Tivasi gangsters.

She tightened the chain around her fist, exhaled, and said through the bond, *I can't do this alone. Help me, please.*

An explosion of sheer, unbridled joy surged back at her.

This will hurt, Azia said, *but only a little,* and called for his maayin.

Kavi winced at a sudden heaviness in her chest and limbs, gritted her teeth and waited for the searing pain that had burned her skin away to follow. Then straightened in surprise. *That's it?*

A single petal of emerald-green maayin danced in Azia's palm as he walked up to her and smiled. *You can be really stubborn, you know that?*

Gasps and cries filled the hall of the Caterpillar as more petals of shimmering maayin coalesced out of thin air. This was different from what he'd done at Lathun. This was measured, controlled, a hint of what he was actually capable of, but still more power than any warlock had a right to.

The petals swirled and hovered protectively around the Taemu and the rickshaw drivers, who stared at Azia in awe while the petals hung, menacingly still, over the cowering Tivasi gangsters.

Don't kill anyone, Kavi said. *I'll need them when this is over.*

I wasn't planning to.

He snapped his fingers, and the petals scattered. They sliced through the gangsters, left them with shallow cuts on their arms and backs as they fell to the ground pleading.

Thank you, she said.

Azia nodded, withdrew his maayin, and stepped back to stand at her shoulder.

'Do you yield?' Kavi said, walking up to the prostrate gangsters.

Cries of 'Yes!' 'Mercy!' and 'Please!' answered her.

'Then get the fuck out of my way,' she growled, and they scrambled away from her.

Make sure they don't change their minds, she said through the bond, and turned to face her people.

They'd been rejected by the city. Stripped of their purpose and sent back to the slums. They'd lost their homes and their purpose. But when this was over, they wouldn't need the city or rely on its people to survive; they would no longer be a part of this grotesque structure that shackled them to the bottom and moulded them for failure. They would own Azraaya from the inside out. 'Let's go,' she said, and walked into the kitchen.

She stopped by the dirt-coloured door that led to the corridor and the den beyond, and waited, panting as she caught her breath.

Footsteps pattered into the kitchen behind her, and she cast a tired glance over her shoulder: Hazeen, Mozhi, and Bola — followed by the Taemu and rickshaw drivers still able to fight.

'In there?' Mozhi asked.

Kavi crouched and picked up a hammer that looked like something the rickshaw mechanics used. 'Through the door, staircase down,' she said, 'then corridor, and another staircase up. He'll be there.'

Bola yanked the door open, and the four of them peered down the staircase.

The sweaty faces of more Tivasi gangsters stared back up at them; from the chatter and cursing coming from further down the corridor, more waited behind.

'Fuckers are like ants,' Bola said, and glanced at Kavi's hammer. 'Nice hammer.'

'Thanks.' She frowned. What was she planning to do with it, anyway? 'You want it?'

Bola grinned, and Kavi passed it over.

'Take a moment,' Mozhi said, patting Kavi on the shoulder. 'Catch your breath.'

Hazeen nodded. 'We'll go first.'

The sisters stomped down the staircase.

Bola's hammer made a series of wet *smacks* as it connected with flesh.

Hazeen lifted a gangster and flung him down the corridor.

Mozhi roared as she grabbed a man by the hair and smashed her elbow into his face.

Kavi took the stairs one at a time. Tested her footing on each step before moving on to the next one. Her legs were on fire. Her arms were going numb. The air in the narrow corridor was stifling: it reeked of sweat and tamakhu and the stench of bodies trapped in a small space.

Gods, she was sick of all this violence. Sick of getting hit and hurting people; exhausted from the constant state of alertness she needed to keep herself in. Maybe if she was smarter, she could've resolved this without bloodshed. Massa would've thought of something underhanded and cunning; he would've brought Grishan down without a single punch being thrown.

Will that satisfy you? Her mother's voice whispered in her ear. *Is that what you promised Nariga?*

Kavi's lips trembled. The screams, the fire, *my baby, my baby.* No, Amma.

Then keep fighting.

She stepped into the corridor, squeezed past Bola, smashed an uppercut into a gangster's jaw, stomped down on another's knee, stumbled forward, backpedalled to dodge a slashing knife, and fell into her boxing stance. She could do this.

One punch at a time.

Crack. A right hook into the knife-wielder's ribs. She took a step forward.

Smack-thud. Her fists blurred, a woman fell, the whites of her eyes exposed as they rolled up into her skull.

Kavi took another step forward – she winced, staggered as a mallet connected with her biceps, and snarled and punched the gangster in the jaw. His head ricocheted off the wall with a wet *crunch*.

By the time she arrived at the second staircase, the one leading up and into the anteroom outside the Tivasi den, the chain around her fist was soaked in blood, and stuck between its links were now pieces of shattered teeth and clumps of hair still attached to scalp.

Her own hair was damp with sweat and plastered to her face and neck. Her jaw ached from a punch that had slipped through her guard, and her gums bled a persistent metallic tang into her mouth.

She panted, leaned against the wall.

Almost there.

All she needed to do was put herself in front of him, and the berserker would handle the rest.

She checked on the sisters: they looked exhausted, but all three were still standing. And behind them, the rest of her people nursed their wounds and waited.

'Coming?' Kavi rasped, pointing up the stairs.

'Don't ask stupid questions,' Hazeen said. She groaned as she rotated a shoulder.

Mozhi's left arm was covered in blood and hung limp at her side, so she used the other hand to flash a thumbs-up. 'You're spending too much time with Bola.'

'Hah?' Bola wiped her hammer clean on a gangster's shirt and frisked his pockets.

Thank you. Kavi nodded, and started up the stairs.

A terrified man stood beside a wooden stool in the anteroom. He took one look at Kavi and the sisters and stepped aside;

bobbed his head and gestured to the large door behind him that led into the den.

She ignored him, shoved the door open.

A spike of adrenaline coursed through her body, numbed the pain, made the edges of her vision flicker, narrow, and tunnel past the crowd of silent gangsters to focus on the man seated in the massive chair at the end of the hall.

Her lips, of their own accord, pulled back, and she stepped inside.

Chapter 39
Boss-II

The gangsters parted, allowed her to cross the floor while Grishan watched, and waited.

The pounding in her ears drowned out the sound of her footsteps. Her fists clenched and unclenched. *Almost there.*

Their eyes met, and Grishan smiled. 'Do what you want with her,' he said, his voice echoing through the hushed chamber. 'But keep her alive.'

The gangsters closed in.

A loud, high-pitched whistle cut through the air like a siren and brought the gangsters up short. They froze, exchanged glances.

'Leave her,' Deva's familiar, gruff voice commanded, and the gangsters shuffled back and away from Kavi.

She continued walking until she was only a couple of strides away from Grishan. The man paid her no attention. Instead, he'd turned his cold, dead eyes on Deva, who stood off to the side, watching Kavi with a quiet intensity.

Deva snapped his fingers. 'The Taemu in the back, bring them here. The ones coming through the Caterpillar, let them in.'

'Yes, bhai.' A group of gangsters rushed to obey, the rest spreading out to let the Taemu and rickshaw drivers – who were trickling in from the corridor – join them in the den. She sensed Azia's presence among them, and reached out to him through the bond.

Azia —

I know, he said, *they need to see you do this alone.*

If I fail –

You won't.

'Is this who you're betting on, Deva?' Grishan said.

Deva spat at Grishan's feet, and retreated to a safe distance. He knew what was coming. He'd been there at the chokepoint when Kavi had fought the Kraelish.

Grishan grunted and turned back to Kavi. 'I don't know how you won him over, but I'm impressed.'

'Chotu,' Kavi said, without taking her eyes off Grishan.

'Akka,' he responded.

'Keep our people away from me, don't let them get too close.'

'Yes, Akka.'

'Deva,' she said. 'The same goes for your men.'

'I know,' he said, backing away and gesturing for his men to do the same.

Grishan watched the crowd retreat, bemused, curious, but not perturbed. 'Do you understand what you're doing?' he asked.

She reached for the berserker, and froze at the spiking of Azia's horror and revulsion.

Kavi, don't—

I'm sorry, she said, and blocked him out.

'I will kill you,' Grishan said, matter of factly. 'And then I will kill every single Taemu in this city.'

'Fuck you.'

She reached for the berserker's chains, and one by one, snapped them in half.

The pressure in her core detonated. Sent waves of raw emotion screaming through her body: grief, rage and an overwhelming, nauseating, desire for vengeance. It reached up, wrapped itself around her throat and shoved her aside. Kavi went without a fight; she found a quiet corner inside her head, hugged her knees to her chest, and watched as the Berserker took control.

Grishan shot to his feet, closed the gap between them with one massive stride, and snapped both hands around the Berserker's neck. He squeezed.

The Berserker twisted, opened her mouth and tried to breathe, but found her throat sealed shut. She dug her nails into Grishan's wrists. Punched and bit and kneed and kicked and gouged at his eyes.

But he was ready. His hands never left her throat, but his skin contracted as he strengthened each part of his body a split-second before she made impact with it.

The Berserker's fist, her knuckles and the chain wrapped around it, crunched into Grishan's cheekbones. His temple. His neck. His jaw.

But the hands around her neck would not yield. They got tighter, heavier, as Grishan threw his weight into it, and inch by inch, he forced the Berserker to her knees, and then, to the ground.

The Berserker struck out indiscriminately, but the flesh her blows found was always hard as stone. Soon the rage began to dim and was replaced by a sensation she had never experienced before.

This was not how it was supposed to go. Nothing could stop her. She *was* rage. She was the Berserker, right? *Right, Kavi?*

Kavi?

Spittle dribbled down her face as Grishan bared his teeth, forced his fingers into her neck and drew blood.

Kavi? I don't understand. What is this — this feeling?

It's called fear, Kavi said.

The Berserker's mouth worked; her body went limp. She called Nilasi, sent the hungry blue threads of maayin searching for something to use, something to heal her with. But there was no one in range except Grishan, and he was a mage, her maayin would not work on him.

I'm sorry, the berserker said, her voice barely a whisper as she hobbled and retreated into what was once its prison, and forced Kavi back out into her asphyxiating body.

Kavi stared up at where Grishan had been, where now she saw only a blur. Her emotion spent, her body pushed to its limits.

So, this is how it ends.

The more you enjoy living, Bithun coughed and said, *the more afraid you will be of dying.*

I'm not afraid, sahib. I am calm.

She blinked. Her vision cleared. Warm tears trickled past her temples, into her ears and briefly muffled the slow thudding of her heartbeat, the violent thumping of Grishan's and the harsh gasps he made with each laboured breath.

Why are you out of breath?

She blinked again. He was hurt. The right side of his face was a bloody mess. One eye was sealed shut. There were fresh bruises and wounds on his jaw and over the pale scars that circled his neck. Chunks of flesh were missing from the back of his trembling hands. He was hurt.

The berserker had hurt him.

So, it was not the end after all. The berserker had been too blinded by fear to realise what she'd done.

The pressure on Kavi's neck eased, not enough to let her breathe, but enough to indicate that Grishan thought it was over. She had, after all, stopped fighting back.

Darkness crept along the edges of her vision. She tested her fingers, her toes. She could still move. But she'd only get one chance. And she was okay with that. She was calm. She was empty. She was not afraid.

Kavi twisted her right arm, and with every ounce of strength she could summon, smashed her elbow into the bloody half of Grishan's face; at the same time, she flung a knee up and into his groin.

Both blows connected. The fingers around her throat, for just a heartbeat, lost their grip, and – coughing, choking, gasping for air – she scrambled away from him.

Grishan nursed the side of his face and watched her but made no attempt to chase after her.

Kavi sat on her haunches, panted as she caught her breath. The exhaustion and pain from all her injuries returned with a vengeance. She ran her fingers down her neck and winced. His hands must have been made of iron. She spat, groaned, forced herself upright, and met Grishan's eyes.

He waited and watched her with that cold, curious look in his eyes.

Now what?

Thunk. Thunk. Thunk. The familiar, wooden sound of Chotu's crutch hitting the ground cut through the silence in the hall. And in its wake, a scraping rustle and an occasional clunk. He was dragging something along the floor.

'Akka,' he said, flinging a sack at her feet. Its contents squeaked and hissed and clacked against each other. 'Finish it, Akka.'

She glanced at the sack, then up at Chotu. At the unbridled fury on his face as he glared at Grishan. And from somewhere in the back of the den, the soft, gentle sound of humming found its way to her ears.

She froze. Her eyes widened.

The humming got louder as more Taemu – and they had to be Taemu, no one else would know this melody – joined in.

The words are lost, but we remember the tune, Amma said. *It was once sung by the families left behind by warriors gone into battle, to remind them of their sacrifice. To remind us what they fought for.*

The Taemu in the den thumped their chests as they hummed, just like Amma had, all those years ago. It was mournful. It was angry; it was unyielding. And it sent Kavi back into the past, where she found the little girl hiding inside a crack in the wall. She found the young woman frozen on her knees.

She pulled them up.

She held their hands and led them away.

The little girl she led to a lush green park, with swings and slides and see-saws, and she watched over the girl while she played.

The young woman she led to a quiet, empty beach, and she watched over the woman while she sat in the shade of a coconut tree and wept.

And when she was sure they were safe, she went back. She found the ones who'd hurt them, and she ripped the skin off their flesh, and the flesh off their bones.

A low growl left Kavi's throat as she called Nilasi. *Heal me.*

The blue threads of maayin tore their way out of her body, writhed and fought each other to get to the rats in the sack.

Grishan stared, eyes bulging, mouth hanging open, as her cuts and bruises, all the gashes and wounds, sealed themselves up.

Kavi cracked her neck, rolled her shoulders, and unwound the chain around her fist. 'You're not the only monster here,' she whispered.

She lunged, and using the chain like a whip, snapped it around his neck.

It caught, spun around his throat. She leaped past him, turned on her heel, and with both hands on the lower half of the chain, dug one foot into the small of his back, and – teeth bared, spittle flying, eyes bulging – pulled with all her might.

He choked, gagged; his back arched. His hands fought for purchase on the chain.

The veins on her neck stood out, her muscles burned, and a guttural roar tore its way out of her throat as—

Clink snap! The chain broke. Sent Kavi tumbling away and Grishan coughing-gasping for air.

She found her footing, rushed back to him, dropped to her knees and slid across the floor. As she ducked under a wild swing she grabbed the back of his knee to kill her momentum and, with her other hand, hammered her knuckles into the tender bone under his kneecap.

He grunted. She sensed him channel his maayin, felt the bone and muscle on his leg harden, and grimaced as he grabbed her by the hair and hit her in the face. But she didn't stop. She had his scent now; she could smell his fear. She punched his knee again. He punched her in the head again.

They exchanged blows until his knee shattered with a loud *crack!*

He gasped, staggered. Fractured white bone jutted through the torn red flesh on one knee.

She switched to his other leg. And started over.

He howled and rained down blows on her head, her face, her shoulders – he tore out her hair and her scalp, pulled half her ear off, but she didn't stop.

She would deal with the pain later. She was good at that. For now, she had a promise to keep.

Crack-crack-crunch – his kneecap twisted, popped, and tore through his skin. He cried out in pain and fell flat on his arse.

She wheezed. Stood. Spat out blood and shattered teeth. She was not done with him. She could still hear Nariga's shrieks as her baby burned to death. The sound of her choking on her sobs as she slapped her own head with both hands. Over, and over, and over again.

Kavi lifted one of Grishan's enormous arms as he moaned and whimpered. And smashed his elbow out. Then she moved on to the other arm.

Crack!

He screamed.

Still wheezing, she took a step back from Grishan and studied her own broken hands. Her fingers were splayed at odd angles, the bones jutted through skin, and her left wrist, she was sure, was fractured.

End it, Kavi, Amma said in her ear.

Grishan muttered to himself as he stared at his ruined arms. He'd aged at least a decade, and there was this strange curiosity in his eyes. As if he wanted to know what happened next. A man like him would never repent, or regret; he would never ask for forgiveness, because he lacked a conscience and believed he had done nothing wrong to begin with.

She had nothing to say to him.

Her fingers were useless, she could no longer make a fist, so she smashed the base of her palm into his nose.

The bone collapsed, was forced back into his head, and punctured his brain.

He was dead before he hit the ground.

Kavi stepped around him, stumbled, and collapsed into Grishan's large chair.

It's done, Amma. It's done.

She coughed, spat out more blood, and – with one eye sealed

shut – gazed out at the Taemu, the rickshaw drivers, and the gangsters watching her.

Standing in the front row, with a crutch under one arm, tears unashamedly streaming down his cheeks, was Chotu. For the first time since they'd found each other, he smiled.

Kavi wiped the blood off her mouth with the back of her hand. *You have a nice smile, little brother, I'll make sure I see it more often.*

And on Chotu's right, with a drainpipe clutched in both hands, a purple bruise on his face, and eyes full of concern, was Nabo.

I'm all right. She smiled at him. *Don't look so worried.*

And behind them, with arms slightly extended to both sides and a pair of translucent green petals hovering over each palm, was Azia. He flicked his wrists, and the maayin disintegrated.

Thank you for watching out for them.

He nodded.

Deva snapped his fingers, gestured to Grishan's body, and a trio of gangsters rushed up and dragged it away.

Once the body was clear, he strolled up to the chair, got on one knee, and offered her a beedi.

She parted her lips. He gently placed a beedi between them and lit it with a matchstick.

'Boss,' he said, and stood at her side.

As if on cue, a chorus of *Boss!* burst out across the den.

The gangsters saluted. 'Boss!'

The rickshaw drivers lowered their heads with respect. 'Boss!'

The sisters and the Taemu, faces flush with pride, joined in. 'Boss!'

Her eyebrow twitched. *What happened to Akka?*

She gestured for Deva to come closer.

'Boss?'

There was still work to do, but as of this moment, she was one step closer to securing a real future for her people. A future where her people would never have to worry about being caught in the wrong neighbourhood or lower their eyes and bow and scrape just to survive. She'd start with the Dolmondas and wipe the other gangs off the surface of this city. The rot in Azraaya's heart had been cut away, and now she could begin unclogging its veins and arteries. But first, 'Deva, we're going to change the name of the gang.'

'To what?'

She took a drag, exhaled, and looked up at him with her one functioning eye. Massa would be so proud.

'The Imperial Rickshaw Company.'

EPILOGUE

Ze'aan

I wrapped the dupatta around my head, over the lower half of my face, and hailed a steam-rickshaw.

'Memsaab, where?' the driver asked, cocking his head, waggling his eyebrows, and jabbing his thumb at the sky. His manner would've drawn gasps in Kraelin. But here, in Azraaya, it meant the man was being considerate and respectful. I'd had drivers yell their price at me before I'd even told them my destination; I'd had one announce that I would have to share the backseat with their aunty who they had to pick up from the fish market; I'd even had a man look me up and down, purse his lips, and *slurrrrrp* his saliva while he bobbled his head.

The other notable thing about the rickshaw driver was that he was a Taemu.

'161 Gulab Chamcha Road,' I said.

His demeanour changed. He released the clutch, twisted the knob that turned off the engine, and squinted at me. 'Imperial Rickshaw Company office?'

'Yes.'

'What business you have there?'

'I—' There was no point in lying. He was a Taemu, he would know her, and I'd already decided during the interminable journey – on the steamships from Balthour, to Hamaka, to some godsforsaken port in the Tholar delta, and then on the bumpy bullock cart ride to Azraaya – that my life would be in her hands. 'I'm an old acquaintance of Kavithri's.'

He sat up straight. 'You know the boss?'

The what? 'I know Kavithri, yes.'

'Sit, no charge, I'll take you.'

I hid the surprise from my face and shuffled into the backseat.

He pumped the lever to start the vehicle, checked for traffic, honked his horn for absolutely no reason, and accelerated into the street. As he drove, he adjusted the side-view mirror and offered me a glimpse of my own reflection: gaunt, unkempt, a shadow of what I'd been when I lived in this city. But despite all that, there was life in my eyes again.

Maybe it was all the nights I'd spent on the steamship – the hum of the engine, the whisper of the waves, the gentle, almost imperceptible rocking that never failed to lull me to sleep. Maybe it was the clarity of purpose that came with the choice I'd made. Or maybe I felt alive because I could see her again.

There was no going back for me. Senior Warlock Ackerman was dead, his spine severed by a dagger of my maayin, and so were the guards at the dorms. I'd had no choice. The captain of the steamship – my route to freedom – was a collector, and when I told him about the items in the Kraelish repository, he'd agreed to allow me onboard if I could pilfer a bagful of relics for him.

Kraelin's eye still remained in Balthour. A strange compulsion *not* to take it, or an eerie premonition of what might happen if I did, had stayed my hand.

'Dubey!' My driver shouted and waved at a rickshaw going the other way, and this Dubey waved back.

I frowned at the back of the man's head. Taemu driving

rickshaws, Taemu being greeted by other Raayans – what was going on?

'Any news on the Nathrians?' I asked. The last I'd heard was that they'd been pushed back to Draghal. I told the driver as much.

'Same, memsaab,' the driver said. 'Fighting-fighting, then retreat, fighting-fighting again, then retreat. Soon they will be back on their side of the border.'

'That's good,' I said. One day, in the not-so-distant future, the Kraelish would return with their makra and their armies and turn this city into rubble, but the thought no longer gave me the satisfaction it once would have.

I picked at the skin around my nails. How would Kavithri react? Not just to my presence, but to what I knew about the blood banks and the emperor's grand intentions. Would she even let me speak? Would she hand me over to the Raayans? Or would she kill me herself?

I swallowed. Took a deep, expansive breath and slowly exhaled as the rickshaw stopped to allow a group of zobhanatyam dancers to scurry across the street.

I stared at their colourful outfits, their kohl-lined eyes and hennaed hands, the jasmine flowers in their hair, the thick anklets that jangled with each step.

My mother used to send me to zobhanatyam classes. I'd loved watching the older girls dance; loved learning the intricate choreography and the meaning behind each gesture and eye movement and the stories behind each dance. I'd dreamed of being on stage – lit up while the audience watched from the dark.

I'd given up after six months. I wasn't good enough.

Loving something doesn't mean you'll be good at it, my teacher had said when I told her I wanted to quit. *Just like loving someone doesn't mean they'll love you back. But it's because you love something that you will persist when things get rough.*

I guess I hadn't loved it as much as the others.

The rickshaw turned into a street with a worn-down sign that said *Gulab Chamcha Road,* and a sudden wave of dizziness pitched through my head. I squeezed my hands together to stop them from shaking. I lowered my head and blinked until the bright spots in my vision disappeared.

I was a traitor to both Raaya and Kraelin.

I had killed and murdered to get what I wanted.

And despite what I'd done to her, Kavithri was the only one I could trust.

'Office is upstairs,' the driver said, and saluted a man who stood – purse tucked under one arm – outside a shop called *Reddy's Dead Body Disposals.*

What the Hel?

'Looks like boss is out, but you can wait in the office,' the driver said, gesturing for me to disembark.

'Thank you.' I hopped out, distracted by the inexplicable shop sign. It had to be a joke, or a front for something else.

The man with the purse watched me take the stairs up to the office of the Imperial Rickshaw Company. I ignored him, focused on mastering the flutter in my belly.

The door to the office was open, and a man – a Hamakan, from his piercings and facial structure – sat behind a desk, reading.

'I— excuse me,' I said. 'I'm here to see Kavithri.'

He looked up at me and smiled.

'Please, have a seat,' he said, his accent forcing him to linger, not unpleasantly, on each word. 'She should be back soon.'

There was a newspamphlet on a table by the divan, and I read for a while without really comprehending the meaning of the words and sentences and put it away. I glanced at the Hamakan, who—

The scuff of footsteps, a loud burp, then:

'Little brother,' a woman with a deep, bassy voice said. 'Take that as your lesson, you can't have your samosa and eat it too.'

'Akka,' a boy said. 'Can you please tell her to stop.'

'One does not stop a force of nature,' the same woman said again.

'Did she just call herself a force of nature?' A different woman.

'Meshira have mercy.' Another one.

'Chotu' – my mouth went dry; it was her, she was here – 'you shouldn't have offered her a bite of your samosa. You knew she'd eat the whole thing, right? See, look at Azia, he ate the entire thing by himself without sharing with anyone.'

The Hamakan at the desk smiled to himself.

'That's because you called me skinny and forced me to eat it.' A softer, more sullen voice, also a boy.

'Learn from the warlock, little brother.'

'Bola, please—'

Kavithri was first into the office. She grinned at the Hamakan, who tilted his head at me.

Our eyes met.

The blood drained from Kavithri's face.

Her mouth worked. Her hands clenched and unclenched.

Behind her, a boy with a scar that ran down his face mirrored her reaction. 'You,' he whispered.

I'd never met him before, why was *he* so angry? So repulsed?

I ignored him, turned back to her.

My heartbeat thundered in my ears and the bundle of fear and doubt and longing in my chest overwhelmed my desire to fall to my knees and beg for forgiveness. Before I knew what I was doing, my lips had curled into that cruel, cruel smile my mother had warned me about and the words came tumbling out of my mouth.

'Hello, Kavithri.'

END

ACKNOWLEDGMENTS

A heartfelt thanks to:

My agent, Ernie Chiara. My editor, Brendan Durkin, and the wonderful team at Gollancz.

My father and brother. My wife. My mother who I miss every day.

My in-laws, whose kindness and generosity gave me the space to write this book.

And to the readers who read and loved *Kavithri*; thank you for your kind messages, it means so much.

Credits

Aman J. Bedi and Gollancz would like to thank everyone at Orion who worked on the publication of *City of Jackals*.

Editor
Brendan Durkin

Copy-editor
Abigail Nathan

Proofreader
Margot Gray

Editorial Management
Jane Hughes
Charlie Panayiotou
Lucy Bilton

Audio
Paul Stark
Louise Richardson
Georgina Cutler-Ross

Contracts
Dan Herron
Ellie Bowker
Oliver Chacón

Design
Nick Shah
Rachael Lancaster
Deborah Francois
Helen Ewing

Rights
Rebecca Folland
Tara Hiatt
Ben Fowler
Alice Cottrell
Ruth Blakemore
Marie Henckel

Finance
Nick Gibson
Jasdip Nandra
Sue Baker
Tom Costello

Inventory
Jo Jacobs
Dan Stevens

Production
Paul Hussey
Katie Horrocks

Marketing
Javerya Iqbal

Publicity
Jenna Petts

Sales
David Murphy
Victoria Laws
Esther Waters
Karin Burnik
Anne-Katrine Buch
Frances Doyle
Group Sales teams across
Digital, Field, International
and Non-Trade

Operations
Group Sales Operations team

BRINGING NEWS FROM OUR WORLDS TO YOURS . . .

Want hot-off-the-press info about the latest and greatest SFF releases?

Look no further than the Gollancz newsletter! Your one-stop shop for news, updates, discounts and exclusive giveaways.

Sign up now:

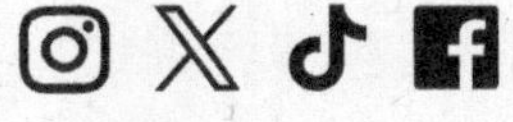

@gollancz